RISING TIDE

DI JAMIE JOHANSSON BOOK 2

MORGAN GREENE

ALSO BY MORGAN GREENE

The DS Johansson Prequel Trilogy:
Bare Skin (Book 1)
Fresh Meat (Book 2)
Idle Hands (Book 3)

The DS Johansson Prequel Trilogy Boxset

———

The DI Jamie Johansson Series
Angel Maker (Book 1)
Rising Tide (Book 2)
Old Blood (Book 3)

Death Chorus (Book 4)
Quiet Wolf (Book 5)
Ice Queen (Book 6)

BOLSTAD-B OIL PLATFORM

LOCATION: NORWEGIAN SEA

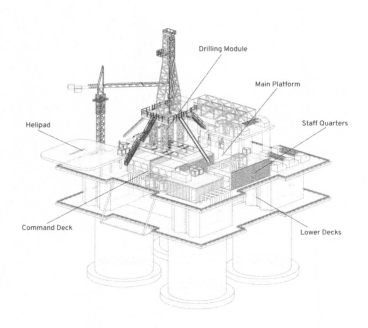

CHARACTERS

Stockholm Polis

- Jamie Johansson — Kriminalinspektör (Detective Inspector)
- Anders Wiik — Kriminalinspektör (Detective Inspector)
- Julia Hallberg — Polisassistent (Detective Constable)
- Ingrid Falk — Kriminalkommissare (Superintendent)

Bolstad Industries

- Arnold Wallace — Senior Risk Advisor
- Tim Ehrling — Bolstad B Head Of Operations
- Vogel — Bolstad B Deputy Head Of Operations
- Sven Rosenburg — Head Engineer
- Orn Møller — Senior Engineer
- Grzegorz Kurek — Safety Engineer
- Dima Boykov — Drill Technician

- Colm Quinn — Driller
- Sasha Kravets — Driller
- Miroslav Lebedenkov — Driller
- Alejandro Reyes — Driller

Helsinki University Researchers

- Noemi Heikkinen
- Paméla Sevier
- Ashleigh Hooper

RISING TIDE

1

LAND WAS 342 MILES AWAY.

The sea stretched endlessly around, boiling and rolling, the crash of the waves against the hulking iron legs of the Bolstad B drilling platform an endless rush of white noise below.

A cold wind whipped across the surface of the ocean, sending a spray of saltwater into the air. The hatch to the lower submersible platform creaked open and a man stepped out onto the catwalk. He screwed his face up against the cold, swore under his breath.

He fought his way forward in the wind, the air making his eyes ache. It was eight below zero, and despite the fast-approaching spring, the sun still set here at five. There were just a few dregs of light left in the sky, a dim glow spread out along the horizon.

Everyone else was in their cabins by now. No one else would be stupid enough to be out here.

'Hey,' the man called, staggering towards the outer rail.

A woman stood there, staring out to sea.

The platform ended ten feet behind her, and above, a

crane arm hung over the open water, a hook swinging from it. The contraption was designed to lower a submersible pod into the water a hundred feet below.

But there was no pod.

Which meant there was no reason anyone should be out there.

The exact reason they chose it.

The woman turned her head, her bright red coat buffeting in the wind. She smiled at him. Her skin was pale, her electric-blue eyes burning in the dying light. She had white-blonde hair, and it was clear she'd been crying.

He approached quickly, kissed her, and then took her in his arms. They hugged tightly, and when they parted, she looked as though she was about to cry again.

'How long?' she asked, voice strained.

'Not long.' He forced himself to smile. 'Tomorrow morning. Before sunrise. It's all worked out. There are just a few more things to clear up, and then ...' But he didn't get to finish. Her eyes had strayed from his, over his shoulder.

The back of his neck erupted into gooseflesh and he turned quickly, shielding her behind him.

The hatch was open, and an inky shape was stepping through it.

His heart began to race and he felt the woman's fingers curl into the fabric of his coat.

He moved her backwards, knowing there was nowhere to run. 'Please!' he called. 'Don't! We can fix this!'

But the person who had just stepped onto the platform wasn't listening. Something glinted at their side and the man's eyes went there, seeing the outline of a knife turning in the frozen air.

The man felt the girl's fingers tighten in his coat, and he knew there was only one way they were getting out of this.

He charged blindly, fists raised, teeth bared like a rabid dog, and swung with everything he had.

His knuckles sailed in a vicious arc but hit nothing.

Then he felt a sudden warmth in his stomach, felt something spill from his lips.

He dragged in a ragged breath and looked down, seeing the knife slither out of the folds of his coat.

Something splashed onto the toes of his work boots, shimmering black in the twilight.

He swayed, stumbled, and then fell backwards. His fingers clutched at his stomach, the pain blinding suddenly. He felt tears on his cheeks as he craned his head backwards, searching for her, knowing that he was about to watch the woman he loved die.

Except the platform was empty.

Heavy footsteps moved around his head and then down the catwalk. They paused at the rail as the attacker looked over, searching the empty space below, finding nothing except a concertina of whitecaps.

She must have jumped.

There was nowhere else to go.

The man stared up at the figure above him and watched as its gaze lifted to the hook swinging from the crane above.

He felt the tears warm on his face then, watching as the figure walked back towards him.

The knife rising slowly at its side.

IT WAS the first time Jamie had seriously grappled with the idea of Anders Wiik dying.

As she watched his face turn red, the veins in his neck bulge, and his chest heave, she wondered if he was about to collapse then and there.

Detective Inspector Jamie Johansson eased off her pace and slowed to a stop. She glanced down at her watch, seeing her heart rate holding at a steady 125, and then brushed the errant strand of ash-blonde hair off her forehead, shaking out her long plait as she caught her breath.

Behind her, Kriminalinspektör Anders Wiik of the Violent Crimes department of Stockholm Polis stumbled to a halt and bent forwards, hands on knees, panting and wheezing.

She thought saying that there were just another four kilometres to go wasn't going to help things. Especially since they'd only done one so far.

'*Är du okej?*' she asked, looking around. Are you okay? The streets of Stockholm were quiet, the sun not long up. Rush hour wouldn't kick in for another hour or so yet.

He nodded quickly, but Jamie knew he wasn't. If he'd

tried to speak, he'd probably have emptied his stomach all over the pavement.

Well, you asked for it, she felt like saying. Though she doubted that would help either. She didn't think he'd make another bet with her any time soon. Especially not one that involved shooting.

Julia Hallberg, Wiik's – and now, she guessed, hers as well – *polisassistent* had told him that Jamie was a good shot. But she figured male bravado got the better of even men like Wiik every now and then. Jamie hadn't been excited to make it a competition – and if anything she was getting more than a little tired of Hallberg fawning over her to Wiik. But the girl meant well. No, the *woman*. Hallberg wasn't that much younger than her. Damn. Why couldn't she shake that habit? She hated that she felt closer to Wiik's age than Hallberg's despite him being more than ten years her senior. He was nearly fifty, and though he looked good for it, he couldn't run for shit.

'Ready?' Jamie asked, taking a step closer to him. She watched as her heart rate fell with every passing second.

'One second,' he choked out, finally pulling himself upright.

Wiik was nearly a head taller than Jamie, with a strong, square jaw and nose, and perfectly groomed, slicked-back hair. Though it looked a little bedraggled now, his clean-shaven cheeks red and blotchy. 'Am I really meant to believe you do this for *fun?*' he asked in Swedish.

'*Lägg av,*' Jamie laughed. Leave off. 'Come on,' she continued, turning and kicking out her toes to loosen her quads. She was glad Wiik had overestimated his skill with a pistol, or she'd have been forced to choke down a burger that he'd described as 'a heart attack in a bun'. He'd been going on about the place since she'd officially started her loan from the London Met and couldn't understand how she didn't eat food like that.

She couldn't understand how he could.

Supposedly, he wanted to take her out for a 'welcome to the city' burger. She'd asked if a 'welcome to the city' salad was on the table.

Apparently, it was not.

'Wiik?' she asked, turning back to see if he'd finally mustered the strength to go on.

But he wasn't looking at her. He was staring down at his phone, his slowly rising and falling shoulders and focused stare telling her that something was up.

'What is it?' she asked, measuring him as she approached.

He met her cool blue eyes. 'We've got a body. Falk wants us in as soon as possible. It's a weird one.'

Jamie inspected the lines on his face, not seeing the usual stony confidence that she'd come to know so well over the last few months. 'Weird how?'

He locked his phone and pushed it back into his sweat-pants, narrowing his eyes at her a little. 'You can swim, right?'

Jamie walked out of the stairwell and onto the seventh floor at Stockholm Polis HQ.

She glanced left and right, but there was no sign of Wiik yet. Hallberg, on the other hand, was there early, as always.

'Inspector,' she said, jumping up from her desk. 'Falk is waiting for you.'

Jamie smiled at her, then glanced over at Kriminalkom-missarie Ingrid Falk, who was more than visible through the glass wall of her office. She was behind her desk, reading something on the screen of her computer, squinting slightly. A cup of coffee steamed next to her.

'Thanks, Hallberg,' Jamie said, nodding. 'Wiik not here yet?'

'No,' Hallberg confirmed.

He would want to shave, shower, redo his hair again. He could be asked, but not rushed. He liked things a certain way, and Jamie had quickly learned it was easier to just let him get on with it than try to fight him.

'You know what this is about?' Hallberg asked, grabbing Jamie's attention.

'No.' She shook her head. 'Wiik said a body had been found on a drilling platform in the Norwegian sea. Swedish owned – apparently they want to keep it quiet until they know what's what.'

'And they're flying us out there?'

Jamie bit her lip. 'I don't know, Hallberg. The text didn't say a lot. But Falk will know more.'

'Right,' she said. 'Can I get you a coffee or anything?'

'Sure,' she said. Usually she didn't like to ask anything of Hallberg – especially since Wiik seemed to ask *everything* of her. He called it 'her education'. Jamie called it abusing Hallberg's accommodating nature. But this morning, Jamie didn't feel much like making idle conversation. A coolness had descended so quickly over Wiik when he received the text that Jamie was on edge now. Calls that came in like that were never good, and the fact that this was landing at her and Wiik's feet meant that whatever the details of the case were, they were serious.

What the protocol was for incidents like this she didn't know, but judging by the conflicted look on Falk's face, it wasn't going to be an easy ride.

Jamie exhaled, trying to shrug off some of the tension in her shoulders, and headed for the office.

She knocked once and then entered. It was just after eight, and the office was still practically empty, apart from a few early-risers ticking away at their paperwork before the day officially started.

'Johansson,' Falk said, looking up. She smiled briefly, then gestured to one of the seats in front of her. She let out a long sigh, pulled off her reading glasses, and then massaged the bridge of her nose. Her features were fine, her pointed chin and prominent cheekbones magnified by her dark hair. It was pulled back over her ears, flicking out at the nape of her neck.

Jamie could already tell this was going to be a shit-show. 'What is it?' she asked.

'Ever heard of the Bolstad Company?' Falk met her eyes now.

'No,' Jamie said truthfully.

'They're a Swedish-owned oil company operating in the Norwegian sea. Among other places.'

'Ah,' Jamie said, crossing her legs. 'And what does that have to do with us?'

'One of the crew members of the Bolstad B platform was killed last night.'

Jamie didn't feel like asking the same question twice would do her any good. 'Who was the victim?'

'Alejandro Reyes. A Spaniard. Twenty-seven years old,' Falk said, glancing back at her screen, at what Jamie had to guess was the information she had so far on the case.

'Then why are we dealing with it and not the Spanish police? Shouldn't Bolstad have looped them in on—'

'Under normal circumstances, yes. Probably. Definitely.'

Falk filled her lungs, closed her eyes for a moment, and then looked at Jamie again.

'But these aren't *normal* circumstances?' Jamie raised an eyebrow.

'Bolstad is a Swedish company. Their head of operations is Swedish. As is their head engineer.'

'Did either of them kill Reyes?'

'No. I don't know.' Falk seemed strained by the whole thing. She was usually so calm and collected.

'So then what's going on?' Jamie asked, leaning forwards a little now. 'Why us? Why Wiik and I?'

'Bolstad is hanging by a thread. The company is about to go under.'

'Right?' Jamie didn't understand the concern. 'An oil company isn't doing well. Surprise, surprise. The world is changing.'

'They had four platforms operating in that sector – Bolstad A through D. Over the last five years, three of them have dried up. Bolstad B is the last remaining. But only barely. Every six months, there's a complete crew change. All of the workers are flown back to the mainland, and a new crew takes over. That happens in five days.'

Jamie watched her closely.

'Usually, in these circumstances, the timeline would be moved up. The crew would be brought home, everyone would be arrested upon arrival, questioned, and an investigation would take place.'

'And that's not the best way to do this? How many crew members are there? Surely it won't be difficult to find out who—'

'Which is exactly why you're going to go there.'

Jamie had hoped that wasn't coming.

'They've offered to fly you and Wiik out there before the

crew switchover. The Spanish authorities haven't been informed yet. The platform is locked down. No communication going in or out. And Bolstad want to keep it that way.'

'How can they?' Jamie stared at the woman she'd thought she'd come to know over the last few months. The honest, straight-laced, protocol follower, who now seemed to be completely fine with not only throwing standard procedure out the window, but also with bending international maritime law to breaking point. 'Keeping the death of a citizen from their country of origin is—'

'I know,' Falk said, swallowing. 'But ...' She seemed to grapple with her own words. 'But it's just five days. Bolstad want to keep it quiet until then. They want my best detectives – and I know that I can trust you and Wiik. Can't I?'

'Of course,' Jamie said, eyeing Falk carefully.

'Good. So then go there and find out who did this. There are a lot of families waiting to see their sons, their husbands, their fathers ...' She seemed to let the last word linger before she went on. 'And as far as they know, in five days, they will again. Bolstad's stakeholders are already selling up, and if word of this gets out, the company won't be able to withstand the media backlash. The vultures are already circling.'

Falk still hadn't answered the question Jamie wanted to know the answer to more than any other. Why Bolstad? Why them? Why Falk – and why like this? Murder was murder. And this platform was now a melting pot of scared, trapped people who just wanted to get home. And if Bolstad – and Falk – had any scruples, they'd make that happen. As quickly as possible.

Jamie stared hard at Falk. 'What have they got on you?'

'Who?' she asked, lifting her chin to meet Jamie's eye directly.

'Bolstad,' she said flatly. 'You know what they're asking

here isn't right. But you're going along with it? What aren't you telling me?'

Falk remained silent, maybe weighing up what to say and what not to. Maybe figuring out how she could brush this all off as some weird joke and actually do what she was supposed to. Tell Bolstad to shove it, and then put everyone on board in handcuffs.

'Your father,' she said, her eyes sharpening.

Jamie narrowed hers. 'What about him?'

'You're asking questions about the last case he worked before he died.'

Jamie's knuckles flexed.

'But you're not getting anywhere, are you?'

She didn't figure Falk for the game-playing type, but there was more going on here than Jamie knew. And she didn't like it.

'I was there, you know,' she said, almost aloof now. She leaned back in her chair, gazing off to the side. 'I could point you in the right direction – towards the cages you should be rattling.'

'But you're not going to,' Jamie said, her voice cold.

'You know how this works, Jamie,' Falk said, the familiarity leaving a sour taste in Jamie's mouth. 'You've been doing this long enough.'

Jamie nodded, trying not to sneer too much. 'I just never expected it from you.'

Falk's mask slipped a little, the fear, the angst underneath shining through. She didn't want to do this, play this card. But it was all she had. 'Do this for me, no questions, and I'll see what I can remember about his case. Do we have a deal?' She turned her head slightly, weighing Jamie up.

Jamie hated this. She wasn't the sort of person to be strong-armed. And definitely not the sort of person to be blackmailed. But Falk was right. Every lead she'd followed up on, every name she'd tracked down, she'd had nothing but doors slammed in her face. Missing paperwork for concurrent cases, things being misfiled. No one seemed to have any recollection of him working on anything at the time. She was at a loss.

But Falk knew something. And she knew what it was worth to Jamie.

'You could just tell me what the hell's really going on,' Jamie said, folding her arms. 'That would just be easier.'

Falk stared across the desk at her. 'I could – and don't take this the wrong way – but I don't know you well enough yet. And even if I did …' She trailed off, shaking her head, that same look of fear coming over her again.

Jamie was about to open her mouth again when Hallberg walked in holding a pair of coffees.

She sat next to Jamie, a curtain of silence falling across the room. She put the coffees on the desk and pushed one in front of Jamie, looking from her to Falk.

'So,' Hallberg said, bright as ever. 'What did I miss?'

3

THAT WAS THE DEAL. The killer for a name.

Jamie didn't like it, but it was what was happening.

Luckily for Jamie, Wiik wasn't thrilled about the situation either and drove in silence towards Stockholm Arlanda Airport, where Bolstad had a helicopter waiting for them.

They would be flying north to Trondheim, refuelling, and then making the five-hundred-mile journey out to the Bolstad B platform, which lay 342 miles west of the nearest land – an inhospitable, frozen Norwegian peninsula that housed a tiny village called Sørland. But there wasn't an airport there. Or a hospital. Or anything of any use if they got into trouble.

Basically, they were all alone in the middle of a turbulent ocean with nothing but their wits and a shaky sat-phone signal.

The nearest help would be nearly four hours away. And that was only if you could scramble a helicopter and a pilot from Bergen and they flew full-throttle across nearly five hundred miles of open ocean. Which Jamie guessed they wouldn't. Because doing that would burn too much fuel and would cut the range on the chopper down to the wire. Which meant that if anything went wrong, there'd not be enough fuel to get back to land and it would plunge straight into the sea. And Bolstad no doubt valued their property more than their people's lives. Which was why Jamie and Wiik were in this mess in the first place.

No, they'd not be risking a thirteen-million-pound helicopter unless they had to. And even then they'd be doing it carefully, flying efficiently. Safely.

Unhurriedly.

So basically, if anything went wrong, Jamie and Wiik were screwed.

Her stomach was tying itself into knots just thinking about it.

Jamie exhaled and stared out of the window, watching the last of the buildings move past in a wash. The sky was grey and dull overhead, the spring looking more like winter as the day wore on.

And she was having such a good morning, too, watching Wiik suffer.

They arrived at the airport and were greeted by two guys from Bolstad. Security, Jamie guessed by their ex-military air and taut black suits. Both of them were six-foot-plus. Both of them looked like they were made from stone. And both of them were as silent as it, too.

Wiik parked his car in the short-stay lot – optimistic, Jamie thought – and they were led into the airport with just a small duffle bag of fresh clothes each. Enough for a few days. Both of them hoped they wouldn't be there that long.

After all, how hard was this going to be? It wasn't like the killer had anywhere to run.

They followed the guys through to a private part of the terminal Jamie didn't even realise existed. It was through one of those doors that said *No Entry To Unauthorised Persons*, and contained a few rows of chairs, as well as a pair of gates. They were archways, half blocked by desks, and beyond, were sliding doors that led directly onto the runway. One of the desks was empty, the other was manned by a single woman in a grey pencil skirt and white blouse, her hair tied back behind her head.

The two Bolstad guys walked straight through without a word and paused by the sliding door, turning back to face the empty waiting room as though there was no one there at all, their eyes fixed on some indeterminate point on the far wall.

Jamie and Wiik slowed up at the desk and offered their passports. The woman smiled at them briefly, took them and held them against the scanner for a moment, tapped a few things into the computer in front of her, and then handed them back without so much as a word.

She smiled briefly again, then locked the computer, side-stepped around the desk, and headed for the main terminal.

The door hissed closed and locked behind her. And then it was just Wiik and Jamie. They glanced at each other, neither at perfect ease, and turned towards the door ahead.

The two suits both stepped to the side and proffered the runway, and Jamie and Wiik stepped forwards into the unknown.

The silence of the terminal was broken by the wind blowing across the tarmac. It had picked up in the last few minutes, the flat grey sky now swirling in the distance. The rotors of the H155 Eurocopter jostled gently in the moving air. Its sleek black body and tinted windows reeked of corporate expense accounts. The thing was devoid of branding. It was as low-profile as she suspected helicopters came. Then again, oil companies weren't the epitome of glamour anymore. There was nothing sexy about climate crisis. Or about oil-chugging private air travel.

The security duo overtook Jamie and Wiik on the walk out, striding quickly, their suit buttons straining against their wide chests. Jamie glanced down as the one on her left passed, his suit fluttering up in the wind, exposing a pistol holstered under his ribs. Jamie just caught sight of the bottom of the leather sleeve before he took hold of the hem and pulled it tight against his hip. But it was enough.

She looked at Wiik, and his eyes, fixed on the heavy's midriff, told her he'd seen it too. He met her gaze then, face lined with apprehension.

As they got close to the chopper, Jamie noticed that a pilot was already on board. And as the suits pulled open the side door and waited for Jamie and Wiik to climb in, the rotors started spooling. It would be a few hours over land to Trondheim, and then from there they'd be heading over the water.

By the time they got to Bolstad B, it would be dark, and the clock would have started.

Five days to catch a killer.

The thought struck her again – how hard could it be?

But as the rotors reached lift-off speed and dragged the sleek black Eurocopter into the buffeting wind, and Jamie stared at the two bulls in two-pieces sitting across the plush leather cabin, pistols hanging at their ribs, the thought waned in her mind.

She decided it was better not to think about it.

4

THEY SIDLED down towards Trondheim and settled onto the tarmac of the small airport to the south of the city. Though calling it that was generous. It was a quaint and picturesque town with pretty buildings and a beautiful seaside locale.

Jamie had heard nice things about it.

Though she never thought she'd be seeing it through the window of an oil company's private helicopter.

Though their visit would be brief. A quick refuel, and then they would be setting off again.

The engine whine died and the rotors began to throb over-head as they slowed.

Jamie had her weight against the window when the door opened in front of her and slid sideways. She lurched forwards, into space, and if it hadn't been for Wiik's hand shooting out and taking her by the back of the coat, she would have flopped right onto the runway.

A man was standing in the gap now, looking in, seem-ingly surprised to have almost had a woman throw herself at his feet.

Jamie nodded her thanks to Wiik, dusted herself off, and

then settled back into the leather seat as the man got in and slotted between the two suits, pushing a duffle bag into the baggage space between his heels.

He was in his late fifties, with grey, curly hair, a pointed, pronounced nose, and round glasses. He was in a tweed suit with a brown paisley tie and smiled warmly at them, extending a hand over the top of his leather briefcase. 'Arnold Wallace,' he said warmly, his voice betraying him as a public school boy. His twang was classic southern England. Sussex, Jamie guessed. But who he was and what he was doing here was another thing entirely.

Wiik narrowed his eyes at the bespectacled man. Jamie took his hand and shook. 'Morning. Detective Inspector Jamie Johansson,' she said in English.

'Kriminalinspektör Anders Wiik,' Wiik grunted after the fact, keeping his hands on his lap.

'Oh,' Wallace said, raising his eyebrows and bouncing between the two suits as the clank of the fuel hose being inserted into the hull sounded somewhere under Jamie's seat. 'A Brit!' he said, looking at Jamie, seemingly gladdened by the fact.

Wiik snorted. He didn't agree with that supposition, it seemed.

'Something like that,' Jamie said, waiting for him to elaborate as to his identity.

After a moment, Wallace caught on. 'Oh,' he said for the second time, prompting Jamie to hope that every sentence wouldn't start with it. 'Of course. You must be wondering who I am.' He laid his hand on his chest like he was about to lay down the soliloquy from *Hamlet*. 'Arnold Wallace,' he reiterated. 'Senior Risk Advisor, Bolstad Industries.'

Wiik scoffed this time.

'Something the matter?' Wallace asked.

Wiik could be extra abrasive when he wanted to be. He was a good detective, but lacked social grace at the best of times. Or more accurately, didn't really care what people thought of him, and gave little credence to tact.

'Seems a little late,' Wiik said, his English impeccable, if not expectedly dry and Swedish-accented, 'for a risk assessment.' He narrowed his eyes. 'Considering someone already died.'

Wallace smiled at that, amused by it.

Jamie clicked then. 'You're not that kind of risk advisor.'

'Right,' he confirmed, still smiling at Wiik as though being in the presence of a *lesser mind* was funny to him. 'Corporate risk. A whole different beast.'

Wiik's jaw flexed, temple vein bulging.

Jamie checked her watch. Almost midday. Wiik didn't usually get rubbed up like this until mid-afternoon when the caffeine started to wear off. But it was by no means a record.

'So you decide,' Wiik said airily, 'how much damage something like this does to a company's bottom line.' He nodded in understanding, his hands curling into loose fists on top of his knees.

Wallace kept smiling, but the two Bolstad guys clocked it and stiffened in their seats.

Jamie didn't feel like getting into a brawl in the back of this very expensive tin can.

Especially not on account of Wiik's natural prickliness.

And the two suits looked like they were paid to be on a hair trigger.

She cleared her throat. 'Mr Wallace—'

'Call me Arnold.'

'Mr Wallace,' she said again, looking at the side of Wiik's head now, 'is here to do a job, *Wiik*.' He looked at her then. 'Just like we are.' She turned back to the man in tweed. 'Bolstad needs to manage the situation their way – and we won't think to pass judgement on or interfere with that.'

Wallace grinned at her.

'So long as they let us manage the situation *our* way. And don't try to interfere in an official police investigation.' She looked at both suits, her voice cool.

Wiik shifted and sank lower in his seat, the temple vein abating.

Jamie wanted to let him know they were on the same page on this one.

They felt like they had their arms twisted up behind their back. But Falk wasn't budging, and she knew her way around Wiik. She could make him go, just like she'd made Jamie. And the fact that he hadn't been forthcoming about what Falk's methods had been was just fine with her. She wouldn't ask about his as long as he wouldn't ask about hers.

As much as she respected Wiik, her private investigation was too personal to let him into.

Just yet, at least. If she was going to find out what happened to her father, by the way Falk was spinning it, she'd have to knock on some questionable doors, turn over some heavy stones. And she'd already lost one partner through her determination to grind her own axe on company time.

She wasn't about to put another in the firing line, too.

'Right,' Wallace said, breaking the awkward silence. He unfastened his briefcase and dug inside it. 'Bolstad furnished me with these before I left the Bergen office,' he said, taking hold of a stack of manila folders and dragging them free. 'They asked me to pass them on to the detectives investigating the, er, *incident*.'

'The murder,' Wiik said flatly, glancing down at the folders as Wallace handed them to Jamie.

She looked down at them and Wiik pulled the one off the top without asking and opened it.

Jamie followed suit. A printed picture of a young woman with sharp eyes was paper-clipped to the top of what looked like application forms and other photocopied documents. Wiik had a picture of a man with a beard in front of him.

'What are these?' she asked, closing the one in front of her and lifting the cover of the next to confirm they were all the same.

'Employee dossiers,' Wallace said, looking impressed with his use of the word *dossiers.* 'Everyone on board the Bolstad B drilling platform.'

Jamie ran her finger down the spines of the folders. 'How many?'

'Ten employees, three researchers.'

'Researchers?'

'Yes. Three young women from Helsinki University. Staying on board the platform, conducting a three-month study into the effects of deep-sea drilling on ocean life.'

Wiik looked up. 'Is that normal? To have civilians on board?'

'Not unheard of,' Wallace said. 'Not common, though.'

'The ten crew members,' Jamie said. 'Have they been spoken to? Separated? Interviewed—'

Wallace cut in. 'Confined to quarters. Drilling has ceased. All communication in and out has been cut off except with head office. When we arrive, we will be greeted by the head of operations – Tim Ehrling – and his second in command, Helene Vogel. They've been instructed to sit tight until we are on-site.'

Wiik drew a slow breath, filling his lungs. 'Is there any other information you can give us? Any suspects?'

Wallace nodded to the stack on Jamie's lap. 'Everything

we have, everything we know – it's all in there. A file on every person on board, along with a master folder containing crew rotas, the layout of the platform, and everything else you could need to know. This is your investigation, Inspector,' Wallace said, turning his attention to Jamie. 'And as your partner so eloquently iterated – we'll do our very best to not step on your toes. Bolstad is glad to have the assistance of Stockholm Polis. And we're assured that you are their finest representatives. I have no doubt that you'll find the culprit without any trouble. And of course, should you need any more information, both myself and the Bolstad company are at your disposal. If there's anything you should need or want, ask, and we will do our very best to accommodate.'

Wiik closed the folder on his lap and dropped it back on Jamie's pile. 'Well, in that case,' he said, the temple vein returning. 'I want to get off this helicopter and go home.'

Wallace chuckled through closed, thin lips. 'Very good, Inspector Wiik. You'll do well to remember your sense of humour when we're aboard. Things at sea can often be difficult.'

'I wasn't joking,' he said.

But then it was too late. The hose was being removed, the engine was spooling up again, and the rotors were beating at the sky overhead.

'Nice try,' Jamie said, nudging him with her shoulder, her voice swallowed by the growing drone of the engine.

'Can you blame me?' Wiik asked sourly.

'No,' Jamie said, feeling her stomach sink as they lifted off. 'I can't.'

5

WIIK LOOKED like he regretted asking the question almost immediately.

They were about a hundred miles off the coast when Wiik pulled a pair of headphones off the rack above his head and put them on.

'Why are we flying so low?' he asked, looking out of the window at the whitecaps below. They were still a few hundred metres up, but by no means anywhere near the cloud line.

The answer he got wasn't what he was expecting, or something he wanted to hear. 'It's a safety protocol,' the pilot said. 'In case of engine failure. If we have to ditch, there's far less chance of the chopper breaking up on impact and all of us dying.' His voice was calm in Jamie's ears. The pilot wasn't done, though. 'This far from land, if we go down, it's a long time for anyone to come pick us up. And trust me, you don't want to be hitting the water at two hundred miles an hour. At least this way we'll have a chance to get out and tread water until rescue arrives—' Jamie removed her headset then. She didn't need to hear any more.

Wiik looked suitably horrified, but kept listening.

Jamie didn't need to. She was trying her best to keep her mind on the task at hand and sort out the situation unfolding in front of her. Because right now she had the feeling that her and Wiik were sitting in the back of a private chopper that, if it did go down, wouldn't have their names on the flight plan. And that didn't put her at ease.

Jamie sighed and leaned her head back, an open personnel file in her lap, assessing the situation. What did she know?

One: Someone was dead, and a killer was running free. Okay. That was her domain.

Two: Bolstad were keeping it quiet. They were halting all communication, in or out. They hadn't informed the Spanish police of the crime, or the victim's next of kin.

Three: They'd reached out to Falk personally to have this handled. And she'd strong-armed both Wiik and Jamie into the case on a moment's notice. Hallberg had been told the bare minimum – that she was to handle all of Wiik and Jamie's active cases while they were gone. That they had been requested for a specific assignment. And that was it.

Four: Bolstad was in trouble. If this got out, it could end them. *Would* end them. So that couldn't happen. And to assess the potential risk, the damage, even, they were sending their own man. This Wallace guy. And two heavies to protect him. Armed heavies. Ex-military heavies. Who looked a lot like the shoot-first-ask-questions-later type.

Jamie swallowed.

This didn't bode well.

She had no idea what to expect, but whatever the situation was on board, she didn't think she was going to like it. There was no turning back now, though. They were here, they were in it, and all they could do was solve the case, and get out cleanly.

She exhaled, closing the file, and then her eyes.

The quicker they found the guy and arrested him, the quicker Bolstad could ship the killer off to Spain to face charges – no doubt pay off a couple of people to keep it out of the news while they were at it – and preserve the precious few years of wrecking the planet that they had left. Helping Bolstad keep their business going was already leaving a sour taste in her mouth. But this was the game. She had underestimated Falk. She remembered the woman as a clean-nosed pencil pusher. A brown-nose for all intents and purposes. But it seemed that she wasn't as clean as Jamie thought. She was mixed up with Bolstad, with whatever her father had been, and who knows what else. But she knew something, and it was something that Jamie wanted. Sadly, she knew the value of it, too. And she wasn't afraid to drop Jamie right on the block to save her own skin.

She couldn't even begin to imagine what they had on her to force her hand like this. But Jamie knew one thing – she wasn't about to go into this thing half-cocked.

So, providing they didn't plunge to an icy death in the ocean before they arrived, she'd be walking in there cautious and focused. And by the time the sun came up tomorrow, she'd have someone in cuffs.

Of that much, she was sure.

6

BOLSTAD B SWELLED into view through a veil of cold fog that moved across the ocean in waves, like another sea reflected above the one below.

Waves roiled, leaping up the iron legs, swirled and battered by the wind.

The helicopter's engine whined and dipped, then whined, then dipped as the pilot manoeuvred it upwards, swinging high above the platform and into the worst of the elements.

He was seasoned – no doubt about that. But the way he was wrestling the thing around didn't make Wiik or Jamie feel any better. They both buckled up and held on to the support handles next to them.

Wallace chuckled softly at the sight, neatly wedged between his two bodyguards, who would provide ample cushioning should the pilot lose his mettle and send them careening into the side of the platform.

The landing gear whirred down under their feet, the platform disappearing beneath the belly as they descended with a sickening lurch.

Lights flashed below, flaring through the mist, and then the wheels hit concrete, squeaked, and held fast.

The chopper jostled, settling and swaying on the landing pad, and the pilot wasted no time killing the engine.

The rotors slowed above them as Wallace unbuckled and leant forwards. He pulled his duffle from between his knees and unzipped it, withdrawing a black raincoat printed with the Bolstad logo and throwing it around his shoulders.

It wasn't raining as far as Jamie could see, but as soon as Wallace opened the doors, she understood why he'd put a coat on.

The ocean spray hit her and Wiik square in the face, and they both winced, the sudden onslaught of nearly unbearably cold wind and water enough to beat away any semblance of lethargy that had set in on the flight.

Jamie wasted no time in unbuckling and getting out, determined to be out of the weather as soon as possible. She pushed the stack of files under the hem of her coat, buttoned-up, and braved the elements.

Her feet hit the concrete and two figures filled her field of vision. Wallace had already disappeared, the two heavies moving quickly after him.

'Inspector!' one of the figures in front of her yelled, his voice snatched away by the wind. 'Thank you for coming!'

The gale howled in Jamie's ears, threatening to knock her off balance. She figured that would be par for the course out here.

She looked up at the man in front of her. He was thin, not much taller than Jamie, clad in a heavily insulated and waxed black parka. He had a thin layer of stubble and sandy-coloured hair that was thinning on top. It moved in wispy circles on his head, despite his hood. He was holding it up with one hand, the other extended towards Jamie.

'Happy to help!' Jamie yelled back, taking it, thinking for a second how far that was from the truth.

'Tim Ehrling! Head of Operations!' he called, nodding and forcing a smile between winces. The air really was that cold. It felt like Jamie's skin was about to peel from her cheeks.

'Jamie Johansson!' she said.

Wiik was next to her now and took Ehrling's Hand. 'Anders Wiik!'

'Glad to have you,' Ehrling screamed. 'This is Deputy HOO Helene Vogel!'

The figure next to him stepped forwards, her coat done up to her nose, her hood pulled tight by the drawstrings. She extended a slim hand and shook Jamie and Wiik's in turn. It looked like she was about as thrilled to be out there as Jamie was.

'Shall we go inside?' she shouted through her collar, squinting at them.

Wiik didn't need another invitation and took off in the direction that Wallace had gone. Jamie fell in behind, with Ehrling and Vogel close on her heels. There was a single steel staircase leading down under the helideck, the metal rungs singing as the wind moved between them. At the bottom of the stairs, an open catwalk clinging to the main body of the platform split left and right, a sign on the wall in front of them offering the choice of decks. Wiik stopped, squinting, his once perfectly coiffed hair now a mad tangle of wet strands. Jamie didn't think she was any better. Neither were in waterproof jackets. Wiik was in his long black woollen coat and Jamie, her usual slate-grey peacoat. She'd thrown a packable kagoul in her duffle, but she didn't think it would be any more use in this spray.

Ehrling overtook Jamie and Wiik, and turned right,

following a sign for the command deck. Vogel, right on his tail, and then Jamie and Wiik.

Ehrling followed the path around and they exited from under the helideck, keeping close to the body of the platform.

Jamie stole a glance down through her feet and her stomach turned over. Twenty feet below, there was another catwalk. And another below that. And another below that. And then it was the ocean. Hundreds of feet down. Hitting the water at that speed would be like hitting concrete. The thought came to her quickly and made her unsteady for a second.

She breathed through it, feeling the sting of the cold air on her face, and then looked up to see Ehrling holding a steel door open for Vogel and Wiik. Jamie went in third, and he pulled it closed behind them.

Jamie lifted her hands, the ocean spray dripping from her fingers, and pulled her plait over her shoulder, wringing it out.

The water splashed on the concrete floor, two stairwells in front of them. One led up, another down, deeper into the bowels of the platform.

'This way,' Ehrling said, accent apparent, gesturing up the stairs. Jamie could tell now that he was Swedish. 'Please,' he added, beckoning them with him.

They all climbed, leaving a dark trail of water on the concrete behind them.

Ahead, Tim Ehrling was fumbling a key card from his pocket and swiping it through a card reader. The stencilled lettering above the door at the top of the stairs read *Command Deck*.

An electric bolt slid back somewhere inside the door and Ehrling pushed it open. Wiik was next and then Jamie, with Vogel behind, who closed the door behind her.

It locked instantly, and then they were all inside the command deck. Jamie got her bearings quickly, looking left to see the room laid out in front of her, a set of windows running the full length of the wall, giving a panoramic view of the platform and the helideck. Jamie cast her eyes across it all – the main body and drilling platform, an Eiffel Tower knockoff that housed the drill. And a separate module that lay off the main platform, connected by an exposed bridge – Jamie didn't know what it was for, but she'd find out. And the helideck. Which Wiik was taking a particular interest in.

'What is he doing?' he asked, struggling to keep the alarm from his voice. He rushed forwards, nearly pressing his nose against the glass, watching as the rotors of the chopper began to spin up again.

Jamie gritted her teeth and peeled her eyes away, looking around the rest of the room as the helicopter lifted off the helipad and dived over the edge. A few seconds later, the noise was swallowed up by the ocean and the fog, and the helicopter was gone. Along with any chance of a quick escape they might have had.

Wiik pushed the hems of his coat back and put his hands on his hips, hanging his head.

Jamie hadn't thought it was going to stay there for the next five days, but seeing it leave still made her feel a little cold. Colder than she already was, that is.

In the centre of the room sat a huge, crescent-shaped control desk. There were two chairs behind it, facing six screens and more knobs and dials than Jamie had seen outside of an aeroplane cockpit.

Vogel was sitting down in one of the chairs and booting up the screens. The black veil displaying Bolstad's logo – a pair of cradling hands, supporting a magnificent wreath-adorned 'B' – disappeared, and a series of readouts, gauges, and measurements appeared, displaying all the statuses of the systems on board.

Jamie didn't know how long the platform had been here, but this equipment looked relatively new.

'What's through there?' Wiik asked from behind her.

Jamie turned to see him standing at the window, arms now folded, nodding towards a set of double doors at the back of the room. They were wooden – or at least wooden-cladded – and protected by another card reader.

Ehrling fielded that one, walking over from the stairs where he'd hung his raincoat. He was wearing a tired sweater, a pair of reading glasses hanging around his neck on a thin string. 'Those are the—'

'The executive quarters,' Wallace cut in, appearing from a stairwell on the opposite side of the room. He crested the top step, smiling at Jamie and then Wiik, flattening his tie against his chest. He looked dry and comfortable. The two guards behind him, however, didn't. They both looked sodden, and one was carrying Wallace's coat for him. The other had his bag. 'It's where I'll be staying,' Wallace finished, approaching and swiping a key card from his breast pocket.

The doors opened, revealing a palatial room. The floor was wooden throughout, a bed sitting on a raised platform at the back. To the right, a large leather corner suite sat on top of a plush rug, a flatscreen television suspended on the wall in front of it. Next to that, there was a desk with a leather armchair. Abstract oil-in-water artworks adorned the walls. On the opposite side, Jamie could see a kitchenette with gleaming black worktops and marble-tiled floors. A dark wooden table and chairs was set up before it, and two more doors led off from the room.

Wiik and Jamie walked forwards, following Wallace as he

entered, taking off his suit jacket and tossing it onto the silk bedspread.

He began rolling up his sleeves, utterly unhurried.

Jamie glanced at the two doors off the kitchen. The rooms beyond were in darkness, but Jamie could make out a bathroom through one, and a pair of bunks through the other – that's where his guards would sleep.

'Right,' Wallace said, grinning again. 'Welcome to Bolstad B.'

Wiik made a grunting sound, his arms still tightly folded. Though they hadn't seen their own sleeping quarters yet, Jamie guessed they wouldn't look a damn thing like this. No doubt, Wiik had arrived at the same conclusion.

She stole a glance over her shoulder at Ehrling and Vogel, who were scowling from the control deck. Jamie doubted they were living in luxury either.

'Before we go any further,' Wallace said, grabbing Jamie's attention again. 'Weapons.' He raised his eyebrows, looking at each of them.

They both tightened their grips on their duffle bags instinctively. Neither was carrying on their person, but they both had a case in their luggage that held a SIG Sauer P226 semi-automatic pistol. Along with two seventeen-round magazines.

'Please,' Wallace said, lifting his hands.

Neither Jamie nor Wiik moved, but a second later they realised he wasn't speaking to them.

A hand landed on both of their shoulders at the same time, and Jamie felt the weight of one of Wallace's heavies behind her.

She tensed, glancing at Wiik, who looked like he was ready to swing a punch.

His temple vein was throbbing again.

She wondered what his blood pressure was.

High, by the colour on his face and the flexing of his jaw.

A moment later, the guards took the initiative and pulled the duffels from both Wiik and Jamie's grip.

She let go. Wiik didn't. He seemed totally unable to tell when to pick his battles.

'Don't,' he said coldly, pulling back on the handle.

The bodyguard – who must have been about six foot one, with shoulders like a bull's, a square head, and a nose that seemed to occupy 80 per cent of the real estate on his face – turned slowly, his hand still firmly around the strap, and looked at Wiik.

'Inspector,' Wallace said, with a sigh. 'Come now.'

Wiik held firm. 'Let go,' he said to the guard.

A flicker of a smile crossed the big man's face.

'Surely,' Wallace went on, clasping his hands. 'You understand, Inspector Wiik, that we can't have you running around the platform with a firearm in your possession. This is, of course, an *oil* drilling platform. So apart from being a huge incendiary risk, there's also the added issue of there being a murderer on board. And adding a firearm into that mixture can only make the situation worse.'

But Wiik wasn't budging.

The second guard, who had Jamie's bag, stepped towards Wallace and laid it at his feet, then turned and closed in on Wiik. He lifted his right hand and put it on Wiik's shoulder so that he was standing between them, dwarfed and outmanned.

Jamie looked at Wallace, the wry smile on his face betraying the fact that he'd have no problem watching his two meat-heads rough Wiik up for the bag.

She decided it wasn't worth it.

Whether they were officers of the law or not, Bolstad was

in charge here, and its vessel was Wallace. Insufferable as he was.

'Wiik,' Jamie said, looking at him.

He didn't look back.

'Wiik.' She said it more firmly this time, and he met her eye, not turning his head.

She nodded slowly, and he drew a slow breath, sizing up the two guys in front of him.

After a second, he let go and raised his hands in surrender. 'Fine,' he said bitterly.

The bag was gone then, and sitting next to Jamie's an instant later. The two guards took their place at Wallace's flanks and gathered their hands into knots in front of them.

Arnold Wallace, with his curly grey hair, pointed nose, and glasses, clapped, and then breathed a sigh of conde-scending relief. 'Now, isn't that better? Now that we all know where we stand.' He chuckled at his own humour, safe and sound between his two bodyguards, both of whom were still armed despite the apparent incendiary risk. Both of whom would have no qualms about beating the shit out of a police officer on the order of their master.

Wiik and Jamie were both statues, watching Wallace, his beady eyes calculating and scheming behind his glasses.

After a few seconds, he seemed to make up his mind on whatever decision he was pondering and parted his still-clasped hands. He kept his knuckles towards Jamie and Wiik and shooed them out like cats. 'Well,' he said still grinning. 'Go on then. Ehrling and Vogel will bring you up to speed on the situation. I've got work to do. And you two have a murder to solve.'

7
_____

WHAT WORK Wallace had to do in that plush room, Jamie couldn't have guessed, but considering the way that last exchange had gone down, she didn't think that he was as soft and gutless as she'd first thought.

It was an easy assumption – he hardly looked the cut-throat type. But then again, the worst ones rarely did.

The doors slid shut and bolted behind Jamie and Wiik, and they were faced with the control room, the panoramic windows, and a thousand miles of open ocean.

Jamie suddenly felt very small.

'Sorry about that,' Ehrling said, coming forwards, running his hands through his thinning hair.

Jamie didn't think he had anything to apologise for. But she appreciated the sentiment. 'We've dealt with worse,' she said. Though she didn't like that she and Wiik had been stripped of their weapons.

Wiik had resigned himself to a moody silence. And Jamie didn't really blame him.

But if the events since their arrival had reinforced anything, it was that she wanted to make as much headway in

the investigation as she could and be out of here before the
sun was up.

Jamie unbuttoned her coat and pulled the stack of files
out, resting them on the corner of the crescent desk.

Ehrling looked down at them, his shoulders stiffening.
'Right,' he said, exhaling slowly. It was as though he'd been
putting off facing the reality of the situation. Jamie suspected
that up here, locked away and protected from the rest of the
platform, it was easy to pretend things were okay.

'What is the state of things here?' Jamie asked, taking off
her coat now and letting it hang from her hand. Her long-
sleeve T-shirt underneath was damp, and her hands were still
nearly numb. But the air inside the command deck was warm,
at least.

'We're still locked down,' Ehrling said, nodding. 'Crew
are confined to their quarters, drilling has stopped. Nothing is
moving. When the body was found, we called it in and were
told that law enforcement would be arriving to handle the
situation, and that we should expect a *Bolstad representative,*
too.' He cast an anxious look at the double doors to the executive quarters.

'Do you get many of them visiting?' Jamie asked carefully. 'Representatives, I mean.'

Ehrling shook his head. 'No,' he replied. 'Bolstad doesn't
send anyone unless they have to.'

'And I suspect that door remains locked until they do?'
Jamie nodded in the direction Ehrling had looked.

'We don't even have the right access cards,' he said,
almost incredulous. 'As though sleeping in any sort of
comfort is some sort of crime.' He laughed a little at his own
joke, then caught Jamie's eye and cleared his throat quickly.
'Sorry, that's not appropriate considering the circumstances,
is it?'

Jamie smiled briefly but didn't reply. 'Where is the body of the victim now?' she asked.

'He's still ...' Ehrling trailed off, his jaw quivering. He wasn't a hardy man, Jamie thought. Which struck her as odd, considering he was the acting head of operations.

'He's still hanging from the crane on the lower submersible platform,' Helene Vogel, Ehrling's deputy said frankly, spinning around on her chair.

Jamie looked at her. She had short black hair, a slim build, and piercing green eyes. Her features were fine, feminine, but she looked stern and unmoving. It clicked then that she was the spine, and Ehrling was ... Jamie glanced back at him. She didn't know what he was. But by the expression on Vogel's face, he was the one thing standing in her way of being in charge of this whole place.

Jamie cleared her throat and addressed Vogel. 'Did you say hanging from a crane?' Not much phased her these days, but hearing something like that still set her teeth on edge.

Wiik seemed to perk up then, too, and joined Jamie.

'What happened?' he asked.

Vogel and Ehrling exchanged glances. 'You haven't been told?'

Jamie shook her head. 'Only that someone had been murdered. We weren't given the details before we were flown out.'

Ehrling had circled towards the files Jamie had put down and laid a hand on them. 'And these are?' He looked almost nervous.

'Personnel files,' Jamie said, narrowing her eyes. She'd read through them all quickly on the flight, but hadn't spent much time looking at Ehrling's. By the way he was pressing down on the stack, she wished she had.

'Right, right,' he said, nodding. 'Of course.' He paused for effect and then shrugged. 'Though you won't need them.'

'And why is that?' Wiik asked, homing in on the man.

'We all know who did it.'

Vogel fired him an icy look.

Jamie observed them both.

Wiik bit his bottom lip, eyebrows crumpling towards each other. 'And who might that be?'

'Quinn and his lot.' He tsked and shook his head. 'Bad news from the off.'

'Colm Quinn?' Jamie confirmed. Now that was a file she *had* read.

'You know all about him then.'

'I'd prefer to hear your version of events,' Jamie offered.

She could see Vogel's hand had tightened around the arm of the chair. A quick look at Wiik told her he'd seen it too. The woman was all but seething.

Ehrling was looking as nonchalant as possible, but Jamie could see the pulse in his neck doing double time. 'Since he and his ... *cronies* – Kravets, Lebedenkov – arrived, they've been nothing but awful. Sloppy, rude, aggressive ... violent ...'

Vogel sucked air through her teeth and cut in. 'Just because you don't like them doesn't make them killers,' she said, her voice hard.

'You think they're innocent?' Jamie asked.

'I didn't say that,' she replied just as evenly. 'But they were friends with Alejandro – the victim. They had no reason to kill him.'

Jamie measured the woman, taking the names in. Colm Quinn. Sasha Kravets. Miroslav Lebedenkov. They were all drillers. The roughest, most dangerous job on board. And the victim, Alejandro Reyes, he was one too. But what pricked

Jamie's ears wasn't that. She looked back at Vogel now. 'Who was the ringleader out of their group?'

'Quinn,' she said without hesitation.

'Quinn.' Jamie confirmed. 'And the others ...' She trailed off as if she didn't remember the names, waiting for Vogel to help her out.

'Kravets and Lebedenkov.'

'Right,' Jamie nodded. 'They got brains of their own?'

'Are you asking if they'd follow Quinn's order to kill?'

'I wasn't. But now I am.'

She narrowed her eyes at Jamie. It was the kind of look that said, *I don't appreciate being interrogated when I'm trying to help you.* But Jamie had what she needed. For now at least.

They'd get to Quinn and his cronies. And to Ehrling's file and whatever was hiding there. But first, they needed to see the body. That would tell them something. A lot, Jamie hoped. About the nature of the crime. Hung from a crane? That's a message if she ever heard one. The question was, to who? And who had sent it?

'The lower submersible platform,' Jamie said to Ehrling. 'Can you take us?'

'Vogel can show you,' he said, smiling at her.

Wiik picked up on Jamie's lead. 'My partner asked *you.*'

Ehrling seemed less inclined to argue with Wiik. He was still soaked, bedraggled, and eight different types of pissed off. Plus, it looked like a buzzard had tried to nest in his hair. Jamie doubted she would have stood up to him either.

Wiik seemingly hadn't missed Ehrling's interest in the files and wasn't keen on leaving him alone with them either.

'Of course,' he said, finally taking his hand off the stack. 'Just let me, uh,' he sighed, 'get my coat.'

Jamie and Wiik nodded their approval.

'Vogel,' Jamie said, realising that neither her nor Wiik had a bag to put them in – until Wallace was done with their holdalls, at least – and they didn't even know where they were sleeping yet. 'Do you have a spare bag for the files? Waterproof, if possible.'

She stayed right where she was on the chair, as if deciding if she could say no or not. Then she got up. 'Of course,' she said tiredly. 'Anything to help.' She walked in the opposite direction to Ehrling and stopped at a metal locker next to the stairs that Wallace had come up. She opened it, revealing a rack with four bright orange jackets and trousers inside. They had high-visibility stripes on them and were splattered with grime and oil. On a shelf above, Jamie could see hard hats. And at the bottom, there were waxed satchels.

Vogel pulled one out and lifted the flap, pulling a toolbox out and laying it in the bottom of the locker. She turned it over then and emptied out the rest of the contents – loose screws, a filthy rag, and some other small tools. Screwdrivers, Allen keys.

Then, she was walking towards them and hurled the bag at Jamie. 'Here,' she said, as it spun towards her.

Jamie grabbed it out of the air, moving her head back so it didn't hit her in the face, and lowered it, just as Vogel passed. 'Thanks,' she said.

'Don't mention it,' Vogel replied, feigning a curtsy. She was maybe an inch or two shorter than Jamie, but she held herself powerfully. But then again, she figured you'd have to in order to survive in a place like this. How Ehrling got the post, she didn't know.

He was eyeing them as he pulled on his raincoat.

But then again, if Bolstad was on their way out, the company all but belly-up, did they really have a lot of choice?

Still, Ehrling's installation as head of operations struck Jamie as strange. Digging into his file might tell her more.

She wasted no time in grabbing the folders and pushing them inside. Then she zipped it up, latched the flap, and slung it across her body. Wiik gave her a little nod, and then they were waiting on Ehrling.

He came back over, fiddling with his hood. 'Okay,' he said, sighing emphatically and screwing his face up at the lashing of spray blowing across the flood-lit helideck. 'Ready when you are.' He gestured to the stairwell by the locker. 'That leads down to the staff quarters. As well as to—'

But he didn't get to finish.

A loud, dull banging echoed from the direction of the stairs, and then a muffled voice came with it. 'Ehrling, Vogel! I know you're up there. Where's Noemi? Ehrling!'

Jamie picked the words out between the thudding. Someone was beating on the door at the bottom of the stairs. A woman by the pitch of the voice.

'What about Noemi—' Jamie began, turning back to Ehrling, who'd now shrunk back behind the desk.

'Oh for God's sake,' Vogel growled, glaring at him while she headed for the stairs. She disappeared down it, and then a second later, the banging stopped and a woman appeared, her face a mixture of rage and disgust.

She was maybe five foot eight or nine, and well built. She had pale, freckled skin, and thick, curly red hair. Her eyes were ablaze, jaw set. Her plaid shirt billowed behind her, heavy leather boots tramping across the concrete floor as she crossed the space towards Ehrling like a charging bull.

By the look in her eye, she was about to tear his head off. Jamie couldn't decide whether it would be verbally or literally.

'Ehrling!' she growled, pointing at him, her voice

betraying her as English. Northern, Jamie thought by the twang. But she couldn't be sure. 'You fucking git!'

Yeah, definitely Northern.

'Where is she? I'll fucking kill you!'

Jamie decided. It was literally. 'Hey,' she said and stepped into the woman's path, raising her hands to try and calm her down.

But she wasn't stopping.

The redhead gave Jamie the most cursory of glances, sized her up, sized wrong, and then tried to shove her aside with her arm. Hard.

Jamie's hand came up and caught the woman's forearm. She slowed momentarily, ready to turn and throw her off, but Jamie wasn't there. The next thing she knew, her wrist was folded up between her shoulder blades.

The woman grunted, stumbled, and then stupidly, tried to wrestle free, throwing her other elbow backwards, aiming for Jamie's cheek.

Wiik stood back and observed, arms folded. He seemed to enjoy watching Jamie do this.

And if she wasn't in the mood to be fucked with before, she definitely wasn't in the mood now.

Jamie swerved backwards out of the elbow's path, sighed, and then hooked the toe of her boot around the woman's shin, pulling hard.

The woman's legs splayed and then Jamie drove her forwards, slamming her down onto the desk in front of the cowering Ehrling.

The woman squealed in shock, and tried to buck like a bronco. 'Get the fuck off me!' she howled. 'Who the fuck are you? I'll fucking—'

But then she stopped, because Wiik had appeared and was holding his badge six inches from her nose. 'You want to try that again?' he said, looking down into her reddening face.

Jamie let go of the woman's wrist, purple finger marks glowing on her porcelain skin. The newcomer immediately brought it round in front of her, rubbing it with her other hand as she pushed herself upright with her elbows.

Jamie gave her space and the redhead took note of her for the first time, looking her up and down. Wondering how the hell she'd just been folded up like a deck chair and taken down by a woman half her size.

'You're the ones they sent then?' she asked, her voice still hot with anger.

'Detective Inspector Jamie Johansson,' Jamie replied.

'Kriminalinspektör Anders Wiik,' he said from the other side of the desk, next to Ehrling, who'd moved behind him. 'And you are?'

'Ashleigh,' she said. 'Hooper.'

'Well, Ashleigh Hooper,' Wiik went on. 'You want to tell us why you were about to "kill" Ehrling here?' He hooked a thumb over his shoulder.

Ehrling had practically disappeared completely behind Wiik now.

Ashleigh straightened her shirt. 'Because that piece of shit isn't doing a damn thing about Noemi!'

'Noemi Heikkinen?' Jamie confirmed now, stepping back around the desk so she was next to Wiik. She recognised the name from the files. 'What do you mean he's not doing anything about her?'

Ashleigh shook her head in confusion. 'She's … aren't you here to … to find her?'

'Find her?' Jamie asked, narrowing her eyes a little. 'What do you mean *find* her?'

'She's— she's missing.' She looked from Wiik to Jamie

and back again. 'That's why you're— Isn't that why you're
... *here*?'

Jamie and Wiik looked at each other.

Wiik spoke first. 'We're here investigating the murder of
Alejandro Reyes.'

'But you're saying,' Jamie finished off, 'that Noemi
Heikkinen is missing?'

'Yes,' Ashleigh said, laughing incredulously. 'I can't
believe this.' She put her hand on her head and walked in a
circle. The fury had gone from her eyes now and they'd
begun to shine. 'You didn't even ...' She glanced at Vogel,
who'd come back to the desk, and then back at Jamie. 'They
didn't even tell you, did they?'

Jamie and Wiik both remained quiet.

'Fucking Bolstad,' Ashleigh said under her breath. 'Of
course they didn't. Why would they?' She threw her arms up
now, verging on tears. 'It's not like they give a shit about
anything except fucking *oil.*'

Jamie went over the files in her head. Noemi Heikkinen
was twenty-two years old. Petite, white-blonde hair, dark blue
eyes. She was studying ecology at Helsinki University. She
was one of three students here on Bolstad B.

The second, Ashleigh Hooper, studying marine biology,
was standing in front of her.

The third, Paméla Sevier, was studying oceanography.
They were all here doing research for a shared paper on the
effects that deep-sea drilling was having on the ocean's
ecosystem. It had seemed odd right from the off to Jamie that
Bolstad would put themselves in a vulnerable position like
that – that they would allow researchers the opportunity to
prove what they were doing was harming the environment.

'When did Noemi disappear?' Jamie asked.

'Last night,' Ashleigh said.

Ehrling seemed to grow a pair of testicles then. He cleared his throat loudly and peeked over Wiik's shoulder. 'We don't know for certain that she's even missing yet,' he said, trying to downplay it.

Ashleigh fired him a scornful look. 'Fuck you,' she growled. 'You *know* she is.'

'Why does Ehrling *know* she's missing?' Jamie pressed.

'Because her and Reyes were … They were …' She couldn't seem to find the right word.

'Involved?' Jamie asked.

Ashleigh nodded, the tears welling in the corners of her eyes. She touched her knuckles to her lips now. They quivered behind her hand. 'And now he's *dead* … and probably so is … Noemi is …' And then the floodgates opened.

Ehrling was talking again. 'Vogel, why don't you escort Miss Hooper back to her quarters?'

Vogel met his eyes for a moment, and then came forwards. Before her hands even touched Ashleigh's shoulders, she shrugged them off. 'Don't touch me,' she spat, tears hot on her cheeks. She fixed her eyes on Ehrling now. 'Whatever has happened to Noemi, it's on *you.*'

Ehrling stared back at her, expression blank. Vogel came forwards again and laid a single hand on Ashleigh's shoulder this time. She tried to shrug it off again, but Vogel was squeezing.

Slowly, Ashleigh allowed herself to be steered back towards the stairs, and then she was gone.

Jamie watched her go, taking it all in. Processing.

Alejandro Reyes was dead. Strung up from a crane somewhere below them.

Helene Vogel knew more than she was letting on.

Noemi Heikkinen was missing.

Colm Quinn had been named as suspect number one.

And Tim Ehrling, the unassuming, soft-eyed head of operations, still partially hiding behind Wiik, until he was absolutely sure that Ashleigh Hooper was gone, was at the centre of it all.

She looked at him, measuring him, weighing him up to see what he was made of. She'd dissect his file later. And if what she wanted wasn't in there ... Well, there were other ways to find the truth.

And out here, she didn't feel like the same rules applied.

She met Wiik's eye, and he gave her a look of quiet reassurance.

And then, they turned their attention towards the door and headed into the gathering night.

8

EHRLING LED them deeper into the labyrinth.

The stairs that fed into the command deck swirled down into the lower levels, and Jamie and Wiik and he went round, and round, and round until they came to the lowest deck of all.

Deck 1 was still eighty feet off the water. And though it was high enough that falling from here would be like hitting a solid slab of steel, the noise of the ocean was still deafening, even before they got outside.

Ehrling opened a hatch and stepped into a corridor streaked with rust. The air was damp and salty, the steel-grated floor suspended over pipes that ran the length of the hallway.

Jamie glanced left and right – seeing a door on either end. The one to her right had the words *Maintenance* stencilled above it. The one to the left, which looked more like a submarine hatch than anything – solid steel with a porthole window, and a two-handed lock that, when turned, would shunt two thick steel bars against the frame, sealing it – had the words *Lower Submersible Platform* above.

Ehrling moved quickly, kneading his hands in front of him. As he neared the hatch, he stopped and glanced back at the still-damp Jamie and Wiik. He reached out for a storage locker positioned before the door. He pulled it open and reached inside, withdrawing two heavy red Bolstad parka coats. 'Here,' he said, throwing them to Jamie and Wiik. 'These should fit.'

Jamie and Wiik both caught them out of the air and looked inside the collars. The coats were dirty, a little damp themselves, and had a distinctly metallic smell, but Jamie could tell by the sheer weight that they'd be necessary to keep the cold at bay. Even in here their breath was frosting in front of their faces. And now that the sun had gone down, she shuddered to think how cold it would be outside.

'You can leave your coats in the locker,' Ehrling said. 'Grab them on the way back in.'

Wiik reached over and checked the label of the parka Jamie had in her hand, and then without asking, pulled it from her grasp and shoved his own into it.

'You had a large,' he said, shrugging out of his wool over-coat and slipping into the fur-hooded jacket. He grimaced as he did. Wiik liked things clean. He liked things neat. And these coats were neither.

Jamie followed suit, a little apprehensive, and donned the huge jacket. Ehrling was shifting nervously in front of them, and she didn't know if she liked the vibe he was giving off. But she trusted Wiik, and he was watching Ehrling like a hawk. He had been since the command deck.

Ehrling bit his lip now and folded his arms. 'He's, uh, he's out there,' he said, nodding over his shoulder at the lower submersible platform. 'Reyes, I mean.'

'After you,' Wiik said gruffly, not moving a muscle.

Ehrling laughed nervously, then cleared his throat. 'I thought I might, uh, stay in here, actually.'

Wiik and Jamie both narrowed their eyes at him.

'And why would you think that?' Wiik asked.

Ehrling swallowed. 'It's just, I've, you know, *seen* him already. And, well, I, er, don't really, uh—'

Wiik started forwards, shoving Ehrling in the shoulder so that he began moving towards the hatch.

He quietened and unlocked the hatch, taking a breath before he pushed outwards.

The cold hit Jamie like a wall. The spray of the ocean, the bitter wind. It stung her face like someone had raked needles across it.

'Jesus,' she muttered, zipping her parka up hastily and bracing against the onslaught.

'I'd say you get used to it!' Ehrling yelled now, the corridor filled by the crash and wash of the waves on the struts below. 'But you don't!'

They stepped out and Ehrling pushed the hatch to.

Wiik hung back to make sure he wasn't making a break for it, but Jamie advanced, towards the grizzly scene before her.

The lower submersible platform was about thirty feet long and six wide. It was a suspended catwalk bolted onto the side of the main platform. The steel grate rattled underfoot as the icy wind whipped through it, and the support struts groaned under the stress of the crane arm.

It extended from the platform at a forty-five-degree angle and lanced twenty feet into the open air. The guard rail ended beneath it and gave way to a locked gate with a yellow hazard symbol on it. *Caution. Danger of Death* was written on it with a little symbol of a stick-man plunging to his doom.

Jamie approached, grimacing.

Just behind, a small precipice stretched out. And then, nothing. Just the air. And the ocean far beneath.

Jamie swayed in the wind, looking up at where a submersible pod would hang.

Except there wasn't one.

In its place, a body was hanging. Alejandro Reyes.

Jamie stared up at the man, the floodlighting over the walkway making the blood staining his shirt and trousers shine black.

He was twenty-seven, well built. He had a shock of dark, tousled hair, and Jamie remembered from his photograph in his file that he was handsome.

But he didn't look it now.

He looked beaten, brutalised.

The thick, braided cable that was designed to hold up the sub was knotted around his neck. His face was gaunt, cut by blows, bruises clinging to the skin where the blood had soaked into the tissues. He was hanging limply. A red parka – identical to the ones Wiik and Jamie were wearing – hung from his shoulders, the tips of his fingers poking out of the ends. The jacket was open, his shirt beneath – a grey T-shirt – was dotted with knife holes. Jamie stared up at the massacre in front of her.

Alejandro twisted on the rope as the wind caught him, his legs swaying, heels clicking as he swung back and forth.

Jamie counted sixteen distinct slits on his torso before he turned away from her. She'd need to inspect the body fully, take photos, send them back to Falk and Hallberg to pass on to a pathologist, see if they couldn't get an expert's opinion. But first, they'd need to get Reyes down. And that would be no small feat.

Built to accommodate a sub, the crane hung a good ten

feet away from the platform. Which meant Alejandro Reyes' body was out of reach.

Jamie set her jaw, steeling herself against the cold. 'Wiik,' she called, motioning him over.

He pushed Ehrling along the platform so he was on the far side of them, away from the hatch, and then came to Jamie's shoulder.

'Give me a hand with this?' she said, turning to the pulley system set at the base of the crane. There was a winch there, with two rubberised buttons, one bearing an upwards pointing arrow, the other a downwards arrow.

Wiik nodded and knelt next to the panel, pressing the down button.

Nothing happened.

'Dead,' Wiik said.

Jamie fired him a look.

'Sorry, poor choice of words.'

Ehrling spoke up then from his position against the wall of the platform. 'It's off. As we don't have a submersible on board, we shut off the power to this walkway.'

Wiik sighed, eyeing up the handle next to the winch instead. He cupped his hands over his mouth and breathed some warmth into them before taking hold of it.

With a grunt, he pushed down on the handle. It groaned a little at first, and then gave. Jamie could see the muscles in his neck pulling taut as he wound it around, letting out the cable.

In front of her, Alejandro Reyes slowly began to lower. With no power going to the winch, it would take a strong person to drag Reyes up there. Jamie cast an eye over her shoulder at Ehrling. Unless, of course, you knew where the switch was to bring the power back.

Wiik grunted on her left and she turned back, seeing Reyes draw level with her eye.

'That's good,' she said, looking out at him.

He swung gently, coming closer and then moving further away.

Jamie measured the distance. It was too far to reach, and she didn't really like the idea of clambering out onto the precipice and stretching across space to try and grab a fistful of his bloody jacket.

She trusted Wiik to keep a hold of her, but still, that was just asking for trouble. The steel looked slick, and the wind blowing across the surface of the ocean must have been thirty, maybe forty miles an hour. She could hear it howling in her ears.

She thought back then to the locker in the command deck. 'Ehrling,' she shouted, looking back at him.

He perked up, still wrapped up tightly in his own black Bolstad jacket. It didn't look as bulky as Jamie or Wiik's, but it did look newer, and cleaner.

'Is there a boathook in that locker?' She nodded back towards the door. 'Something they use to bring the submersible to the gate?'

Ehrling thought for a second. 'Yeah, I mean, I think so. We've never used it, but there's something. I'll get it.' He moved quickly, and Wiik stood up just as fast, intercepting him before he could get there.

Ehrling stopped, looked at each of them in turn. 'What?' He laughed then. 'You think I'm going to trap you out here?'

Wiik said nothing. Jamie didn't either. But that was what was at the back of both of their minds. They'd been out there no more than a few minutes, and Jamie's hands were already numb, her jeans soaked, skin prickling from the cold. The thought of being locked out was nothing short of terrifying.

Ehrling approached the hatch, paused, and then looked back at Wiik, who was hovering anxiously.

Jamie held fast at the rail, trying to avoid locking eyes with Reyes.

Ehrling smiled briefly, and then reached out for the lock. It was a vertical bar, mirrored on the inside.

As Jamie watched him take hold of it, her blood ran a little cold, her breath catching in her throat.

She didn't remember Ehrling closing the door behind them when they'd come outside.

He pushed on the bar, but nothing happened.

'Sorry,' he said, turning his body to the side so he could get his weight behind it. 'These can get a little sticky.'

Jamie watched from the rail, holding her breath.

Ehrling jerked at the metal, switching sides so he could try pulling instead. His teeth bared themselves as he tried again, straining at the locking mechanism.

But it wouldn't budge.

He looked up at Wiik, his eyes full of fear.

'Move,' Wiik commanded, shouldering him out of the way. He took hold of the bar, tightened both hands around it, and heaved. But it didn't move. At all.

Wiik stared at Jamie, the realisation striking home.

'Jesus,' Ehrling said, the little colour that remained in his face draining away. 'We're locked out.' He flung himself against the door, pressing his eyes to the porthole. 'Shit, I can't see anything!' he yelled, his breath fogging the glass. 'I don't ... Who would have? Who would have *known* ...'

Jamie could already see the panic in him.

She was struggling to keep it inside herself.

She took a breath, focusing. Shit, it was hard in the cold. Her entire head was aching from it. It must have been well below zero. How far, she didn't know, but with the wind and the spray, too cold to survive the night. She knew that much.

Jamie closed her eyes, listening as Ehrling's yelling reached fever pitch, as Wiik took hold of him and told him to calm the fuck down. She reached into the pocket of her jeans and pulled her phone out, forcing herself to look at the screen.

No signal.

Of course not. This far out, there wouldn't be.

She glanced at Wiik. He had his out too, and was shaking his head at her.

Shit.

'Ehrling,' Jamie said, coming forwards. He was back at the bar, ripping at it like a madman. 'I'm guessing you didn't bring a satphone with you?'

'You think I'd be doing this if I did?' he roared, spit flecking from between his teeth. His hair flopped back and forth wildly, wet with the spray.

Wiik stepped away from him and Jamie let herself be guided towards the end of the platform. Wiik wasn't easily rattled, but Jamie could see his eyes wide, his mind whirring around behind them, searching for an answer. Jamie knew they couldn't just sit and wait and hope for someone to come and rescue them.

'What are you thinking?' Wiik asked, lowering his voice as much as he could without it being lost in the wind.

'I'm thinking someone *really* doesn't want us here.' Jamie looked over at Ehrling, who'd now collapsed against the door. For someone who was supposed to be running this place, he wasn't much use in a crisis. Jamie reached down and felt at the satchel at her hip, the files safe inside. She was glad then she'd brought them, then. 'I'm thinking that someone saw the chopper come in, put two and two together, and then followed us down here. They saw us out here, and they took their opportunity – closed the door, jammed it.'

'Hoping we freeze to death?' Wiik lifted an eyebrow and leaned in, his once impeccably groomed hair now parting in the middle and falling into thick strands around his face.

'Or just to send a message,' Jamie said.

'I didn't see anyone following us.'

'Me either. But then again, I wasn't looking.'

'Vogel knew we were coming down here.' Wiik inspected Jamie's face for any sign of confirmation of his theory.

'I don't know.' Jamie sighed. 'She doesn't strike me as the type.'

'They never do,' Wiik added.

Jamie knew he was right. But Vogel was Ehrling's second in command. And judging by the way Ehrling was losing his shit by the door, and how she'd faced up to Hooper when she'd come barrelling into the command deck, Jamie thought that Vogel was probably the one keeping this place going. So if it was Ehrling out here alone, maybe locking him out in the cold would let her settle into the captain's chair. But to condemn two detectives to a cold and horrible death? That wasn't going to reflect well on either her or Bolstad. They were doing their best to cover up one death, but four? No, Vogel didn't fit the bill. And plus, she wouldn't have the strength to haul Reyes up there. And on top of that, she'd called him Alejandro. And everyone else by their surnames. Which meant there was more to Reyes' and her relationship than met the eye. He was involved with Noemi, though. And while jealousy wasn't out of the question as a motive for murder, stabbing someone sixteen times in the gut and then stringing them up from a crane didn't make any sense at all.

'Johansson?'

Jamie looked up at Wiik. 'Yeah, sorry,' she said, shrugging off the train of thought and looking around. 'We can figure out who did this later – right now, we need to get off this walkway.'

Wiik nodded in agreement and turned back to Ehrling. 'Hey,' he called, walking over. 'How do we get off this thing?'

Jamie let Wiik deal with the head of operations while she turned to the sea. Reyes swung lazily in her peripheral as she looked down into the waves, the faint outline of the whitecaps staring back up at her from below.

What was the reason for Reyes' death? And if he was out here, why not just toss him over the rail? No one would have known, then.

This was a message.

Her mind kept coming back to that.

Jamie screwed her eyes closed, feeling like her eyeballs were about to freeze. And where was Noemi? Had she gone over?

Hooper said she'd been missing since last night. Thought she was dead, same as Reyes.

Had they been out here together? This place wasn't exactly *on the way* to anywhere. It was secluded. Which made it a poor place to hang a body for someone to just *find*. But it made it a good place to meet a lover in secret. But why were they keeping their relationship a secret?

And where the hell was Noemi?

Had they tossed her over the side? Was Reyes the target here? And Noemi just collateral? Had she jumped to escape a worse fate? Or had she been taken? Jamie turned back to the platform. Was she inside, somewhere? Chained up, maybe? Or strangled to death and stuffed in a storage locker?

Shit, they'd have to search the place, top to bottom. If they could find her, she might be their only witness.

Or, she might be dead. Either way, they needed to find her.

'Hey,' Wiik said, appearing at her shoulder again. 'You okay?'

Jamie turned, shivering. 'Freezing, but I'm alright. What did Ehrling say?' She looked around him. He was still on his ass, face buried in the collar of his coat.

'You're not going to like it.'

'I bet,' Jamie said. 'But we're running out of time.'

Wiik strode off towards the far end of the platform, and Jamie followed wordlessly.

He slowed as he neared the far rail, the corner of the main platform coinciding with the edge of the catwalk. He leaned over it, staring around the corner, into the darkness.

Jamie didn't like this already.

She reached him and leaned out as well, following his gaze.

Around the corner of the platform, Jamie could see a blank concrete wall.

Above, another catwalk jutted out from the side, but it was thirty feet up. Ahead, Jamie could see another one on their level, but it must have been fifty, maybe sixty feet away.

'That,' Wiik said, pointing across at it – dimly lit in the distance. 'Is Emergency Stairwell Six, Ehrling said.'

'Right.' Jamie's heart was already beating faster.

'It's a fire escape that leads to a ladder stretching down to an emergency platform at sea level.' Wiik pointed down into the darkness below Bolstad B. 'The stairs also lead right up to the helideck, with a hatch on each level.' He looked at her. 'Including this one.'

'Right.' Jamie's voice had quietened, her eyes fixed on the stairwell catwalk that seemed *very* far away. She was dreading what was coming next.

'It leads into maintenance, which connects back to the corridor we came out here from.'

'I remember.' She didn't want to ask the question. But she knew she had to. 'So how do we get over there?'

Wiik stepped back from the rail and Jamie's stomach turned over.

Running along the wall, level with their feet, were a set of thick armoured cables. They sat in a metal tray no wider than six inches. About six feet above that, a single cable was tacked to the wall. Jamie followed it. It fed into the floodlight hanging over their head, stretching out into the blackness going the other direction.

Wiik looked at her for a while, and then spoke. 'It's our only chance.'

'I know,' Jamie said quietly, looking down at their shoes. At Wiik's fashion-conscious leather boots. The ones with barely enough tread to hold on to a frosty pavement. At her lightweight trail boots with the ultra-grippy rubber soles. The ones designed to clamber over frozen rocks and up muddy mountains.

'Do you want me to go?' Wiik asked.

She looked up at him, knowing that if she said yes, she'd just have to watch him struggle, slip, and then fall to his death.

'No,' she said, finding the few remaining ounces of strength and warmth she had inside her and summoning them. She flexed her hands in her pockets, willing blood into them, and stared up at the cable overhead. She doubted she'd be able to do more than pinch it between her fingertips. 'I'll do it,' she muttered, raking in a shaking breath and meeting Wiik's eye – she hoped not for the last time. 'You want to give that door one last try first? You know, just in case?'

9

Wiik was squeezing Jamie's hand so tightly she thought he was going to crush it.

As she stepped up and onto the rail, he was right there with her. One hand in hers, the other on her back, steadying her against the wind.

It beat at her flank, stung her face, threw her off balance. She had one foot on the middle rung of the rail, the other on the top. She could feel the raw, slick steel against the arch of her boot, could hear the spray pelting the side of the platform's legs.

She swallowed, trying to steady her heart, but it was no good. No matter how much she tried to distance herself from the fact, there was no getting away from what she was about to do.

Shimmying eighty feet, balancing on a board no wider than her foot, pressed against a soaked wall with nothing but a wire to hold on to.

She exhaled, whole body shaking, wind threatening to knock her off before she even started.

Wiik tightened his grip as she wobbled. 'At least,' he said, looking up at her, his eyes as full and fearful as she'd ever seen, 'the wind is blowing *into* the platform.'

She couldn't muster a response. It didn't make her feel better.

'I mean, instead of a crosswind, or—'

'Just shut up, Wiik,' she muttered. She wasn't sure if he heard her or not, but volume wasn't something her throat could produce just then.

Jamie reached up, feeling bulky and awkward in her parka, and grabbed for the wire overhead. Her nails scraped against the concrete, a dull pain shooting through her frozen hands, and her grip slipped.

She swore and then reached up again, not wanting to stretch or risk her balance.

Wiik lifted his hand, trying to give her better leverage, but it was futile. This was suicide any way she spun it.

But as she looked down into Wiik's face, his cheeks red and blotchy from the cold, and then over at Ehrling, who was now sat in the corner of the catwalk, cradling his knees, trying to conserve warmth – or who knew what else – she knew there was no other option. They could wait, sure – but for how long? And soon, Jamie wouldn't have the strength to attempt this. It was now or never.

And she chose now.

Jamie gritted her teeth and reached to her chin, unzipping her parka with her free hand.

'What are you doing?' Wiik called up to her.

But Jamie wasn't able to answer. She was in full focus mode. And she knew that she couldn't do this wrapped up in so much bulk. No, she could barely move in that thing, and she needed to feel everything. She needed mobility, and she needed to be able to press herself to the wall.

She was still on the rail when she pulled her hand from Wiik's grasp and shed the coat and satchel completely. Wiik took them, his knuckles white in the fabric, breath held between his teeth as Jamie pushed upwards and sank her fingers into the wire, forcing her nails down behind it. The pins holding it to the wall strained, but they would hold – she hoped.

She lifted her left leg, her right still over the rail, and planted her foot on the trough. She had to move fast now. Without the coat, her core temperature would plummet. But she hoped that was going to spur her on.

Jamie pushed up onto the metal tray, letting it take her weight. It groaned a little, bowed under the stress. But she was light. And thinking about the strength of the brackets designed to support a few *wires* wasn't going to do her reasoning for trying this any good.

She took one last look at Wiik and then drew her back leg over the rail, putting all of her weight onto the tray.

The sudden transference made it undulate, the force rolling down it and then back up like a wave.

She glanced at her feet, toes tight to the concrete, nothing but space and boiling ocean beneath her heels, and her head swam, her stomach threatening to expel what little was inside it.

Acid clawed its way into the back of her throat. But she couldn't turn back now.

She nodded to Wiik and then offered him her free hand – the one closest to him.

He looked at her quizzically, but took it.

She smiled at him, squeezed for a moment, and then pulled it free and closed it around the wire next to the other.

And then that was it. She was alone up there.

And with each shimmying step, Wiik got smaller, and smaller.

She fought with wind, tracing the wall with her toes, heart in her mouth.

It seemed to take an age.

She couldn't think about anything. Anything except falling. Anything except what it would be like to hit the water from this height. About how long she could swim for if she survived. About which way the current was moving and how quickly she'd be swept away. Whether she'd lose sight of the platform before she drowned. Whether they'd ever find her body.

Jamie slid her left foot over, gaining another few inches, and stumbled.

It caught on a stray screw sticking out of the wall. Her toe just nudged it, but it forced her heel back, the treads on her boot slipping.

She was pressing her body against the wall so hard it forced her foot backwards, sending it arcing into space.

Her right knee sang under the sudden strain, her thigh burning.

Her grip slipped, nails bending backwards.

She called out, not sure if she even made a noise, and felt her ankle connect with the metal tray.

Pain surged up through her leg, and then suddenly, she didn't know if she was falling or not.

Her world span, balance totally gone.

Jamie forced her eyes open seeing her hand flat against the concrete. She was breathing hard and traced the wall back up, teetering on the tray as it rolled beneath her, moving up and down like the sea below.

Her fingers made contact with the wire then and she slowly hooked them over it, forcing herself to breathe.

With all the strength she could find in her right leg, she forced herself to stand straight, sweat beading on her forehead despite the blistering cold.

Her left leg came up then and found its place next to her right.

She looked back along the line of the wall, only now realising how dark it was here. From either end, it looked bright enough – lights drowning both their catwalk and the emergency stairs. But from where she was now, it was inky. Thick. Impenetrable. Wiik was just a murky figure, bathed in white in the distance. He was hanging over the rail, threatening to climb out there himself. She could see his mouth open, his head shaking. But she couldn't hear anything. The wind and the roar from below were swallowing his words.

What was he saying? Are you okay? Come back? Keep going?

Jamie looked the other way, frozen to the bone. She was just halfway. Fuck. What was she thinking? Was she really doing this? She was going to die up here.

No.

No. She couldn't think like that. She wouldn't.

She'd faced down killers and traffickers and gunmen and everything in between. She wouldn't be brought down by a locked door and a shaky fucking plank bolted to a wall.

She had to keep moving. Before she got too cold.

She'd fought off hypothermia once, and if it set in again, she'd not be able to stand, let alone make it to the other side.

She had to move, and she had to move now.

Jamie shimmied. Her hips ached. Her shoulders creaked and throbbed. Her hair was soaked, her skin cold and blueing before her eyes. She could feel her shirt sodden, her skin shrivelling and constricting as the blood retreated to her organs. Her boots were wet now, too, her heels squelching in them as she moved.

But she was *moving*. And that was all that mattered.

She kept her eyes fixed on her hands, trusted what little tactile feedback she had in her feet to keep her on the right track.

And then she was squinting, the light searing her dilated pupils.

Fuck, she could barely see anything. She wished the light would just go away, so she could open her eyes, see what she was ... Wait, light?

Jamie dared to turn her head, saw that she was no more than ten feet from the catwalk now.

Her heart raced, relief flooding her veins. She felt her jaw quiver, her eyes fill. Jesus, she didn't think she'd ever been so happy to see a goddamn handrail!

Almost there. Just a little ... further ... just ... almost ...

Jamie let go, lurched sideways, and felt the rail hit her square in the chest. It hurt, like hell, punched all the wind out of her.

Her knees scraped metal, her toes scrabbling for grip, arms locked into hooks. She sprayed spittle through her teeth, sodden plait waving behind her as she shunted her boot into the corner of the catwalk and an upright rail support. And then her other foot was under her and she was climbing.

Her weight transferred and she flopped forwards, felt the cold metal bar slide down her stomach and hit her hip, sending her spinning onto her side.

She landed with a clang, breathing hard, tears warm on her face.

Jamie coughed and curled her fingers through the gaps in the grate, her eyes fluttering open.

She could just make out Wiik in the distance. He was still, still at the rail. He lifted a hand and waved to her.

She lifted hers and waved back, unable to move her fingers.

Jesus, she was cold.

She needed to get inside.

Jamie forced her knees up under her and then pushed up on numb hands until she was upright. She squinted into the wind and spray and looked around, getting her bearings, and then did a double take.

The stairs ahead – the emergency ones that led all the way to the helideck. She could have sworn there was someone on them.

A dark figure, cut out against the indigo sky.

But now they were gone.

No, it was a trick of the light. Her mind was working against her. No one would be crazy enough to be out here now.

Her eyes traced the wall to the bottom of the stairs and stopped at the hatch there.

Yes. That was what Wiik said – a door to the maintenance deck, which led through to the corridor that led to the lower submersible platform.

Okay, now she just had to get up. Inside, she'd be able to get to her coat, get it on, let Wiik and Ehrling in, and then get something warm to eat and drink.

She had a plan, and with the little strength she had left, pushed herself to a shaky stance, wobbled, and then started moving.

Her feet seemed heavy, glued to the ground, and her skin had numbed now that she couldn't even feel the wind anymore.

She looked down and could see her hands wrapped

around her body. Damn, she thought they were hanging at her sides.

The door loomed towards her. On the left, a staircase led down to a ladder, and in front, another staircase stretched up and wrapped around, winding into the darkness above. A floodlamp burnt overhead, forcing her to squint. She looked up at the flat section of the staircase, at where she thought she'd glimpsed the figure. The spray moved through the glare of the light, waves of mist swirling through it, too. It must have just been a trick of the light. Must have been. She was basically out of her mind with the cold as it was. She could barely focus on what she needed to do.

Jamie blinked twice, wondering how long she'd just been standing there, and then forced her hands from her ribs and onto the bar in front of her.

As she willed her numb fingers to close around it, she feared it was going to be locked. Jammed like the other one. She swallowed, her throat folding awkwardly, and then she pulled.

Her shoulders hurt, her skin hurting as she jerked.

Jamie shuddered violently, her knees quaking, and then pulled again, and again.

And then it moved, and she felt a wave of emotion so strong it nearly broke her.

The mechanism began to shift, and then it clanked horizontally. The door opened heavily as Jamie dragged it into the wind, and then she lurched inside, grabbed for the inside handle, and pulled it shut.

It swung quickly and banged into the frame, pinned in place by the wind.

She collapsed against it and twisted the bar back into the locked position, breathing hard.

Her back prickled with the sudden onslaught of heat and her chest tightened, the air thick.

She could smell oil, grease, hot metal.

Maintenance.

Jamie turned to face it, already feeling the sweat pushing through her skin, the heat coming off the pipes around her palpable. She didn't know what she'd expected, but hypothermia wasn't going to be an issue anymore.

She could just make out vertical pipes ahead. They ran down through the floor and catwalks moved between them, offering access to each set. The bodies of boilers rose out of the darkness on both sides – two rows of them, burning the oil that the platform pulled from the earth to keep the place running. They chugged and whirred, and somewhere towards the back of the cavernous room, Jamie could hear the whining revolutions of electrical generators.

She squinted into the darkness ahead, feeling claustrophobic, trying to get her bearings.

And then she froze.

As her mind returned to her, she became aware of herself. Of the blood returning to her extremities. Of the wet cloth against her skin. Of the heavy rise and fall of her chest as she choked on the steam-filled air.

And of the sound of footsteps echoing between the ker-thunk of the boilers.

Her brain replayed the snatched image of a figure at the top of the stairs.

It replayed the moment they realised they'd been locked out.

It replayed the moment Jamie realised that someone didn't want them here.

And then it told her that the type of person who was going to take a shot like that – who was going to try to kill off the director of operations and two police officers without hesitation – they weren't about to leave the outcome up to chance.

And now, Jamie was on her own.

In the dark.

And they had the home-field advantage.

10

JAMIE FORCED HERSELF TO BREATHE.

Her heart was beating fast, and she could feel the hot blood pouring down her arms and into her hands, making her skin prickle painfully. Her muscles were lubricating, her adrenal glands wringing themselves out like sponges.

She was sharpening, warming with every passing second.

From where she was standing, there were three paths – right, left, and straight ahead. If she stayed right here, she could see whoever was coming. She could take them down – of that much, she was certain. Her size worked for her. Not in a physically advantageous way, but in that no one expected her to be able to put her heel into the temple of someone six feet tall. So if they came at her, she could take them.

She thanked the years of taekwondo and her trainer for that.

She settled herself.

If they came for her here, she'd be ready. But she didn't think *they* would be.

They'd locked all three of them outside, and Jamie knew that they knew that she would need to let them in. That being stuck out there, they'd just freeze. The killer had time. They could wait. They could just stay right where they were, hidden in the darkness, and let Wiik and Ehrling die out there. And then it would *just* be Jamie to contend with.

She swallowed.

She had to get to that door. And quickly. So that she had Wiik watching her back.

Jamie squinted into the darkness ahead and traced a step forwards. The footsteps had stopped now.

The catwalk rang softly under her boots as she moved.

Ahead, a wall loomed into view – except it wasn't a wall, but the hot body of a giant boiler that split the path in two.

Jamie stopped at the junction and glanced both ways. Not only did she not know where she was going, but she also didn't know how far it was. The door she needed to get back to Wiik was somewhere ahead of her. So she just needed to keep her bearings. But damn it was dark, and hot, and sweat was dripping into her eyes and making them sting.

Jamie chose right, hoping the paths would converge on the other side, and moved further from the meagre shaft of light coming in through the porthole behind her.

She could hear her breathing in her ears now, her pulse in her neck.

Progress was slow, and the layout here like a maze. It was laid out in rough grids, but paths would suddenly end, surrounded on three sides by a control unit or valves and pipes – little maintenance inlets designed to give access to specific modules. Or to confound detectives trying to avoid getting their skulls caved in by murderous drillers.

Jamie backtracked and turned to the left now, hoping she was moving in the right direction.

She came to another rail, a flat wall beyond, and reached

out, laying her hand on the cool concrete. Shit. Outer wall. She didn't think she was going that way.

Jamie looked left and right, wondering if it was the wall she'd shimmied along, or if she had somehow got herself completely turned around.

She hung her head, her clothes clinging to her, soaked and now sticky from the steam.

The boilers kept clunking behind, turbines whirring. But between the throb, her ears detected something. Her body tensed all at once, the back of her neck erupting into gooseflesh.

Footsteps.

She shoved herself back from the wall, turning just in time to see a shadow lurch out of the darkness, running right at her. Its hands were out, its bulk enormous – she didn't know if it was a giant man, a bear, or just someone in a Bolstad parka, but whichever it was, they were going for her throat.

Jamie got her hands up and threw a twisting block, deflecting the incoming attack with her forearms, stepping to the side while she did.

The assailant moved past her and clattered into the rail, hands hitting the metal like gongs.

Jamie wasted no time, dancing onto her left foot and sending a roundhouse square into where she guessed their kidneys would be. It was hard to see in the dark, but a hard kick there would stun an opponent.

Except her shin connected and seemed to rebound off.

The padding of the jacket, or just the assailant's bulk – she didn't know. But as she came back down onto both feet, fists raised in front of her, they pushed off the rail and turned, advancing quickly.

Jamie swallowed, moving backwards, the shape swimming towards her in the darkness, hands loose at their sides.

Her mind raced, and she stole a glance over her shoulder, wondering if she could risk a crescent or even a high side kick – really knock their head off their shoulders. Big or not, a boot to the face would rock anyone's world. But she didn't dare. They were too big, sidling side to side, and it was pitch dark, and with every inch Jamie took up, her heels clipped the intentionally rough steel grating underfoot, threatening to trip her up.

No, this wasn't the place, and she wasn't about to get herself strangled to death. Not after what she'd just been through.

She made the call then, stepping a little wider, bouncing from foot to foot, baiting them to come faster. And then she stopped and lunged in.

Her right knee rose and as she touched down with her opposite foot, she pivoted forwards and lashed out in a fierce push kick.

Her heel landed square in the middle of her attacker's body and stopped them where they stood.

Jamie's knee twinged under the force, but the desired effect was achieved.

The figure staggered, and Jamie sprang backwards, turning a full one-eighty in the air and taking off running.

She didn't know where she was going, but it was her only shot just then. This wasn't the place to get into a fight, and if the first kick didn't put them down, she'd have a battle ahead.

Jamie needed to cut right, and risked slowing down just enough to look at each turning she passed.

Inlet.

Inlet.

Inlet.

Walkway.

Shit. Jamie slammed on the brakes, grabbed for the rail on her right, and halted herself, stretching her shoulder out as she came to a sudden stop and then pulled herself back towards the gap.

She glanced up as she rounded the corner, seeing her attacker coming towards her again, closing the gap.

Jamie plunged on, cutting right, then left again.

Footsteps thundered behind her.

The boilers thumped at her flanks, the whir of the turbines enough to make her wince.

There. Ahead. She could see light. A dim glow. A porthole. To the corridor! Yes, she was there. She was safe.

Jamie came to another T-junction, knowing the door was just on the other side of the last row of pumps and pipes, and hung a left. She took hold of the rail with her right hand and swung herself around the first corner. Just one more right and she was – trapped?

Jamie's hands came up to protect her face and she collided with a solid wall of metal, a large globe valve set on a thick horizontal pipe.

She drew back quickly, feeling the metal hot in the air in front of her, the momentary touch enough to set her skin tingling.

Jamie snatched a breath and tried to gain a sense of where she was, turning as quickly as she could.

But it was too late.

The shape loomed into view in front of her, trapping her in the box of catwalk she'd chosen.

She swallowed hard and looked over her shoulder. Over the pipe, she could see the door. It was right there. Ten feet. No more. Shit.

Jamie looked up at the figure in front of her. The jagged

shape of a fur hood cut itself out of the darkness, the contours of the face still obscured and shadowed.

Then her eyes moved down, to their hand, at the shape *there* catching the light.

Her blood ran cold as the figure raised the knife in their grip. It turned slowly and Jamie's eyes fixed themselves on it, imagining what it would be like to feel it piercing her skin.

Her body shuddered, the figure a step away from thrusting it right into her gut.

Jamie dragged her eyes away from it, searching for an out.

Her back touched the valve behind her and the metal stung her skin, even through her shirt. The pipe was filled with pressurised steam.

To her left and right, bright yellow railings glowed in the darkness, pipes reaching up towards the ceiling behind them. No escape.

Shit.

This was it.

Pain.

That was all she could think of.

How much it would hurt.

But pain was better than death.

And she chose to live.

Jamie made one last move, turning and stepping up onto the middle rung of the railing.

The figure jumped forwards.

Jamie jumped up.

Her other foot hit the top rail and propelled her into the air.

She arced like a high-jumper, her back landing on the red-hot pipe, and brought her legs upwards, rolling backwards over it.

The knife whistled through the air, the tip just nicking Jamie's calf as the attacker swiped at her disappearing legs.

Torn fabric.

Cut skin.

Pain.

Jamie's eyes flashed with all the colours of the rainbow and then some, and then she was landing.

Her back was stinging. All down her right arm, too. And her leg – throbbing.

Jamie's toes hit metal and then her hands did.

She grunted, feeling pain everywhere. But she couldn't waste a second.

Jamie forced herself upright and turned, dragging her leg lamely behind her, feeling the hem of her jeans flapping around her left ankle.

She managed to get her foot to behave after a few steps and shoved down the deep throb erupting up her leg with every stride.

And then she was at the door, the light stinging her eyes as she pulled herself level with it, grabbed the bar, and twisted with everything she had.

The metal squeaked and then gave, and she flopped into the corridor beyond, blinded by the light.

Jamie stumbled forwards, throwing a kick behind her to shunt the door closed, and then started forwards, loping like a wounded animal, bouncing from wall to wall, breath ragged in her chest.

The sudden switch from hot to cold was enough to make her wheeze.

But she was there now.

She could see it ahead.

The door.

The door to Wiik.

And she could see the bar – it was horizontal, shut, and she could see a metal boathook wedged diagonally across the doorway.

Jamie kept her eyes focused ahead, not trusting her balance enough to turn and look behind.

Her right arm was wrapped around her body and felt like it was on fire. She dared not look down.

She had no doubt she was a mess now, and she could feel the blood trickling down her calf.

But the door was right there.

She reached out for it, her good hand taking hold of the rod that was stopping the mechanism from moving, and pulled. She jerked it upwards and it came free, swinging around in front of her.

It was six feet long and had a metal hook on the end.

The locker it lived in was open on her right.

Jamie threw it down angrily and took a breath, grabbing the bar. With gritted teeth, she jerked it upwards. It didn't move.

'Come on,' she growled, pulling again.

Again, it didn't budge.

Jamie exhaled, her head pounding, blood roaring in her ears, and yanked.

This time, it flew upwards, out of her grip.

The door swung wide before she realised what was happening, and Wiik filled the gap.

'Johansson,' he said, the shock on his face apparent. He stepped in, taking her by the shoulders, and wheeled her backwards while Ehrling followed and closed the door behind them, whining about how he nearly died.

Jamie barely registered it.

She was focused on Wiik – on his bright red cheeks, on the fear in his eyes.

'What the hell happened to you?' He stepped back, looking her up and down. 'Jesus, you're bleeding,' he said, homing in on her tattered trouser leg. 'And your hand,' he said, grabbing it from its position across her stomach and holding it up to inspect it. The skin along the heel of it had already begun to blister.

She hoped the story wouldn't be the same up her back.

'What happened to you?' Wiik asked again.

Jamie laughed, then felt her eyes begin to well up. She looked up at Wiik, resisting the urge to throw her arms around his neck, and hung her head. 'You don't even want to know.' She exhaled then. 'For fuck's sake,' she muttered.

'What is it?' he asked, following her eyeline.

She lifted her left leg gingerly, her hem hanging off her bloodied ankle in ribbons. 'These were my favourite jeans.'

11

'So, you couldn't pick them out of a line-up?'

Jamie hissed in pain as Wiik pulled the bandage tight around her calf. 'No,' she said through gritted teeth. 'They had a coat on – maybe a mask, even.'

'But they were big?' Wiik stared up at her from his position on his knees. 'A man?' He paused, trying to catch her eye. 'A woman?'

Jamie glanced at him now, knowing he was alluding to Ashleigh Hooper. Who'd already proved to be quick to violence.

They were in their 'quarters'. Which were far from luxurious. Nothing in comparison to Wallace's stateroom. When they'd finally made it back upstairs, Ehrling had wanted to find Vogel and brief Wallace on the situation, but Jamie had refused and fired him one of those looks that said, *Try it and see what happens.* She didn't like to intimidate people into doing what she wanted, but sometimes, there was no other choice.

Instead, Ehrling had shown them to their room. Singular.

But that was the least of Jamie's worries right now. There

were two bunks in there, and a private bathroom. Which was more than the crew here had. There were four rooms on this deck – the upper crew quarters. Ehrling occupied one as the head of operations. Vogel had the one next door. Jamie and Wiik were in the third, across the hall, and in the one next to them were the three girls on the research trip. Correction, *two* girls. Noemi Heikkinen was still missing. But the fiery, red-headed Ashleigh Hooper, and the yet-unmet French oceanographer Paméla Sevier, were there. Jamie could hear them talking through the wall. It was solid steel, a thick sheet, and cold.

Jamie let the pain subside and unset her teeth, sighing. 'Yeah, they were *big*. A man, I think. I don't know, Wiik. It was dark – and I was more concerned with getting out of there alive than his suit size.'

Wiik looked up at her, a mix of concern and anger in his eyes. Jamie could see an *I should have been there* on his lips. But it always seemed to be that she got cornered on her own. Though she didn't particularly like how that was the case.

'Look, I love getting chased by a knife-wielding murderer as much as the next gal,' Jamie said coolly, 'but it's not something I'm keen to repeat just to get another look at this guy.' She patted him on the shoulder and then levered herself to her feet, putting weight on her foot. Her calf hurt like hell, but she thought she could still run if the situation called for it. It was a deep slice, but not into the muscle, thankfully.

'If you had your gun, you could have just put two bullets in the guy, and we'd have been out of here *tonight,*' Wiik said sourly.

'Don't go connecting dots that aren't there, Wiik,' Jamie said, seeing the cogs turning in his head.

'You don't think it's odd that Wallace takes our weapons and then you're getting attacked an hour later?'

'I think that we would have been locked out either way,'
Jamie said. 'But if he'd seen a gun in my hand, maybe he'd
have thought twice about trying it on in the boiler room.'
Jamie stared into space, processing the situation, wondering
how that would have gone down, and if Wiik was right – if
they *would* have been on a flight out that night. 'Then again,'
Jamie added, playing her own devil's advocate, 'there's no
way to know whether the person who locked us out was the
same person that killed Reyes.'

Wiik scoffed. 'I bet Wallace's in on it.'

'Based on what?' Jamie lifted an eyebrow at Wiik as he
stood up and looked down at his knees, grimacing at the
layer of grease or whatever had now cemented itself to his
jeans.

He sighed and ran his hand over his head, smoothing his
hair down into his impeccable coif. 'Based on the fact that
he's a shifty little weasel who stripped us of our weapons at
gunpoint.'

'We weren't at gunpoint.'

'You think those Bolstad goons wouldn't have drawn on
us if that had gone on any longer?'

Jamie couldn't argue with him there.

'We're not here to solve this case,' Wiik said. 'We're just
window dressing. We're a fixture to show that Bolstad is
doing things by the book.'

'What are you talking about?'

'Wallace is what, a corporate risk assessor? Why does he
need two armed guards? Come on, Jamie, tell me you're not
buying that?' Wiik folded his arms tightly and stared her in
the eyes.

'I can't say I know enough about him or his position to
say any different,' she answered diplomatically. She wasn't
into conjecture.

'No, we're here to make it look like this is getting *solved*. Wallace and his heavies are here to make sure it gets *fixed*.'

Fixed? Jamie measured Wiik. 'You think he's about to, what, cull the crew so this doesn't get out?' She kept her voice low, aware of the solid walls and the ears that might be pressed against them.

'I don't know,' Wiik said. 'But mark my words that he's going to say he's on our side, but his actions will tell a different story. I haven't had a look at the rest of the crew yet, but you know who I *know* is big?'

Jamie gritted her teeth.

'Wallace's guards.'

'You can't seriously be suggesting that they flew us all the way out here to just murder us? Do you even hear what you're saying?'

'I don't know why – but what I do know, is that someone beat and stabbed Alejandro Reyes to death, then strung him up from a crane by his neck. Not a day later, we're out here investigating, under pretty fucking *suspect* circumstances.'

Jamie inspected Wiik closely as he said it, still trying to discern how Falk managed to goad him into coming.

'And then someone's trying to kill us, too?' he continued. 'Someone had a score to settle with Reyes, but surely they can't be stupid enough to try and kill two police officers *and* the head of operations, as well? They'd know that would create one colossal fucking shitstorm. Sweeping one death under the rug when you've got the killer in police custody is one thing. But two civilian deaths and two detectives, too? No, something's up, Jamie. And I don't like it. Not one bit.'

Jamie let him finish and weighed it all in her head. She couldn't disagree. Reyes was dead, sure. And that was heinous. But it felt like the tip of the iceberg. And Wiik was right – she did feel like they'd been brought in here and let loose just for sport. But whether it was something to do with *them,* something to do with Falk, or they were just collateral damage in all this, she just couldn't say. But their badges meant nothing, that much was certain. And if they sat on their hands, things would just get worse.

A killer was running free, and he'd already proved that he wasn't fond of having Jamie and Wiik on board.

'Okay,' Jamie said, nodding slowly.

'*Okay* what?'

'Okay, we operate under the assumption that we can't trust anyone.'

'You did before?' he scoffed.

She ignored him and went on. 'First, we find Reyes' killer. But we do it quietly, and without ruffling any feathers. We need to make it look like we're not making any headway. We gather information and we formulate the case. They'll expect us to reach out to home – to tell them what happened, to get support from Falk, from Hallberg, from anyone.'

'But we don't?'

'I don't know if we can trust Falk right now. If we've been hung out to dry here, then either she's in on it, or she's just too shit-scared of Bolstad to have stood up to them.'

Wiik shook his head now. 'I've known Falk for a long time—'

She cut him off. 'Until we're back on solid ground, we can't take that risk. Everyone I trust in the world right now is standing in this room.'

Wiik restrained a hint of a smile.

'Falk got me to come here by dangling something in front of me she knows I want. But I have a feeling that if I don't make it home, it solves *two* problems for her.'

Wiik bit his lip, but didn't ask or interrupt again.

'So as far as it goes, we're on our own, alright?'

Wiik nodded. 'So where do we start?'

'Noemi Heikkinen.'

'The missing girl?' Wiik looked a little surprised.

Jamie nodded. 'If she was out there with Reyes when he was killed, then she could have seen the killer.'

'You saw that platform, Jamie. There was nowhere else to run.'

'She could be dead, you're right. But she could have escaped. We did.'

'Not everyone's like you,' Wiik replied, voice restrained. 'But if she did escape, why hasn't she turned up yet?'

'She's afraid for her life. She could be hiding. I would be.'

'I doubt that.'

Jamie ignored that, too. 'That's where we start. We find Noemi, or we find out what happened to her. Quietly. We make it seem like we're not even interested. Like we're just going down the list, and the only thing we care about is going home.'

'That won't be hard.'

He was full of it tonight. 'We do the rounds, talk to the crew. We gather information. And then when everything's laid out in front of us, we make our play.'

'Which is what, exactly?' Wiik was the one who lifted an eyebrow now.

'I don't know yet. But I'm envisioning fighter jets, explosions, commandos abseiling down onto the platform from helicopter gunships. The works, you know?'

'Sometimes I can't tell whether you're joking.'

Jamie laughed a little now. 'You know what? Me neither.'

12

THE HITS just kept on coming.

When Jamie decided that a hot shower was the only thing in the world that she needed, it seemed out of reach. She cranked the tap on and let the desalinated water run for a good five minutes before accepting that it wasn't going to warm. Why, when it seemed there were a hundred boilers running below, piping steam up from maintenance, that was the case, Jamie didn't know. But either way, it did nothing to improve her mood.

Jamie exited the bathroom, still dressed, to share her anger with Wiik, and found him standing over his open duffle bag. It was sitting on a steel chair that was perched in the corner, and he was staring down into it.

'What's wrong?' Jamie asked, slowing.

'They've been through this,' he grumbled.

'Who?'

He sighed and ran both hands over his head, glancing over at her. 'Wallace. His goons. Does it matter?'

Jamie went to her bag and lifted the flap. She came to the same conclusion. Everything she'd put in there was now back in upside down. She'd put her underwear on the bottom, and now it sat proudly on top. What they were looking for, Jamie didn't know, but Wiik was right. Someone had been through their belongings.

'Well,' Wiik said, laughing and slapping the lid down onto his bag. 'At least it can't get any worse.'

Jamie harrumphed. 'I wouldn't bet on it. There's no hot water.'

She expected a cold shower to wake her up, but sleep came surprisingly quickly.

It wasn't pleasant or particularly restful, but it held on to her until six the next morning, when she was woken by a shuddering that rocked the entire room.

Jamie sat bolt upright, and then a loud bang from beneath her, followed by Wiik's swearing, told her that he'd just done exactly the same, forgetting he'd requested the bottom bunk.

Jamie swung her legs off the scratchy sheets, the plastic-covered mattress groaning beneath her, and dropped to the floor.

A bolt of pain shot up her leg and then it immediately resigned itself to throbbing painfully. Jamie ground her teeth and tottered sideways, cursing herself for being so stupid.

Wiik pulled himself upright next to her, rubbing his forehead, and looked around. 'What the hell is that?'

Jamie narrowed her eyes, listening as the noise joined the vibration. It was a distant rumble, pulsing slowly. She didn't think she'd ever heard it before, but her mind worked quickly, the throes of sleep blasted from her mind. 'They've started drilling again.'

'Drilling?' Wiik asked, turning to face Jamie.

They stared at each other for a moment, and then each

looked down at the same time, realising that neither were dressed from the waist down except for their underpants.

Jamie and Wiik turned their backs on one another quickly and Wiik stared at the ceiling as though he hadn't just seen more of her than Jamie preferred anyone to.

She put her head in her hands and let out a low groan. She wondered then whether this name was going to be worth it. Falk had better deliver.

Five minutes later, they were out of the room, fully dressed, both in desperate need of coffee, and some fucking answers.

They weren't supposed to be drilling. Operations were supposed to be suspended. But Jamie had a feeling this wasn't Ehrling's doing.

They exited the room, and Wiik crossed to Ehrling's door, banging on it with the heel of his hand. 'Ehrling,' he called.

But there was no answer.

Jamie figured he was already up and upstairs on the command deck. Along with Vogel.

A noise to her left pulled her attention away from Wiik's slouched shoulders and incessant banging.

She looked down towards the room next to theirs and saw a face in the doorway she didn't recognise. A woman was standing there. She had shoulder-length brown hair and a full, unkempt fringe. Keen eyes peaked out from under it.

Paméla Sevier.

Jamie met her gaze for a moment, and then turned and started towards her. Sevier closed the door quickly, and the bolt thudded shut behind it.

'Hey,' Wiik called after her, noticing she was heading down the corridor. 'Where are you going?'

'I was just …' Jamie said, stopping and looking back. She glanced at the locked door again.

'Ehrling's not here. He must be upstairs,' Wiik decided, already taking off. 'You coming?' he called.

Jamie stole one last look at the locked door and then relented. She could come back to Hooper and Sevier later. As much as she wanted all the information on Heikkinen and Reyes' relationship she could get, Wiik was right that they needed to corner Ehrling first and find out why operations had started again.

She still hadn't dug into his file, though she wished she had.

Jamie trailed Wiik to the command deck and listened as he banged on the door again. At least he wasn't shouting this time. Jamie's leg was still smarting like hell and her brain was fuzzy. It was early, she'd slept like shit, and a deep, nagging ache had embedded itself at the base of her skull.

After the fiftieth bang, the door opened in front of them and revealed Vogel. She was looking out at them, her face a picture of alarm, her short black hair sticking up at odd angles. Jamie didn't know if it was supposed to look like that or she'd just not brushed it since she got up.

'Where's Ehrling?' Wiik asked, stepping through the gap and walking past her.

Vogel did a double take, watching Wiik stride up the stairs in surprise. She turned back to Jamie then.

'Yeah, he does that,' Jamie said, sighing. She smiled tiredly at Vogel. 'Don't think too much into it.'

Vogel proffered the stairs to Jamie as well and she hauled herself up it.

Ehrling was at the desk, but rose quickly as Wiik approached, glancing over at Vogel, who was next to Jamie, for some sort of backup. His mouth started flapping before Wiik even said anything, but no sound came out.

'What the hell are you doing?' Wiik demanded. 'Operations are supposed to be suspended until—'

'That,' Wallace said, the door to his stateroom opening dramatically, 'is my doing.'

Jamie narrowed her eyes at him. There was no way he heard Wiik through his vault door. The room must be monitored. She didn't doubt there was a full security suite in there, so Wallace could watch Ehrling as he watched everyone else.

'Well,' Wiik said, turning, 'why am I not surprised.' He took a step forward and Wallace's two guards appeared at his flanks like attack dogs.

He gave the smallest gesture of his hand and waved them down, not bothered by the look on Wiik's face, it seemed.

'You may not understand how business works, Mr Wiik,' Wallace said, pushing his hands into the pockets of his chinos. He'd forgone the jacket this morning and had on just a plain blue shirt. The sleeves were rolled up his forearms, and his little round stomach pulled the buttons taught. He seemed perfectly at ease, and was even smiling at Wiik. 'But things can't just come to a halt because of one issue.'

'One *issue*?' Wiik spat. 'A man is dead, still hanging from a crane—'

'Yes, don't you'd think you'd better see to that?' Wallace raised an eyebrow. 'In fact, weren't you supposed to deal with that yesterday evening?'

'We *were*,' Wiik growled, his teeth clamping together. 'Until *someone* locked us out there and tried to kill—'

'Look,' Wallace said, cutting in lightly. 'I can't be held responsible if you locked yourself out of—'

'We didn't lock ourselves—'

'Nevertheless,' Wallace said, his voice cooling, the guards

drawing in line with him again. 'A man is dead, and that is a tragedy. But if you haven't noticed, there are only a finite number of people on this place, and they're not going anywhere. And with Bolstad's fate resting on your shoulders – along with the some six-thousand-odd jobs that go along with it – I would think you might be a little more obliging.' He chuckled to himself. 'You can't seriously expect us to stop the entire operation because of one man? The quarter ends in just a few days, and Bolstad B is yet to hit its quota. Losing days while you parade around here harassing employees – who I might add are already stressed and scared enough without you tormenting them further – is just not an option.' He glanced at Jamie, smiled at her, and then went back to Wiik.

Jamie's skin crawled.

'You have your assignment,' Wallace said, 'and I have mine. So, if you'd stop intimidating my head of operations, and get back to your investigation, I'd be much obliged.'

Wiik was seething.

The worst thing of all was that Wallace was doing the exact thing Wiik hated most of all. He was telling him how to do his job.

Wiik was the definition of anal-retentive. Not to a point of obsession, but he had an opinion on how things should be done, and while he wasn't wont to verbalise it often, when people forced him to deviate from the neat little path he traced through the world, it was like nails on a chalkboard, a blade through plasterboard, or any of the other things that makes your head want to fold down into your neck and your spine to kink like a hose pipe.

Jamie was staring at Wiik, waiting for his heels to ignite and for him to blast into orbit.

'This *is* part of the investigation,' Wiik squeezed out, the vein in his temple bulging dangerously. He wasn't a violent man. In fact, he hated violence. He had a fierce loyalty to the law and its ruthless application. So when someone stood between him and that, it irked him more than anything else. 'Ehrling is the first person we want to interview in regards to Reyes' murder,' he said, measuring Wallace, who seemed perfectly prepared for this outcome.

'There is no need,' Wallace replied. 'He has a rock-solid alibi.'

'Oh yeah?' Wiik huffed. 'I bet he does.'

'To call Mr Ehrling's integrity into question is to question mine also, Mr Wiik.'

Wiik stared at him, not sure what he was saying. Jamie wasn't sure either. But watching this was like being at the theatre. Only with worse acting.

'You see,' Wallace doled out, 'Mr Ehrling was on a conference call with myself, and two other members of the Bolstad IPC.'

'Bolstad IPC?' Wiik asked, knowing Wallace wouldn't relent until this was all played out.

'Internal Performance Committee. A regular monthly review. This one falling a week before the end of the quarter, to make sure Bolstad B was on course to hit its target. Which we've already established,' he said, smirking, 'it was not.'

'That's assuming we know what time Reyes was murdered,' Wiik retorted.

'Not necessary,' Wallace replied, seemingly amused by it all. 'Because Reyes was on shift until six p.m. on the night of his death – and our meeting didn't start until five thirty.'

'Seems late for a business meeting.'

'Bolstad is a multi-national corporation with offices all around the world. The IPC members were conferencing in from Canada, the South China Sea, and Oman. Do you need some help working out the time differences?'

Wiik swallowed, his jaw flexing.

'The meeting,' Wallace continued, 'went on for some …
four or so hours?' He looked at Ehrling now.

'Five,' the man added.

Jamie restrained a smirk herself. More bad theatre.

'So there you have it,' Wallace said. 'There's no need to interview Mr Ehrling.'

'Reyes could have been killed after—'

'Not possible,' Wallace said, shaking his head. 'Miss Vogel informs me that Ms Sevier, one of the researchers here, reported Ms Heikkinen's supposed disappearance to her at nine that evening. That she had left their room at a little after seven and not returned, which was highly out of character. Vogel accompanied Ms Sevier and Ms Hooper on a search following this report, and a little after ten, Reyes' body was discovered.'

Sevier. She's the one who reported Noemi Heikkinen missing.

Jamie's mind went back to the face in the doorway.

Wiik listened to everything Wallace was saying, albeit begrudgingly. It was all very, *very* useful information. If it was accurate and reliable, that was.

'And if you don't believe me, I can, of course, get the testimony of the three others who joined us in that meeting – or you could ask Vogel.'

Wiik turned to look at her.

She was staring back at Wallace, a sour look on her face at being thrust into the spotlight. 'Me? I was in my quarters,' she said plainly. 'All night.'

'Exactly,' Wallace replied. 'And they are next door to Ehrling's, and you can clearly hear through those walls. Solid, but thin sheets of steel.' Wallace rolled back and forth on his heels, his expensive loafers squeaking. His grey, frizzy hair shook gently as he turned to face Wiik again. 'I have no doubt she can attest to that meeting beginning before Reyes' shift ended, and going on until after Ms Heikkinen was reported missing. Can't you?' His eyes fell on the deputy head of operations again.

Vogel straightened. 'Whenever Ehrling is in a meeting, I usually just put my headphones on.'

'Because ...' Wallace encouraged her, offering a hand.

'Because,' she said, seemingly unhappy to do so, 'you can hear everything through these walls.'

Wiik was looking from the railroaded Vogel to the smug Wallace to the brow-beaten Ehrling and back, stuck in the middle of all three.

'So then,' Wallace said, clasping his hands together in front of him. 'I hope that clears everything up. Ehrling and Vogel have lots to do. We've already lost a day, best not lose another one.' He lifted his still-raised hand higher. 'You've got plenty to get on with, and you've already been given the name of a likely suspect, I believe? Mr Colm Quinn. I suggest you start with him, and stop pursuing leads that I can *guarantee* won't work out for you.'

Wiik didn't say anything, the statement hanging in the air. Wallace's face now one of consternation as he directed them to the door.

Wiik ran his hand over his head and let out a long breath, turning to look at Jamie.

She nodded that it was over.

'Come on,' Vogel said, reading the room and clearly wanting to be out of it as much as any of them. 'I'll show you out.'

She led the way down the stairs and pulled the door open,

ushering Jamie and Wiik back into the damp corridor that fed down into the crew quarters.

She closed it behind them and folded her arms. 'I really was in my room all night,' she said, lowering her voice so it was barely above a whisper. Jamie had to watch her mouth to pick the words out over the constant whirring and thudding of the drill. 'And Ehrling was in his room – in a meeting.' Vogel's voice was clearly tinged with a German accent, but her English was impeccable.

'But you had your headphones on?' Wiik asked, watching her closely, too.

She nodded. 'Yeah. They go on for a long time. Easier just to tune it out, you know?'

'Why aren't you in these meetings?' Wiik pressed. 'As deputy head – and clearly the one with the backbone to run this place – it seems odd to keep you out of the loop.'

Vogel glanced at Jamie to see if that was supposed to be some sort of compliment. She got that look a lot from people. And it wasn't.

'Uh,' Vogel went on, shaking her head. 'I don't know. Boys club? Or maybe Ehrling just wants to make sure that no one else catches onto that fact.'

'That you're the one running this place,' Jamie said.

Vogel smiled as humbly as she could. 'I don't really want to speak ill of my boss.'

'Please do,' Wiik said.

Vogel sighed. 'If you haven't noticed, this place isn't exactly the kind of place you're put in charge of running if your career is on the up.'

Wiik nodded. 'So Ehrling screwed up and running this place is his punishment?'

'Something like that,' Vogel said. 'He had a contract

running a drill site in the UAE, but something happened there, and then he got transferred here.'

'A long way from the Emirates,' Jamie said, looking at Wiik. He nodded. Neither of them knew much about the oil scene in the Middle East, but they called it 'black gold' for a reason, and it was one of the wealthiest places in the world because of its oil reserves.

'So what did you do to get stuck out here?' Wiik asked, focusing on her now.

'Believe it or not,' Vogel said, 'I volunteered. Though I didn't expect to be trapped on board with a murderer.' She shook her head in disbelief.

'Why did you?'

'Bolstad has thirty-one heads of operations at drill sites and on platforms around the world. Guess how many of them are women?'

'None,' Jamie said.

'Exactly.'

'So you're paying your dues?' Jamie asked, measuring the woman in front of her. She was slight, but Jamie could see a sharp mind behind her eyes.

'Something like that.' Vogel stole a look at the door behind her, mindful of time. 'Bolstad B is the last working platform of four that were built out here. This is the only one still drilling, and the longer I keep it that way, the better that reflects on me.'

Jamie understood.

'And when the oil runs dry … Hopefully Bolstad take into account what I did.' She stepped back towards the door. 'Look, I've got to get back.'

'Okay,' Jamie said. 'Thank you. We'll need to talk again, okay?'

'Sure,' Vogel said. 'Find me later – I get off at seven. Oh, and Quinn's out working the main drill.' She disappeared through the door and it locked behind her.

Wiik opened his mouth to speak, but Jamie motioned him after her down the stairs, and opened a hatch on the next landing. The cold air hit them both like a sledgehammer, and they winced, totally unprepared for the unsparing ocean wind.

Jamie stepped onto a catwalk that offered up a staircase leading down to other decks, as well as other doors back into the crew quarters. Once Wiik seemed sure they weren't going to get trapped, he closed it behind him.

Jamie hoped they wouldn't be so easily overheard out here.

'So what do you think?' Wiik asked, studying her expression.

'I think …' Jamie said slowly, turning and leaning on the rail. She was just in a thermal long-sleeve and the wind was already making her cheeks ache. 'That Wallace made a real point of making sure that Ehrling was protected.'

Wiik nodded his agreement. 'Convenient that his meeting seemed to miraculously coincide with Reyes' death.'

'Not for Reyes.'

Wiik laughed sardonically. 'I suppose not.' He thought for a moment. 'How did Wallace know that Vogel had head-phones on?'

Jamie thought on that, but didn't have an answer. Though she could see where Wiik was going with it. 'You think Ehrling slipped out of his room during the meeting, went downstairs, killed Reyes and strung him up from a crane, and then slipped back in without Vogel realising he was even gone?'

Wiik shrugged. 'I've had crazier theories that have panned out.'

'But what reason would Ehrling have for going after Reyes?'

'If they were using the meeting to cover it, then Wallace would be complicit. Maybe he ordered it, has something on Ehrling?'

'Why would the brass want one of their own employees taken out? And like that, too?'

'Maybe Reyes crossed the wrong person?'

'But for them to string him up like that? He was just a kid. What could he have possibly done?' Jamie couldn't wrap her head around the idea. She stared down over the scene in front of her. 'I'll go over their files again later.'

The main drill was dead ahead, the framework above it piercing the sky. A few figures in bright orange jackets and white hard hats milled around the drill itself. Colm Quinn. And probably Sasha Kravets and Miroslav Lebedenkov. 'Notice how we've been pushed towards Quinn twice now?'

'Think there's something to it?'

'Don't know,' Jamie said. 'But whether it's a diversion or they really do think it was Quinn, we need to speak to him. And the girl.'

'Sevier?'

'Paméla, yeah,' Jamie confirmed. 'If she reported Heikkinen missing, then she was probably closest to her. And if she was closest to her, she probably knew the most about her and Reyes' relationship.'

Wiik stared down at the drill too. 'Let's deal with Reyes first,' he said. 'We can't leave him hanging out there forever. And it doesn't look like Ehrling's rushing to get him down. Especially not after last night.'

Jamie scoffed. 'That frightened-kitten act all for show, you think? The way he broke down when the door was locked? Was that one of Wallace's goons just shoring up his story?'

Wiik stuck his bottom lip out. 'Maybe. But they couldn't have counted on you finding a way back around. How would they ensure Ehrling didn't freeze but we did?'

'Electric underwear?' Jamie offered.

Wiik cracked a wry smile.

'I don't know. Maybe they weren't intent on saving him. Ehrling doesn't seem like the type to hold up under questioning, so maybe they were tying off a loose end. Would certainly explain the extremeness of his reaction if he realised he was being double-crossed.'

Wiik let out a long breath. 'It's a theory. But right now, we don't know enough about this. Let's get Reyes' body down, then we can go see Quinn. See what he thinks of Ehrling and the fact that he's having the finger pointed at him.'

Jamie nodded slowly, thinking of Sevier, and the clock that might be ticking on Heikkinen's life if she was still alive. 'Or we could split up? You take Quinn, I'll track down Sevier.' She turned to look at him, not keen on leaving any lead unpursued. Even for a minute.

Wiik laughed now and pushed back off the rail. 'Yeah, right,' he said, motioning her to head back inside. 'You think I'm letting you out of my sight again? Every time we split up, you nearly get your head blown off or get chased by a knife-wielding maniac.'

Jamie paused at the door and met Wiik's eye. 'I wouldn't say *every* time.'

He laughed a little. 'Come on, let's get inside before we freeze to death. Again.'

13

As they descended into the bowels of the platform, heading for the lower submersible platform, the temperature began to decline.

The warm air drifted up through the vents and stairwells, mounting in the crew quarters at the top, while the lower levels remained cold and damp, regardless of how hot those steam pipes were.

Jamie rubbed her arm through her sleeve, the surface burns on her skin beginning to itch, and then pushed through into the corridor that joined maintenance and the platform.

They'd left in such a hurry to get Jamie attended to that the chaos from last night still remained.

Jamie stepped forwards, seeing thin splatters of blood on the painted steel walls where she'd flicked it off her boot and leg.

The floor was lined with grates, but below it the rust-speckled steel was also doused in her blood. It stared up at her as she walked.

Jamie grimaced and looked at the door instead. Both her

and Wiik's parka jackets lay there in a heap, the boathook used to wedge the door shut lying on top of them.

Jamie stooped and picked it up, feeling her hands curl around the six-foot pole. It was made of lightweight aluminium, weighted on the head-side. She moved it in her hands, looking at it, thinking about how it had almost cost her and Wiik their lives.

'Okay?' he asked, coming up behind her. He knelt and pulled their jackets into his arms, proffering hers.

Jamie took it and threw it around her shoulders, staring at the door in front of her.

'Let's get this over with,' Wiik said, taking the initiative.

He pushed through and cold air flooded into the corridor, stinging Jamie's nostrils and making her chest tighten. It had to be close to freezing outside, if not below.

She screwed her eyes up against the wind and stepped onto the platform, seeing Reyes swinging in stark contrast to the pale sky.

Jamie stopped in her tracks just outside the door, the pained look on his face apparent now in the light of day.

'You want to stay by the door, or should I?' Wiik said, keeping his hand firmly on the handle.

Fool me once, Jamie thought. 'I'll watch the door,' she replied, handing the boathook off to Wiik. She wasn't shy about the job at hand, but Wiik had six inches and probably four stone on her. And Reyes wasn't that small.

He nodded and moved towards the edge.

Jamie lingered at the doorway, checking the corridor every few seconds as Wiik lowered Reyes to a point he could pull him in. He leaned over the rail and Jamie watched apprehensively, not daring to pull her heel from its spot under the door.

The hook found Reyes' jacket and Wiik drew him closer, and then pulled him over the platform and against the rail.

She could hear Wiik swearing as he held onto the body. Jamie could smell Reyes from the doorway. She didn't want to imagine what was going up Wiik's nose.

It looked like rigor mortis had worn off. Reyes was flopping around as Wiik wrestled with him. But Jamie could see that he'd not let the line out enough and bit her lip, glancing back down the corridor again to make sure it was clear.

She dashed over and took hold of the winch, winding it out a little further, sending Wiik backwards, and Reyes with him.

The sudden shift in weight as Reyes' feet went over the rail made Wiik stumble and he thudded against the wall of the platform, grunting and releasing the dead man in his arms.

The line snapped tight around Reyes' neck and he hung there in the air over Wiik for a second, legs buckled under him on the steel catwalk, and then gravity took hold and he spun sideways and slumped face down onto the metal. Jamie wound out the winch to give it some slack, and Wiik got up and dusted himself off.

Jamie stared down at Reyes, stepping backwards to check the corridor again, and then met Wiik's eye. 'Well, that went well,' she said, sighing. She didn't think she'd ever worked a case like this, and the way Wiik was grimacing at the substance that had smeared itself on his coat, she didn't think he had either.

Here was a body – a murder victim. And they'd not done any of the things that they should have. That the law demanded. They'd not secured the scene, no crime scene technicians had been through, no evidence had been collected. Next of kin hadn't been informed. A cordon wasn't set up. No pathology lab was ready to accept the body. And they'd not interviewed a single witness.

Jamie let out a long sigh and glanced down at Reyes's bulging, bloated face.

'Now what?' Wiik asked.

Jamie swallowed.

She didn't really have an answer.

After five minutes of deliberating, they laid Wiik's Bolstad parka over him, and then carried him inside and up the stairs. It took nearly twenty minutes to get him to the medical bay – a series of three interconnected rooms that offered medical care to the crew members. There wasn't a doctor on board – Jamie knew that for cargo ships, you didn't need one by law unless there were twelve crew members. She expected it was the same here – but both Ehrling and the head engineer were qualified first aid practitioners. What use that was going to be if someone had their arm ripped off by the drill, Jamie didn't know, but then again, she figured that risk came with the territory.

Sadly, it seemed that while there were no protocols in place for dealing with a murder, if someone did manage to get their arm ripped off, their body wasn't going to be left outside to rot.

There was no sign of anyone to ask, and it took Jamie longer than she would have liked to find a body bag.

She pulled it from a cabinet on ground level and brought it over to the steel table where they'd laid Reyes. Jamie and Wiik worked in silence, lifting Reyes in shoulders first, then legs, and then zipping him up.

There was a secure storage room in the medical bay that they needed a key card to unlock. And though they wanted to put Reyes in there, neither of them really wanted to see Wallace again while trying and get hold of Ehrling or Vogel's card. The wider berth they could give him, the better.

For a few seconds, they lingered, looking down at the body.

There was nothing to say, nothing to do. There was no one to tell. All they could do was leave him here, as bitter a taste in their mouths as that left.

Wallace had begun operations again, but it looked like everyone else was keeping to their rooms. Whether that was still the mandate or people were staying confined for fear of something else, Jamie couldn't say. The arrival of Wallace, two detectives, and the presence of a murderer was no doubt keeping people from roaming anywhere alone.

If they had any sense, at least.

Jamie and Wiik stopped off at their room to grab their own jackets, along with the bag containing the personnel files, and then they set off. The door had a simple mortise lock, and Ehrling had given them a key to it before they'd headed down to see Reyes' body the night before. But Jamie she didn't trust Wallace or anyone else enough to leave the files unattended. They'd already rifled through their clothes. And for all she knew, they'd been in there and messed with the files already. She had no way to know if the key she and Wiik had was the only one, or if Ehrling had a master key that opened every room in this place.

Either way, she'd be keeping the files on her person from now on, or at least until she had time to go over them with a fine-tooth comb.

Jamie had wanted to stop in with Sevier to find out about Heikkinen, but with Quinn's name popping up again and again, and his friend and co-driller's blood still on their hands – literally – they couldn't ignore him any longer.

He'd been on shift for four hours already, and it was wearing into late morning.

As Jamie walked, she struggled to believe that. It felt like they'd been on the move all day.

She realised then that she'd not eaten or drunk a thing for nearly twenty hours too. She was missing water, sustenance, coffee.

And judging by the scowl Wiik was sporting, he was, too.

And to make things worse, it took them much longer than expected to find the right exit.

They both paused at the door to look at a sign that depicted a piece of metal lodged in someone's head, and relented to the *Helmets Must Be Worn At All Times* instruction, each taking one from the rack next to the ominous sign.

Jamie and Wiik strode out into the frigid morning air, fighting the wind with every step. The sky was layered with pale grey cloud. It moved quickly above them like a mirror laid above the sea below.

The thunk of the drill rode up through Jamie's knees and made her injured calf throb with every step. It was doing little to lift her mood. And Wiik seemed to be feeding off it.

The drill platform was wide and open – a hundred feet of concrete hemmed in by a yellow rail. The tower rose above them, right in the middle of the platform, criss-crossed iron that housed a colossal winch and rig hoist – the device that lowered the drill and casing into the ocean below.

Stairs wound up around it to another midway platform, and Jamie could see a guy moving around up there, his white hat and high-vis vest glowing. She didn't know who it was.

Ahead, she could see two more figures. One was of average build, the other larger and wider.

Jamie and Wiik slowed as they got close, the two men's backs showing to them.

One was working a control unit, moving levers up and down, which sounded like they modulated the speed and pressure of the drill. He watched a screen in front of him intensely as he worked.

The other was standing just to the side, at another control unit. He had a dial in one hand and was pressing buttons with the other, tapping the screen and then flicking switches.

Jamie didn't know a lot about deep-sea drilling, but she could see thick plastic pipes running into the riser pipe and down out of view. They seemed to jolt and move as the big man pushed buttons. So she guessed that something was being piped down into the bore-hole, though she didn't know what or why.

She and Wiik stopped, neither keen to interrupt what was going on in front of them.

They looked at each other after a few seconds, unsure of what to do.

Knocking on doors, running down suspects, interviewing them, compiling evidence – these all seemed trivial now that they were standing here, three hundred-odd miles from land. From the country where their badges and titles meant anything.

The big man looked up, his large, flat face and angular cheekbones giving him away as Lebedenkov. He was one of the drillers. Bulgarian. Jamie remembered his face from the file. It was hard to forget.

He narrowed his eyes at them and then called out to the man working the levers. His voice was swallowed by the howl of the drill.

The second man looked up, then turned his head.

Jamie only caught a portion of his face over his shoulder, but she knew this to be Quinn.

He had pale green eyes, a narrow face, and a rough,

gingery beard. There was no mistaking him, either. He looked like the kind of guy who thought getting punched in the face was the sign of a good night out.

He returned to his control unit, backed off the levers, and then slammed his gloved hand down onto a big red button.

An ear-splitting alarm blared and the noise of the drill died altogether.

Lebedenkov stepped away from his unit, pulled his own gloves off, and cracked his knuckles in front of his broad chest, staring Wiik down. He shifted next to Jamie, his leather boots squeaking as he met the big man's eye.

Quinn slipped his gloves off too, and reached to his chest, unzipping the dark red Bolstad overall he was wearing. He pushed the gloves half inside so they hung out a little, and then he sauntered forwards, grinning at Jamie with crooked teeth.

'Well, well, well,' he said, his broad Irish accent unmistakable. His piercing eyes roved up and down Jamie and made her skin crawl. 'And here I was thinking we'd just lost a bird from this place, and then suddenly, here you are. One out, one in.' He grinned, dancing from one foot to the other, gesturing left then right.

He knew about Noemi Heikkinen. Word had spread then.

'Ain't we just the luckiest lads in the world,' Quinn went on, laughing now.

'Watch it,' Wiik growled, advancing a step.

Quinn met his eye and stopped, measuring him. 'Sorry, lad,' he said, not a hint of remorse in him. 'Just havin' a little fun. You know how it is out here at sea, eh? We don't get to see many lasses out here.' His eyes flashed. 'Specially not ones that fill a pair of jeans like her, eh?' He nodded at Jamie.

She reminded herself not to let Quinn get to her. He was playing the fool – the debased dog – but she could see through it from a mile off. He was just trying to get at Wiik. And he was succeeding.

'That other lass,' he went on, Wiik's temper visibly growing with every second. 'Scrawny little bird she was, eh?' He glanced at Lebedenkov, who leered back, breaking into a grin that showed off the gaps between his teeth. 'Nutt'in' to her. All skin and bones, you know?' He was within lunging distance of Wiik. Which meant Wiik was in lunging distance of him. And he knew it. Knew his angles and reach-distance perfectly. He was a brawler, a boxer at best, but he knew how to fight. Jamie could tell that from the way he was standing. A quarter on, weight on the balls of his feet, right hand hung at his hip, ready to knock Wiik's head clean off his shoulders the second he stepped in. 'Me, I like a girl with a bit of meat on her. One who can really *take* what you're doling out. You're the same, eh, lad? I'm sure you're no slouch,' he said directly to Wiik now. 'The question is, are you enough for *her?*' He kept his eyes locked on Wiik, whose teeth were about to shatter against each other. His temple vein was bulging dangerously.

But Jamie could tell he was outmatched and had no intention of watching him get hit. So, instead, she stepped between them and shoved her badge in Quinn's face. 'Detective Inspector Jamie Johansson,' she said flatly, keen to get this over with as quickly as possible. She could feel Wiik at her shoulder, burning a hole into Quinn with his gaze. 'Need to ask you a few questions. You're Colm Quinn, right?'

'Know my name already, do ya? Should I be flattered, or worried?' he asked fluidly, focusing on Jamie now, not a hint of fear in him. He held her gaze.

She held his. 'You tell me,' Jamie retorted. 'Did you kill Alejandro Reyes? Because we've had your name twice now from people who think you probably did.'

'No,' he said lightly, seemingly unphased by the news or the accusations. 'Shame about that, though.'

'A shame that you didn't kill him?'

He cracked a smirk. 'Shame that he's dead.' He strung the last word out. 'Was a hell of a worker, and now that Ehrling's got us playing catch-up, it's gonna mean double shifts for us to make the difference up. I reckon that's the opposite of motive, eh?'

Jamie didn't return his smile. 'Or a good cover story.'

'Or one of those,' he said, shrugging. 'Guess that's for yer to work out, eh, birdie?' He winked at her. Jamie felt Wiik move closer behind her. 'Oh,' he went on. 'Yer man's got a thing for yer, I reckon.' He looked up at Wiik and then down at Jamie again.

She threw an elbow into Wiik's gut and he grunted, stepping back. 'Where were you two nights ago between five and nine in the evening?' Jamie asked Quinn.

He sucked on his teeth, glanced at Lebedenkov, then back. 'In my room, with this ugly fucker. Laying down cards.'

'All evening?'

'Far as I remember,' he said lightly. 'Kravets, too.'

'The three of you.'

Quinn nodded. 'Aye, I reckon so.'

'Anyone corroborate that?'

'What, the three of us ain't good enough for yer?' he laughed, and Lebedenkov joined in.

'Not if all three of you conspired to kill Reyes.'

'And why would we do that?'

'You tell me.'

'You're the detective, eh?'

Jamie took a breath. This was going nowhere. 'So you didn't know where Reyes was that night?'

'Well, he started out with us, first off.'

'What do you mean "he started out with you"?'

'Like I said, we were playing cards.'

'You said three of you.'

'Aye, first there was four – then there was three. Reyes left. Early. Ran off to be with his lass.'

Jamie narrowed her eyes at Quinn, looking for chinks in the armour.

'You chatted to her friends yet?' Quinn said, not letting the silence sit.

'Whose? Heikkinen's?'

'They didn't much like that match – reckon it didn't do a lot for their "research".' He put the word in air quotes and Lebedenkov snickered in the background. 'See, we're just hard working lads, tryin' to do our jobs. Them lassies arrive, all high and mighty, doin' their fancy tests and analyses. And then suddenly, one of them's shacking up with one of us. Really didn't sit too well with them. 'Specially that French lass. Got a real fire in her. And yer already met the redhead, I suspect?'

'How do you know that?' Jamie narrowed her eyes at him.

Quinn laughed. 'Take that as a yes, then. Let's just say she's got no qualms about voicing her opinion. Yer can't fookin' move in this place without hearing her trampin' around, yellin' about this 'n' that. So let's just call it an educated guess, eh?'

'So you're saying that Sevier and Hooper had the most to gain from Reyes' death?' Jamie watched him carefully. He'd been no stranger to the law, and was driving the conversation every which way from where Jamie wanted it. He might not look much, but there was more to Colm Quinn than met the eye.

'I don't know,' Quinn said, shrugging. He pulled his gloves from his overall and smacked them on his thigh, sending dust into the air. 'But what I do know, is that the lads and I were playing cards. Reyes was supposed to be playing with us, 'cept that little lass came to the door, asking for him. And off he scampered, leaving us one short of a decent game.'

'Noemi Heikkinen came to your room before Reyes was killed?'

'No, the French lass.'

'Paméla Sevier?'

'If you say so.'

Jamie processed it all. So Reyes was with Sevier, not Noemi? She swallowed, trying to get back on track. She'd see who was in the room next to Quinn, whether they could confirm their alibis. 'Reyes left with her, and you stayed in your room all night?'

He nodded. 'Aye. There anything else, or can we get back to work?'

Jamie took a breath, crossing the t's and dotting the i's. 'Was there anyone else who had any motive to go after Reyes? Anyone he'd fallen out with? Anyone who'd threatened him?'

Quinn seemed to find this more amusing than anything. 'Who *didn't?*'

Jamie's blood ran a little colder.

'Let's see,' he said, holding up his hands to count on his fingers. 'There's Kurek, the safety officer – bit of a bastard with the cards and dice. Me and the lads knew to leave well enough alone. Reyes didn't have what you might call "common sense". Got into him for a good bit of cash. And he's not got much of a sense of humour, that one. Reckon a discussion could have gone sour nice and fookin' fast there.' That was one finger.

'Then there's Møller – Orn Møller. He's an engineer – big bastard, can't miss him. He had the hots for Reyes' little bird. Fancied her for himself. Him and Reyes had some words over it more than once. Lad had some opinions on Reyes' *sort,* if you know what I mean?' That was two fingers.

'I don't,' Jamie said. 'Want to spell it out for me?'

'Handsome lad, Reyes was. Got that tall, dark, and big cock combination you lasses love.'

Wiik grumbled in the background but knew well enough to keep his mouth shut and let Jamie work.

'And with so few birds on board, at sea for a long time …'

'Reyes and another crew member?' Jamie raised an eyebrow.

'Aye, I never knew what he saw in that up-tight bitch, but as I said, out here, any hole's a goal, if you know what I mean.'

'Vogel.' Jamie had suspected it since her and Vogel first talked, but it was good to have her suspicion confirmed, and would give her the upper hand when they spoke next.

Quinn nodded. 'Oh, aye. They were making the beast with the two backs from the off. Not my type, but we've already established what I like, eh?' He grinned at Wiik again and Jamie didn't have to turn around to know he was glaring back at Quinn. 'But when that blonde piece came along,' Quinn continued, clicking his tongue. 'Reyes gave Vogel the thumb pretty damn quick. Brutal, even by my standards.' That was finger number three.

'So Vogel and Reyes were sleeping together, but then Reyes broke up with her when Noemi Heikkinen arrived?' Jamie confirmed.

'You hard of hearing, lass?' Quinn asked her, furrowing his brow.

'No,' Wiik interjected this time. 'You're just barely speaking English.' He grunted.

Jamie spoke again, keen to keep Quinn's focus on her and for the two of them not to come to blows. 'Just making sure I have my facts straight,' she said. 'It's a lot to take in. So Reyes owed Kurek money and wasn't paying up? Møller thought Reyes wasn't good enough for Noemi and wanted her for himself – and wasn't shy about it. And Reyes broke up with Vogel to pursue Heikkinen? Is that about the sum of it?'

'It's about half of it.'

Jamie suppressed a groan. 'There's more?'

'Sven Rosenberg.'

'Head engineer?' Jamie remembered the name from the file. 'What grudge did he have with Reyes?'

'Not with Reyes, but with his bird.'

'Noemi?'

Quinn nodded. 'Aye, they had a big blowout a few weeks back. Real nasty, said he was gonna kill her.'

Jamie's body stiffened a little. 'What happened?'

'Lass was doing something for her research – something to do with the amount of waste mud and oil that leaked into the ocean – so she was up there' – he nodded at the midway platform overhead where they'd seen Kravets – 'checking the seals on the riser and drill casing. And she finds they're about to give.'

'As in blow?'

'Give, blow, suck, whatever you prefer.'

Jamie did her best to ignore the crassness of the comment. Again. 'Okay? And that annoyed Rosenberg?'

'Oh, aye – the guy had supposedly inspected them and signed them off two days before. So when Heikkinen went to

Ehrling and told him, he came down hard on Rosenberg, wrote him up. His fuck-up could have cost the entire operation. If the main seals went, it'd make a hell of a mess. And from what I heard, Bolstad's not exactly in a great position. Spill like that could mean the end of everything.'

'Where did you hear that?'

He shrugged. 'People talk, you know? But if it could be traced back to a single engineer not doing his fookin' job right – well, no one'd be keen to hire him again.'

'But it's not Noemi's fault if he didn't do his job.' Jamie was doing her best to follow Quinn's complex, rambling storylines.

'That's the ticket, eh? Rosenberg stands by his report – reckons that those seals were in good nick when he signed off on them.'

'He thinks they were tampered with.'

Quinn grinned again. 'You're sharp, lass, you know that?'

'I've been told.' Jamie brushed it off. 'But who would want a seal to break?'

'Seems coincidental that she'd check it right then, eh?'

'You're saying she knew about it?'

'I'm not saying anything,' Quinn said casually.

'But that's what you're intimating. Except Heikkinen wouldn't know how to tamper with a seal? And even if she did, why would she do that and then report it to Ehrling?' She bit her lip, looking at Quinn, who seemed to be holding back a grin.

'Beats me,' Quinn said. 'All I know is that Rosenberg checked it, then Noemi Heikkinen checked it, and went scarpering off to Ehrling right before it blew. Pretty good fookin' timing, if you ask me.'

'You think Reyes tampered with the seal and then Noemi found out and reported it?'

Quinn shrugged. 'Be useful if you could ask her, eh?'

It would, yeah, Jamie thought. 'Who would want to cause a spill out here?' she asked, not especially to Quinn.

He sighed lengthily. 'Your guess is as good as mine.'

'It would be an international incident,' Jamie added, thinking back to when news broke about the oil spill in the Gulf of Mexico and how much attention that attracted. 'It would destroy Bolstad.'

'Aye, that it would. Put them in the ground for sure, I reckon. And who'd want to see that happen, eh? Who's got the environment at the top of their priorities list, I wonder?'

'The girls,' Jamie said. 'You're talking about eco-terrorism? But surely they wouldn't knowingly want to manufacture an oil spill? It would be devastating to the ocean.'

'Aye, you'd think so. But one spill from a small rig like this – controlled – maybe it's not that big of a deal. Especially if they got the data to show exactly how much damage it would do.'

'Which is exactly what they were researching out here …' Jamie swallowed. 'And if there was a spill, Bolstad would be finished. For good. And one less oil company in the world wouldn't be a bad thing. Jesus,' Jamie said.

Quinn laughed a little. 'Your words, not mine.'

'So Rosenberg came at Heikkinen, accusing her of making him look inept? And how did Reyes react?'

'As you imagine when someone threatens yer lass.' Quinn counted off finger number four.

Jamie exhaled hard, looking at Quinn's remaining digit. 'Anything else?' she asked, a little apprehensive.

'There's Boykov – Dima Boykov – the drill tech.'

'And Reyes what, slept with his mother?' Jamie asked tiredly.

Quinn chuckled. 'No, he just didn't like how Reyes handled his drill. Not a euphemism.'

'Didn't think it was.'

'Aye, said he was too rough. Was gonna wear it out.'

'And you think that'd be motive enough to kill Reyes?'

'Guess you'll have to meet Boykov and tell me. Lad takes his job seriously, you know.' That was finger five.

Jamie sighed. 'Great. Thank you – you've actually been really helpful.'

'Don't sound so shocked. Colm Quinn's got a lot to offer if yer take the time to get to know him.' He winked at Jamie, and she did her best not to shudder.

She turned away, and Wiik followed her lead, seemingly keen to put ground between himself and Quinn.

'Detective,' Quinn called, before she could get five steps. 'Watch your back out here – I reckon whatever Reyes started, it's not over.'

Jamie didn't say anything, processed that, and then nodded.

Quinn returned it and then went back to work.

'Quinn,' Jamie called.

He glanced over his shoulder.

'Don't go anywhere, okay? We'll need to talk to you again.'

He laughed. 'Aye, I didn't fancy a swim anyway.'

14

'WHAT WAS THAT ABOUT?' Wiik asked when they were out of earshot.

The drill struck up behind them and the incessant vibration rang through Jamie's heels. 'What was *what* about?'

'"Don't go anywhere",' Wiik parroted and then tutted.

Jamie resisted the urge to roll her eyes. 'It was just a joke,' she said.

'Exactly. I've known you for nearly three months, and I don't think I've heard you make a single joke in that time.' He strode quickly, forcing Jamie to jog to keep up.

'Maybe you're just not the laughing type,' Jamie said, grabbing his shoulder and turning him around. 'Hey, wait.' She came to a stop just short of the door and looked Wiik dead in the eye. 'What is this? Quinn's been the most helpful person we've spoken to since we've got here. He just gave us a whole bunch of leads to chase down.'

Wiik scoffed. 'I'm surprised you didn't take his head off the way he was speaking to you.'

'I almost did,' Jamie replied, trying to catch his eye now. He wouldn't look at her. What was this? Jealousy? She felt like taking *Wiik's* head off. 'Come on, Wiik. Quinn is a piece of shit. Anyone with a nose could tell that from a hundred yards away. But he's also the only person we've met so far who's been forthcoming with information. I don't know if he's innocent, or if he's just spinning stories to throw us off, but you can be damn sure we're going to interview every single person in this place to find out. I may not like the guy, but unlike you, I'm not trying to make enemies of every person I meet. If you haven't noticed, we're pretty fucking outnumbered here.'

Wiik ground his teeth. 'I'm not trying to make enemies,' he said sourly.

'Really? Because that's the second person you've almost got into a fight with in as many days over, what, the size of your dick?'

Wiik looked down then and made an ugly face.

Jamie was surprised to hear it come out of her mouth, too. She rarely got worked up over anything. But she wasn't keen on seeing Wiik getting the shit kicked out of him over a petty pissing contest.

'It's just ...' he started, trailing off. 'I don't like this.'

'What?'

'This place. The investigation. Wallace. Ehrling. Quinn. Any of it. It doesn't feel like we're here to solve a crime. It feels like ...'

'Like what?'

'Like ...' He was wrestling with the words.

'Spit it out, Wiik.'

'It feels like Reyes was bait.'

'Bait? For who?' Jamie watched him closely.

'For us. Maybe not *us* us. But us. Police officers.'

'I'm not following.' She really wasn't, and usually she was sharp.

'Bolstad want nothing more than to sweep this under the rug and keep the company going. A single death isn't that hard to cover up. Especially on an oil rig. Dangerous places. A few payoffs, a couple of non-disclosures. You could bury it. But the deaths of two police officers? There's no getting away from that kind of shitstorm.'

'Wait,' Jamie said, catching up. 'You're saying you think someone killed Reyes knowing Bolstad would try to cover it up, with the express intention of killing the police officers who came to investigate?'

Wiik shrugged slowly. 'I don't know. Just a feeling. One I can't shake.'

'But who the hell would have reason to do that?' Jamie asked, her mouth going a little dry.

Wiik met her eye then. 'Who would want to shut Bolstad down? If Quinn's information is reliable, then we already know the answer.'

'Sevier. Hooper.' Jamie bit her lip. 'Shit.'

Wiik nodded. 'From what Quinn said, Heikkinen reported the seals as ready to burst. Rosenberg maintains they were fine a few days earlier. If they were trying to cause a spill, then either Heikkinen wasn't in on it, or more likely she was and got cold feet.'

'Which explains why she miraculously chose that moment to check the seals.'

'It's one theory.'

'So Hooper and Sevier make a move to cause a spill. Heikkinen gets cold feet, sabotages their plan. And then they have to think of something else ...'

'Sevier goes to Quinn's room, lures Reyes out under the guise of meeting Heikkinen. And then they kill him.'

'And Bolstad try to cover it up.'

'They call us in.'

'And then they act on it, turning one concealable death into an international scandal,' Jamie finished.

Wiik nodded grimly. 'We don't know Heikkinen was with Reyes that night, only that Sevier reported her missing to Vogel, *after* calling on Reyes herself.'

'So they, what, killed off their friend to cover their tracks?'

'If Heikkinen was in love with Reyes, there's no way she'd let Hooper and Sevier get away with it. Love trumps friendship.'

Jamie shook her head. 'As does not going to prison.'

Wiik cast his eyes across the deck of the platform. 'And we already know Hooper's not afraid of throwing a punch.'

'So with Ehrling, asking about Heikkinen, that was all a charade to throw us off the scent?'

Wiik didn't answer this time. He just let the theory sit.

'Okay,' Jamie said, processing it all. 'Let's go and speak to Hooper and Sevier, see how they remember it. And Wiik?'

'Yeah?'

'Try not to get into a fight with them too, okay?' She winked at him.

He cracked a smile. The first she'd seen since they left Stockholm. 'If I remember correctly, last time you and Hooper crossed paths, it was *you* who was slamming her face into a desk, not me.'

Jamie returned it. 'Oh, yeah. I guess that was me,' she said, and then headed for the door.

. . .

Back inside, the temperature was mercifully warmer. Jamie
and Wiik were both rosy-cheeked, hands stuffed deeply in
their pockets, shoulders hunched around their ears, as they
climbed back up towards the staff quarters.

They got off a floor lower, following the signs for the
cafeteria. It was getting into the late morning, and Jamie's
eyes were heavy.

A dingy corridor with a tiled floor offered up a set of
double swing doors that opened into a wide room.

A set of four long bench-tables stretched from the door to
the far wall, each capable of sitting eight, or even ten people,
Jamie thought. On the left wall, a series of posters were
displayed, perpetuating the idea that oil was the lifeblood of
the world. Four people of different races shaking hands and
grinning in hard hats, a family running through a meadow, a
picture of a deer on a wooded hill, flower buds pushing
through dark earth. Jamie pulled her eyes away from the
propaganda and homed in on the thing producing the smell of
coffee.

Wiik was already walking towards the kitchen-end of the
room. A long table sat against the wall with a tray-rail in front
of it. On the table, a large silver still was steaming, and next
to it were plastic bowls covered in cling film. As Jamie
approached, she could see they were filled with scant portions
of different cereals. A small glass-fronted fridge sat at the far
left, filled with little single-servings of juices and milk. There
was a service window behind the table, giving a view of a
small kitchen with a grease-splattered cooker. Jamie watched
as Wiik went in, hunting for real cups. There was a stack of
paper ones next to the coffee still, but he hated drinking from
them. He was one of those people who had to drink their
coffee nuclear hot. And a paper cup didn't keep it that way
long enough, he said.

Jamie's eyes passed over her partner to a clipboard hanging on the wall. As she went in, she could see it was a list of names. There were three columns labelled breakfast, lunch, and dinner. Under each column names were written, arranged by date. All the names of the workers. This wasn't a large platform by any stretch, and it looked like everyone had to pitch in and do their share.

It struck Jamie as odd that the cafeteria would hold thirty, maybe forty people, and there were just ten workers on board. And that they did their own cooking. She didn't know a lot about oil rigs, but she'd always thought they'd had their own kitchen staff at least.

Wiik closed a cupboard in frustration behind her and kept looking. The noise brought Jamie back to reality, and she ran her finger down the list.

This morning, it had been Quinn and Kravets' turn to handle breakfast. They'd filled some bowls with oats and cornflakes and turned the coffee pot on, then gone out to their shift.

She picked the clipboard up and flicked back to two nights previous, scanning down the dinner column for the names there. Sven Rosenberg and Dima Boykov. It was hardly an airtight alibi, but at least if it could be proved they were in the kitchen cooking, that would rule them out of the investigation.

'Ah,' Wiik said suddenly.

She turned to see him holding up two white cups.

He went out of the kitchen and filled them quickly. 'Milk?' he called. 'They don't have skimmed.'

But Jamie didn't answer.

'Johansson?' he called again, coming back into the kitchen. 'What is it?'

Jamie's eyes were fixed on the counter top across the kitchen. Specifically at the knife block there.

Specifically at the empty space where one should have been.

'There's a knife missing,' she said, nodding at it. Her calf throbbed through her jeans.

She took the coffee from Wiik, turning back to the kitchen rota, looking for the names of the people working last night.

Jamie reached up and put her finger on a name there.

Wiik followed it. 'Orn Møller,' he said. 'You think he's the one that locked us out? Chased you through maintenance?'

Jamie let her finger fall and took a sip of black coffee. It was hot, and bitter, but that suited her just fine. She looked at Wiik, the corner of her mouth curling into her cheek. 'Only one way to find out.'

Wiik and Jamie reached the upper crew quarters, topped off with caffeine and stale bran flakes, and slowed. Jamie had been thinking all through breakfast, about how to handle this. Hooper was the antagonistic sort, she already knew that, and if Sevier had been involved with Heikkinen's death, then she wasn't to be underestimated either. But despite that, she didn't think having Wiik there was the best solution. If the girls' room was the same size as theirs, then four bodies in there would be no fun for anyone.

Plus, if anything did go down, Jamie didn't want to be falling all over Wiik.

'Hey,' she said, turning and stopping him at the end of the corridor. 'Why don't you go up, speak to Vogel.'

'Vogel?' Wiik asked. 'Why?'

. . .

'She didn't tell us about her relationship with Reyes. And she made a big point of corroborating Ehrling's alibi by giving us her whereabouts. But there's nothing to say that she didn't slip out during that meeting and go after Reyes.'

'She'd have motive to get rid of Heikkinen, too.' Wiik was nodding slowly. 'So far she's seemed like the only stable person we've met.'

'Let's see how stable she is when you tell her you know about her and Reyes. She's the only one who we know has lied so far. I want to know what happens when we call her out on it.'

'Only if Quinn's story holds up,' Wiik added. 'You want to head up there before we speak to Sevier?'

'No,' Jamie said, glancing over her shoulders at the girls' room. 'You should handle Vogel on your own. It's clear that she feels underappreciated here, that she thinks she's the one doing everything with no recognition for it. You'll have a better chance of making her feel … *appreciated* if I'm not there.'

Wiik raised an eyebrow slowly. 'You're suggesting I try to … *seduce* her to get the truth?'

'If I thought seduction was a tool you had in your wheel-house, I would have said it.'

'You're full of it this morning.' He tried to suppress a look of mild offence.

'Sorry,' Jamie said, exhaling and brushing a few loose strands of hair over her ears. 'Just tired.'

'You and me both.'

There was silence between them for a few seconds.

'Look,' Jamie said. 'We already know Hooper is fiery, and I don't know a thing about Sevier yet, but if you're there,

I think there's a good chance they'll just shut down. They're surrounded by men here as it is. Maybe they'll be more relaxed with just me.'

Wiik couldn't argue. On either count. Vogel hadn't responded warmly to Jamie's presence thus far – Jamie suspected it was because they were probably quite alike. Like two repelling magnets. And if the girls were innocent and they'd just had their best friend killed off by a man on board, maybe sticking another guy in the only place they felt safe was the wrong way to go about this.

'Fine,' Wiik said eventually. 'But if *anything* goes wrong, you yell, alright? And I'll come running.'

'Sure,' Jamie said. For a second she was going to say, *Nothing will go wrong, don't worry.* But she didn't feel like tempting fate. 'Now, go charm Vogel into telling us what really happened with Reyes.'

'Alright, alright,' Wiik said, holding his hands up. 'I get it, I'm not the most personable guy.' He gave her a weak smile and then slinked away like a wounded puppy.

She was mustering the energy to call after him, to tell him she didn't mean it like that. But then he was gone and Jamie was alone in the corridor.

15

JAMIE HOVERED at the door for a few seconds, listening for any hint of movement inside.

She could hear voices, low. Kept purposefully low to stop anyone from overhearing, she thought.

Jamie knocked, and waited.

A few seconds later, the door opened a few inches, stopping abruptly against Ashleigh Hooper's boot – which was wedged firmly in place.

She didn't look surprised to see Jamie, but she didn't look pleased either.

'Yeah?' Hooper asked, narrowing her eyes a little.

'Detective Inspector Jamie Johansson,' Jamie said. 'We met upstairs.'

'I remember,' Hooper said dryly.

Jamie didn't mean it like that. Damn, she was really screwing things up today. 'Can we talk?'

'About what?'

'Noemi Heikkinen.'

'You found her?'

'No.'

'Then, no,' Hooper said, trying to close the door. But it didn't budge.

Her foot was one side, Jamie's was the other.

'It doesn't work like that,' Jamie continued, her patience already wearing thin. 'I need to speak to you about Noemi Heikkinen and her relationship with Alejandro Reyes.'

'I don't know anything about that,' Hooper said, sticking her bottom lip out. 'Me and Noemi weren't that close.'

'What about you and Paméla Sevier? Are you close with her?' Jamie asked casually.

The quiet squeaking of plastic rang through the gap. Someone shifting on a mattress inside the room. Someone perking up hearing their name.

Hooper swallowed, not knowing what the correct answer was.

'Because,' Jamie went on, 'I've got three eye-witnesses who say that she came and called on Alejandro Reyes the night that he was murdered. Which makes Paméla Sevier probably the last person to see him alive.'

Hooper stayed quiet.

'So which will it be? You want to cover for her, lie to me, aid a potential murderer? Obstruct justice? Or do you want to open the door so we can straighten all this out and I can go catch who really did this?'

There was a whisper through the door, and Hooper glanced over her shoulder. She released her foot. 'Fine,' she said, pulling the door wide.

Jamie stepped inside and met the redhead's eye. 'Good answer.'

Hooper sneered at her, but Jamie was already looking at Sevier. She'd come back to Hooper in time, but Sevier, so far, was an unknown.

Jamie sized the girl up as Hooper closed the door on her right. She made sure to keep her in her peripheral.

Paméla Sevier was a little over five feet, slight in build, with a full fringe of dark hair. She glowered up at Jamie through it, her mouth an acrid pout.

Jamie held her gaze for almost a minute straight before she spoke.

'What?' Paméla asked, her English good, but heavily accented. 'What do you want?'

'Let's cut right to it,' Jamie said. 'Why did you go to Colm Quinn's room to call on Reyes?'

She folded her arms. 'Because Noemi asked me to.'

'You're going to have to do better than that.'

'Because Noemi was afraid of Quinn and his … *friends.*'

Jamie noted the disdain in her voice. 'They gave Noemi some trouble?'

Sevier swallowed, broke eye contact for the first time. There was anger in her, fear too. 'Noemi was beautiful. A girl like that, here, with these … *men.*' She shook her head. 'Everybody wanted to be with her.'

'But you weren't scared of them? Quinn, Lebedenkov, Kravets – they're big guys.'

'I can handle myself.'

'I'm sure you can,' Jamie said. The girl was small, but Jamie knew that didn't always mean helpless. She glanced at Hooper then. Neither of them looked like they'd take any shit. Especially not from the likes of Quinn. But Noemi? Was she the weak link? 'Tell me what happened that night.'

'We were here – Ashleigh and me. We had been down on the floating dock, collecting some algae and water samples. Noemi was with Vogel – getting hold of some data for us. We came back up here at about six, I think, and about twenty minutes later, Noemi arrived – nearly in tears.'

. . .

'She was crying?' Jamie asked, thinking about what Vogel had said. She was supposed to be in her quarters since five, before Ehrling's meeting started. 'What happened?'

Sevier shrugged. 'I don't know. She seemed angry, I think. She said that she needed to see Alejandro – I mean, Reyes.' She looked up at Jamie, as though being on first-name terms with the victim was going to implicate her.

Jamie nodded for her to go on.

'She asked me if I would call for him. He had finished his shift but hadn't gone to eat yet. He was in Quinn's room, playing cards.' She glanced at Hooper then, who was a statue behind Jamie, leaning against the wall, arms folded. Sevier cleared her throat and went on. 'So I did. I went down there, knocked on their door, and told Reyes that Noemi wanted to see him.'

'Then what happened?'

'I came back here, and Noemi was already gone.'

Jamie looked at Hooper now. 'That right? You were here?'

'Noemi left just after Pam,' Hooper said grouchily. 'Went down to their "secret meeting place".'

The inflection was unmissable. 'You knew where it was?'

She snorted. 'Of course.'

'Who else knew?'

'Who didn't,' Hooper said, shaking her head. 'Like Pam said, Noemi was a catch. Reyes couldn't help but brag to his friends. Quinn, Kravets, Lebe-dick-face.' She sneered again. 'I bet he couldn't wait to tell them all about where they'd …' Her bottom lip started to quiver, her tough-girl facade cracking once more.

Either she was a good enough actress to cry on command, or she genuinely had nothing to do with Heikkinen's death.

Jamie collected herself for a second. 'So Quinn, Kravets, Lebedenkov – they were jealous of Reyes? For being with Noemi.'

'You could say that,' Sevier answered now.

'Jealous enough to kill Reyes?' Jamie stared her dead in the eye.

'If they were,' Sevier said, looking at the ground, 'I hate to think what they were planning to do to Noemi afterwards.'

'For her sake,' Hooper said, cutting back in. 'I hope she jumped. If she had any sense, with one of those fucking animals coming at her, she would have. If not, well …' She cleared the lump in her throat and met Jamie's eye. 'She'd have suffered a fate worse than death. And then they would have tossed her over, anyway.'

16

'Is THERE anything else you can tell me about—' But Jamie didn't get to finish the sentence.

She lifted her head and pricked her ears, a thud resounding up through the floor.

Then there was a loud crash. Jamie took a few steps back, lifting her heels and staring at the thin carpeted floor between them.

Sevier and Hooper looked at each other, and then at Jamie. She met the girls' concerned gazes and then froze as a blood-curdling scream rose from the floor below.

Jamie turned and tore the door open, jumping into the hallway, looking left and right for the quickest way down. She chose right and started moving, listening as the girls slammed and bolted their door behind her.

As she reached the end of the corridor and the stairs there, she heard footsteps on her left and watched Wiik descending quickly from the command deck. His wide eyes told her he'd heard the scream, too. And they both knew what that kind of scream meant.

He fell into step with her and they both plunged down to the main crew quarters, swinging a hard right into the narrow corridor. Jamie bounced off the wall, her calf throbbing under her, and made for the only open door in front of them.

It was four down on the left, directly under the girls' room.

Jamie's heart was in her throat as she slowed, glancing down at the vinyl tiled floor underfoot, at the trail of blood leading out of it.

Wiik shouldered past her and into the doorway, putting his hands against the frame.

Jamie came up next to him, knowing what she was about to find.

Wiik shoved back out of the door, jostling past her for the second time, and followed the blood, swearing as he went. But Jamie wasn't listening.

She stepped into the doorway and looked down at the scene in front of her.

Dima Boykov, the drill technician who'd had a problem with how Reyes was using the drill, who she recognised from both the name on his door and the photograph in his file, was lying slumped against his bed, arms limp at his sides, legs tangled in front of him, eyes wide and staring at the ceiling. His mouth hung open, his nose swollen, crooked, and bleeding – broken. His teeth were bloodied, too. But it was his torso that Jamie's eyes were drawn to, and the white shirt he was wearing, littered with holes, soaked red.

A pool of blood was spreading beneath him.

And while Jamie's first instinct was to launch herself into the room and try to stem it, there was no point.

She could tell that he was dead, even from the doorway, a cluster of wounds in the centre of his chest, right through the heart.

Jamie felt bile rise in her throat and listened as doors began to open around her. She swallowed hard and looked at the faces that now swum in the corridor. For a moment, they were all strangers, and then she began to recognise them, her mind pulling up the photographs from the files.

There was Sven Rosenberg the Swede, head engineer. He was tall, had short black hair and dark, dark eyes sitting above a long, hooked nose.

Orn Møller the Dane, senior engineer. He was shaped like a bison, with mousy-brown hair and close-set eyes, a small mouth, and wide cheeks.

Grzegorz Kurek, the Polish safety engineer. He was lean, with dark, tousled hair and wide, sunken green eyes that had heavy circles under them. His hand was clenched around the doorframe, eyes darting wildly, teeth dug into his bottom lip.

Jamie looked from one to the other, and then down at the blood trail that ran into the corridor and towards the end of the hallway. It petered out short of all of them. Which meant it could have been any of them.

One of them could have been the person who killed Reyes. And one of them could have killed Boykov, too.

They all stared back at her. Was she staring at a killer?

A bang resounded, and Jamie jumped.

Wiik strode through the door at the far end of the crew quarters and it bounced off the wall. He ran his hand over his head, pressing his hair flat to his scalp, and let out a long breath. 'Nothing,' he called out to Jamie.

He slowed, noticing the three people hanging out of their respective rooms. He was right in the middle of them. Wiik pulled his badge, flashed it around and walked back towards Jamie. 'In your rooms,' he commanded, gesturing them back in. 'And stay there until we call for you.'

They exchanged tentative glances, and then Kurek

nodded at the blood trail leading from Boykov's room. The three men looked at it, and then one at a time shrunk back into their quarters, closing the doors.

Wiik approached Jamie and put his hands on his hips. 'No sign of anyone,' he said. 'Place is a fucking maze. Could have been anyone.'

Jamie looked down at Boykov. 'It wasn't Hooper or Sevier. What about Ehrling and Vogel?'

'They were on the command deck,' Wiik said diligently. 'And Wallace was in his room.'

'His cronies?'

Wiik shrugged. 'Don't know. The door was closed. Though with a killer on the loose, I wouldn't expect them to leave his side.'

Jamie didn't want to comment on that. She just kept looking at Boykov, not quite sure what to do next. It was about now they'd lock down the scene, call in the crime scene techs, canvas the area. But none of it felt like normal. Jamie felt powerless. Just a bystander in what was quickly turning into a bloodbath. 'What did Vogel say?' she asked, not wanting to address the situation.

'She confessed to being with Reyes. But she said that the breakup was nothing. That they were just sleeping together, that was it. She wasn't looking for a relationship, and apparently neither was Reyes.'

Jamie nodded. 'It doesn't gel with Quinn's story. But that's not surprising.'

Wiik let out a long breath, did the thing with his hand and his hair again. 'Jesus, what a fucking mess.'

Jamie swallowed, watching as the pool of blood seeped across the thin carpet, closer to the toes of her boots. 'Yep,' she said, struggling to find her voice. 'A real fucking mess.'

. . .

As much as Jamie hated to admit it, she was out of her depth. And so was Wiik.

It was easy to think that you were the one and only mind working on a case, but they were just the tip of the spear. And without the support of the SPA behind them, Jamie and Wiik felt all but castrated.

Wiik had gone to get Ehrling, and minutes later, Wallace arrived with his heavies in tow. He stood stoically in the background, and then retreated to his stateroom in silence.

'You have a satellite link here?' Jamie asked Ehrling.

He nodded. 'Of course.'

'We need to call this in.'

Ehrling swallowed. 'Okay. What can I do?'

Jamie glanced at Boykov. 'Get us another body bag.'

Thirty minutes later, Jamie had taken photos of the scene, the body, and the blood trail, and Ehrling and Wiik had carried him off to the infirmary to join Reyes.

There were only six people who could have killed Boykov — Rosenburg, Møller, or Kurek — the three men in that very corridor. Though it'd take some serious balls to stab a man to death and then just slip right back into your room like nothing happened.

Or it was Quinn, Kravets, or Lebedenkov. Who were all still on shift outside — she guessed. Though the security footage that covered the platform would hopefully confirm or deny that and make their lives easier.

But first, Jamie headed back upstairs to speak to Vogel about getting on a call to Falk. This had gone too far now. They needed to get out of there, and they needed to call the cavalry in instead. Crime Scene Techs to sweep the whole place. An army of uniformed to wrestle everyone into handcuffs and manhandle them back to the mainland. That's what needed to happen.

Jamie banged on the command-deck door with the heel of her hand and a minute later, it opened, revealing Vogel. She looked tired and unhappy. Jamie shared the sentiment.

'You know there's a buzzer, right?' Vogel said, lifting her chin to Jamie's right.

She glanced down at the card reader and noticed there was a button underneath it with a little bell icon.

Jamie flashed Vogel an apologetic smile. 'I'll remember for next time. I need to call the mainland,' she said, stepping in without invitation.

'Sure,' Vogel said to her back, closing the door behind her and following her up the stairs. 'Not like I was working or anything.'

Jamie stopped on the steps and turned to face her. She stared down at the women. 'Two – maybe three – people are dead. You know that, don't you?'

'I didn't kill them,' Vogel said, as though that was what Jamie was inferring.

'I just meant …' Jamie shook her head. 'Never mind. Just … just show me how to work this.' She gestured to the control desk.

Vogel breezed past her towards the work station, sitting down in the chair. She reached across to a keyboard in the middle of the desk, tapped a few things, and minimised the window displaying weather patterns. Then she pulled a mouse forwards from the back of the desk, clicked open an application that displayed a big phone, and offered the chair in front of it to Jamie. 'Just type the number in the box and hit the button,' Vogel said, already sitting back at her own desk. She put a pair of headphones on and began searching through a list of data that Jamie could only guess the meaning of.

Jamie sat and wasted no time typing in the number for

Falk's office. She clicked the phone icon as instructed and a little window popped up on the screen with a loading bar. The words *Establishing Connection* flashed gently, and then suddenly, it was dialling.

She picked up almost immediately, her voice ringing tinnily through the small speakers on either side of the screen. *'Hallå, Kriminalkommissarie Ingrid Falk,'* she said.

'Falk,' Jamie all but barked.

'Johansson?' she sounded unsure if it was her.

'You've got to do something,' Jamie said, near breathless. She prided herself on being able to keep a cool head, but with every passing second, she was getting the feeling they'd been locked in a cage with a rabid dog. And more often than not, when Jamie got feelings about cases, they were usually right. 'We've got another body.'

'Hello? Jamie? I can barely hear you – did you say you've got another body there?'

'Another crew member, yes – stabbed, same as Reyes, and—'

'The line is really bad,' Falk interjected, her voice beginning to crackle now.

'Falk! Listen to me,' Jamie said, growing in volume. 'This is getting out of hand – Wiik and I can't—'

'Johansson? Speak slower, I'm not—'

'You've got to get us off this thing. Speak to Bolstad and—'

'I can't do that, you need to—'

'I'm not fucking around,' Jamie growled now. 'People are dying, Falk. *Call Bolstad.* Get these people out of here. Get *us* out of here.'

There was silence on the line, just a faint crackling in the air. The phone icon in front of Jamie strobed slowly.

'Falk? Are you there?' Jamie asked.

'I'm here,' she said after a few seconds, letting out a slow breath. 'Okay,' she said. 'I'll speak to Bolstad, explain the situation, try and get a chopper out there tonight, and—'

'Uh,' came a voice from Jamie's right. 'That's not going to be possible.'

She turned to look at Vogel, who was sitting at her desk, holding her headphones around her neck.

'I wasn't listening in,' Vogel confirmed quickly. 'But I couldn't help but overhear ...'

'What is it?' Jamie asked, her voice colder than she intended.

Vogel weighed Jamie for a second, and then took her headphones off and slid her chair across towards her.

She reached out and pulled the keyboard over, then tapped a few things. The phone window minimised, and she pulled up the weather patterns she was looking at before Jamie came in. 'This is what,' she said, gesturing to the screen. 'There's a low-pressure front moving down from the north. It's already swept past Svalbaard and will be hitting us in the next four or five hours, judging by the wind speed. If it continues to pick up pace, maybe less. No way to tell.'

'Meaning?' Jamie asked, knowing the answer already.

'Meaning no chopper. No one gets out, or in. Not until the storm passes, at least.' Vogel looked apprehensive to share the news, but didn't seem phased by the imminent threat of death at the hands of whoever was stacking up the bodies downstairs.

'For how long?' Jamie forced the words out, her heart thudding in her chest.

Vogel exhaled, tilted her head back and forth. 'Two – three days. Maybe? Sometimes in the wake of these cells, the winds can keep up and—'

'Jesus,' Jamie muttered, cutting her off. 'What about a ship? Or—'

'It'd take a ship that long to get here – especially in that weather. And you'd need a warship to brave the swells. They can get up to thirty, forty metres – sometimes more. Wind speeds up to a hundred and twenty, hundred and thirty kilometres an hour. We're trapped here. For now, at least.'

Like rats, Jamie almost said. The word *trapped* made her stomach twist into a knot.

'We're already seeing the first effects – high-altitude cloud formations – it's why the satellite signal is so spotty.'

The line still crackled in the background as Falk listened to the information being laid out.

'Will we still get a signal when it hits?'

'Unlikely. Not for a call at least.' Vogel said. 'But it's a queued-upload system.'

'Let's just pretend for a second I don't know what that is.'

Vogel's jaw flexed.

Jamie wasn't in the mood.

'It means that whatever you want to send will automatically queue itself up and wait for a signal. As soon as it receives one, it'll begin transmitting. It will be intermittent, but you might be able to send and receive messages.'

'Images?'

'As attachments?' Vogel inspected the look of desperate focus on Jamie's face. 'If you want to send them, I'd do it quickly. In a few hours, it might be too late.'

Jamie swallowed and nodded. 'Falk – you get all that?'

'I got it. What do you need?'

Jamie was glad she sounded a little bit more onside now. Whatever Bolstad had on her – whatever they were using to get her to go along with this whole thing – it wasn't more important than the lives of the crew, or the lives of her and

Wiik. And she couldn't help but feel better about that. Even if it meant exactly nothing right now. 'I'm going to send over some photographs of the scenes. I need a pathologist to look at them and tell me what they see.'

'Okay.'

'Can you get Claesson to do it?'

'Peter Claesson?' Falk seemed surprised.

'Yeah.'

'Uh, okay. I can try. Why?'

Because I trust him. And I don't know who else we can right now, Jamie felt like saying. 'I know he's good at what he does. And we need all the help we can get,' she said instead.

'I'll see what I can do. Anything else?'

'Is Hallberg free? I need her to dig up some information on a few people. There are three girls on board here – research students from Helsinki University. One of them is missing.'

'Missing?'

'Yeah, a girl called Noemi Heikkinen. She was with Reyes when he was killed. There's no sign of her. Possibly dead, possibly … worse. I don't know. I have some info on them, but I was hoping Hallberg could work her magic.'

'I'll have her start right away. Just send me their names. Anything else?'

Jamie glanced at Vogel. She also wanted Hallberg to look into Ehrling and Wallace, but saying that with Vogel sitting next to her and Wallace in the next room, no doubt with a glass to the door, felt like a stupid move. Jamie's hand automatically went to the satchel she was still carrying, containing the personnel files, and squeezed it. 'No,' she said. 'That's everything. If I think of anything else, I'll email you.'

'Okay, and Johansson?'

'Yeah?'

'Look after yourself, alright?'

Jamie swallowed. 'I'll try.'

17

JAMIE WATCHED the progress bar creep slowly towards completion, the pictures from her phone joining the upload queue.

Vogel sat with her arms folded, in silence.

It seemed neither of them felt much like talking.

The wind was already beginning to pick up, buffeting at the windows that overlooked the helideck. The clouds had begun to brood on the horizon. They morphed, heavy and dark, growing with each passing moment.

Jamie thought that four hours seemed very generous.

She had resigned herself to quiet thought. Realistically, they had two options. Either they hunkered down and tried to ride this out – which was probably going to result in more deaths as the killer crept around unseen and free. And that plan was also going to be completely useless if Wallace insisted on keeping the drill going the whole time, too, which Jamie figured he would. And that would mean everyone would have to work, moving around the rig, unsupervised, vulnerable. There was no way Jamie and Wiik could police that.

It was clear that he didn't give two shits about the people on board. All he cared about was the bottom line, and no doubt managing this platform to his next bonus.

Or the second, and only realistic option, was that Jamie and Wiik grew some collective balls, gritted their teeth, and hunted down this motherfucker before he could put a knife in anyone else. But that came with its own risks. And she didn't think Wallace was about to let them have their weapons back.

And with the size of this place, and the fact that it was running on a skeleton crew, added up to one massive fucking maze with a thousand places to hide, making their task near impossible. And probably quite dangerous.

And that wasn't even the worst of it.

'I need to see the CCTV,' Jamie said, still watching the clouds. 'So we can figure out who went after Boykov.'

'We have cameras that cover the command deck, helideck, the main drill platform, and the cafeteria.'

'Just four cameras on the entire platform?'

'This isn't exactly what you'd call usual circumstances. This is the sixth rig I've worked on. Nothing like this has ever happened before. If you ask me, it takes a special kind of idiot to want to kill someone when they've got nowhere to run.'

If there was one thing this killer wasn't, it was stupid, Jamie thought. No, something was going on here. A plan of some kind. A motive. A train of thought that had led to Reyes' death, and then to Boykov's. And if she could figure it out, she could anticipate who was next, and stop the killer before they got to them.

But that was a lot of *if*s, and they weren't exactly on the offensive.

Yet, at least.

The moment the upload bar hit 100 per cent, Jamie pulled

the cord from her phone, typed in Falk's email address, and hit send.

She pushed back from the desk and stood up. 'Can you get the footage together from the night of Reyes' death – between six and nine p.m.?'

'There's not a camera on the lower submersible platform,' Vogel said.

'I know – but if we can catch anyone else on film at the same time, we might be able to rule them out as suspects.'

Vogel's lack of enthusiasm told Jamie she didn't think that was going to be that helpful. Neither did Jamie, really. But it was about all they had.

'And the footage from the last hour or so, to cover Boykov's death.'

'Of course,' Vogel said. 'I'll, uh, put it on a flash drive for you.'

'Great,' Jamie said. 'I'll be back.'

Vogel forced a smile. 'I'll be here.'

'And you should stay that way – this is probably the safest place on the rig.'

Vogel thought on that, then nodded. 'Thanks, but I can look after myself.'

'Let me know when the footage is ready.'

'Will do. And, Inspector?'

'Yeah?' Jamie said, already on the stairs.

'Good luck.'

Jamie descended the stairs back towards Boykov's room. The smell of blood hung thick in the air.

Wiik was standing outside it, arms folded, lips curled down into a grumpy grimace. If Jamie was having a bad time out here, Wiik was having an even worse one. And why was he even here, anyway? What did Falk have on him?

As she approached, it struck her just how little she knew about her partner, really.

Anders Wiik was six feet tall and fastidious about his appearance. She knew his age, that he was divorced, that he had a son, an old partner who'd moved on – whose shoes she had filled. But otherwise … not much else. They'd been working together a few months now, but she didn't know where he lived, what he did after work, or even what kind of music he liked. She knew that he couldn't run for shit, and that he had a sharp mind and an uncanny memory. That he had the social skills of a cactus. But those were observations anyone could make ten minutes after meeting him.

She didn't think she'd ever asked him a personal question.

'Hey,' she said, approaching. 'Who's your favourite band?'

'My favourite band?' He lifted an eyebrow in confusion.

'Yeah.' She smiled. 'Music, you know?'

He looked at her oddly. 'I don't really listen to music. Why are you asking that?'

'Just …' She sighed. 'Just trying to lighten the mood.'

He shrugged it off. 'You get through to Falk?'

Jamie nodded. 'Yeah, but we're not getting off this thing any time soon.'

'She wouldn't send a chopper?'

'She couldn't. There's a weather front rolling in – we won't be able to get out for a couple of days. Maybe three.'

Wiik swore under his breath and hung his head, lacing his fingers across the nape of his neck. 'So, we're stuck here?'

'Just you, me, and a knife-wielding madman.'

He cracked a smile at that one, and it made Jamie feel a

little warmer. Wiik looked up, his eyes going to the three doors that had opened when Boykov was killed. Kurek. Møller. Rosenberg. 'Which one first?' Wiik asked.

Jamie approached the first door – Grzegorz Kurek's, the safety engineer that Reyes had owed a gambling debt to – and lifted her knuckles. 'Unless you'd prefer to start elsewhere?'

He proffered his hand for her to continue.

Jamie rapped hard. 'Kurek,' she called through the wood. 'Detective Inspector Jamie Johansson, Stockholm Polis. We need to talk to you.'

There was no response.

Jamie glanced at Wiik, and he nodded for her to try again.

She banged with the heel of her hand now. 'Police,' she called. 'Open the door.'

But again, there was nothing.

The door on her left opened instead, and Orn Møller stuck his head out – the big Danish engineer that supposedly had a thing for Noemi Heikkinen. 'He's gone, I think,' he said in thickly accented English. The large man looked tired.

'Gone where?' Jamie asked, reaching for the handle.

Møller shrugged, standing half in the doorway, and then folded his arms. 'I don't know. I just heard his door close and then footsteps.'

Jamie looked at Møller, pushing down on the handle to Kurek's room and letting the door swing open. 'You don't seem very broken up about your friend just getting stabbed to death.' She glanced inside. It was far more spartan than her own. A single bunk was placed against the left-hand wall, a writing desk bolted against the back. A small shelf with some books on it sat above, and on the right, a narrow door led into a tiny shower room.

'Who said he was my friend?' Møller answered.

Jamie stepped back from Kurek's door, confident he

hadn't been murdered in there. 'You sure that's the stance you want to take on the guy who just got murdered?'

Wiik was standing next to her now, but Møller didn't seem phased by their presence or their question.

'I didn't kill him, but that doesn't mean I had to like him.'

'So who might have wanted to?'

Møller shrugged again. 'Don't know. Boykov wasn't exactly the most popular guy. Bit of a know-it-all. Thought he was smarter than everyone else.'

'Was he?' Jamie asked, trying to size up the big man in front of her.

Møller smiled then. 'Doesn't really matter now, does it?'

'So, you didn't do it?'

'No,' Møller said flatly. 'I didn't.' He held his hands up. 'No blood, see.'

'Could have washed them.'

Møller sighed, as though bored of the conversation.

'And you were in your room the whole time?' Jamie asked.

Møller nodded.

'See anything? Hear anyone?'

He shook his head. 'Nope. Not until Boykov screamed.'

'And you didn't come running?' Jamie studied his face.

He looked at her as though it were a stupid question. 'After one of the crew got stabbed fifty times and strung up from a crane by the neck? I didn't really want to risk being number three on that list. I got up, ran to the door, and held firm on the handle until I heard the commotion you two were making.' He nodded at Wiik now.

'You must have heard *something* then?' Jamie asked, trying to keep the desperation from her voice.

'Boykov's door being thrown open. Someone running away. Then, nothing.'

Jamie gritted her teeth, tried to keep her reserve as steely as she could. They were supposed to be the ones in control here.

Wiik spoke now, seemingly sensing Jamie was running out of steam. 'So you weren't aware that anyone had any specific reason to go after Boykov?'

Møller shook his head.

Wiik pressed on. 'Boykov had a grudge with Reyes, we heard – didn't like the way he was using the drill.'

'You think Boykov killed Reyes?'

'We're just trying to get our facts straight,' Wiik said, playing the diplomat.

Møller took his time answering. 'I don't know anything about a grudge. I just do my job, that's it. I try not to get mixed up in petty squabbles.'

'Sounds like the smart choice,' Jamie said.

'It is,' Møller replied. 'I've been doing this long enough to know that tempers run high at sea. And that making enemies out here means the months pass a lot more slowly.'

Jamie nodded. 'So why did you make a point of crossing Reyes then?'

Møller looked from Jamie to Wiik and back. 'Who said I crossed Reyes?'

'We were told that you took issue with his relationship with Noemi Heikkinen. Threatened him,' Jamie said, pressing.

'I never threatened him,' Møller said, standing a little straighter and tempering his voice. 'But Reyes was a piece of shit. I'm not saying he deserved to die, but what he was doing with Heikkinen … She deserved a better man.' His voice quavered on the last part, and Jamie watched as he swallowed.

Noemi's fate was still unknown – at least to Jamie and

Wiik – and though Møller was hiding it well, he seemed to be taking that hard. Jamie didn't know if that was because he knew something more about it or not.

'A man like you?' Jamie took a step closer.

Møller narrowed his eyes. 'You going to accuse me of something, or just stand there talking about it?'

'Do we have any reason to?'

Møller grunted and went back into his room, moving to close the door.

'Hey,' Jamie said, walking up and putting her hand against it. 'We're not done talking.'

Møller stared down at her for a moment. 'So arrest me.'

And then he shoved it closed in her face.

'Don't mind him,' came a softer voice from over Jamie's shoulder.

She and Wiik both turned to face a man standing in a doorway opposite. Two rooms down from Boykov's.

'Sven Rosenberg,' Jamie said, matching his face to the one she'd seen in the files. 'Head engineer.' Sven Rosenburg was one of two Swedes on board – along with Ehrling. Sven had been with the company for years, and was pretty much the only person on board that didn't seem to have an axe to grind with Reyes. Though Quinn did say that Rosenburg had argued with Heikkinen … threatened to kill her … Though Boykov was an integral part of his engineering team – or at least used to be. And a threat against someone who was missing didn't necessarily mean he had anything to do with the two murders that had occurred. Still, no one was being ruled out at this point.

Rosenburg smiled broadly, with wide, off-white teeth. 'I hope that's not what they'll put on my gravestone, but yes.'

He was in his late fifties, and had a thick head of white hair, a kind, lined face. He stepped out of his room and offered Jamie his hand. He had a thick, Northern Swedish lilt that made his English sound like a song.

She took it and shook, and then Wiik did the same.

'Sorry about Møller,' Rosenberg said. 'He's been upset since Noemi Heikkinen disappeared.'

'You knew that he liked her?' Jamie asked.

'Everyone did. He wasn't shy about voicing his opinions about Reyes.'

'Did you know Reyes?'

Rosenberg nodded. 'Yes. I make a point of knowing everyone on the drill team. I'm tasked with making sure that everything runs smoothly when it comes to the selection of the sites and the excavation. So, I don't let just anyone onboard.'

'So, you chose Reyes? Quinn, Kravets ... Lebedenkov?'

'Chose? No. But I'm given some files, and if I have a problem with any of them, I say, and we look for alternatives,' Rosenberg said. 'It's not exactly a job people are lining up for, though. It attracts a certain type of person.'

'And what kind of person is that?'

'The kind of person who thinks being stuck three hundred miles out to sea on a floating bomb is better than what's on shore. Usually, they don't have the same view on the world as everyone else, or there's something they want to be very far away from.'

'And which was Reyes?'

Rosenberg thought for a moment. 'He was an odd one. A nice enough boy, by all accounts. Quinn, Kravets, Lebedenkov – they've worked together for years now. A strong team. They had a fourth – but he got out of the drilling game. Everyone tires of it sooner or later. This was Reyes' first posting. Naturally, he fell in with Quinn. Didn't have much choice, there.'

'We've had the pleasure of meeting Colm Quinn and his merry band of men,' Jamie said. 'They're definitely of a sort. But Reyes wasn't like them?'

'Who can say?' Rosenberg offered them an apologetic shrug. 'We don't tend to mix. They see the engineers – myself, Møller, Kurek, Boykov – as the stuck-up sort. Overly educated. Afraid to get their hands dirty. You know?'

Get their hands dirty. Interesting choice of words, Jamie thought. 'And they see themselves as …'

Rosenberg smiled warmly. 'When you were in school, were there those kids who used to hang around by the bus stop, or behind the bicycle shed, smoking cigarettes? Rebels without a cause?'

Jamie and Wiik both nodded in unison.

'I have a feeling some of them grew up to be Colm Quinn and his crew.'

Jamie was surprised by the aptness of the metaphor. But appreciated Rosenberg's candour. He was the most helpful person they'd met so far.

'But they keep themselves down,' Rosenberg went on. 'Bolstad offer training, schooling if they want. They could have trained up to become engineers if they wanted to. I thought Reyes might have gone that way – he asked me about it the first week he was here.'

'He wanted to move up?' Jamie said. 'Get an education?'

'I think so. It's a natural progression. Better pay. Better opportunities. And a damn sight safer than being a driller all his life.'

Wiik decided to do what he did best then, and sour a friendly conversation. 'I suppose they're only one blown seal away from death, right?'

Rosenberg's expression changed.

Jamie could have kicked Wiik. But she'd already thrown an elbow into his gut that day, as well as told him he was about as enticing to women as a porcupine. So she didn't want to try her luck.

'Yes,' Rosenberg said. 'They are. But not on my rig. My seals are well maintained, checked regularly.'

'That's not what we were told. Supposedly Noemi Heikkinen found evidence that a seal on the drill was due to burst any second.'

'And went behind my back to report that nonsense to Ehrling, too.'

'Behind your back, or over your head?' Wiik was staring Rosenberg dead in the eye now.

'It doesn't matter, because it was a set-up from the start.'

'So tell us your version of events.'

Rosenberg's nostrils flared. He didn't look happy to be telling the story. 'There's nothing much to say. I checked that seal and signed off on it not forty-eight hours before. And then, for seemingly no reason, she decides to inspect it as well. It had no bearing on their research from what those girls had told me about their project, and to my knowledge, the Heikkinen girl wouldn't have even known what she was looking at. So, *how* exactly she came to the conclusion that it was worn out is beyond me.'

'Was it?' Jamie asked, feeling like no one had actually addressed that point yet. Strangely.

Rosenberg swallowed. 'Yes,' he said curtly.

'But you checked it.'

'Yes.' His nostrils flared again.

Wiik's eyes bored into him.

'So how does that happen?' Jamie asked. 'A seal wearing so quickly?'

Rosenberg drew a slow breath. 'There are two options. Either the seal is damaged – which it wasn't. Or someone sabotaged it. But, of course, talk of sabotage was quashed the moment it came out of my mouth. Much simpler to believe I'm simply inept at my job. Not like I've been doing it for more than two decades.'

'Sabotage?' Jamie let the word hang in the air. 'And how would someone do that?'

Rosenberg thought for a second, looking like he was trying to work out whether anything he said could be self-incriminating. 'You could intentionally damage the seal,' he said then. 'That would be the fastest way.'

'But the seal was *worn,* not damaged?' Jamie confirmed. She felt like there was a distinction there.

'That's correct.'

'So why would that be?'

'I suspect because they knew what they were doing. At least enough not to get caught. A damaged seal can't lie. Evidence would be clear. But a worn seal could give out at any moment. Naturally. So, it's likely if someone sabotaged it, they would have got away with it, the responsibility for the ensuing damage, spill, casualties landing squarely at my feet.' Rosenberg's throat tightened, words squeezing. He cleared it and then swallowed. He was clearly angry about the whole situation.

'What do you do with the worn seals that are replaced?'

'They're stored in the lower decks, and then disposed of when a resupply ship picks up the waste.'

'And who has access to that storeroom?'

'Everyone, I should think. There's nothing in there worth stealing.'

'Unless you're trying to sabotage an oil drill.'

They were silent for a few seconds, everyone thinking on it.

Rosenberg spoke again then. 'I checked that seal. I've got no reason not to do my job. If I didn't, and it blew, I'd never work again.'

'I believe you,' Jamie said. 'Which is why you need to be careful.'

'Careful?' His eyes widened a little then. 'What do you mean "careful"?'

'If someone *was* trying to sabotage the drill, and you were the person to take the blame, then it could mean—'

It clicked for Rosenberg then. 'They might have been doing it to frame me.'

'Anyone on board that might want to ruin your career?'

Rosenberg bit his lip but didn't answer.

'Look, we don't know what's going on here yet, but it's clear that there's someone on board with an axe to grind. Whether what happened with Reyes and Boykov were grudges coming to bear, or something else …' Jamie looked at the man, trying her best to show concern. 'Just … just be careful. Try not to go anywhere alone. Stick to well-trafficked areas. Stay in your room when you can.' She nodded her reassurance.

Rosenberg shook his head and huffed at having just been told he could be the next target of a murderer and that his best bet was to stay in his room. 'Fat lot of good that did Boykov. Goodbye.' Then he stepped back across the threshold, and he too closed the door in Jamie's face.

She sighed and turned to Wiik. 'I'm getting really sick of that.'

Wiik smirked, seemingly amused by it. 'Weird,' he said, heading for the door. 'I'm not.'

18

JAMIE AND WIIK were sitting in the cafeteria.

Or at least Jamie was. Staring at the screen of the laptop that Vogel had just loaned her. Vogel had come down the stairs just after their interview with Rosenberg, beaten-up old laptop in her arms, power cable trailing, and handed it to Jamie, along with a flash drive containing the footage she wanted.

Jamie squinted down at it now, watching the feed from the cafeteria on the night that Reyes was killed.

Wiik came over and put a cup of coffee down in front of her.

It was lunchtime now, but the place was empty. Jamie suspected that no one really wanted to risk going anywhere just then.

She glanced up at him. 'Thanks,' she said, taking a long, hot draught.

'Anything?' Wiik asked, slotting one leg over the bench and sitting next to her.

'No,' Jamie said tiredly. 'Nothing conclusive. We know that Reyes was killed between six and nine – but that's a pretty big window. Rosenberg and Boykov come in around ten past six and start making a batch of ... something. It's not exactly in frame.' Jamie pointed to the screen and then nodded towards the corner of the room. A single camera sat there, facing into it from the ceiling. But the door to the kitchen was at the very top right of the feed, and was almost completely out of view. 'They don't leave the kitchen until after seven. At which point, Boykov eats a quick bowl of food, and then leaves. Around seven fifteen.'

'So he could have killed Reyes?'

'And then stabbed himself to cover his tracks, sure.' She sighed. 'Sorry.'

Wiik waved her off. 'Just because he's dead now, doesn't mean he didn't kill Reyes.'

'No, it doesn't,' Jamie said. 'But that would mean there are two separate killers, both wielding knives, both cornering their victims in a place they believe is safe, both stabbing their victims multiple times. It's a pretty specific MO.'

Wiik conceded. 'Okay, so we discount Boykov. For now, at least.'

Jamie nodded in agreement.

'Rosenberg?'

Jamie drew a breath and scrubbed through the footage until she found what she was looking for. 'Møller comes in around six forty, and then Rosenberg joins him around seven. They eat together, talk for a little bit, then they play some cards. Uno, I think, judging by this. But I can't be sure.'

'Uno?' Wiik looked at her.

'Yeah, you ever play?'

He shook his head. 'No, never. Any good?'

'I don't know,' Jamie said. 'Never played either.' She thought it was easier to leave it there than to explain that a group of students in her uni halls played it continually, but that she never got invited to join in. 'They, uh, play that until about quarter past nine, and then leave, too.'

'So Møller and Rosenberg are out. They didn't kill Reyes. Unless Møller ran downstairs, murdered Reyes just after six, then ran back up here to play Uno with his friend.'

Jamie wasn't sure if he was serious or joking. 'Timing would be tight, and he's not exactly built for speed.'

'Plus, murdering Heikkinen's boyfriend in front of her probably wouldn't improve his odds much. So let's assume he's clean. For now, at least.'

'Well, that's three people down.' Boykov, Rosenburg, and Møller.

Wiik cracked a smile. 'Got to start somewhere. Who else is on here?'

'Uh,' Jamie said, scanning through the footage at speed. She had the files of the crew laid out in front of her. 'Around eight fifteen, Ashleigh Hooper and Paméla Sevier come in. They eat, and then about half an hour later, leave. That chimes with their story about reporting Noemi Heikkinen missing. They go down to dinner, come back. She's not there, they call on Vogel.'

'What about Vogel? Ehrling?'

'Not on here at all. They say they were in their rooms all evening. But that's going to be impossible to verify, and if they wanted to avoid the cameras, they'd know how to. But I don't know if Ehrling has the stomach for murder, or the physicality to overpower both Reyes and Boykov.'

'Vogel either, I wouldn't think,' Wiik added.

'We can probably count them out too, then.' That didn't leave many suspects.

Wiik nodded, doing the maths in his head too. 'What about Quinn? Kravets, Lebedenkov?'

Jamie exhaled. Three names that kept coming up. 'They

come in around nine, eat their fill, hang out for an hour or so, then leave.'

'But we can't confirm their alibi before that?'

'Only if you believe that they were together in Quinn's room until then.'

'Which I don't,' Wiik said flatly.

'You think they had something to do with Reyes' death?' Jamie watched him closely.

Wiik narrowed his eyes at her. 'I know you were somehow *charmed* by Quinn, but—'

'I wasn't charmed by anyone,' Jamie interjected.

'—the guy is a piece of shit. Trust me. I've known enough of them.'

'And I haven't?' Jamie's jaw flexed. 'I was a detective before I met you, Wiik. You know that, right?'

His shoulders stiffened a little. 'I'm not questioning your professional capabilities, Johansson.'

'So what are you questioning?'

Wiik seemed to detect the coldness in Jamie's voice, and didn't respond right away.

Their two coffee cups steamed between them, but they were both statues.

'All I'm saying,' Wiik said, 'is that Quinn knows his way around police questioning.' He lifted his chin at Quinn's folder. 'What's his file say?'

She had Ehrling's open in front of her – which didn't contain anything untoward or out of place. He was about as mundane as people came, with seemingly nothing to hide, or even worth hiding. She hadn't got into Quinn or the others' yet.

Jamie broke eye contact and pulled it towards her, flipping it open.

Wiik grabbed Kravets' and Lebedenkov's.

She looked past Quinn's photograph – that looked suspiciously like a mugshot – and ran her finger down his work history. There was a four-year gap in it, and on the next page, a copy of an official transcript from Cork Prison, stating that Colm Quinn served four years of an eight-year sentence for aggravated assault. The notes section outlined how the charge was pleaded down from assault with intent to kill and possession of a deadly weapon. Jamie let out a long breath and closed the file, wondering if it was a knife.

Wiik closed Kravets' file then, too. 'Quinn a convict?' he asked, barely phrasing it as a question.

Jamie gave a slight nod.

'Kravets, too. Seven years for assault, resisting arrest, attempted arson.'

'A real charmer then.'

'Lebedenkov was remanded to custody pending a charge for attempted manslaughter, but was let out, the charges eventually dropped. It doesn't say why.'

'A real nice bunch then.'

Wiik stayed quiet, but kept watching Jamie, waiting for her to come around.

'Okay,' she said, leaning forwards, holding her hands out. 'So, if it was Quinn – Kravets' and Lebedenkov, too – Sevier calls for Reyes at their door, and he goes down to meet Noemi. Quinn and the others slip out after him, follow him down there. Then they confront him, beat him, stab him, string him up. Noemi, terrified for her life—'

'And worse.'

'—leaps to her death,' Jamie said, carrying on. 'We show up, they try and lock us out, too. When I climb around, one of them chases me through maintenance, tries to finish the job. That about the sum of it?'

Wiik nodded. 'Sounds plausible to me. They've got the

nerve for it. The credentials, too. And you said the guy who chased you was big. Quinn is small, but Kravets and Lebedenkov both fit that bill.'

'But to what end?' Jamie asked, as much to herself as to Wiik. 'I see means and opportunity, the credentials to match – but no motive. And like Quinn said, Reyes was one of them. There was no benefit to killing Reyes for them. And all the fingers immediately started pointing at them. And with their history, they'd know that. Know that getting away with it would basically be impossible. And while they don't strike me as university graduates, Quinn's not stupid. Not stupid enough to kill someone on an oil rig and think they could get away scot-free.'

'Sevier said that Noemi was afraid of them. It can get lonely at sea, I bet. And maybe it wasn't Quinn – he could just be covering for his friends. Maybe Kravets or Lebedenkov finally gave in. Maybe both. The jealousy just finally overcame them.'

'I don't buy sexual motivation. What the killer did to Reyes – that was brutal. It was a message.'

'To Heikkinen – this is what we'll do to you if you try and run.' Wiik was insistent.

Jamie shook her head. 'No, it would have taken *time* to do that to Reyes. But I don't think it was to show Heikkinen. Not when she was cornered. They could have just run her down right there. No one would have been able to do anything, hear anything. They could have done whatever they liked to her, and then tossed her over the rail afterwards. But the crime was focused on Reyes. If they wanted him out of the way, why go through all the pageantry?'

'Maybe Noemi didn't get away in time. We don't know what happened down there.' Wiik met Jamie's eye then.

'So they tossed Noemi over the rail, and did that to Reyes after the fact to, what, cover it all up?'

Wiik raised an eyebrow, stuck out his bottom lip.

'Why not just throw Reyes over the rail, too? Would have taken far less time. Less effort. Less chance of getting caught.'

Wiik didn't have an answer for her. 'So you think they're being framed?'

'No. I don't know. Maybe. What I do know is that we can't make any assumptions about either Reyes *or* Heikkinen right now. But whatever did or didn't happen to Noemi, our priority is Reyes. We just need to ignore Heikkinen for the time being' — it pained Jamie to say that. But it was the truth — 'and go by the evidence we have in front of us. Someone murdered Reyes, and they strung him up for the world to see. Why? Why do that? I don't think this is personal. Reyes was a message to someone else. But to who, and *from* who ...' She shook her head. 'I don't know. And then there's Boykov. Killed in the middle of the day. In a hallway that wasn't exactly deserted. In his room, of all places.' Jamie leaned over, rested her elbows on the table, resting her chin in her hands, staring at the grainy feed in front of her.

'If his door was locked,' Wiik mused, 'it's likely that the killer knocked and Boykov opened it. That Boykov knew the killer.'

'There's ten people on this crew,' Jamie said through her fingers, 'everyone knows everyone.'

'Just trying to make some observations.'

'I know,' Jamie said, closing her eyes, 'I'm sorry.'

'It's fine,' Wiik replied, 'let's just work this together,

okay? I know you're used to doing things on your own, but I'm good at what I do as well.'

Jamie swallowed. He was right. He was Falk's best detective before she arrived. And he still was. It was easy to forget that, though she didn't know why.

'We can surmise,' Wiik went on, 'that whatever the killer's reason for going after Reyes, that it was connected to Boykov, too. That he was involved in whatever Reyes was. Or that the killer was afraid that Boykov could name him. Or that Boykov had some information that the killer didn't want getting out. But whatever it was, Boykov was a loose end that needed tying up. And the killer, once more, wanted to make a statement with it.'

Jamie processed that. She didn't disagree with any of it. 'And the other thing,' she said, 'is Kurek.'

'Kurek?' Wiik perked up a little now. 'The safety engineer that Reyes owed money to?'

Jamie nodded. 'His room was closest to Boykov. He ran before we could question him. And he's not on this tape. So as far as we know, he doesn't have an alibi for Reyes' death. We have the supposed whereabouts of everyone except Kurek. And he had a motive to kill Reyes.'

'You can't get money from a dead man,' Wiik said.

'So, he tries to rough him up a little. It goes too far, he accidentally kills him,' Jamie said, 'panics, stabs and strings him up to make it look like someone else did it.'

'Maybe.'

'Or he corners the two of them – Reyes and Heikkinen – goes after Heikkinen to make Reyes pay up. Maybe he wants his *payment* in another way. Things get heated. Reyes steps in. They fight. He kills Reyes by mistake. Then stabs him and strings him up to cover his tracks.'

Wiik didn't even offer her a maybe this time.

The theories were getting messier by the minute. Jamie couldn't disagree with that.

They just sat in silence, both ruminating on what they had so far. Which was a wide pool of suspects, all with viable motives, a loose set of 'facts' and alibis, two dead bodies, a conspiracy to sabotage the drill, and no clear reason for any of it.

It was times like this you needed to step away. Needed to clear your head. Jamie wanted to run. So badly. She wanted to lace up her trainers, and hit the road, put twenty kilometres between her and the case. And then come back to it with perspective.

But she couldn't.

They were trapped here.

And there was nothing either of them could do about it.

19

JAMIE AND WIIK sat in silence for a few minutes before the air around them crackled. They both picked their heads up and looked at the door, at the tannoy speaker there.

Vogel's voice echoed in the room. '*Johansson, Wiik – you're needed on the command deck.*'

The line cut off, and Jamie and Wiik looked at each other before stepping out of the bench and heading for the door. Jamie stopped, doubled back, scooping the files into a pile and shoving them into the satchel. She threw it over her shoulder and dashed through the door Wiik was holding open for her.

They wound up towards the command deck, both breathing hard by the time they got there, and Wiik made to hammer on the door.

'Wait,' Jamie said, grabbing his arm.

Wiik looked at her quizzically, then saw her reaching for the call button. She pressed it, and he lowered his hand. Almost instantly, the door opened.

Vogel stood there. 'Good, you're here.'

'What's wrong?' Wiik asked, his voice that cool-yet-apprehensive tone that said, *Please tell me there's not another body.*

'Your boss is on the line,' she said. 'And the weather is closing in. Connection is shaky – come on.' She motioned them in, and they followed her up to the screen where the pulsing phone icon was displayed once more.

Wiik and Jamie pulled out the two empty chairs at the desk.

Vogel hovered in the background with her arms folded, but Ehrling was nowhere to be seen.

'Falk,' Wiik said.

'Wiik,' came the reply, even shakier than when Jamie had spoken to her. Every second or two, the connection seemed to drop for a moment. But even through the interference, Jamie could hear the relief in Falk's voice to hear that they were safe. 'Johansson with you?'

'I'm here,' Jamie said, her eyes fixed on the glass in front of her. What had once been distant storm clouds had now erupted into a column of charcoal. It rose up in front of the rig, blotting out the pale sky behind, a curtain of wind and rain and darkness that was about to swallow the platform whole.

The sea had reduced itself to an eerie calm, but the small waves that rippled the surface were rolled into a white layer of froth by the wind. It rattled the windows in the frames as the storm drew the ocean into its grasp.

'Johansson?'

Jamie snapped to attention. 'Yeah, sorry – what was that?'

Falk had been talking all the while.

'I asked if you got the email from Claesson?'

'Uh,' Jamie said, looking around as if it was going to materialise in front of her.

Vogel appeared at her shoulder, reached over and

grabbed the mouse, and opened a browser window. Jamie nodded a thanks as she retreated, and then navigated to her email account. It took a few seconds to load and then she was already reading it, scanning through Claesson's thoughts.

'Yeah,' Jamie called. 'I got it. Tell him thanks, will you?'

There was static on the line, and then a grinding noise. 'Johansson?' Falk asked. 'Are you there?'

'Yeah,' Jamie said, speaking a little louder. 'I'm here – can you hear me? I said I have the email.'

'That's … good … I … Hallberg is here … dug up some … on Hooper, Sevier, and … —kkinen.'

Jamie strained her ears to catch the words between the dips.

Vogel had come forwards a little now, piqued by the mention of the girls. She didn't really want any of the crew knowing what routes they were taking into the investigation, but perhaps having Vogel onside and in the loop, could give them an edge here. Unless she was the one who killed Reyes, of course.

Though Jamie didn't think she'd have the strength to string him up like that.

Still, she'd been wrong before.

'Hallberg,' Wiik said now. 'What do you have for us?'

'Hey … it's … —llberg.'

'Yes,' Wiik repeated. 'What have you found?'

'It looks like … Hooper, Sevier, and Heikkinen … all studying in Helsinki University … marine biology, ecology, oceanography … but they … activism group … arrested last year for … demonstration turned violent … released without charge.'

Wiik glanced at Jamie.

She was doing her best to read between the lines. 'They

were part of an activist group and were arrested last year at a demonstration?'

'Yes ... refusing to disperse, resisting arrest ... no charges brought. Apparently, the law firm that dealt with their release was ... big company ... handles corporate law ... on retainer for ... called Heikkinen Investments.'

'Heikkinen?' Jamie asked, wishing the signal would clear. The first flashes of lightning had begun showing through the gathering storm now. So she didn't think it was about to. 'As in Noemi Heikkinen?'

'Her father, Simon Heikkinen ... stakes in ... automotive, manufacturing ... oil. Including Bolstad.'

'Noemi Heikkinen's father has a stake in Bolstad?' Jamie asked, as surprised as anyone else in the room. She looked over at Vogel who shook her head, signifying she didn't know.

'Yes,' Hallberg replied. 'Heikkinen Investments ... funding the trip'

So, Heikkinen Investments was paying for the research trip. And Noemi's father had stakes in the company. It explained how he managed to get Bolstad to go along with it, despite it not exactly being in the company's best interest.

And by the sounds of it, Hooper, Sevier, and Heikkinen were hell-raisers. Or at least politically active. To the point of being arrested.

Jamie exhaled hard. 'This is great work, Hallberg, thanks.' A picture began to form in her mind. Hooper, Sevier, and Heikkinen hatched a plan to take the fight right to the oil industry. Sabotage the drill, take Bolstad out of the game entirely. Sink them once and for all. Heikkinen uses her father's connections with Bolstad to get them out here under the guise of a research expedition.

Except they don't know shit about drills. But Reyes does.

Jamie set her teeth, her mind working furiously.

So, Heikkinen seduces him, gets him to go along with their plan. He changes out the seal on the drill after it was inspected – swaps new for old – but then ... Heikkinen changes her mind? She reports the seal to Ehrling, cuts the legs out from her own plan ...

For what? Fear? No ... love. Jamie swallowed. Heikkinen is young. Reyes is a charmer.

The girls find out that Heikkinen has crossed them, and they follow her and Reyes down to the submersible platform. They go after Heikkinen, Reyes gets in the way. Hooper is fast, she's strong. She's as big as Reyes is. Sevier goes after Heikkinen. Maybe they fight. She throws Heikkinen over? Jamie swallowed. And then, their plan gone to shit, they need to think of another way to get Bolstad shut down. An international scandal? They string Reyes up between them, cause a stir, hope that it'll get out. Bolstad keep it quiet, bring Jamie and Wiik in. They try to lock them outside, kill the two of them, knowing Bolstad won't be able to keep that quiet.

It was a lot of extrapolation, but it fitted. It was possible – and with this new information ...

'What was the demonstration in protest of?' Jamie asked, picking her head up.

'The importation ... oil products ... Norway ... Norwegian Sea drilling ...' The line crackled horribly, and Jamie and Wiik both winced. Lightning flashed in the distance. The clouds roiled. ' ...The Finnish government ... signed new ... import deal ... Norway.'

All the pieces seemed to fall into place. They were protesting exactly what Bolstad was doing. Right under Jamie's feet. They go to the rally, get all riled up. Get arrested. They get bailed out by Noemi's father – whose very livelihood is made from the thing they were protesting. It leaves a sour taste in their mouths. They start hatching a plan to create change. Real change. Have a real impact.

Jamie had already seen Hooper's temper. How quickly she'd go to physicality. And Sevier was calm. The level-headed one. The brains. And Noemi … Noemi had the connections. And she had the looks. She could get the right person to fall for her. The one that could make their plan real …

'Wiik, Johansson?' It was Falk again now. 'Vogel says … about to … lose signal … the storm.' The line crackled again. 'Is there … anything … we can do?'

Jamie and Wiik stared at each other for a few seconds.

'No,' Jamie said. 'We can handle this.' She nodded at Wiik, and he looked back at her and then returned it.

'Okay,' Falk said. 'Just look after—'

Another flash streaked through the cloud bank, suddenly much closer than before.

A roll of thunder came after it, making the whole platform shake.

And the speakers dropped to a quiet drone of static.

A message popped up on screen, displaying the words *Connection Lost.*

Vogel came forwards, leaned over, and closed the window, sighing. 'That's it then,' she said, her voice quiet. 'We're on our own.'

The words send a shiver down Jamie's spine. Wiik had become stone next to her.

Jamie, Wiik, and Vogel all jumped a little when the door buzzed at the bottom of the stairwell and opened.

Wallace appeared on the steps, followed by his two guards, and then Ehrling brought up the rear.

Vogel snapped out of her trance first. 'Where the hell have you been?' she barked at Ehrling.

He shrank a little. Then looked at Wallace, who answered for him.

'He's been with me,' Wallace said.

'Doing what?' Vogel pressed. 'I've been up here on my own for hours. The storm is playing havoc with our instruments and readings and the surface currents are causing the drill to—'

Wallace held up his hand to silence her. 'Nothing you can't handle, I'm sure. Ehrling says you're very capable.'

Vogel's mouth hung open, but she didn't say anything else. She was caught off guard by something she wasn't sure was a compliment or an insult of some kind.

'He's back now,' Wallace said, lifting his eyebrows and smiling. 'So crisis averted.' His eyes drifted to Jamie and Wiik then. 'Ah, Detectives,' he said, using emphasis that seemed to come in lieu of air quotes. 'How goes the investigation? Any *solid leads* yet?'

Jamie could see the tension in Wiik.

She put on her best for-the-public smile. 'Just checking all the facts, gathering evidence.'

'Wasn't that what you were doing yesterday?' Wallace asked lightly.

'Unfortunately, it's about ninety per cent of our job,' Jamie said with a sigh, feigning boredom. 'We speak to people, we watch CCTV, we check alibis. And most of the time, the culprit just sort of ...'

'Falls into your lap,' Wallace said, amused. 'Well, I hope this case proves just as trivial for you. Now, if you don't mind.' He nodded to them all and headed for his stateroom-cum-bunker at the back of the command deck.

Jamie watched him go, but Wiik seemed more interested in one of his bodyguards.

'That's a nice bruise,' he said loudly. Directly. To the guy in the suit at Wallace's left shoulder.

He kept walking.

'Hey, blockhead,' Wiik called. 'I'm talking to you.'

The guy slowed a little, but refused to look over.

Wiik rose from his chair then and moved to intercept. 'I only ask,' he said, 'because the guy we just found dead downstairs had bruised knuckles.' Wiik was within arm's reach of him now. 'Wouldn't know anything about that, would you?'

Wiik was bluffing – hard. Jamie had seen Boykov's hands. They were clean of any defensive marks. She figured that Wiik just had a chip on his shoulder, but what targeting Wallace was going to get him, she didn't know.

The ex-military contractor, who had a few inches on Wiik, as well as a few jacket sizes, turned to look at him now.

Wallace seemed bored with the conversation already and motioned the other guard to follow him into his quarters. He seemed to have no doubt that the remaining bodyguard could manage Wiik without issue. Jamie felt inclined to agree.

Blockhead turned to face Wiik, lifting his chin so that his bruised cheek caught the light. 'This?' he asked, his voice throaty and gruff. Jamie thought Scottish, but she wasn't sure what part. 'Walked into a door.'

'I'm tempted to believe you're that stupid,' Wiik replied. 'But when bodies are piling up left and right, I'm inclined to question that.'

The guard shrugged slowly, looking about as disinterested as anyone ever had.

'Why don't you tell me what really happened?'

'Like I said, walked into a door.'

'You stab it afterwards?'

The guy huffed, curling a wry smirk, and then opened the hem of his blazer, showing off the butt of the pistol tucked against his ribs. 'Wouldn't need to.'

Wiik stuck out his bottom lip. 'Guns are loud.'

'So's your wife.'

Jamie watched as Wiik's hands curled at his sides. 'Watch your mouth. I'm a kriminalinspektör with the Stockholm Polis.'

'Are you?' he asked. 'I don't see a badge.'

Wiik, dumbly, took the bait. 'No? Then what the fuck do you call this?' He pulled it from his jacket pocket and shoved it in the guy's face.

Before he could even get his arm out straight, the goon in the suit snatched it out of the air and pocketed it.

There was a moment of stillness – of shock. Wiik didn't know what to do.

Neither did Jamie.

They were all catapulted back to the playground without warning. And the biggest, meanest bully had just taken Wiik's toy, and there were no teachers in sight.

All Wiik had now were his fists. But judging by the way that he'd just relieved Wiik of his badge, he wasn't going to let Wiik punch him. Not even close.

And a big part of Wiik knew that.

Enough not to take a swing for him then and there.

After a few seconds, Blockhead pulled the badge back out – causing Wiik to flinch – and slapped it against his chest, pinning it there with his fingers. 'Take it,' he whispered. 'Go on.'

The way the muscles in Wiik's jaw were flexing and the way his temple vein was bulging, he was either going to do it, or explode.

Slowly, he raised his hand.

Blockhead seemed utterly unphased. Loose. Relaxed.

Wiik's fingers touched the badge and Blockhead took his off Wiik's chest.

Wiik clutched the leather billfold against his breast, and the goon shouldered past him, making a point of barging him out of the way.

Wiik stumbled, regained himself, and then lifted his chin. 'What's your name?' he asked, not turning to watch him go.

But he didn't answer.

'Hey,' Wiik said now, turning to speak to Blockhead's back. 'I asked for your name.'

The guy paused at the threshold to the door and looked back. 'See you soon,' he said, and then puckered his lips and blew him a kiss.

Then the door closed, and it was just Jamie, Wiik, Ehrling, and Vogel standing there.

Jamie took a step forwards, still reeling from what had just happened. 'Wiik ...' she said, reaching out for his shoulder.

He threw his arm up, batting it away, and then stormed down the stairs and out through the door.

Jamie stared at the steps, wondering if she should go after him, or just leave him be.

Vogel was standing next to her then, and laid a hand on her shoulder, squeezing gently. Just a small human gesture to show Jamie that she'd witnessed what had just happened, too. The pure brutality of it.

Jamie caught something out of the corner of her eye then and turned her head, seeing Ehrling grinning to himself.

She couldn't help herself and was in his face a second later. 'Reyes. Boykov. You know what they were?' she hissed.

He leaned backwards, trying to get out of her orbit, smile fading by the second.

Her eyes searched his face for every tell. 'Loose ends,' she said, making sure to keep her voice barely audible. Quiet enough to not be overheard by the camera she knew to be covering the command deck.

Ehrling's brow crumpled as his brain tried to compute it.

'They're being tied off,' Jamie said. 'I don't know why, and I don't know who's doing it. But whatever the *fuck* is going on here, the only person walking out of it alive is the one pulling the strings.'

Ehrling swallowed, tried to break eye contact. But Jamie kept moving forwards, eating the space between them.

'If you know something, you should pick a side, and fast. Because I can tell, just by the smell of you, that two minutes in an interrogation room with a conspiracy charge hanging over your head will have you singing.' Jamie's lip quivered with rage, her fists balled so tightly her nails threatened to draw blood from her palms.

Ehrling's eyes darted around her face. But he found no weakness.

Somewhere behind her, she heard a door open, and Ehrling's gaze moved over her shoulder for a second, and then back to Jamie.

'It's a good thing, then, Inspector,' he said, voice shaking, 'that we're a long way from Stockholm.'

Jamie didn't have to look around to know that Wallace had appeared on the command deck, coming to Ehrling's rescue.

She let out a breath, let her shoulders drop a little, and then she laughed to herself, lowering her eyes and shaking her head. 'We won't be for long, Ehrling.' She looked up now. 'And then we'll see what's what.'

He let his grin return, the sight of his master enough to embolden him. 'Sure … if you last that long.'

20

JAMIE DESCENDED THE STAIRS QUICKLY, seething, and whirled into the upper crew quarters.

She damn near kicked the door open and stepped into her and Wiik's room. He was pacing in circles, and she fell into step behind him. They moved around the room like clock hands.

And then Wiik stopped, stood with his hands against the top bunk of their bed, and lowered his head so that it dipped between his elbows. His back arched out, legs semi-bent, knuckles white around the painted steel frame.

He emptied his lungs of air and then stood up and ran his hand over his head, pressing his hair against his scalp. He looked at Jamie, still scowling. 'What are you so worked up about?' he growled.

'Ehrling,' Jamie said, surprised at how venomous her voice sounded in her ears.

'What did that little worm do?'

'All but threatened me. And you too, I guess.'

'Piece of shit,' Wiik muttered.

'Hey, look,' Jamie started, 'about what happened up there—'

'Forget it,' Wiik said, more as an order than anything else.

Jamie nodded. But she wouldn't.

'So what now?' Wiik said.

Jamie thought on that for a few seconds. 'Now we decide how we want to approach things.'

'Okay.' Wiik folded his arms now.

'I'm pretty fucking sure by now we're just window dressing – as you said. A way for Bolstad to make it *look* like they're doing things by the book.'

Wiik snorted in agreement.

'Whereas Wallace and his two goons are the ones who are actually here to deal with things.' Jamie walked over to the desk in the corner of their room and leaned against it. 'Whoever killed Reyes … we know it wasn't Wallace or his dogs.'

Wiik nodded. 'Right. They arrived with us, so that rules them out.'

'The question we need to answer first, is whether the same person who killed Reyes killed Boykov. Or whether Blockhead cornered Boykov, got him to admit that he killed Reyes, and then killed him for it. Cleaning the whole thing up neatly. If that's how it went down, then as far as Wallace is concerned, this whole thing is mopped up and as soon as the storm clears, they'll be out of here.'

'But why make Boykov's kill look like Reyes'?'

Jamie drew a slow breath. 'To confuse us? To keep us looking for the "real killer" until they can get off this place? I bet they'd be on a chopper right now if they could be.'

'Plausible,' Wiik said, sitting on his bunk. 'So what happens when the changeover happens and the crime isn't "solved"?'

Jamie bit her lip. 'Bolstad put a fat bonus in everyone's

pockets, make them sign an NDA, and then send them on their way, confident in the knowledge that a killer isn't walking off this thing.'

Wiik watched her, nodding slowly. 'You think they'd go for that?'

Jamie shrugged. 'Depends how big the cheque is.'

'What about the girls? Think *they'd* go for that?'

'Probably not – if they're innocent – but then again, life at sea is dangerous. And I'd bet they signed a waiver to say if they got into an accident of some kind there'd be no legal ramifications …'

'You think Wallace would kill them?' Wiik asked, glancing at the wall to Jamie's right. The one they shared with Sevier and Hooper.

'I don't know,' Jamie said honestly. 'But Bolstad is hanging by a thread, and I wouldn't put it past him. I think his title as a risk assessor is nothing more than that. Wallace's a corporate fixer. He's here to make sure that this mess gets cleaned up. And if that means killing everyone who might talk … I'm just not making any firm assumptions.'

'So then, that's it?' Wiik asked. 'It's done. Boykov killed Reyes. Wallace had Boykov killed.' Wiik clapped to illustrate the finiteness of it.

Jamie shook her head, screwing her face up. 'No, it can't be that simple. Because Boykov was on kitchen duty the night Reyes was killed. We saw him.'

'But he left just after seven. Plenty of time to go and kill Reyes.'

'But how would he know where he was if he was on kitchen duty? Conceivably, anyone else might have seen them go down and followed them, but Boykov was in the kitchen. So unless someone told him where they were … which means there's more than one person in on this …' Jamie's head was spinning.

People were being ruled out and then ruled back in by the minute.

Wiik sighed, rubbed his head. 'Right. So who *doesn't* have an alibi?'

'Kurek is the only one not accounted for.'

'What about Quinn?'

'In his room, playing cards. With Kravets and Lebedenkov.'

'If you believe them.'

'We've got no reason not to.'

'Do we know where they were when Boykov was killed?'

'I have two of them on camera on the drill deck at the time. Not sure which two.'

'So one of them *isn't* accounted for?'

'Along with everyone else on the crew who isn't on camera at that exact moment. Not exactly evidence of anything.'

Wiik leaned over and cradled the back of his skull in his hands. 'So where does that leave us?'

Jamie walked in circles. 'What do we know for certain?'

'Nothing.' Wiik laughed sardonically.

'We *know* that someone tried to sabotage the drill. We know that Rosenberg checked the seal and signed off on it, and then a few days later, Noemi Heikkinen reported it to Ehrling as worn out.'

Wiik said nothing now.

'And we know that it's a big coincidence that Heikkinen chose just then to check that seal. And we also know that when it comes to investigations, coincidences rarely happen.'

Wiik offered her a brief nod.

'So Heikkinen was in on the seal being swapped out. Which implicates Reyes being involved in the plot.'

'Which leaves us where?'

'Which leaves us with the relatively solid assumption that Reyes was killed because the *plan* to have that seal blow up went to shit because of Heikkinen. The only people I can think of who would want to sabotage the drill are Sevier and Hooper. Which means they're our likely suspects. They kill Reyes, and Noemi Heikkinen to cover their tracks.'

'So what does Boykov have to do with that?'

Jamie swallowed and folded her arms. For that one, she didn't have an answer. 'Maybe he saw them coming back up after they did it? That's why they killed him before we could speak to him?'

'It's as likely a theory as any,' Wiik said slowly. 'Though I still like Quinn and his cronies for it more. Doing to a person what they did to Reyes? You really think two university students have the stomach for that kind of thing? Kill their friend, stab and hang a man by the neck? One look at Quinn told me he was more than capable.'

'But Quinn doesn't have a motive. The girls do.'

'So we find the motive. Or we just lock the three of them up, and if no one else dies in the meanwhile, we know we got the right people.'

Jamie thought on that. Not what you'd call a foolproof solution. And she doubted Wallace would let them take the platform's only drillers out of commission.

'Before we do anything else,' Jamie said, 'we need to *prove* sabotage. Once we can do that, we corner Sevier and Hooper and we get them to talk. If we can force them to admit they were responsible for it, then we can press them from there, see what they really know about Reyes' death.'

'And how are we supposed to do that?'

'The seal,' Jamie said, standing up. 'We find the missing seal, and we have our proof.'

'And why wouldn't they have just thrown it over the rail?' Wiik asked.

'Rosenberg said the seals were taken away by a waste ship. Maybe they didn't want to risk one being unaccounted for.'

'That's a big maybe. What do you want to do, go down to the storeroom and hunt around for it?' He raised an eyebrow, hoping he wasn't right.

'Yes, Wiik,' she said. 'That's *exactly* what we're going to do.'

Jamie stopped at a door that read *Storage* and pushed it open.

Wiik slumped off the final step and put his hands on his hips. The corridor beyond was pure darkness.

The hull of the platform groaned around them as the wind continued to build.

She stepped forwards and shivered at the sudden temperature drop. The stairwell wasn't warm, but it was obviously heated. The storage deck, however, didn't seem to be.

'Shit,' Jamie said, pulling her jacket a little tighter.

Wiik had been scowling all the way from the top. And now was no different. He stared down the corridor like there was a bad smell under his nose.

Jamie sniffed the air. Actually, there was a bad smell. The place smelt like shit. Old, burnt rubber and damp pipes.

Wiik reached out to the wall and punched a button with a picture of a bulb on it that was dimly illuminated in the light coming out of the stairwell.

Electricity buzzed overhead, and then a long line of strip lights spluttered to life.

Jamie started forwards, sighing, hating this decision more and more with each passing moment. But they had no other option. The only thing they could do that wasn't this was to just hide out in their room and hope they were right about Wallace's clean-up operation. Cross their fingers that no one else got murdered. Wait for the storm to pass. Then they'd take a ride home in a chopper, face to face with the guy who'd just doled out bloody justice to keep an oil company afloat, and pretend like nothing ever happened.

Or, they could do their fucking jobs, find out who killed Reyes, why, and put them in cuffs.

Noemi Heikkinen had reported the seal to Ehrling – no doubt wanting to halt the plan to sabotage the rig. That much they knew. But where things spiralled from there, and who put a knife in Reyes' gut was still up for debate.

'Hey,' Wiik called.

Jamie stopped and looked back at him. He was hanging through a door they'd passed on the right. He beckoned her back towards him, and she approached.

'In here,' he said, stepping in.

She followed him into the darkness.

He kicked something, stumbled, and then swore.

Jamie felt for around on the wall and found a switch.

She flicked it, the sound of electricity buzzing once more around them, but nothing happened. 'Dead,' she said, flicking it a few more times.

'Typical,' Wiik muttered, fishing his phone from his pocket. He put the torch on and flashed it around. 'Jesus,' he said, staring at all the crap strewn around. Boxes and egg cartons and cleaning supplies and waste bins and black bags and all manner of other things had been thrown in there. 'Guess we know what they're doing with their rubbish.'

Jamie swallowed, not seeing anything that looked like a drill seal. Though she wasn't sure she knew what it would look like if she did.

As Wiik moved through the room, turning over bags of who knows what with his fine Italian leather boots, Jamie stepped back into the corridor and looked down its length. There were four doors on either side. And a lot of space behind each one. And she was under no illusions that every one was going to be full of junk. Just like this one.

'You good here?' she asked him, hooking a thumb over her shoulder. 'I'm going to start on the next one.'

Wiik grumbled something under his breath that she didn't catch. So she took it as a yes and stepped back into the light.

She could hear a dripping somewhere in the distance.

Jamie closed her eyes for a second, reminding herself why she was here. It was for her father. Falk had information about her father that she needed. That was why she'd accepted this job.

She opened her eyes then and gritted her teeth. Did Falk know? Did Falk know that Bolstad would try and cover this up themselves by tying up loose ends? Did she expect Jamie to go along with it? Did she expect her to just roll over and accept that that's how it was? Throw the investigation because Falk was giving her something in return?

Was this just a win-win, either way? If Jamie let it go, Bolstad got what they wanted, covered up Reyes' death, and whatever they had on Falk was either handed over, or she just bought a little more favour for them. But if Jamie *didn't* let it go …

She swallowed.

She'd be one of those loose ends.

She wouldn't make it home, and Falk wouldn't owe her shit anymore.

Could she really believe that she'd been sent here to die?

No. She'd been sent here to make a trade. Information she needed from Falk for looking the other way when it came to Bolstad.

Jamie could still hear Wiik swearing behind her.

Whatever way she cut it, they were trapped here for the next few days, and she was making a lot of assumptions. She just needed to keep her head down, try not to put too big a target on her back, and ride this out.

She and Wiik could gather evidence, make their decisions, and if they couldn't arrest whoever was behind this out here, they'd damn well do it when they were back on dry land.

Ehrling's words rang in her head then.

If she made it that far.

21

JAMIE'S HANDS WERE NUMB.

They'd been down there for around forty minutes, had cleared five of the eight rooms, and so far had come up with nothing.

There seemed to be a loose system as to which room things were put in. Some seemed purely for recyclables. Others for rubbish. Textiles. Contaminated waste. Even dried and tinned foods. But they were yet to run into the one that contained the seals.

Jamie stepped out of storage room number six to find Wiik standing outside the door opposite.

'Anything?' he asked.

Jamie shook her head, lowering her phone torch. 'Nope.' She stamped her feet, willing some blood back into them. 'Just shelves and shelves of vacuum-sealed powdered foods.'

'Sounds appetising.'

Jamie shrugged. 'I guess they have to be prepared for anything. Provisions enough to keep the crew alive in case of emergency.'

'Like a knife-wielding murderer running around in the middle of a storm that prevents any sort of rescue?'

'Yeah,' Jamie said, laughing a little. 'Something like that.' She looked at the final two doors. 'Come on, let's get this over with and get back upstairs.'

Wiik nodded and headed for the door to his right. Jamie took the one on her left.

They both pushed in, torches up, and set about locating their prize.

The room was the same size as the others. About five metres deep, and as many across. In front of her, a row of shelving units spanned the width of the room. And beyond that, there was another one. She flashed her torch across what was on them.

Paint cans, tins of grease and oil. Boxes of ... she didn't know what. Chinese characters. Russian characters ... She walked down the length of it, then found a box with the words *actuator valve* on it, followed by a string of numbers and letters. Machine parts. Boxes of machine parts.

The light caught something on the next shelf along, and she squinted into the dark, seeing a crate full of what looked like tools. Welding torches. A welding mask.

Her heart quickened a little, the smell of oil thick in the air.

Jamie kept moving, holding her hand up, searching for the word *seal* or anything else that might clue her in to where the hell this thing was.

'Seals, seals, seals,' she muttered, eyes stinging from the dust in the room. Her breathing was laboured, the air like liquid.

And then she paused, seeing a filthy-looking bin against the wall. It was square, nearly the size of a refuse sack, and filled with a tangled mass of shimmering black.

Jamie approached quickly, her breath misting in front of her face, and held the light on it.

She stared down at what had to be them.

They looked like cross sections of rubber piping. About forty centimetres across, maybe a little more, and thick. Like big, black bagels.

She inspected the ones on top. They were all chewed up, covered in stress cracks, worn thin and rough at the edges. Changed before they blew.

But she couldn't see any that weren't.

Her breathing was slow, but her heart beat quickly against her ribs. 'Come on,' she said. 'Come on ...'

Then she stopped, the light hovering near the far side of the bin.

Jamie reached in, past one of the worn-out seals, and closed her fingers around one which was half-buried. It was greasy to the touch and she felt the thick liquid squelch in her grip, oozing between her fingers as she pulled the thing free, wiggling and tugging at the same time.

Sweat beaded on her brow as she reached across the bin, trying to drag it out, the edges sharp against her palm. Sharp. Not worn round. Sharp. And new. This was it.

She was totally focused, the squeaking of rubber on rubber, along with her heart and strained breath enough to drown everything else out.

Until she heard it.

Jamie froze.

Footsteps behind her.

Her breath seized in her throat, the hair on the back of her neck standing on end.

She jerked backwards as hard as she could, immediately aware of how vulnerable she was. The seal came free in her hand and she swung it instinctively, the heavy rubber whistling through the air.

The torch flashed, illuminating the raised arms of someone standing right behind her, shielding their face from the blow.

Jamie only caught it for an instant before the weight of her makeshift bludgeon threw her off balance. It came up short, sailing right in front of the figure, missing completely, but only by inches.

Jamie stumbled, swearing, and felt the greasy seal come free of her grasp. It bounced on the ground and came to rest on its side.

Jamie pulled the torch back up in front of her as quickly as she could, searching for whoever had tried to attack her.

Her eyes struggled to focus, the strobing of her torch and the darkness in the room enough to make them ache.

Nothing. She saw nothing in front of her.

Movement.

Beyond the shelves.

They were making a run for it.

'Wiik!' Jamie yelled out, taking off after them. 'Wiik!'

She heard clattering across the hall, Wiik's voice.

Jamie burst into the corridor, looking left and right.

The door at the end – the stairwell, was swinging closed.

Wiik emerged from the storeroom opposite, covered in dust. 'What is it?' he called at Jamie's back. She was already running.

The door flew out to meet Jamie. She could hear Wiik panting behind her already.

She plunged through into the stairwell and stopped, looking up and down, listening for steps.

They echoed below.

Jamie went right, circling down, down, down into the depths of the platform.

Wiik was yelling above her. 'Johansson!'

But she couldn't reply. She had to focus. Had to catch them.

The floors blurred past as she pounded the stairs, heels clanging on the ridged steel.

She leaned over, looking down through the narrow gap between the staircases, saw a hand two floors below, tracing the rail. She was catching up.

Jamie kept going, breathing hard, plait whipping behind her as she ran. She weighed up shedding her jacket. It was slowing her down.

But she'd already experienced the cold outside these walls once before and wasn't keen to repeat the experience.

The floor levelled out suddenly, and there was just one door ahead.

She tore it open and moved into the corridor, at the bottom now.

There was nowhere left to run.

Jamie checked both ways, and then halted, her legs suddenly stiff under her. The sound of her heart filled her head as she realised where exactly she was. On her left, there was a single hatch, the words *Lower Submersible Platform* written above it.

Jamie turned, staring at another lonely door at the other end of the corridor. It was slowly closing.

She could hear the chug and hum of the boilers beyond.

She didn't need to read the sign to know what was through it.

Her calf throbbed, the heel of her hand burning at her side, eyes fixed on it.

Jamie's brain revolved in time with the turbines in the

maintenance room as she considered her options.

There was noise on the stairs behind her, the distinct sound of Wiik's breathing. And then he was at her side. 'What—' he started, screwing his eyes up, trying to catch his breath, 'what happened?'

'There was someone,' Jamie said, her voice calm then.

'Someone? Who?'

Jamie peeled her eyes from the maintenance door. 'I don't know. But I lost them.'

'Lost them?' Wiik asked.

'Yeah,' Jamie said, shaking it off. 'They must have ...' She swallowed. 'Must have gotten off on a different floor.'

Wiik glance at the lower submersible platform hatch, and at the now-closed maintenance door. 'Shit,' he said, 'any ideas who it was?'

One of Wallace's hitmen? Ashleigh Hooper or Paméla Sevier? Kurek?

'No,' she said. 'But they were in the storeroom where the seal was. Probably looking for it themselves.'

'Why?'

Jamie shrugged again and motioned Wiik back through the door towards the stairs. 'I don't know,' she said. 'To get rid of the evidence?'

Wiik finally caught his breath. 'Then we'd better collect it before they come back.'

'Yeah,' she said. 'I think we'd better. I just hope they don't come looking for it again.'

Wiik paused on the bottom step and looked over his shoulder at her. For the first time, she saw uncertainty in his eyes. The first thing which had genuinely unnerved her since she arrived. 'You and me both,' he said. And then walked on, upwards into the innards of the platform, and the storm that lay ahead.

22

IT WAS dark when the alarm sounded.

The noise of the storm had risen to a deep and ominous howl as it swirled through the towers outside, forcing the whole platform to sway on its titanic legs.

But the alarm was something else.

Jamie and Wiik both sat bolt upright in bed again.

Jamie felt her mattress jolt a little as Wiik once more planted his head on the underside of her bunk and swore loudly.

A red light was flashing above their door, painting the whole room bloody.

'What now?' Wiik called, voice laced with rage.

Jamie squinted at the faintly glowing face of her watch, forcing her eyes to focus. It was just after 4am. She let herself down off her bed a little more carefully this time, and Wiik rose next to her, rubbing his head.

Voices echoed from outside. Footsteps followed.

They glanced at each other for just a moment before reaching for their clothes. Pulling their boots on, they made out the door. Ehrling and Vogel's doors were both wide open, their rooms empty across the way.

Jamie looked left, saw Hooper and Sevier's door firmly shut. The alarm kept blaring. A deep, echoing drone.

Fire? Some other type of emergency? She didn't know.

Wiik tapped her on the shoulder and headed for the stairs that led up to the command deck. She fell in behind him, heart thundering. In the stairwell, Wiik started up, but Jamie grabbed his arm.

She could hear shouting from below, snatched between tones.

Wiik followed her down, and then they were in the staff quarters.

The doors were open. She could see Rosenberg and Møller in the gloom ahead, talking from their doorways opposite one another.

Jamie started forwards, ready to call out, and froze, looking at the floor in front of her.

There was a dark liquid splattered all along it, shining black in the deep red lighting.

Her eyes followed the trail back to a door on her right and her blood ran a little colder, seeing the same, shimmering black tar coating the frame, the door. Handprints. Smears.

In blood.

Jamie steeled herself and looked ahead.

The trail led outwards. She just didn't know where to.

As she began moving, Møller and Rosenberg looked up.

'Rooms, now,' she ordered, pointing them back inside. 'And lock your doors.'

They looked at each other, and then gave in, shuffling back inside.

Jamie pressed on, following the trail, watching as the liquid dripped and ran down the walls at her flanks. Through each door, through the maze of corridors, the screaming got louder. Screams of pain. They were distinct. Haunting.

Wiik was breathing hard behind her, right on her shoulder.

They moved like wolves, stalking, watching each other's backs the whole way. They were in someone else's territory, and with each passing minute, that became more apparent.

Jamie followed the trail to the infirmary, the screams filling her ears.

There was an open door ahead, leading into the main treatment room. The howls echoed out. Jamie just didn't know whose.

A blinding light exploded from within and they shielded their eyes, squinting into the brilliance as they both reached the doorway.

The scene beyond was a frenzy.

Colm Quinn was flat on his back on the table in the centre of the room. He was shirtless, a wound just above his right hip spilling blood over his midriff, soaking his grey boxer shorts.

His legs flailed and kicked as Tim Ehrling, the closest thing to a doctor they had, tried to pin him down and press a wad of gauze to the wound.

The *stab* wound.

Jamie's eyes moved across Quinn's body to the other side, to the diagonal slash that moved up from the middle of his stomach, across his ribs.

Blood was pouring from that, too, and Helene Vogel was doing her best to staunch the bleeding.

Behind them, holding Quinn's shoulders down, was Sasha Kravets, one of the other drillers – a tall Ukrainian with broad shoulders, and shaved, black hair and a wide, full-lipped, downturned mouth. His arms were covered with blood, his white vest sodden from the sternum down. He looked like he was the one who'd carried Quinn in here.

Lebedenkov appeared from the other room, holding a metal case. He was bloodied, too, but nowhere near as badly as the others. He set it down on a rolling surgical table and lifted the lid. Ehrling turned and said something to him that Jamie didn't catch between the incessant alarm and Quinn's deafening writhing.

They switched positions and Quinn roared as Lebedenkov pressed down hard, an extra spurt of blood running down onto the table before the bleeding slowed.

Quinn spat flecks of saliva into the air through bared teeth as Ehrling drew a clear liquid into a syringe he'd pulled from the case. His eyes were wide, his hands red, smearing blood across the label on the bottle he was holding.

Jamie couldn't make out what it said.

She and Wiik could only watch.

Ehrling turned, approached Quinn, standing between Lebedenkov and Kravets, and said something to the both of them.

They pressed Quinn flat, pinning his arm in place.

Ehrling raised the needle.

Jamie's heart stopped for a moment as she stared at him, wondering if the man that had all but threatened her life was about to inject Quinn with something that wasn't going to save him, but would instead do the opposite.

The syringe looked damn full.

And then he was bringing it down.

Jamie started forwards, felt Wiik's hand on her shoulder, pulling her back. She looked up at him, unable to read his hard expression in the half-light as he watched the scene unfold. He didn't even meet her eye.

He did nothing

Not even twitch as Ehrling forced the needle into Quinn's arm and pressed down on the plunger.

The man continued to buck, continued to scream. Ehrling turned away, put the syringe down, and went to the sink at the back of the room, began washing his hands.

Jamie watched him closely.

He seemed calm.

For someone who'd been so easily shaken at the beginning of the investigation, he didn't seem to be frantic. And she expected he would be. Not the sort of person you could rely on in a situation like this. And yet, Ehrling seemed practically unphased.

And Jamie couldn't figure out why. But she knew he was dirty. Somehow. In some way, he had his grubby little fingers in all of this. Reyes' death, Noemi's disappearance, Boykov's murder, the sabotage plot. And now this.

She so wanted to rush in, shove his head against the counter, and make him talk. *Make* him.

But Wiik was squeezing her shoulder hard enough that her eye was twitching.

Ehrling finished washing himself, took a paper towel from the counter, dried off, and went back to the case, taking a pair of latex gloves out of a box inside.

As Quinn's kicking lessened and the noise began to fade, Ehrling threaded a hooked needle.

And then Quinn fell still, his breathing fast and shallow as whatever Ehrling had injected him with took hold.

Kravets lifted his hands from Quinn's shoulders at Ehrling's word, and then, with a plastic bottle in one hand, stitching needle in the other, he moved Lebedenkov off.

The big Bulgarian took the gauze away and Ehrling sprayed what was in the bottle – a cleaning solution, Jamie guessed – over the wound, put it down next to Quinn's hip, and then pinched the wound together and began stitching it. Quickly. Yet not unskilfully.

Jamie was surprised.

And then she felt eyes on her.

She turned her head to see Vogel looking directly at her, her own expression conflicted. Frightened, Jamie thought.

A minute later, Ehrling was applying a dressing, and then he was around the table and next to Vogel.

He shooed her out of the way silently, and she peeled back from Quinn, looking down at him.

Jamie didn't know that she'd ever met a man so unbalanced as Ehrling was. She recalled the first meeting with him – how uncertain he'd seemed. Like he wanted nothing more than to be off this place. How he'd immediately fingered Quinn for Reyes' death. And now how he was here, saving the man's life. How he'd done everything in his power *not* to go down to the submersible deck. And then how he'd broken down into tears when they got locked out.

How he'd been nervous of the personnel files, despite there being nothing untoward in his.

And how he'd quivered when Jamie came at him, but then hardened when Wallace had poked his head out. How he'd threatened her.

And now, how he was sewing up a man. He was first aid qualified, but she didn't read about any formal medical training. But he obviously wasn't short on it. Which told her that his file was shortened. That she was only seeing what they wanted to her to see.

She just couldn't put her finger on Ehrling. But she knew that he was going to be hard to anticipate. There was a part of her that thought he was unhinged. Psychotic, even. Slingshotting back and forth between stable and unstable. Between calm and frantic. Between submissive and dominant.

Jamie's eyes met Vogel's, and the answer fell into place.

Vogel.

She'd been here, working with him. Right alongside him.

If anyone would know who he really was, it would be Vogel.

She stood there, still holding the bloodied wadding she'd used to stop the bleeding, wide-eyed with shock.

Jamie saw the opportunity, and took it.

'Vogel,' she said, moving forwards. 'Come with me, let's get you cleaned up.' She said it loudly enough for everyone to hear, took Vogel by the elbows and guided her quickly from the room, catching Ehrling watching from the corner of his eye as he worked on Quinn's slashed torso.

As she got into the corridor and headed for the cafeteria, she heard Wiik's voice from behind her, asking the room important question. 'Who did this?'

The reply came in the form of just one word that followed Jamie down the corridor, but did nothing to help her solve this puzzle.

'Kurek.'

23

JAMIE STOOD in the kitchen of the cafeteria, stirring Vogel's tea, keeping an eye on her as she scraped Quinn's blood from between her fingers with her thumbnail.

'You okay?' Jamie asked, the spoon clinking softly on the sides of the cup.

She nodded, then sighed. 'Yeah, just … intense, you know? Unexpected.' Her German accent brought a certain formalness to the statement. But Jamie knew that it had hit her hard.

'Tell me about Ehrling,' Jamie said then. 'Sugar?' She looked up at Vogel, who realised then that she was asking about the tea, not calling her that.

'No, thanks,' she said, accepting the cup. She put it down on the steel counter, and then pulled a plastic crate off a shelf overhead, taking out a few disposable UHT milk pots. 'What about him?' She emptied them into the liquid and then grabbed a wooden spoon from the utensils rack at the back of the counter and used the handle to stir the milk in.

Jamie leaned against the counter, arms folded, and

watched the door. Wiik had hung back and was standing outside it, ready to signal her if anyone came.

Two against one was never a good way to get information out of someone freely.

'What's he like?' Jamie asked.

'He's, uh,' Vogel started, sipping the tea. 'He's okay.'

'Okay? How long have you worked together?'

'We both got here around the same time – about ten, no, eleven months ago?'

Jamie offered her a compassionate smile. 'You've been out here all that time?'

She nodded. 'Yeah, every six months, the crew changes – they go home, to their families, their wives, their kids. The head of operations and the assistant stay on. Few weeks off a year while Bolstad does necessary maintenance and overhaul on the rig.' She shrugged. 'Not so bad.'

'You've got no one waiting for you back home?' Jamie tried not to make it sound as lonely as it seemed to her.

Vogel shook her head. 'No, this line of work doesn't exactly attract *attached* people.'

Jamie nodded. 'I know the feeling.'

Vogel was the one who smiled now. 'You get used to it, you know? Being out here. It becomes as good as home.'

Jamie also knew that feeling. But she wasn't here to play *'Who has the saddest life?'* 'And Ehrling's been here all that time, too?'

She nodded.

'And you said you applied for the job?'

She nodded again.

'Where did you see it advertised?'

'I was working for Bolstad already – as a systems analyst,' she said.

Jamie knew that already, from her file. But wanted to hear it again.

'There's an internal Bolstad employees intranet that's used for all sorts of stuff. Managing contracts, holidays, payslips, that kind of thing. There's also an opportunities page.'

'You didn't want to apply for the head of operations position?' Jamie asked it casually, but it was an important question.

'I would have if it was advertised.'

So it wasn't, then. Ehrling was installed here.

'Weird that they'd change the head and assistant head at the same time.' Jamie stuck out her bottom lip. 'Makes sense they'd want to keep on someone with experience. Do you know who was the head before?'

Vogel looked at her questioningly, wondering what she was getting at. 'No, I don't. And I don't know if that's weird – I don't think so. These kinds of jobs have a high turnover. A lot rides on us. It's stressful. People leave jobs all the time. And it's important that a head and assistant head work well together. Maybe Bolstad just felt that a change of management would be the best decision. I know that our output has been higher than it was before we arrived. The final assessment submitted before we started work was that oil reserves had run dry out here. But we found more.' She sounded proud of that.

'*You* found more, you mean,' Jamie said, reading her tone.

She smiled bashfully and looked down into her tea. 'Like I said, Ehrling and I make a good team.'

Jamie nodded. 'Do you like him?'

'I don't have to. So long as we work well together.'

'Do you?'

'Yes.'

Vogel was a strong woman. Smart. Focused. Jamie could see that. 'He just lets you get on with it?'

'He trusts me to do my job,' Vogel said diplomatically. 'And I respect that. A lot of guys wouldn't.'

'So he's a good boss.'

'He knows I do my job. He doesn't micromanage me. As good as I've had.'

'What's he like as a person?' Jamie often found honesty was the best route into these conversations. 'I'm struggling to get a read on him.' She knew from his file that he was from a town north of Gothenburg, had studied business and management. From there, he'd gone straight to work for Bolstad. His experience set wasn't dissimilar to Vogel's. He'd worked in analytics, then moved up to a supervisory role. He'd worked in site assessment, workflow-efficiency optimisation, a string of other boring, nondescript titles that meant he never went anywhere near an actual drill. And then he'd moved up to management. An assistant-head position here, then as an oil-field supervisor in one of Bolstad's provisional UAE sites. That was until a year ago, when he was moved here. Which gelled with everything Vogel was saying.

She had hoped it wouldn't. That there'd be a hole in the narrative. That Vogel's story wouldn't match up to his file, that she could find what was *off* about him. But there wasn't anything. Not on paper, at least.

'He's ... fine,' Vogel said. 'Not really sociable.'

Jamie took that in. 'Is he kind?'

'Kind?' Vogel looked at her over the rim of her coffee cup.

'Yeah, is he a nice person to be around? Does he get you coffee in the morning? Do the rest of the crew like him?'

'It's very much a them-and-us sort of situation. He's reasonably friendly with Rosenberg, I suppose. They're both

Swedes, so it's not surprising. Møller, too, I guess. Rosenberg and him are friends, I think.'

Jamie processed it all, wondering where Vogel's allegiances lay. She had to be careful here. 'That's good. Thank you. I'm just struggling to work him out. One minute he seems calm, the next jittery. And then, with Quinn, in there …'

Vogel swallowed, watching Jamie carefully.

'I don't know. He just surprised me, is all. I didn't think he'd be the one to act so coolly in a situation like that.'

She collected her thoughts before speaking. 'I know what you mean. It took me a while to get a read on him, too. But … he's okay. He has his off days, sure. Sometimes he struggles to keep his emotions in check. But don't we all? He's got people's lives in his hands, remember. Everyone working out here – on this … *thing*. This death trap.' She gestured to the platform around her. 'Their lives rest on Ehrling's shoulders. If anyone has an accident, or … dies …' She cleared her throat. 'That's on him. Directly. He bears the brunt of it. It's a lot to take on.'

Vogel was right. And Jamie was annoyed she'd not realised that earlier. 'How did he react when Heikkinen told him about the worn-out drill seal?'

'Uh,' she said, a little caught off guard. 'He was … angry, I suppose. It upset him.'

'Angry with who?'

'Rosenberg, I guess. It was his job to make sure that sort of thing is taken care of. If it blew, it could take someone's head off. *Literally*. It's happened. The pressure inside the main chamber is huge. The force of the mud being expelled could kill someone if they were standing in the wrong place.'

'He reprimanded him?'

'I guess so,' Vogel said. 'In private, though. Ehrling's not one to make a public scene. I know they swapped the worn seal out right away, though. Made sure it was all up to spec then himself.'

Jamie was slowly starting to get a picture now, but it was still murky. 'Did he mind having the girls here? Heikkinen, Hooper, Sevier?'

'He didn't have much of a choice. None of us did. One day, a chopper arrived – they got off, letter in hand from head office. Wasn't anything we could really do.'

'But he never said anything to them? Didn't take a liking to any of them?'

'A liking?'

'I hear Heikkinen was quite beautiful.' Jamie cursed herself the moment the words came out of her mouth. Reyes had been with Vogel before she'd arrived and had cast her aside the moment Heikkinen had got there.

Vogel cleared her throat, her posture changing. She grew immediately cold. 'I wouldn't know,' she said. 'What people do off the clock is their business.'

Jamie kept smiling, but inside she was kicking herself. 'Right, of course.' She let the silence sit for a second, Vogel's quiet slurping the only sound between them. 'Does Ehrling have any medical training, do you know?'

'All the HOOs are put through a first aid training course. I suspect that because we're running a reduced crew here that Ehrling was given extra training, just in case. A full crew has catering staff, a doctor, cleaning staff, everything. Sometimes a rig this size will have thirty, forty people on board.'

'Is it unusual to have so few people working?'

'When a rig is on its last legs and oil is running out? Not really. Often they work at reduced capacity.' Her voice was without emotion now. She was just answering as matter-of-factly as she could, ready to get out of there.

Jamie had all but lost her, and she wasn't going to get any more information on Ehrling. 'Okay, thanks. Do you need me to walk you back to your room?'

Vogel shook her head and put her still-full cup down on the counter. 'No, I'm fine. Just want to get back to bed. Inspector.' She nodded to Jamie and then left without another word.

The door closed out in the cafeteria, and then she heard footsteps approaching.

Wiik hovered by the kitchen entrance. 'Get anything?'

Jamie beckoned him in. 'Not really. Just that Ehrling is, by all accounts, a good guy. He and Vogel arrived here together nearly a year ago. She applied. He was put here by Bolstad. They saved the rig from going under, and have been here ever since.'

'Jesus,' Wiik said. 'Twelve months at sea.'

Jamie nodded. 'He reacted as you'd expect someone to when Heikkinen told him about the seal. He was angry. Chewed Rosenberg out behind closed doors. Got the issue sorted personally. Made sure everything was running as it should have been.'

Wiik said nothing.

'Vogel was under no illusion that it's a stressful job. And Ehrling has his up days and his down days like everyone else.'

'And which was he having when he threatened you?' Wiik stared at her.

She swallowed. 'I don't know. But there seems to be a marked difference in him when Wallace is around.'

Wiik nodded in agreement, looked at the floor, and moved what looked like an old piece of salad leaf around with the toe of his shoe. 'Yeah, I noticed. The question is whether that's just for show, or whether that's who he really is.'

Jamie let him speak this time.

'Is Ehrling the guy who collapsed on the submersible deck and went to tears when he thought we were going to die? Or is he the guy who makes threats against police officers?'

That one, Jamie couldn't answer. 'And if it's the first one?'

'Then the calm and collected act is just that. An act. A show.'

'Who for?'

'Us?' Wiik shrugged.

'And if it's the second one?'

He sighed. 'Then we need to take his threat seriously. And watch our fucking backs.'

24

JAMIE STOOD on the command deck, a cup of coffee in hand, and watched the clouds lighten from sodden black to mottled grey.

The storm continued to rage, hurling itself against the glass in front of her in thick sheets of rain.

The posts around the helideck, topped by red lights to guide choppers in the dark, waved madly, and she swore she could feel the whole place moving under her feet.

Though that might have just been the nausea that had lodged itself in her guts since that morning.

Her jaw was beginning to ache from clenching her teeth so hard.

She hadn't said a word in nearly three hours.

After interviewing Vogel in the cafeteria, she and Wiik had gone back to their room to find that it had been searched.

Things were out of place. Clothing moved. Bags rummaged in. *Again.*

And now, the personnel files were missing. Her satchel had been taken. As was the intact seal. The one thing they had that proved foul play.

By Kurek? Trying to cover his tracks? By the mess in Quinn's quarters, he'd snuck in there in the dead of night and attacked him right there on his bunk.

But Quinn had fought him off, yelled out. And then Kurek bolted. Kravets was across the hall, said he leapt out of bed at the noise, saw Kurek fleeing. Lebedenkov was up a moment later. They raised the alarm, carried Quinn up to medical. Ehrling arrived. Then Vogel. Then Jamie and Wiik.

And during that time – the time they'd spent just standing there watching Quinn writhing on the table. That son of a bitch had circled around and ransacked their room looking for the files.

Jamie slurped her coffee angrily.

She'd pored over his file, too.

There was nothing in it.

Nothing of any fucking use. To say why he would do this. To indicate what reason he would have for wanting to sabotage the drill.

Jamie glared at the storm as Vogel and Ehrling clacked on their keyboards behind her.

Wiik appeared at her shoulder, his hair still damp from the shower.

'Hey,' he said, the look of quiet rage also apparent in his face.

Jamie didn't even look up.

Through all this, Wallace hadn't made an appearance.

It was what Jamie was waiting for.

Quinn was being watched over by Lebedenkov and Kravets in case Kurek came back. Though why Quinn had been targeted in the first place was still a mystery to Jamie.

She had all the dots, but couldn't connect any of them.

Had Kurek killed Boykov, too? Had he killed Reyes? If so, why?

Jamie shook her head.

What did they know? Motive. What motive did Kurek have? What did Jamie know about him?

Grzegorz Kurek, Polish national. Educated at Kraków University. Qualified as a safety engineer in 2011. Had been working on rigs since. No wife, no kids. He was unattached, smart. His performance reports noted his focus, his efficiency. He fit the profile for the psycho-loner. Even his work role gave him that classic 'power over people's lives' quality that psychopaths ached for. But that didn't chime for Jamie at all. What did he have to gain from sabotaging the drill?

Jamie closed her eyes, rolling it over in her head. What did she *know?* She knew that the seal was swapped out so that it would blow at any moment. She knew that Heikkinen somehow found out about it, and reported it to Ehrling.

Vogel said that Ehrling then went to … Wait. Vogel said … Vogel said it could take someone's head off. That it could kill someone. She opened her eyes then.

Quinn.

If it had blown, could it have killed Quinn?

Reyes owed Kurek some money, too.

Had he just had enough of their bullshit? Snapped?

He was the safety engineer. He'd be in charge of making sure that everything was … *safe*. The responsibility fell to Rosenberg to make sure everything was up to spec. But it would be *Kurek* who handled safety checks. It was Rosenberg's responsibility to make sure everyone did their job.

Jamie turned then. 'Ehrling,' she said, her voice strange in her ears after so much silence.

He looked up unhurriedly, but didn't say anything.

'Vogel said you had words with Rosenberg after the drill seal issue was reported to you.'

He nodded, barely.

'Was it Rosenberg who signed off on the quality of that seal?'

He nodded again.

'Who changed it?'

He lifted an eyebrow. 'Sorry?'

'Whose job is it to *change* the seals when they get worn out?'

'Boykov,' he said. 'He's the drill technician. Or *was,* at least.'

Jamie swallowed. 'And who inspected it afterwards, Rosenberg?'

'No, Kurek. He performs visual inspections whenever work is carried out to ensure safety of the workers.' He narrowed his eyes, measuring Jamie's stony expression.

Jamie nodded. 'Thank you.' She turned away just as quickly and went back to the window, stepping closer to it to put more distance between her and Ehrling, and so that the rain hitting the glass would block out her lowered voice to the mic she knew was in the room.

Wiik followed her cue and came up on her shoulder again. 'What are you thinking?'

'If that seal was changed by Boykov, and Kurek inspected it, and then Rosenberg signed off on it. They'd have no reason to go back and check again, right?'

Wiik nodded.

'So if Kurek went back in and changed it out a second time, it would have gone undetected.'

Wiik nodded again.

'Boykov was the only other one who would have been able to corroborate Rosenberg's assertion that the seal was in good condition. So taking him out of the picture makes it Kurek's word against Rosenberg's. That's motive against Boykov.'

'If Kurek intended to plead his side of things after this was all over.'

'What if he did?'

'You can't honestly think that Kurek has any plans to walk out of this a free man?' Wiik leaned in, basically whispered it in her ear.

Jamie bit her lip. 'I don't know,' she said, just as quietly, shaking her head. 'But I think the *why* is more important now. What if we had it wrong about this being about causing a spill? What if he was trying to hurt one person specifically?'

'Who?'

'Who's dead, Wiik?' Jamie looked at him.

'Reyes ...' Wiik said. 'But how could he be sure it would blow when Reyes was working it? He could have just as easily got Quinn. Or Lebedenkov, or—'

'But remember what Quinn said about Boykov and Reyes? He said that Boykov took serious issue with the way Reyes ran the drill. That he worked it too hard.'

'Jesus, so Kurek swaps the seal before Reyes gets on the drill, banking on it blowing up in his face?'

'Literally,' Jamie said, folding her arms. Her coffee was now cold, but she slugged it anyway, willing the caffeine into her brain.

'But why? You can't believe it's because Reyes owed Kurek money over *cards.*'

Jamie shook her head. 'Maybe it's more than that. Maybe it's bigger than that. Rosenberg said that it was a them-and-us situation. And Vogel used those words, too. That on one side was the engineers and management, and on the other the drillers.'

'Right?'

'Two groups of guys, at each other's throats, stepping on each other's toes – out here. Møller said it – tempers run high at sea.'

'So you think this is just some feud coming to a head all of a sudden?'

Jamie drew in a slow breath. 'Maybe so. And if there's one sure-fire way to make an argument at boiling point ignite, it's to introduce love into the mix.'

'Heikkinen ...' Wiik swallowed. 'She was with Reyes, but we know Møller liked her.'

Jamie turned to face him slightly, but made sure Ehrling couldn't see her lips moving. 'Right. And we know that Kravets and Lebedenkov gave her enough grief that she was scared to go near them.'

'And Reyes was skipping out on Boykov's card debt.'

Jamie watched beads of water streak across the glass. 'So maybe things just continue to build up. And the engineers hatch a plan to put the drillers in their place. They swap out a perfectly good seal, knowing it will go bang.'

'But then Heikkinen gets in the way of that.'

'The drillers know something is up – probably know enough to see that someone was trying to kill them.'

'Tensions rise. And you think Quinn is the sort of guy to let something like this go?'

Wiik drew a slow breath. 'And you said Heikkinen needed to speak to Reyes the night he died, right? About something important.'

'That's what Sevier and Hooper said,' Jamie said.

'Think she was trying to warn him?'

'Maybe.'

'And then Kurek came down there after them? Killed Reyes.'

Jamie said nothing, but that's what she was thinking.

'And then Boykov was recompense?'

Jamie stayed silent.

'You think Quinn went after Boykov as revenge?'

'I don't know,' she said after a long time. 'But what I do know ... is that this isn't over yet.'

Jamie and Wiik slunk off the command deck with one thing in mind.

The direction of the case had changed more than a spinning compass, but now Jamie felt like the dots had started to line up.

On one side it was Rosenberg, Møller, Kurek, and formerly, Boykov. And on the other, it was Quinn, Lebedenkov, Kravets, and Reyes.

Who had drawn first blood, Jamie couldn't say. But she knew Heikkinen had been mixed up in it all, and now, it was a full-blown blood feud that they were stuck right in the middle of.

And it looked like Bolstad was clued in – or at least enough to dispatch Wallace. Who seemed to have been slithering around here like a snake, attempting to fix things, broker peace, cover things up before the truth got out. Whether he'd given Jamie the files as an empty gesture, doctored versions to keep her busy while he did his job ... she couldn't say. But it had obviously irked him how much they had uncovered, anyway.

So, maybe it wasn't Kurek who took them. Maybe it was Wallace taking them back.

Word of sabotage getting out would no doubt sink Bolstad completely. And that's what he was here to stop happening. So now he was trying to do everything he could to keep this all quiet. Whatever the cost.

Jamie and Wiik walked quickly, heading for Sevier and Hooper's room. They needed to speak to them again – see if they knew anything about this feud that was going on. Hopefully, Heikkinen had let slip about it.

Jamie thought about it all, felt like everything was coming into focus. Møller's feelings towards Reyes made more sense now, too.

Wiik took the lead this time, his patience spent, and rapped hard on the door.

There was no answer. 'Paméla Sevier. Ashleigh Hooper,' he said, holding his face close to the surface. 'This is Kriminalinspektör Anders Wiik, Stockholm Polis. We need to speak to you.'

No response.

He jiggled the handle, but it was locked.

Wiik swore under his breath then and looked back at Jamie.

She didn't want to jump to any conclusions, but it was hard not to imagine the worst.

'Come on,' Wiik said, 'let's keep moving. They've got to be here somewhere.'

Jamie gave a brief smile, though she didn't know if she sold it. He was right. Vogel had kept them abreast of the situation with the storm: hundred-and-forty-kilometre-an-hour winds, minus twenty-degree wind chill. The rain was all but snow, and ice had begun to form on the metal carcass of the platform. Windswept spikes clinging to the girder-work. Which meant that drilling had been suspended – much to Wallace's dismay, no doubt – and everyone was inside.

If the girls had any sense, they'd stay where they could be seen and not be snuck up on.

Jamie hoped that they'd be outside of the war going on,

but Heikkinen had got sucked in, and there was no telling if they had, too. If nothing else, they were potential witnesses … and potential loose ends.

Wiik led them back down to the staff quarters, heading for the cafeteria.

They passed Quinn's bloodstains and kept moving quickly.

But then Jamie slowed down, an ajar door on her right catching her attention.

She tapped Wiik on the shoulder, and he stopped and looked back.

Jamie hovered in the gap, pricking her ear for any sound of movement.

This was Møller's door.

She heard a hiss from inside, a grunt, someone muttering something under their breath.

Jamie laid her fingers against the wood and pushed gently inwards, willing it not to squeak. Mercifully, it didn't, and Jamie stepped inside, following the sound.

She could see Møller through the open bathroom door. He was standing in front of the mirror, leant over, spitting what looked like blood into the sink.

She paused, watching for a few seconds as he cupped his hands under the tap, took some water in his mouth, swished it around, and then spat it out, grunting once again, touching his face tentatively.

He practically filled the tiny bathroom.

Jamie felt Wiik's hand on her shoulder, and she looked at him. He had his head turned, and she followed his eyes to the bunk against the wall. On it, Jamie could see Møller's massive Bolstad parka, and lying on top of it was a bowie knife fit to butcher a mammoth.

Jamie's calf throbbed, and she wondered if she'd seen that

knife before. Her heart kicked up a gear, the hairs on the back of her neck standing on end.

And then she heard a worse sound. Silence.

Jamie turned to see Møller standing in front of the mirror, staring at Jamie in the reflection.

The water was off, and his face was a mess.

She could see his cheek was swollen and bruised, his lip split in the corner. His opposite eye was black, too, the white violently bloodshot, the eyebrow cut.

His knuckles whitened around the edges of the steel sink, and Jamie watched as his eyes flitted to Wiik, who had moved behind Jamie now, and then came back to her.

Jamie kept her stare locked, and tried to wave Wiik away. She could hear his breathing tighten, feel his weight shift behind her.

It was one of those moments where everything was balancing on a razor's edge, ready to tip. Where disaster was just an incremental shift in any direction.

And then it happened.

Wiik moved.

Møller moved.

Jamie reacted.

The big Dane with the close-set eyes and a mess of bruises on his face pushed back from the sink and rushed into the room.

No one had time to assess his intentions before Wiik shoved Jamie sideways and met him head-on.

She'd never seen Wiik react like that. He had a temper, sure, and a short fuse most times, but she'd never seen him resort to physicality.

And yet, he cocked back his elbow like a javelin thrower and tried to sock Møller square in his already beaten-up face.

But Møller was too low and too fast, and slammed his

shoulder into Wiik's midriff, picked him up, and drove him clean back across the room and into the wall above his bed.

Wiik made a strange wheezing mewl as he hit the wall, sending the books on the shelf over the bed sprawling sideways.

Two of them fell down as Wiik crumpled into a heap and made a scrabbling grab for Møller's coat.

But the big man was fast, and only had one thing on his mind – getting the knife.

He snatched it off the bed and tried to take his coat with it, but Wiik's hand closed around the fur hood.

From nowhere, Møller's left hand swung in a wide arc and open-handed Wiik in the side of the head.

The clap resounded around the room as Jamie lifted herself off the ground.

Wiik must have lost his grip, because by the time she was on her feet, Møller had his coat in his hand and was lumbering towards the door.

Jamie knew better than to put herself between him and it – the guy was twice her size and weight, and wouldn't hold back to get away.

Wiik's eyes bulged in her peripheral as she swung into the hallway after him and chased him down.

She'd only have one shot at this, and she needed to catch him off guard.

If it was Møller that had come after her in maintenance, she wasn't about to make the same mistake twice.

He rushed towards the door at the far end of the corridor, and Jamie kept pace, steadying her breathing, calculating the distance, the angle, how she was going to do it.

And then they were there.

Møller slowed, reached out for the handle with his left hand, his coat and the knife still in his right.

Jamie came up behind him, weaved past his right shoulder and stepped into her right foot, bracing her weight.

The door opened towards her, and she lunged forwards with her left heel raised, shunting it closed, and free of his grasp.

Møller was stunned for a second, eyes wide.

And Jamie took the opportunity.

She planted her left foot, twisted into the balls of her feet, and then hooked her right steeply upwards.

Her knee rose level with her chest and then she unwound, slingshotting the Kevlar-capped toe of her boot in a tight arc up past Møller's still-outstretched arm and over his shoulder.

The force of the impact sent reverberations all through her ankle and knee, right up to her hip.

But she struck true.

Jamie went one way, and Møller sagged the other, his ear as good as cleaved in two.

His cries filled the hallway, and he went to a knee, instinctively throwing his free hand to the side of his head, blood already spilling from under it.

In the distance, Wiik came staggering out of Møller's quarters, loping towards them, clutching his stomach, bouncing from one wall to the other, face the colour of beetroot.

Jamie was back on her feet then and coming at Møller again before he had time to do anything.

A swift kick to his right wrist sent the knife spinning to the floor. And then Wiik was there, snatching the now-free hand from the air and folding it roughly up between Møller's shoulder blades.

Jamie heard Wiik drive his knee into the small of his back, and then force him to the ground.

And he went.

His yells had now stifled, and despite the blood still pumping down his face, he had fallen silent.

His cheek rested against the floor, his blood beginning to pool around his chin, but his lips were firmly closed, and he wasn't thrashing to get Wiik off him.

He just watched, staring up at Jamie with eyes full of fury.

It was usually around this time they started talking, denying everything, threatening, swearing to every god they could name that they'd get out of this or get revenge.

But Møller didn't do any of that.

He just lay there, and then lowered his eyes and accepted whatever came next.

And Jamie could have sworn, just before he turned his head away, that she saw a tear form on his cheek. But then he did, and she was looking at the back of his head.

She glanced up, checked all the doors on the corridor, saw they were all closed, and cleared her throat. 'Get him up,' she said quickly. 'We need to move. And fast.'

ORN MØLLER, the six-foot-something Dane with the mousy-brown hair, bruising all over his face, and now a two-piece left ear, sat on a chair with his hands cable tied behind his back.

Jamie had found a first aid kit in a supply cupboard at the end of the hall, and then they'd bundled him into an empty bedroom two floors down from where they'd collared him in.

Vogel herself had said it – the rig was designed to house forty people. Which meant three floors of crew quarters. Only the top one of which was being currently used.

Still, if he yelled, someone might hear.

But he didn't seem inclined to do that.

He was just sitting quietly, his left eye half-obscured by the bandage that ran around his head, holding his ear together.

Jamie looked down at her boot, saw there was blood on the toe, and then rubbed it on the opposite calf before clearing her throat and meeting Wiik's gaze. They were standing outside the room, doing their best to figure out what the hell was supposed to happen next.

'What are you thinking?' Wiik asked.

She stared up at his steadily reddening face. Møller had really slapped him. 'I think he wasn't trying to hurt you,' she said then.

Wiik did a double take. 'What? He tackled me. Then he punched me,' Wiik said, pointing to his face. 'And shoved you, too.'

'No, *you* shoved me, Wiik,' Jamie said, trying to keep her voice even.

Wiik's temple vein was bulging.

'He did tackle you, but then, he slapped you – to get his coat.'

'And knife.'

Jamie nodded reluctantly. 'Yeah, and that.'

'Why are you defending him?' Wiik sounded all but disgusted.

'I'm not,' Jamie said. 'But I think we need to look at the bigger picture here.'

'The bigger picture is that Orn Møller assaulted a Stockholm Polis detective. Resisted arrest. Tried to run. While in possession of a fucking *knife.'* He pointed at Jamie's leg. 'The same knife that probably sliced your fucking leg and murdered two crew members!'

Jamie gritted her teeth. 'Don't swear at me, Wiik,' she said coolly. She could see him getting worked up, and nothing defused him like calling him out on his lack of manners.

He blew out a long breath and put his hands on his hips. But didn't apologise.

'All I'm saying,' Jamie went on, keeping her voice calm now, 'is that maybe we should hear Møller's side of it before we jump to any conclusions. Because running away from two detectives is different from locking them outside to die and then trying to gut one like a fish.' She stooped a little to catch his eye. 'Yeah?'

Wiik swallowed, and then dropped his hands and pushed the door to the bedroom open. 'After you then.'

Jamie did her best to ignore the sarcasm in his voice, and instead focused on Orn Møller, who, judging by the way his eyes were fixed on the door, had just heard every word they said.

She just hoped it wasn't about to influence what he was going to say.

Because if nothing else, she could really do with hearing the truth at least once in this case. It would sure be a big fucking help.

Jamie and Wiik entered the room in silence, and Jamie stopped short of Møller – outside of lunging distance – and folded her arms, staring down at him. Wiik sat on the plastic-mattressed bed and kept quiet, watching Jamie as much as Møller.

Jamie lifted her chin and gestured loosely to Møller's beaten-up countenance. 'What happened to your face?'

'Some bitch kicked me,' he said gruffly, staring up at her from under the bandage.

Jamie let that one slide. 'Before you were stupid enough to run away—'

Wiik cleared his throat behind her.

'—and assault a police officer,' she added, 'your face was already a bit of a fucking mess.'

'Bad genes, I guess.' He looked away. 'But we have to play the hand we're dealt.'

'Cut the shit,' Jamie said, shifting her weight uneasily. She knew every minute they spent down here was one where every other person left in this place was open to getting their throats slit. 'Who did it to you?'

Møller stared back at her wordlessly.

'If you don't start talking,' Jamie said, 'we can't help you.'

He huffed in amusement. 'You can't help me anyway. You can't help anyone. You can't even help yourselves.'

'So you help us then.' Her voice was stricken with humanity. 'If you haven't noticed, things are going to shit here. Hell, they've already gone to shit. Two people are dead. Two are missing. And I think we're one bad moment away from an all-out bloodbath. So if you know something, you need to tell us. Right now.'

He shook his head slowly, his thick arms folded down behind his back. 'Jesus, you have no idea what's going on here, do you?'

Jamie's nostrils flared a little and she felt her spine stiffen. 'Why don't you tell us?'

He kept his head down and didn't answer.

'Møller – I don't know if you realise the gravity of the situation here, but you were found in possession of a deadly weapon – one which might have been used to attack a police officer … *me.'*

He looked up at her now but said nothing.

'And when we found you in possession of that weapon, you tried to run. You tackled and then struck my partner, and no doubt would have done the same to me, to get away.'

More silence.

'And now you're in police custody, and if you don't start telling us what you know, then I really don't think I can help you.' Jamie was all but pleading with him.

He seemed to think on it for a few seconds, and then answered measuredly. 'And what if I don't? You just going to leave me tied to this chair for the next three days?'

Jamie swallowed. 'If it means no one else gets killed, I'm thinking about it.'

'And what if someone comes in here? And kills me? I'm guessing you're not going to sit here and watch me until the helicopter arrives to take us home.'

'You'll be safe. No one knows you're here.'

He scoffed.

Yeah, she didn't believe it either. 'Honestly, the answer is that I don't know.'

Wiik cleared his throat again behind her, but she wasn't going to stop. It was the truth.

'What I do know is that there's a war of some kind going on. And we're stuck in the middle of it.' She gestured to Wiik. 'Reyes getting killed, then Boykov ... now Quinn. You show up with a knife and a heap of bruises. Wallace is here with his two attack dogs ...'

Møller's ears seemed to prick up at the mention of Wallace, and Jamie's mind went back to Wiik's exchange with Blockhead – the bruise on his face, too.

'Did Wallace's man do that to you?' Jamie asked.

Møller had turned to stone now.

'Who attacked you, Møller?'

Nothing.

'Who were you going to use the knife on? Or was it for protection?'

Still nothing.

'Where were you running to?'

He lowered his head and stared at the floor between his feet.

'Goddammit, Møller!' Jamie practically yelled, started walking in a tight circle, running her hand through her hair. 'You want to get fucking killed? You need to talk to us!'

But he'd made his choice.

Wiik was on his feet then, and took Jamie by the shoulder, guided towards the door.

She walked, defeated.

'Let him think it over,' Wiik said, squeezing her on the arm. The gesture was a kind one, but it felt awkward, like it might as well have been a pat on the head. 'He'll come to realise the position he's in. Few hours at most, I'd say.'

'You want to just leave him down here?' She kept her voice hushed to try and make sure Møller didn't hear through the door.

'Do we really have another choice?'

She hated that they didn't.

'Like you said – no one knows he's down here. So unless he starts screaming, we'll come back in a while and find him right where we left him.'

Jamie didn't like this at all. She wanted them to wait right there. But that would just waste too much time. And she didn't feel like that was something they had a lot of right now.

She nodded slowly. 'Okay. So what now?'

'Now we hide this,' he said, holding up Møller's knife. 'Then we find Hooper and Sevier, and hope they can tell us something.' He gave her a weak smile and then headed for the stairs.

Jamie lingered for a second or two, looking back at the door. And then she swallowed the sick that felt like it was rising in her throat and went after Wiik.

They were standing in the empty cafeteria, choking down freeze-dried oats and water, when the tannoy crackled behind them once more. '*Inspector Wiik, Inspector Johansson.*' It was Vogel. '*Can you come to the command deck?*' The line clicked off, and while the voice wasn't laced with alarm, Jamie and Wiik wasted no time in heading up there.

There was still no sign of Hooper or Sevier, and they were both growing uneasy.

The place seemed deserted, in fact. With the storm going on, there was no drilling, which meant that everyone was inside. But 'inside' was proving to be pretty expansive, with plenty of places to hide.

They suspected that Quinn, Lebedenkov, and Kravets were all still in the infirmary.

Safety in numbers, Jamie thought. But that was fine with her. If they were there, it meant they weren't somewhere else. And that was something.

Kurek was still at large.

That was their main problem.

Ehrling and Vogel had sense, and they both wanted to survive this. So they were basically living on the command deck.

The only other person that left at a loose end was Rosenberg, the head engineer. But with a wife and kids waiting for him at home, Jamie hoped he'd stay put in his quarters and had the sense not to come out. If it was her, she'd have barricaded the door.

They passed his room on the right, and Jamie slowed.

'What is it?' Wiik asked.

'One sec,' she said, pausing and listening at the threshold. She lifted her knuckles and rapped gently. 'Rosenberg, you in there?' she called through the wood. There were a few seconds of silence, and Jamie's heart began to beat a little harder. 'It's Inspector Johansson,' she said again. 'Are you okay?'

'Inspector?' Rosenberg answered then. 'Is everything alright?'

She breathed a sigh of relief. 'Yeah. Just checking.'

'You don't need me to come out, do you?'

'No,' Jamie said quickly. 'Just … just stay put.'

'I will,' he said, the strain in his voice apparent even through the wood.

Jamie wished she had something better to tell him. But for now, knowing he was there was enough.

Wiik was hovering, waiting for her to move again.

He seemed on edge.

But she couldn't blame him.

A minute later, they were at the command deck.

The door opened a few seconds after they buzzed, and Vogel appeared in the gap, looking worried.

Jamie's heart sank. 'What is it?'

'We need to check something out,' she said.

Wiik spoke then. 'We?'

Vogel nodded. 'Yeah – usually I'd go and do it myself, but …'

'Say no more,' Jamie interjected, holding her hand up. 'Let's go.'

Vogel breathed a little sigh of relief. 'Okay, great.' She looked them both up and down then. 'But you may want to grab your coats.'

26

JAMIE AND WIIK stood at Vogel's shoulder while she wrestled the bar on the door vertical and then drove it open.

They were both squinting before she did it, in preparation, but neither could have anticipated what was going to blow through the gap.

Jamie and Wiik staggered backwards, throwing their hands up to shield their faces.

In the last few hours, Jamie had done her best to block out the noise of the storm, and with everything going on, had reduced it to little more than a background din.

But there was no escaping it now.

They cursed, widened their stance, and waded out into the maelstrom, holding their hoods to their heads.

Vogel was leading them onto a catwalk one storey up from the main drilling platform that gave a panoramic view of the drill and the skene module – a separate tower with its own support situated off the main body, connected by a narrow catwalk. Jamie wasn't exactly sure what a 'skene module' did, but there was a large steel tower with a central flume running up it. So whether it was used for burning excess fumes, or as an exhaust-type thing, she couldn't say. But either way it was swaying in the wind like an ear of corn and the catwalk leading out was twisting violently in the storm. It was making her stomach churn.

'There!' yelled Vogel from her right.

Jamie turned to face her and followed her outstretched hand.

The wind and rain lashed at the platform and practically knocked Jamie off balance.

She took hold of the railing behind her and squinted up at what Vogel was gesturing at.

About a metre above the door was an armoured cable, and at its end, Jamie could see the body of a security camera flapping on a wire.

It hung limply, totally at the mercy of the weather.

'Okay,' Vogel said, nodding to Wiik. 'Let's go back inside!'

She and Wiik shuffled back towards the hatch and entered back into the relative safety of the platform. But Jamie couldn't take her eyes off the camera.

She heard Vogel's voice coming out of the door then.

'—wasn't sure if it was the storm or not – they can cause a lot of damage!' She was still yelling as the wind howled through the open door. 'It's usually from debris, or something, but I don't know! Look at this.' She pulled her phone from her pocket and began showing something to Wiik. He leaned over to check it out as Jamie began to turn in a slow circle, inspecting the platform.

Vogel went on. 'See, you can see – it's fine, and then suddenly it goes off.'

Jamie guessed she was showing him playback of the last seconds of footage before the camera was smashed. Because to her, it was clear that was what had happened. She'd seen enough intentionally damaged CCTV cameras to know one when she saw one. And she also knew there was only one reason someone would want to do that: if they were intent on hiding something they were about to do.

'I wanted to check if it was an accident, or if someone meant to break—'

'Hey!' Jamie yelled, not turning around.

'—the camera,' Vogel went on, obviously not hearing her. 'But I can't figure out why anyone would want to—'

'Hey!' Jamie yelled again this time, turning to face them.

They both looked up, and Wiik moved first, reading the look on Jamie's face.

He surged up to the rail and grabbed hold of it, his hood blowing down, sending his hair into a mess of flailing tentacles above his head.

It didn't take him long to see what Jamie was looking at.

A black shape on the near-black tarmac of the drilling platform.

The wind was sheeting across it, the spray from the ocean below making it difficult to see anything.

But both Jamie and Wiik were experienced enough to know what they were looking at.

And that was another body.

27

JAMIE, Vogel, and Wiik all ran out across the surface, swaying and fighting the wind.

Each of them was squinting through the rain to try to get a better look at who it was lying face down, but they were no more than a dark shape until they were practically right on top of them.

They crowded around so that the body was surrounded, and stared down.

He was wearing a Bolstad parka, and the hood was blown up over the head. But from the tailored suit trousers and polished black shoes, it could only have been one of two people.

Wiik knelt at his side and rolled him over, standing up in shock at what he was looking at. Or moreover, because he didn't *know* what he was looking at.

Jamie's brain registered first – the guy was on his back now and where his head should have been there was a solid black mass.

'It's the seal!' Jamie bellowed, holding her hood over her head.

Wiik and Vogel were staring into the wind, nodding.

Jamie knelt now and wrestled the rubber ring free of the man's neck, feeling him flop limply back to the ground. The temperature was who knows how far below zero and the man's skin was a pale, greyish colour.

Neither Wiik nor Vogel spoke, but they all recognised the man.

It was Blockhead, Wallace's bodyguard, who'd screwed with Wiik.

Jamie weighed the seal in her hands – it must have been close to ten kilos of solid, hard rubber – and judging by the bruise on Blockhead's temple, the grazing on his cheeks, and the blood lodged between his teeth around his nostrils, he'd been hit with it before it was shoved down over his head.

He stared up into the sky with milky eyes. There was no question that he was dead.

But Jamie didn't think he'd been that way for very long.

She inspected the lines of his face, trying to work out what had happened, how it had gone down, and then Wiik was calling her name.

She looked up and saw that he was pointing at the ground between her heels, and that he and Vogel had taken a step back already.

Blood was pooling around her feet, soaking from Block-head's body.

Jamie reached down instinctively, tucked her fingers under him, and felt the still-warm blood running over her fingers.

She lifted them into the air then and let the thick droplets of rain wash them clean.

A wound in the back – maybe multiple. The position he was in, relative to the door. She looked back at the main body, then up at the camera overhead, then back at Blockhead.

The impact mark on his temple. The scuffs on his face, the bloodied nose and mouth. She'd felt the seal come off his head – it wasn't that tight.

She knew how it'd gone down.

And for Blockhead, it wasn't pretty.

She stood then. 'He came out there,' she said, pointing at the door, 'and walked towards the drill.' She gestured to the criss-crossed tower about twenty metres away. 'But he never got there. Whoever killed him came up from behind, quickly, and hit him with the seal.'

Wiik glanced down at it.

'One hard blow' – she gestured to the side of her head – 'to the temple. He stumbles, dazed, and then' – she mimicked a stabbing motion now. A sharp, upward strike, her other hand resting on an invisible shoulder – 'he's stabbed, in the back. And as he goes down, the seal is placed over the head, and forced down. From behind, too, judging by the marks on his face.' It felt so alien to yell out a crime scene assessment, but she was having to so Wiik and Vogel would hear her. Usually, civilians weren't looped in on this kind of thing, but Jamie had pretty much thrown out the rules and procedure book completely at this point.

Wiik began yelling then. 'Whoever killed him was also the one who took the seal from our quarters!'

Jamie gave a quick nod.

'What seal?' Vogel yelled then. 'What happened? Someone robbed your room?'

Shit, they hadn't told anyone about that. 'Yeah,' she said, quickly. 'We went down to the storeroom and found the seal that had been swapped out for the faulty one. Practically new.'

Vogel looked surprised.

'We brought it back up to our quarters for safekeeping.

Evidence!' The storm's intensity seemed to rise for a second or two, threatening to blow them all off the platform completely.

The ocean thundered below.

The skies boiled above.

'Who knew it was there?' Vogel asked. Or at least Jamie thought she did. She had to pretty much lip-read it.

She shook her head now. 'No one, I don't think! Whoever we chased down there I'd guess!' she added, looking at Wiik.

He nodded in confirmation. 'Same person who stole the personnel files!'

'What?' Vogel added, surprised again.

Wiik went on. 'Kurek?' he screamed.

Jamie didn't shake or nod this time. 'I don't know! But why would they want to go after one of Wallace's guys? Surely that's just adding fuel to the fire!'

Wiik screwed his face up against the spray, droplets of freezing rain blowing off his stubbled chin. 'Whatever the reason, Blockhead came out here to meet someone, and then he was attacked!'

Jamie didn't even want to guess who. Or why. Or what would possess *anyone* to go outside in this weather. Except, of course, you needed to meet someone and be absolutely sure you weren't going to be interrupted.

But why the hell was Blockhead meeting with anyone at all?

Jamie didn't know. But she knew who would, and she was sick of tiptoeing around him.

And now it was two on two as well. Wallace's flood wall had just halved in height.

And the tide was rising.

28

FURTHER INSPECTION WAS NEARLY IMPOSSIBLE, not to mention practically suicidal out in the storm.

Jamie got the feet and Wiik the head, and then they hauled Blockhead back towards the shelter of the platform.

Vogel pulled the door open, and then closed it behind them, ordering them to hold on before they put him down.

Jamie stared at Wiik and he stared back, both of them sodden to the bone, carrying a dead body between them. The sort of thing that would usually get someone arrested.

'Here,' Vogel said, having grabbed a fire blanket from an emergency cabinet next to the outer hatch.

She laid it on the ground between them, and they set Blockhead down.

Jamie peeled her haze from the guy's vacant, dead eyes, and started patting him down. They couldn't keep calling him Blockhead; he had to have a name.

Her hand moved over a bulge in his chest pocket and she reached in, pulling out a wallet. She fumbled it open, her fingers numb from the cold, and tried to repress a shiver that erupted through her spine. 'Okay,' she said, teeth chattering as she pulled free his driver's licence. 'His name is Shane ...' but she trailed off, her eyes focusing on what was behind the licence she was holding up.

'Shane ...?' Wiik asked, folding his arms to stop himself shaking. 'Does he have a last name?'

Jamie lowered the wallet. 'Shit,' she said.

'Shane Shit?' Wiik knelt in front of her now, trying to catch her eye. 'Jamie? What is it?'

Jamie swallowed and threw back the hem of the blazer she'd fished in for his wallet. 'Shit,' she said, 'whoever killed him took his gun.'

The fabric slapped limply onto the floor, revealing Shane Reid's empty holster.

Jamie and Wiik both stared down at it.

Vogel came up at their side and joined the silence. 'So that means ...' she said, her voice quiet and strained, 'that whoever killed him ...' She swallowed. ' ... Is now running around this place with a gun?'

Jamie stood up, smiling at Vogel. 'Not necessarily,' she said, aiming for positivity but no doubt falling short. 'He could have taken it out of the holster before he went to the meeting.'

'Do you really believe that?' Vogel asked, measuring her stare.

Jamie thought about her answer for a few seconds. 'No, I don't,' she said, looking down.

'So, what are you going to do?'

Wiik stood up now and ran his hand over his head, slicking his hair against his scalp. 'We're going to come up with a plan to get our weapons back off Wallace.'

'And if you can't?' Vogel looked, sounding genuinely terrified.

'If we can't ...' Jamie interjected, finally facing the reality of the situation. 'Then everyone on board this thing is as good as dead already.'

29

'WE HAVE TO REPORT THIS—'

'No!' Jamie and Wiik both yelled in unison, their eyes snapping up to the frightened woman in front of them. Vogel wasn't the sort of person Jamie would describe as easily rattled, but she looked nothing short of coming apart at the seams. The same way that Jamie felt.

She swallowed, took a quick breath, and then looked back down at Shane Reid – aka Blockhead. 'We need to move the body,' Jamie said, stuffing down all the emotion that was bouncing around inside of her. Fear. Anger. Angst.

'To the med bay,' Vogel said with a little bit of confidence, as though her faith had been restored in the two detectives standing in front of her.

Wiik eyed Jamie.

'No,' Jamie said, meeting Wiik's eye. 'Downstairs.'

He set his jaw and nodded.

'Downstairs?' Vogel sounded incredulous. 'What do you mean downstairs? Downstairs where?'

'To the unused crew quarters,' Jamie answered, already

throwing the corners of the fire blanket over Reid's scraped face and motioning Wiik to pick up his end.

'What? Why?' Vogel came forwards now, reached out as though she was going to grab the blanket from Jamie, but then remembered what was under it and stopped.

Jamie didn't know how to say, *Well, it's already where we're holding one of the crew prisoner, so it makes the most sense.* So instead, she said, 'We need time to work out what we're going to do next – and I don't want anyone knowing that we found his body. Yet, at least.' She forced it out, hefting Reid into the air and beginning the walk towards the stairs, leaving a trail of water droplets behind them.

Vogel started following them. 'Why not? Why aren't we taking him to the med bay? Why aren't we telling Ehrling? Wallace? People need to know—'

'No one needs to know *anything,*' Jamie said coldly, turning to look at Vogel, Reid's body halfway through the stairwell door.

Vogel stopped a few steps short.

'You need to come with us now,' Jamie said.

Vogel stood firm. 'I'm not going anywhere.'

Wiik grunted at the awkward load to hurry Jamie up.

She shifted her weight, hands already aching from holding Reid aloft. 'Do you trust us?' she asked Vogel.

She didn't answer.

'Okay – do you trust anyone else on this thing *more* than us right now?'

'While you're trying to hide a dead body?' She swallowed, voice shaking.

'Look, Vogel – we're all scared, okay? There are people dropping left and right here.' Her voice was beginning to show strain under the dead weight of Reid's body. 'But right now, we need you on side. We can't do this without you.'

'Can't do what without me?'

'Stop whoever is doing this.'

Vogel just hovered, trying to assess the situation.

'Come or don't,' Jamie said, motioning Wiik onwards. 'But remember, you were the one who called us because you were too scared to go walking around this place alone. So you decide. But don't take too long.'

With that, Jamie hustled through the door, and it swung shut behind her on a spring, banging loudly as they started wrestling Reid around the first corner.

Wiik looked up at her, descending backwards carefully. 'You think she'll bite?' he asked.

Jamie stole a quick glance up at the door disappearing above her. 'Don't know,' she said. 'If she doesn't and she goes running back to Wallace and Ehrling, I think we're in trouble.'

'Let's hope she chooses the right side then,' Wiik said, almost tripping.

'Yeah,' Jamie said. 'I just hope that's still us.'

They got another floor down before a door opened above and heels started clanging on the metal stairs.

Vogel appeared above them, breathing hard. 'Okay,' she said, hanging over the rail. 'I've decided.'

Jamie and Wiik paused, staring upwards.

'And what have you decided?' Wiik asked.

'I've decided that I don't want to die – and that you two are probably my best chance at making that happen.'

'Great,' Wiik said. 'Then would you mind getting the door?' He dipped his head over his shoulder. 'Because we've sort of got our hands full here.'

. . .

Jamie and Wiik carried Shane Reid through the door and into one of the empty rooms, dropping his body onto the bunk.

His arm flopped limply out of the blanket and off the side. Neither Jamie nor Wiik rushed to pick it back up.

'What do we do now?' Vogel asked, closing the door behind them.

Wiik and Jamie looked at each other. She knew they had to check on Møller before anything else. He was two doors down, and they definitely didn't want him to alert Vogel to his presence. If they'd only just got her on side, then they couldn't jeopardise that. Jamie wasn't totally sure they could trust her either, but she didn't think that it had been Vogel who had chased her through maintenance and taken a swipe at her. Hell, she'd kicked that person in the back, and though Vogel had some fight in her, Jamie's foot had bounced right off.

So while she wasn't about to throw her lot in with anyone on the crew, Vogel seemed like the least likely culprit, and that's all they had to go on right now.

Jamie tilted her head towards the door and Wiik read her mind.

'I'll be back in a second,' he said hurriedly, going for the door.

'Where's he—?' Vogel started.

'He'll be right back,' Jamie cut her off, grabbing her attention. 'Do you have a way of getting in touch with the command deck?'

'Uh, yeah,' she said, shaking her head and reaching to her belt. She pulled the two-way radio hooked there free and held it up. 'Direct line. Only way out here, really.'

Jamie nodded. 'Good. We're going to need it.'

'Jamie!' Wiik's voice echoed from the corridor and Jamie was already through the door before he'd finished her name.

He was standing in the open doorway to the room they'd put Møller in.

She knew what it was before she got there.

The room was empty, a broken cable tie lying next to the chair.

'Shit,' Jamie muttered, heading inside. She knelt and picked the tie off the floor, inspecting it. She held it up to Wiik. 'Cut, not snapped.'

He backed out of the door and went down the corridor.

Vogel was in the doorway, then. 'Do I even want to know?'

Jamie lowered the cable tie. 'We were questioning one of the crew,' she said.

'With cable ties?'

Wiik appeared at her shoulder then, a little out of breath, and Jamie was glad she didn't have to answer Vogel's question. He held up Møller's knife, having retrieved it from wherever he hid it earlier. Vogel flinched away from it.

'Jesus! What's that?' she said, shrinking into the room to give Wiik space. In any other situation, you could have mistaken him for a knife-wielding killer himself. Dishevelled hair, wide eyes, soaked clothing. He looked like he'd just crawled out of a Stanley Kubrick film.

'That,' Jamie said, standing up, 'is Orn Møller's knife.'

'Møller?' Vogel looked from Jamie to Wiik and back. 'What the hell is he doing with a knife like that?'

Jamie put her hands on her hips. 'Best-case scenario? Protection. Worst case ...'

Vogel swallowed. 'Why the hell would anyone bring a knife like that on board?'

'Møller told us himself that tensions can run high out here. Maybe he felt like he needed it.'

Vogel shook her head in shock. 'And you caught him with it?'

Jamie nodded. 'Yeah, and then he tried to run. We walked into his room. He was cleaning up in the bathroom, his face a mess. Looked like he'd been beaten up.'

'By who?'

'I don't know,' Jamie said. 'But just before that, Reid – Wallace's man – the one lying next door – had come up to the command deck with some fresh bruises on his face. And Møller's didn't look too old.'

Vogel's eyes turned towards the wall that separated them from Shane Reid's body. 'You think Wallace set his man on Møller, and then Møller broke free down here and went after him?'

Jamie looked at Wiik again. 'It's a theory, but he didn't do it alone.' She held up the cable tie once more. 'Someone found him and cut him loose.'

'Kurek,' Wiik offered, only half-inflecting it as a question.

Jamie drew a slow breath. 'Maybe. He's still on the loose. And if we were right about the feud ...'

'Feud? What feud?' Vogel asked, trying to get her head around it all.

'Rosenberg told us that the drillers see it as an us-and-them thing. You used that phrase, too. And it looks like there was some friction between Reyes and Kurek, Reyes and Boykov, Reyes and Møller, Reyes and ...'

'Me?' Vogel said, a little bitterness in her voice.

Jamie cleared her throat. 'And when Heikkinen arrived, it may have sparked something. Our working assumption right now is that Kurek, Boykov, Møller, whoever, changed out the seal, with the hopes that it was going to blow up in Reyes' face. But then, Heikkinen got involved, put a stop to that –

but she not only saved Reyes' life, but also put blame on someone. If she hadn't reported it, the seal bursting could have been chalked up to an accident, or to improper inspection – but not to actual *murder.*'

'And you think that sparked, what, a war between the engineers and drillers?'

Jamie met her eye. 'We don't know. But Reyes' death was a statement. If something was brewing after the incident with the seal, stringing Reyes up like that could have been a message to tell Quinn and his buddies to back off.'

Vogel snorted. 'I can tell you now, Quinn's not exactly the type to back away from a fight.'

'No, I kind of got that,' Jamie said. 'But right now, he's down one friend, and he's lying in a bed with knife wounds to his gut. So whether he's the type to hold a grudge or not, we have nothing tying him to any of the attacks. But what we do have is motive for both Boykov and Kurek for killing Reyes. And now, if it *was* Reid who gave Møller that black eye, we have motive for Møller to have sought revenge.'

'But what about Boykov? Who would want to kill him?' Vogel looked from Jamie to Wiik and back.

'We were hoping you could tell us,' Wiik said then.

'I don't know,' Vogel answered, shrugging and shaking her head. She looked like she was about to break down. 'I don't know why anyone would want to kill *anyone* out here! It's ridiculous! We're all trapped on this thing together, there's nowhere to run. It's crazy!'

'It is,' Jamie said. 'And I don't think that's helping things. Whoever's doing this, whatever the reason, being trapped in here is making things worse. You can't run. You can't go outside. There's no hope of escape. And everyone knows who you are – so you think they'll point the finger, you think you'll get caught. So you need to silence this person, silence that one …' She steeled herself, facing the reality of things. 'Reyes could have been the only intended kill – whether it was calculated or not – but now, things are spiralling. And everyone's on edge. No one wants to die, and everyone knows there's a killer aboard. Maybe more than one. Rosenberg's barricaded himself in his room, Ehrling's probably not left the command deck in two days, Kravets and Lebedenkov have closed ranks around Quinn, and the girls … Sevier and Hooper …'

'Where are they?'

Jamie swallowed. 'We don't know. Hiding … we hope. If they're not …'

'Jesus …' Vogel mumbled, holding her hands over her eyes, squeezing at them with the heels of her hands. 'So what, Møller's on a rampage now, too, and he and Kurek are going on a killing spree?'

Jamie needed to keep a lid on this before it escalated. 'We have no reason to think that.'

'Bullshit!' Vogel snapped. 'You just gave me a hundred reasons why you think that *is* the case! What good are you if you can't keep anyone safe?'

'You're safe, aren't you?' Jamie asked, trying her best not to lose her head. 'Look, we weren't brought here to help. To protect anyone. To solve this. We were brought here so Bolstad had a leg to stand on if anyone found out about this whole thing. They twisted the SPA's arm into getting us out here to make it *look* like this investigation was all above board. When in reality, they sent their own man in to fix things. To *actually* deal with the problem.'

'Wallace …' Vogel said, everything clicking for her.

'Exactly. What, you didn't think it was a little weird that in the midst of a crisis they send in a *corporate risk assessor?*

With two armed bodyguards? Who *immediately* stripped us of our firearms?'

Vogel paled a little.

'Except things aren't going so well for him and his body-guards. Ex-military or not, they've bitten off more than they can chew here, and any attempts they've made to make sure this goes away quietly have backfired spectacularly. Case in point – Shane Reid lying *dead* next door.'

'So what do you propose to do? Bury your heads in the sand?' Vogel asked, on the verge of laughing and bursting into tears at the same time.

'If we had any sense,' Jamie said. 'But that's not how the job works. Whether we were brought here for show or not, people are dying, and where we come from, that's not some-thing you just let slide.'

Wiik folded his arms and nodded affirmatively.

'But we can't do it alone.'

'And I guess this is the part where you ask me to do something to risk my life?' Vogel near enough sneered.

'Not at all,' Jamie said. 'We just need you to distract Wallace long enough for us to sneak into his quarters and find our weapons.'

She scoffed, laughing, not believing what she was hear-ing. 'Oh, is that all? And how the hell am I supposed to do that?'

'Well, for one, you could call up to the command deck and tell them you just found Shane Reid stabbed to death. That should get them down here pretty quickly.'

Her smile faded. 'You're serious?'

Jamie nodded. 'Yeah, we are. If Wallace's guys were all that was standing between this place and total chaos, the body in the next room is proof that's not enough anymore. So unless you want to bear witness to what comes next if we *don't* do something, you're going to make that call.'

Vogel quietened, weighing it up. 'So I just call the command deck and say I stumbled across the body?'

'Maybe with a little more conviction, but that's about the sum of it, yeah.'

Vogel let out a long breath. 'How are you even going to get up to the command deck?'

Wiik interjected now. 'You've got a key card, right?'

Vogel's nostrils flared. 'They'll know I helped you.'

Jamie read the trepidation in her. 'You'll be fine.'

But she didn't look so sure. And Jamie didn't know she could blame her. She wouldn't want to be locked in a room with Wallace, lying about what happened to one of his body-guards. But they needed her to do this.

'Wiik will stay with you,' Jamie said then.

'He will?' Vogel asked, looking at him and then back at Jamie.

'I will?' Wiik asked, as surprised as Vogel.

'Yeah,' Jamie said, forcing herself to smile. 'Make the call, get Wallace down here. Wiik'll be with you the whole time, just to make sure.'

'And you're going to go up to the command deck alone?'

Jamie nodded. 'I am.'

'And how are you going to get into Wallace's quarters?'

'Ehrling.'

'Ehrling doesn't have access,' Vogel said, shaking her head.

'No – he said he doesn't have an access *card*,' Jamie corrected her. 'But he'll be able to get me in there.'

'And if he can't?' Vogel asked, raising her eyebrows.

Jamie tried not to smirk. 'Then I'll make the most of the few minutes I have alone with him anyway.'

30

'OKAY,' Jamie said, 'make the call.'

Vogel let out a shaky breath and then held down the call button on her two-way. 'Command deck, come in. Ehrling? Are you there?'

Jamie nodded for her to go on, trying to smile reassuringly.

The radio crackled for a second, and then Tim Ehrling came over the airways. 'Vogel, are you alright? Where are you?'

'I'm fine – it's just …' Vogel stared at Jamie for a second, fingers flexing around the radio.

She resisted the urge to snatch it from her hand. Come on. Hold it together. Please.

'It's just,' she went on, closing her eyes. 'I've found another body.'

'What? Did you say another body? Whose? Who is it?' Ehrling sounded near frantic, the fear audible in his voice.

'Is Wallace up there with you?'

'Wallace?'

'Yeah, I need to speak to him.'

'He's …' Ehrling's voice drifted further from the radio. 'I think he's here. What's wrong?'

'Damn it, Ehrling!' Vogel nearly yelled. 'Just get him on the damn radio! He's going to want to hear this.'

There was silence for a nearly half a minute, and then another voice came over the radio. 'Ms Vogel,' Wallace said evenly. 'What is it?'

'I think you need to see this,' Vogel replied, egged on by both Jamie and Wiik. 'One of your guards – I've found him.'

'Reid?' Wallace asked quickly. 'Where is he? Is he …?'

'Dead,' Vogel finished. 'Stabbed, I think.'

More silence on the line, then, 'Okay. Stay there. Where are you? I'm coming down.'

'Lower crew quarters,' Vogel replied, barely holding her voice. 'Level one.'

A brief pause. 'I'll be there shortly. Don't move.'

Vogel lowered the radio, shaking.

'You did great,' Jamie said, reaching out and touching her shoulder.

Vogel shrugged it off. 'Just … just make sure you get your weapons,' she said, her voice quiet. 'Because once they realise what we did …'

'It'll be fine,' Jamie said, as firmly as she could. 'Trust me.'

'I am,' Vogel replied, meeting her eye. 'With my life.'

Jamie tried to shake that line off, but just couldn't.

There was a direct stairwell that led from the command deck down to the lower crew quarters, and it was no doubt the one that Wallace would take.

Wiik was standing half through the doorway to it, looking upwards.

Jamie watched him, still, like a statue, her heart beating quiet and fast. And then suddenly he was nodding to her.

Wallace was on the stairs and coming down.

Jamie circled towards the stairwell at the other end of the corridor and started climbing. She'd dried off for the most part now, but her clothes were still damp, and she could feel a nervous sweat clinging to her ribs, the edges of the key card to the command deck pressing into her palm.

When she reached the upper crew quarters, she paused and opened the door, checking the corridor was empty before proceeding. They'd only get one shot at this.

Jamie's fingers began tingling as she headed upwards again, towards the door they'd first used to access the command deck from the helideck.

She reached the electronically locked door and paused, trying to collect herself.

But her heart wouldn't slow, the knot in her stomach not loosening.

She lifted the card and swiped it through the reader quickly, watching as the light turned green and the magnetic lock unfastened itself.

Then she was inside and coming up the stairs.

The noise of the storm still roared outside and the first thing she saw was the full panoramic window being blasted by rain. It looked like the whole thing was going through a car wash.

The clouds outside were mottled and dark, rage-filled and primordial.

Her head turned and she homed in on her target then.

Tim Ehrling.

He was at his desk, fingers hovering above his keyboard, a look of confusion on his face. But not immediately fear.

That came after.

'Inspector Johansson,' he said, his voice wavering just a little. 'What are you doing here? Is Vogel with you?'

Jamie didn't reply, she just walked towards him.

'Wallace?' he asked, the hope in his voice audible then.

She offered him a slow shake of the head, now at his desk.

'Oh,' he said, staring up at her.

'Just you and me, Ehrling.' The nerves had dispelled now, her voice even and firm.

Ehrling swallowed and pushed back from the desk and to the side, but Jamie took another step. She wasn't going to let him out of arm's reach.

He eyed the two-way radio on his desk furtively, his brow already beading with sweat.

'Try it and I break your arm.'

Ehrling stiffened. 'What do you want?' he squeezed out.

'Open Wallace's quarters.'

He shook his head. 'I don't have the key card.'

'I don't care,' Jamie said. 'Open it.'

'I can't,' he pleaded. 'I don't have the card—'

She didn't waste any more time. Ehrling had a few inches on her, but he was slight – and Jamie was strong. And about as pissed off as she'd ever been.

She took hold of his collar before he could react and hauled him out of the chair, throwing her hip into his groin and tossing him over it.

His weight shifted before he could react and he toppled forwards, spinning and landing on his side on the ground. He grunted as he bounced and swore in shock, propping himself up on his elbow to catch his breath.

Jamie came forwards again, hooked the toe of her boot around his arm and kicked it out from under him.

He collapsed, grunting again, and rolled onto his back, staring at the ceiling, panting.

'I'm not fucking around here, Ehrling,' Jamie growled, standing over him.

'Please, I don't have the access!' he wailed, no doubt in the hope someone would hear him, throwing his hands in front of his face for protection.

'You want to rethink that,' Jamie said, meeting his eyes through his splayed fingers. 'Because if you can't get me in there, then this situation is about to take on a whole new dynamic.'

Ehrling stared up, his eyes trying to make sense of that.

Jamie knelt, took one of his hands out of the air by his middle two fingers and twisted, bending them backwards so his elbow folded awkwardly next to his head.

He yelped, his mouth flapping wordlessly, bottom lip quivering.

'Glad I've got your attention,' Jamie growled. 'Now, I'm a little short on time, so you've got two options here. You unlock Wallace's room, and I spend the few precious minutes I have in there, looking for what's mine. Or you don't, and I spend those few minutes out here, with you, finding out everything you know.' She bent his fingers back quickly, the tendons straining, and he mewled a little more. 'One finger at a time.'

'You're – you're a police officer!' he howled, bordering on whimpering.

Jamie guessed she knew which Ehrling was the real one now. And he was lying in front of her, about to burst into tears.

But she couldn't let up, as painful as it was. For both of them. She wedged down the pity rising inside her and leant in closer. 'I don't see a fucking badge, do you?'

He met her eye then and silence fell between them.

'Don't fuck with me,' Jamie whispered, tweaking his fingers again. 'You can't stall your way out of this. Wallace's not coming to save you. So make up your mind. You have until I reach three, and then I start breaking things.'

He kept her gaze, his eyes shining.

'One.' Another tweak.

Ehrling squealed.

'Two.' Jamie tightened her grip, knowing they were about to snap.

His face screwed itself into a mess of wrinkles. 'Okay! Okay!' he whimpered. 'I can get you in!'

She released her grip and pulled him to a seated position. 'Good answer.' She lifted her watch then for him to see. 'You've got sixty seconds. Then we start the whole process over.'

He nodded quickly and scrambled to his feet, massaging his wrist and hand as he went back to his desk.

Jamie followed him, snatching the radio from the surface before he got anywhere near it. 'I'll hold onto this,' she said, clipping it on her belt.

He looked at her for a moment, then nodded weakly and began typing. 'I'll need to open a command window, access the override settings via the admin—'

'I don't care how you do it,' Jamie said. 'Just get it done.' She stood at his shoulder, arms folded, watching the second hand on her clock tick around.

Ehrling typed. At a painful pace.

'Hurry up,' Jamie ordered.

'I'm going as fast as I can,' he said, squinting at the screen. 'This isn't exactly a simple process.'

She held her watch in front of his face. 'Thirty seconds,' she said.

'That's not helping!'

'Twenty-five.'

'Don't rush me!'

'Go faster or you'll be doing it with one hand.'

'I couldn't do it with one hand!'

'This isn't a fucking game!' Jamie's fist smashed into the desk next to his keyboard and everything on top of it hopped an inch in the air.

Ehrling paused and looked at Jamie. She was next to him, face no more than six inches from his own. He read the fury in her eyes.

'People are *dying,*' Jamie said then. 'I don't know why, but there's a killer on board, and at this rate, no one is going to get out alive. One of Wallace's bodyguards is dead. And I have no doubt that the other one is going to be in the cross hairs very, *very* soon. And once he's gone, too, what *hope* do you have of making it off this thing alive? We are *all* you have. So I suggest you start helping me, Ehrling, because when the dust settles, we might just be the only ones left standing.'

He drew a slow breath, turned back towards his screen, and pressed the enter key. 'You're in,' he said slowly.

The door behind Jamie buzzed and then opened, revealing Wallace's stately room.

Jamie didn't say another word before pulling her throbbing hand from the desk and heading into it.

'And Inspector Johansson?' Ehrling called from behind her.

She slowed, looking back.

'For what it's worth, I'm sorry.' He offered her a weak, apologetic smile.

She didn't return it. 'We're way past that,' she said instead, 'but do what I tell you, and you might survive this.'

He nodded gravely. 'Okay.'

'Now stay there, and if you really want to help,' she said, 'let me know if you see Wallace coming up the stairs.'

He smiled again and confirmed that he would. But Jamie didn't trust him.

The only one she trusted was Wiik.

And right now, he might as well have been a million miles away.

Jamie tried not to think about that as she stepped into the lion's den. Or about how the lion could come back at any moment. And if it did, how it would react to find her rummaging through its underwear drawer.

She exhaled, blocked out all the ways Wallace could kill her and make it look like an accident, and then got to work.

31

Jamie stood in the middle of the room and took stock of everything.

She had Ehrling's radio on her belt and glanced back every few seconds to make sure he hadn't bolted. She thought if he did, she'd catch him before he got to the bottom of the stairs and put his head into the wall.

It was probably one of the most violent thoughts she'd ever had. But right now, there was more at stake than her moral compass.

Jamie exhaled and moved left, towards the room that housed the bunk beds. Wallace's guards' quarters.

She pushed the door open, working quickly.

There were two single beds, each with a locker at the foot of it. Otherwise, the room was practically bare, save for a tiny wet room and toilet accessible through a narrow door between the beds.

She knelt at the first locker and opened it, seeing a few pairs of neatly folded white socks and underpants, a few white T-shirts. A toiletries bag. It reeked of military discipline. Everything was perfectly laid out and organised. But there was nothing of note in there.

She closed the locker and moved to the other, finding nearly exactly the same thing.

There was no way to even tell whose was whose.

Jamie got up, running her eyes over the hooks on the walls and the spare suits hanging there. Two of them. She guessed one for each of his guards.

She'd find nothing else here, and headed back into the main room, cursing herself for having wasted that time.

She glanced out and saw Ehrling still in his chair, fingers around the back of it, watching her carefully. She didn't know if he was too afraid to try and make a move, or if he was just waiting for her to fumble through the tripwire and get caught out by a swinging log or spring-loaded arm covered with spikes.

She shook off his gaze and carried on. She needed to focus.

Right. Work the room. One side to the other.

She began on the left, near the bed. Jamie checked the bedside drawers, finding only spare underwear and socks. She grimaced, trying not to picture Wallace in his briefs, and homed in on the bookcase instead. Nothing. Under the bed. Empty.

The ottoman at the foot of the bed. Empty as well.

Shit.

She moved on, towards the dining area. There was a desk there.

Wallace's laptop sat on top and she flicked it open, just in case. Password locked. Of course. And she wasn't about to steal it.

Taking back her own gun was one thing. Taking Wallace's laptop was another. She had no hope of cracking it, and what did she expect to find anyway? A written report detailing all the ways he had his fingers rammed into this case? Unlikely.

She moved on, aiming for the drawers.

She cleared the left side, then started on the right. The top was empty save for a notepad and a few pens.

The second drawer down, however, was double-depth, and locked.

Jamie jiggled the handle, but it wouldn't budge.

'Fuck,' she muttered, getting the feeling then that this was *exactly* the thing she was looking for. 'Ehrling,' she said, turning to him and calling through the open door.

He lifted his head a little, still watching. 'Yeah?'

'Can you open this?'

He licked his lips nervously. 'I don't have a key,' he said.

'There isn't one lying around somewhere?' she asked hopefully, knowing that there would be no reason for one to be.

He shook his head.

Jamie hung hers, staring at the locked drawer.

No, it wouldn't stand in her way.

She got up and strode right out towards Ehrling.

He held his hands up, eyes widening. 'I don't have a key, I swear!' he began to yell.

'Shut up,' Jamie muttered, walking right past him. 'I'm not going to hit you again.'

She began rummaging around on the desk, moving and lifting papers and opening drawers.

'What are you looking for?' Ehrling dared to ask, not daring to leave his seat.

'Ah,' Jamie said, finding a box of paperclips and taking one out. She looked at Ehrling again then. 'Do you have a screwdriver?'

'A screwdriver?' he asked, surprised, a little scared maybe.

'I'm not going to stick it in you.' She resisted the urge to roll her eyes.

'Uh, yeah – try that drawer,' he said, pointing to Vogel's side of the desk.

Jamie was in it a moment later, and was then walking back towards Wallace's desk, hoping to hell that Vogel and Wiik were keeping him entertained.

'What are you going to do?' Ehrling called after her.

She sank to a knee in front of it, stuck the narrow flat-head into the barrel lock on the drawer, and applied torsional pressure.

The straightened paperclip went in next, and she raked it back and forth, trying to get the tumblers to align.

Her hands were shaking, and she could feel sweat beading on the nape of her neck and on her fingers, making the tiny rod of metal slippery.

She blinked quickly, trying to focus, unsure if the distant rumbling she could hear was the thunder outside or her own heart.

'Do you know what you're doing?' Ehrling asked, at her shoulder.

She jumped a little, looked up at him, then went back to raking. 'Yes,' she lied. She did know the fundamentals of *how* to do it. But had she ever actually tried to pick a lock before? No.

'You're going too fast,' Ehrling offered.

Jamie gritted her teeth but didn't reply.

'No, not like that.'

She ignored him.

'Did you bend the paperclip correctly?'

She pulled it out, sighed hard, and turned on him. 'You want to fucking do this?'

He recoiled, then seemed to regain himself a little. 'Not really, but I'd rather get it done and get out of here before Wallace comes back. Because if he comes up those stairs' – Ehrling turned and pointed back into the command deck – 'and we're in here, then he's going to—'

'Jesus!' Jamie said, standing up and shoving the screwdriver and paperclip into his hands. 'There! Fuck, just shut up already.'

She moved out of the way and buried her head in her hands, wondering, once again, how the hell she managed to get herself into these messes.

Jamie didn't know if Ehrling knew what he was doing either or if he was playing her, but she was getting nowhere fast with it and she couldn't think with him breathing down her neck.

Behind her, Ehrling set about trying to pick the lock himself then. She couldn't tell if he was *really* trying to or just doing it for show.

But with both of them in there, Wallace could easily come back up and catch them in the act. And Ehrling was right; she doubted he'd take it well. And with his one remaining guard still armed, and the other now dead, he wouldn't be taking any more chances.

Jamie stepped back onto the command deck and stared into the darkening sky. It was now early evening, and she'd been up since four. Jesus, it had been a long day. Her eyes were heavy now, her back aching, brain fuzzy.

The slashing of the rain against the glass was hypnotic and the thoughts of the case and the culprits all whirled around her head in a blur.

Jamie swayed slowly on her feet and closed her eyes,

hovering behind Ehrling's empty chair, in front of the feed from the camera outside the command deck door.

She breathed slowly, trying to assess their next move. What they were going to do if they couldn't get that drawer open. What they would do if they couldn't get their weapons. How they'd handle things. How they'd catch the killer.

How they'd survive.

Ehrling yelped behind Jamie, and she opened her eyes, turned, and watched him shaking his hand out in pain and then suck his finger. She guessed he'd stabbed himself.

Saved her the trouble.

She shook her head, laughing at the inanity of it, and turned back to the screen, doing a double take this time.

Her eyes swam back into focus, her body stiffening all at once.

'Shit,' she breathed, watching the shapes of Wallace and his one remaining heavy climbing the stairs towards the door.

Her brain stuttered, faltered, and then kicked into life, the tiredness she'd felt moments ago thoroughly dispelled by a fresh dump of adrenaline. Jamie's head swivelled, her eyes searching for an answer, and then fell upon it.

She rushed towards the words *For Emergencies Only*, and then aimed for Ehrling.

'Move!' she called, watching as he turned to see her running at him, fire axe raised and ready to strike.

His eyes widened, and he hurled himself backwards, away from the mangled paperclip jammed into the lock, just avoiding the blade that Jamie wasted no time in swinging.

It swept through the air on a near-horizontal arc, hitting the lock barrel with such force that it sent it flying straight through the wood and into the drawer itself.

Jamie planted her foot on the desk and ripped the axe free, leaving a deep and angry gash behind.

'Hold this,' she said, tossing the axe in Ehrling's general direction and wrenching the desk drawer open.

For a split second, she thought their weapons weren't in there, but then she saw the three letters she'd never been so happy to see. *SIG* was embossed across the top of the gun case staring up at her. She snatched it up, along with the one underneath.

At the bottom of the stairs, the door droned its opening note, the magnetic bolt retracting as Wallace swiped himself through.

'Come on,' Jamie hissed, grabbing hold of the handle of the axe and pulling Ehrling to his feet.

He clung onto it, following Jamie like a weaving caravan, and they ran back onto the command deck, heading for the opposite door.

Footsteps echoed.

Jamie didn't know if they were hers and Ehrling's or Wallace's.

Heels on steps.

Heavy breaths.

Jamie slowed, slinging Ehrling around her and down the staircase first by the axe. With Wallace in such close proximity, she didn't want Ehrling suddenly growing a pair of testicles. Especially not with him behind her with a weapon in his hands.

Ehrling stumbled and then started pounding downwards of his own volition. Crossing Wallace had obviously lit a fire under him, and now he wanted to be very far away from the guy.

She watched him reach the stairs below her and fumble his key card from his pocket, juggling the axe as he did.

And then a shiver ran down her spine and she looked up.

She was only a few steps down, still in plain view of the room.

And Wallace.

He had just reached the top of the opposite stairs, and was now stopped, meeting Jamie's eye across the space.

His narrowed, the skin around them quivering, and then they darted to the open door to his quarters, the broken desk drawer, and then back to Jamie.

He lifted his chin very slightly, and even from thirty-odd feet away, Jamie could see his nostrils flaring, his grip around the handrail tightening like a noose.

She felt like grinning.

Like screaming, *Fuck you!*

But instead, she cracked the wryest smirk, made sure that Ehrling had the door open below her, and held up the pistol case she was holding in her hand for Wallace to see.

And then she made for the exit as quickly as she could.

32

Jamie chased Ehrling all the way down the stairs to the lower crew quarters, and then past them, down to the storage level Jamie and Wiik had visited earlier that day.

They'd arranged to meet there, anticipating blowback from Wallace in some form. Or at the very least, Jamie didn't want to run into him on the lower crew level with their re-stolen guns in hand if they made it out before he'd finished looking at Reid's body.

Ehrling moved into the dark storage corridor, panting, still clutching the axe, and Jamie shooed him along towards the room they'd first found the seal in, hoping that Wiik and Vogel were already there, and that they'd not succumbed to the wrath of Wallace already.

Jamie tapped Ehrling on the shoulder and motioned him towards the door he'd just passed.

She shouldered it open, gun cases under her arm, and stepped into the darkness.

'Wiik?' Jamie said into the room, squinting around.

There was no reply.

She took another step. 'Wiik? You in here?'

'Johansson?' came the tentative reply, accompanied by approaching footsteps.

'Yeah,' she said, sighing with relief. 'It's me.'

Jamie sensed two shapes in front of her and guessed the other was Vogel. A click rang out somewhere near the smudged outline to her right and the narrow strip light above buzzed angrily, threatening to come to life.

It strobed once, weakly, and then brightened.

Jamie saw Wiik in front of her, grinning.

And then his eyes darted, his face changing.

'Jamie!' he said, his hand flying out. He grabbed her by the shoulder and yanked her past him.

She twisted through the air, trying to find her footing, just catching a glimpse of Wiik rushing forwards, elbow rising behind his head.

Ehrling was standing in the doorway, fire axe in hand.

He didn't have time to react before Wiik's fist connected with his face.

A dull thud rang around the room, the sound of knuckles hitting bone, and then Ehrling was sprawling backwards.

Wiik hooked onto the doorframe to stop himself from toppling over, and Ehrling tripped, slumping backwards against the opposite wall, nose streaming with blood, eyes screwed closed. He groaned, dropping the axe, and clutched his face, tears already running down his cheeks.

'Jesus, Wiik,' Jamie said, pulling herself upright on one of the laden shelving units. 'What did you do?'

Wiik turned back and offered his hand. 'He was coming at you with an axe.'

'No, he wasn't,' Jamie said, batting his hand away.

Vogel stood quietly through the exchange, hovering near the light switch. She looked shaken.

'He was,' Wiik reiterated, walking out into the hall. He

picked the axe up and showed it to Jamie as evidence. 'He was right behind you. With this.'

Jamie shoved one of the gun cases into his free hand and then took the axe out of his other. 'Yes, because I brought him down here.'

Realisation dawned. 'You mean ...'

'Yes,' she said, staring down at Ehrling, hoping to hell Wiik hadn't just broken his nose. 'He ... helped. Sort of.'

Vogel appeared in the doorway, gasping lightly. 'Tim,' she said, pushing between them and kneeling at his side. She pulled his hands from his face, and he sobbed, his nose swollen and crooked.

'Christ, Wiik,' Jamie said, hanging her head. 'You broke his fucking nose.'

'He had an axe!' He nearly yelled, then shook his head and stormed back into the storeroom.

Vogel was watching them – no doubt questioning why the hell she'd thrown her lot in with two people who were at each other's throats.

Jamie gave her a quick nod and then followed Wiik.

'Hey,' she said, coming up behind him.

He was pacing, looking at the floor.

'You okay?'

He stopped and looked up, laughing a little. 'No, Jamie. I'm not okay. I'm pretty fucking far from okay.'

Jamie gave him some space. The urge to say, *Take a breath*, or, *It'll be okay*, was strong. But she didn't usually go out for empty sentiments. And Wiik wasn't the type to need them.

Instead, she said, 'Join the club.'

He met her eye. 'This is such a fucking mess.'

She nodded. 'Yeah, it is. But now at least we've got a

chance at making it out in one piece.' She shook her case a little.

He smirked. 'You made sure they're in there, right?'

Jamie's grip tightened a little. 'Don't say that.'

There was a second of stillness, and then they both held the cases up, cracking them open to make sure their pistols were inside.

They laughed then, just a little. Enough to put a crack in the shell of darkness that had solidified around them.

'You know,' Wiik said, 'I really did think Ehrling was about to hit you with that axe.'

She turned to look at him, still on the floor outside. 'He's okay,' she said. 'Just scared, like the rest of us.'

Wiik made a *hmm* sound. 'I don't trust him.'

'We don't have to,' Jamie said. 'We just need to make him talk.'

Wiik moved closer to her, lowered his voice. 'He's working for Wallace. We can't believe a word he says.'

'I know … But he helped me, upstairs.'

'Willingly?'

She bit her lip. 'I did threaten to break his arm.'

'I thought so.'

'But he's just as scared of Wallace as we are.'

'Exactly,' Wiik scoffed. 'Which is why he'll go running back to him the second he gets the chance.'

Jamie shook her head. 'I don't think so. He's crossed him now – that's it. He must have said three times that Wallace would kill him if he found out that he was helping us. I think he's played his hand now. He's with us.'

Wiik deliberated on that. 'We can't be sure it's not a trick – that he's not going to turn on us.'

'No,' Jamie said, sighing. 'I suppose not. But he's afraid for his life with Wallace, I think.'

'He thought Wallace was going to kill him?' Wiik arched an eyebrow, still keeping his voice low as Vogel attended to Ehrling. It looked like she was getting ready to reset his nose.

'Maybe,' Jamie said. 'He's definitely caused waves since he arrived. If he was sent here to clean this mess up, he's done pretty much the opposite.'

Wiik drew a slow breath. 'Yeah – Reyes was one thing. But now Boykov … Quinn … Wallace's own man. The mess on Møller's face. The missing girls. There's something else going on here that we're not seeing. And I don't think we're going to get to the truth unless we find out what that is.'

'I think you're right.' She turned to look at Ehrling, who'd begun groaning again as Vogel got her thumbs into his cheeks.

'But,' Wiik said, grabbing her arm. 'We need to tread carefully. Whether Wallace is trying to keep Bolstad afloat, or just trying to save his own ass, I don't think he's beyond killing to do it.'

'Or at least ordering his attack dog to do it for him.'

Wiik kept her gaze, his hand still on her arm. 'We need to watch each other's backs.'

Jamie smiled at him in the gloom. 'You can count on me.'

His grip loosened. 'Good. Now let's find out what Ehrling knows before Wallace shows up looking to reclaim what you stole.'

Jamie stared at the ceiling and the ten thousand tonnes of steel looming over them. He was up there somewhere, scheming. She knew that much. 'I don't think he'll come at us. Not now. Not here. He'll do it when we don't expect it. When he's got us off guard.'

'Then we'll sleep with one eye open.'

'With our guns under our pillows.'

Ehrling screamed behind them suddenly as Vogel snapped

his nose back into place. His cries echoed through the store-rooms and then faded to nothing.

When Jamie turned back around, Wiik was looking intensely at her.

'We're going to make it out of this, Jamie,' he said.

'I know.' Jamie nodded.

Wiik smiled at her, and she smiled back.

Though she didn't think either of them believed that wholly.

At least she didn't.

But it still felt good to hear.

And right now, they needed all the courage and hope they could get. False or otherwise.

33

JAMIE AND WIIK both thumbed the last rounds into the magazines, and then slotted them into the grips of their SIG Sauer P226 semi-automatic pistols.

Vogel watched carefully from her position in the corner of the storeroom. Ehrling was sitting on a chair next to her, clutching a wad of toilet paper to his bloodied nose.

They'd moved into the storeroom that contained the canned food and bottled water. Jamie and Wiik both decided that it was the safest place for them. They could barricade the door and keep themselves fed and watered for days if they needed to.

Jamie hoped they wouldn't, but it was a lot better than sending them out to die. Wallace had by now, no doubt, worked out that both Ehrling and Vogel had been complicit in the ruse and burglary. Which either put them in his crosshairs, or at the very least, put them outside his sphere of protection.

So, it was up to Jamie and Wiik to keep them safe. Because they'd asked them to cross the only other person who might have been able to.

As Jamie checked and rechecked her pistol, pushing it

into the back of the waistband of her jeans, she realised they'd positioned themselves on the other side of this. Across the battlefield they could see Wallace, and in the melee, it was nothing but smoke and blood.

But they were about to blow that all away.

Wiik was predictably sour about it.

'Quinn's the only person who's been forthcoming about *anything* so far, Wiik.'

'I don't like him, and I don't like this.' Wiik pulled back on the slide of his pistol, chambering a round, and then let it snap back into place.

'I don't either – but it's the only play we have right now. Quinn was targeted, and he'll want to make sure that Kurek doesn't come back to finish the job. If we can leverage that, and he'll help us find him, then we can take Kurek off the board, and make sure no more blood is spilt.'

Wiik didn't seem to like the logic, but it was sound. Wallace was on the hunt for Kurek, too, and had already lost one man to it. Why on earth Shane Reid was outside in the storm, Jamie didn't know. But if they could put a stop to Kurek before he did any more damage, then they hoped they would render this whole blood feud, as well as Wallace's botched clean-up attempt, moot.

Quinn couldn't be moved, and Jamie doubted that Lebedenkov and Kravets would leave his side while he was vulnerable. So that's where they were headed.

Jamie and Wiik moved quickly and quietly, heading up to the medical bay.

There was really no time to lose.

The door was closed when they arrived and they crossed no one's path.

Everyone who had any sense was hiding.

Jamie banged on the door with the heel of her hand.

There was silence from inside.

'Open up,' Jamie called. 'It's Inspector Johansson.'

Wiik had his hand underneath his jacket, fingers around the grip of his pistol, ready to draw it at a moment's notice.

'We're fine,' came a reply, muted through the door. It was Lebedenkov's heavy Bulgarian accent. 'Go away.'

'No,' Jamie said again, banging harder. 'Open the door. We have some questions.'

She heard low murmurings.

She glanced at Wiik. He tilted his head a little, squaring up in front of the door, hand still on his pistol.

Jamie's couldn't help but creep towards her own, her heart beating harder.

'Okay,' Lebedenkov said then. 'You come in.'

Something shifted from behind the door – a cabinet being dragged or something else designed to prevent anyone from kicking their way in – and then it opened a crack.

Lebedenkov's face appeared in the gap, his eyes distrustful and narrowed. He sized Jamie up, then glanced over at Wiik, who looked suitably mean.

Lebedenkov looked back at Jamie. 'Just you.'

Wiik stepped forwards. 'Not a fucking chance,' he spat.

'Then you don't come in,' Lebedenkov answered, making to close the door again.

Jamie's hand landed against it, keeping it open. 'Wait,' she said. 'Quinn? You in there?'

There was a second of silence. 'Where d'hell else am I gonna be?' he called from behind Lebedenkov, his voice strained. 'Let 'em in, fer fuck's sake,' he added.

Lebedenkov thought on it and then moved, beckoning them quickly into the room.

Jamie and Wiik filed through the gap and kept their backs to the wall as Lebedenkov shut the door and locked it.

He moved towards the rear counter and leaned against it next to Kravets. They both folded their arms and eyeballed Jamie and Wiik.

On the other side of the room was a door that led through to where they'd put Reyes' and Boykov's body. But it was barricaded with a filing cabinet, too.

On the counter at the back of the room, Jamie could see empty paper plates and plastic cutlery.

There were two sleeping bags on the floor.

Bottles of water.

And a heavy-looking wrench leaned in the corner. Along with a three-foot-long steel pipe.

Jamie eyes rested on them for a moment.

It didn't look like they'd left this room since Quinn was attacked – except to get food and supplies. It seemed they were intent on sleeping here when the time came. And defending it to the death, too.

'Inspector Johansson,' Quinn cooed, dragging Jamie's attention away from the weaponry in the corner. 'What a lovely surprise.'

Jamie looked at Quinn, lying on the same reclinable consultation chair that Ehrling had stitched him up on. It could have come straight out of a dentist's office. He looked like shit. His shirt was off, his body covered in bandages. There was a dressing over the stab wound with a dark red spot in the middle of it. The entirety of his ribs were bandaged. She had flashbacks to that morning, to seeing the blood pouring out of him and all over the floor.

She could still see smears of it on the vinyl flooring where it hadn't been fully cleaned up. 'We need your help.'

She heard Wiik expel some air from his nose behind her in mild protest at the words. But he kept his mouth shut all the same.

'Oh,' Quinn said, wincing. 'Aren't I lucky. What can I, uh, help you with, exactly? I'm not really in any fit state for a ride, I'm afraid.'

Wiik moved to step away from the wall, but Jamie put her hand on his wrist and he stopped.

Quinn grinned at that. He hadn't lost his touch when it came to Wiik, that was for sure.

'Much as I'd love to,' Jamie said, 'it's strictly business.'

Quinn nodded for her to go on.

'You know one of Wallace's guards just turned up dead?'

He shook his head. 'I don't get out much these days, as you can see.'

'Lose the jokes, Quinn. This is serious, now.'

He held his hands up. 'Sorry, force of habit.'

'I can tell,' Jamie growled. 'With Wallace's bodyguard down, that makes three bodies – that we can find.' She counted them on her fingers. 'Reyes, Boykov, and now Reid – Wallace's man.'

'No great loss to humanity, I'm sure,' Quinn added, unable to resist.

Jamie did her best to ignore it. 'And it was almost four, including you.'

'How could I forget?'

Jesus, she was getting tired of him. 'And you said Kurek did this to you?'

He nodded.

'Grzegorz Kurek.'

'That's what I said.'

'No, you didn't. You nodded,' Jamie said sharply.

'Same fucking thing,' Quinn replied, his eyes flashing.

Jamie could see he was in pain. But she needed to know.

'And why would he do that?' Jamie asked. 'Come after you. In the middle of the night?'

'The fuck should I know?' Quinn snapped, laying his head back. 'Maybe the fucker's gone sideways in the head.'

'You seemed to have a pretty good idea of why he would have gone after Reyes. Wondering if you had any clue why you'd be in line next.'

'You're saying Kurek killed Reyes?' Quinn feigned surprise.

'Drop the act, Quinn. We know that there's some sort of pissing contest going on here, some kind of feud that's been bubbling away. And we just want to get to the bottom of it.'

'Oh, is that what you know, is it? Then why don't you lay it all out for me? Because I'm lying here with a fucking knife-hole in my guts and no fecking idea why!'

Jamie tried to rein her anger in. Quinn was fucking with her. 'Reyes.' She tried to keep her voice even. 'You said that Kurek had a grudge against him over a card debt.'

'That's right.'

'And Boykov didn't like how Reyes was handling the drill.'

'Right again.'

'And Møller didn't like that Noemi Heikkinen had chosen Reyes over him.'

'Three for three.'

'So all the engineers had an axe to grind with Reyes, right?'

'You catch on quick,' Quinn said, closing his eyes and laying his head back. 'I only told you all that, what, two days ago?'

Jamie tried to keep her composure. 'But none of them could do much, right? Because you and the two Easter Island Heads over there all stick together. Reyes included.'

Lebedenkov and Kravets both shifted from foot to foot.

They knew they'd just been insulted, but didn't seem to know how.

'He was one of us, aye,' Quinn said. 'Did our best to look after him.'

'So, here's what I think,' Jamie started, stepping away from the wall and a little closer to Quinn. 'I think that together, Møller, and Kurek, and Boykov, all hatched a little plan to swap out the main seal on the drill before one of Reyes' shifts for a worn-out one. And the way that Reyes was handling that drill – pushing it like he did ...'

Quinn opened his eyes now and looked at Jamie. 'You think they were hoping it'd blow up in his face?'

Jamie nodded. 'I do. I think that Boykov had made his thoughts on how hard Reyes was pushing that drill well known. And if it happened to blow, then it would only prove Boykov right.'

'So they schemed to get rid of Reyes? Fucking bastards,' he muttered, shaking his head.

Lebedenkov and Kravets both grunted their disapproval in the background.

'Yeah – except, before that happened, Heikkinen reported to Ehrling that the seal was worn out.'

'I remember – really got everyone's back up,' Quinn said. 'We all thought it was just an engineer fuck-up. Them being the lazy pricks they are. Never figured they did it to take out Reyes.'

'That's *why* they did it – it would look like an accident.'

'The perfect crime.' Quinn met her eye again, took a slow breath. 'But then, Heikkinen fucked everything up.'

'Right,' Jamie said. 'And we spoke to her friends – Sevier and Hooper – they said that the day Reyes was killed, Noemi disappeared for a few hours. And when she came back, she was nervous, scared, even. And she needed to see Reyes. Quickly.'

'You think she knew they were gunning for him?' Quinn seemed surprised.

'I don't know. But she knew about the drill seal. So it only makes sense that she knew *why* it had been swapped out, too.'

Quinn thought on that. 'That's why Sevier came to my room,' he said, 'and asked for Reyes to meet her. She was going to tell him to watch his back.'

'Except it was already too late,' Jamie finished. 'They met, but they never made it off the lower submersible platform.'

'Kurek,' Quinn offered. 'Always hated that fucker.' The words dripped with venom. 'Sick bastard – stringing Reyes up like that, no doubt to try and warn us off retaliating.' He cast an eye over his shoulder towards Lebedenkov and Kravets, who both looked like they had the stench of shit up their noses.

'Would you have?' Jamie asked. 'Retaliated?'

Quinn looked at his bare feet, then at his bandaged body. 'No, of course not,' he said.

Jamie didn't buy it for a second. 'What do you think happened to Boykov?' She watched him closely.

'I think Kurek probably fucking killed him, too.'

'Why?' Jamie asked flatly.

'I don't know – probably because he was the only other fucker who knew about the plot to kill Reyes.'

Jamie drew a slow breath, processing. 'You think Kurek killed Boykov to cover his own tracks?'

'Why not? Makes sense, doesn't it?'

Committing murder to prevent someone from naming you

in an attempted murder? 'Sure,' Jamie lied. 'But then why come after you, too?'

'Maybe he had a thirst for it,' Quinn said. 'Guy's fucking crazy. You saw what he did to Reyes. Then to Boykov. Probably to Wallace's man, too.'

Jamie swallowed, looked back at Wiik. He was a statue, eyes fixed on Lebedenkov and Kravets, hands loose at his sides.

'Or maybe,' Jamie said, 'he knew you'd figure it out and come for him. So, he came after you first.'

Quinn stayed quiet then. If his theory about Kurek going after Boykov was right, then it explained the mess on Møller's face too, if Kurek had gone after him as well.

Was that what had happened? Had Kurek gone after Reyes, then killed off Boykov to cover his ass. And then targeted Møller? But how did Shane Reid, Wallace's man, fit into that equation?

And where was Møller now? Hunting Kurek or hiding?

Jamie's head was spinning with it all. But she knew one thing. Quinn was scared. And if they had to spend the next three days in this room until a helicopter came to rescue them, then they were prepared to do it.

But that still didn't help the others out there.

Rosenberg was on his own in his room – and if he knew about the plot to kill off Reyes, then he'd be in the firing line too.

And then there were the girls. Sevier and Hooper, who were still … *somewhere*. And with Kurek and Møller both parading around the platform, knives – and possibly guns – in hand, on the hunt for one another …

Jamie opened her mouth to speak again, but before she could, Wiik was next to her, eyes still fixed on the two men at the back of the room.

'You're damp,' he said. Loudly. Accusatively.

Kravets unfolded his arms and met Wiik's stare.

She could see it now. He had on a pair of jeans and an old sweater. It looked a little rumpled, and just around the collar and hem it looked a little darker. Like Wiik said: damp.

She could see it on his jeans, too, just at the pockets.

'Why are you damp?' Wiik asked then.

Everyone else was silent.

Kravets didn't move.

Jamie could see Wiik's temple vein bulging. 'I asked you a question.'

'I went out for cigarette,' the man grunted.

'Bullshit,' Wiik snapped.

'The truth,' he answered, just as coldly.

Jamie's eyes went to Lebedenkov, whose hands had moved from his chest to the counter behind him. He was holding on to the corner, ready to spring forwards, and Quinn's hands had gone to the sides of the chair as well, ready to push himself free of it.

Everyone was still with anticipation.

Jamie tensed.

'Why are you wet? Why did you go outside?'

'For cigarette,' Kravets answered again.

The temperature in the room seemed to have rocketed suddenly.

Jamie could feel sweat beading under her jaw.

Wiik stepped past Jamie now, so that he had a clear line to Kravets. She watched his fingers flex at his sides, ready to reach into his jacket.

Quinn measured the situation carefully.

Jamie's gaze went to Lebedenkov, searching the counter behind him for anything he could use as a weapon. Then she caught him glancing at the pipe wrench leaning against the wall.

Don't do it. She sucked in a deep breath, pushed into the balls of her feet.

'I'm going to ask you *once* more,' Wiik said. 'Why were you outside?'

Jamie could see it in the man's eyes. He was done answering.

Everything seemed to slow down, like the moment of nothing between the flash of lightning and the crash of thunder.

And then it came, rolling through the room with a furious anger that turned everything on its head.

Kravets rushed forwards, hands raised, eyes wild.

Lebedenkov dived for the pipe wrench in the corner.

Quinn flopped off the chair and onto the floor.

Jamie leapt from Kravets's path and ran down Lebedenkov.

Wiik took the brunt of the charge and was driven back into the wall.

Jamie heard the dull thump behind her, the grunt as the air was expelled from Wiik's lungs.

But she was chasing Lebedenkov.

He was bent over, reaching for the wrench.

She had to act quickly. On blind instinct.

Her knee sailed upwards, and she sent it right into Lebedenkov's ribs, bowling him sideways.

She was on him then, her left hand grabbing his shirt at the nape of the neck, forcing him to stay down, while her right tore the pistol from her jeans and shoved the muzzle behind his ear.

The man froze in her grip – seemingly familiar with the feeling of having a gun pressed against his skin.

His hands opened, and he held them away from the wrench, fingers spread, breathing quickly.

She could feel his pulse under the nose of the gun.

'Wiik,' she said breathlessly, looking around.

All she could see was Kravets's back, his elbows at his sides, his hands at Wiik's throat.

'Wiik!' Jamie called this time, still panting. 'You okay?' She stood straighter, craning her neck to get a better look – to see if Kravets had put his head through the wall or not.

Their faces were inches from one another.

Wiik's eyes were fire. And the barrel of his pistol was jammed up under Kravets's chin.

Quinn was slumped in the corner, hands out, one towards Jamie, the other towards Wiik. 'Woah, woah,' he yelled, wincing. Blood was seeping through his bandages. 'Let's all just calm down a second, yeah?'

Jamie didn't move, just readjusted the gun at Lebedenkov's ear to let him know it was still there.

Wiik and Kravets seemed locked in a death grip.

'Everybody calm down,' Quinn ordered. 'Jesus Christ – we all want to walk out of this, alright? No one needs to die here. Fucking hell! Haven't we got enough problems on this thing?'

'No more lies, Quinn!' Jamie yelled, tightening her grip on Lebedenkov's shirt. 'Why is Kravets damp? Did he kill Reid? Did he?' Her voice was cracking, her heart pounding.

'What? Jesus, no!' Quinn said. 'Fuck – no – why would he want to kill him? Wallace is a fucking prick, but he's here to help us!'

'So why was he outside, Quinn? Talk!'

'He was going for the fucking emergency lifeboat!'

Jamie blinked, taking that in. 'What? What boat?'

'There's a boat,' Quinn said, wincing and clutching his

stomach. 'Hanging off the skene module – it's in case of fire, or … or if there's a fucking murderer running around this place.' He coughed, grimaced, and readjusted himself against the wall. 'Kravets was seeing if it was ready to go – what needed to be done.'

'Bullshit! You'd not make it a hundred metres in this storm,' Jamie said, teeth gritted. She could feel the grip of the gun slick under her palm.

'I know, but the storm won't last forever – first sign of it easing …'

'You were going to make a run for it?'

'Fuck aye, we were! Kurek's already made his plans mighty fucking clear. You think I'm gonna wait around for him to finish the job?'

'We're hundreds of miles from land – you'd die.'

'We'd take our fucking chances!' Quinn yelled again now, resting his head against the wall and sucking in a rattling breath.

'When? When was this?' Jamie asked.

Wiik's eyes shifted from Kravets then and fell upon her, still full of rage. *You're not buying this shit?* She could practically hear his voice.

She didn't know if she was, but if Quinn was lying, then they had no choice but to pull their triggers and let the cards fall where they may.

And she didn't think either of them wanted that. Not really.

'I dunno – hour ago, maybe,' Quinn said. 'He was gone maybe fifteen, twenty minutes.'

Jamie looked at Wiik. He stared back wordlessly, Kravets's hands still at his throat, his pistol still at Kravets's.

'Don't believe me?' Quinn asked. 'Check the security

camera. There's one that covers the whole drill deck. You'll see him out there. Just go up to the command deck and—'

'We can't do that,' Jamie cut in. 'Because the camera was fucking *smashed* before Reid was killed.' She hung her head, shook it, tried to think.

Quinn swallowed, looking scared then. 'Look – I know how this looks – I do – but you gotta trust me, okay? We just want to get off this thing alive. That's all. Okay?'

Jamie was still looking at Wiik.

He shook his head at her.

But she had no choice. Whether this whole confrontation had gone to shit or not, it didn't prove anything. Not enough to kill for.

Jamie filled her lungs, refastened her grip on her pistol, and shoved herself free of Lebedenkov, backing up across the room, sights still trained on him.

He stood slowly, raising his hands.

Kravets caught on then and let go of Wiik, stepping backwards carefully, hands next to his shoulders.

He and Lebedenkov both had their mouths twisted into ugly grimaces, but they weren't dead. And Jamie was glad about that. They had enough bodies to deal with without adding two more.

Kravets drew next to Lebedenkov, and Jamie backed up so she was next to Wiik, both of their weapons still raised.

Quinn breathed a sigh of relief. 'Alright then. I think we could all do with a little breathing room here. How about you lower your guns, and—'

'Not a *fucking* chance,' Wiik snarled.

'Okay, okay,' Quinn said, raising his hands. 'I get it – everyone's a little on edge. Understandable, given the circumstances—'

'Won't you just shut the *fuck* up!' Wiik shouted, pointing his gun at Quinn now.

He fell silent for the first time.

This was getting out of control. She needed to get Wiik out of there. Now. Before he did something stupid.

Jamie's pistol was shaking. But she needed to act. And she didn't think it was in the form of keeping her weapon raised.

She lowered it, pulled her gaze away from Lebedenkov and Kravets, and turned to face Wiik. She stood right in front of him, no more than a foot of space between them.

'Hey,' she whispered, looking up at his grim face.

He didn't meet her eye. Just kept his levelled down the barrel of his gun.

'Anders,' she whispered again.

This time, he looked at her.

She never used his first name.

She smiled. 'Look at me.'

He searched her face.

'Put the gun down. We need to go.'

His jaw tightened.

'Come on,' she said. 'We need to get out of here. We still have work to do.' Jamie reached up now and laced her hand over his right arm, pressing down on his elbow, guiding the gun upwards as his arm crooked. He resisted at first.

And then she felt him give in, and watched as his eyes closed.

He said nothing, but Jamie led him from the room wordlessly, her own hands shaking, her throat tight as they wound deeper into the platform.

34

'WAIT, WAIT,' Wiik said, two floors down.

He slowed to a halt on the landing between floors and leaned against the wall, pressing his hands to his forehead, pistol still tightly in his right.

He sank downwards until he was crouching, and then slumped to a seated position, legs splayed in front of him.

Jamie came back and knelt at his side, her hand tentatively reaching out. She didn't know where to lay it. Shoulder, arm, thigh. Part of her wondered if a punch on the arm would do it.

Wiik opened his eyes then and lowered the gun, looking at her. They were shining in the light. He looked broken. 'Jesus, Jamie,' he said, shaking his head. 'What the fuck are we doing here?'

She didn't have an answer that they both didn't already know.

'You can't believe any of that?' he said, looking back up the stairs. 'Really, you can't – surely?'

Jamie swallowed, then shook her head. 'Not a fucking

word. But what choice did we have? Execute the three of them?'

'And put an end to this.'

'We don't know that. Quinn didn't stab himself. So whether it was deserved or not … That's not our job, Wiik. To shoot people.'

'What is our job, Jamie?' He seemed like he was genuinely asking. 'Because I've never felt less like a detective in my whole life.'

Anything she said now would just feel hollow. So she stayed quiet.

'That crap about a lifeboat? No one would be stupid enough to try and get off this thing in the middle of a hurricane.'

Jamie bit her lip. 'I don't think Quinn's telling the truth about why Kurek is after him – maybe not the truth about Reyes, either. And as for Boykov? I don't know. But what I do know, is that there are still people on this thing who are just getting caught in the crossfire. So whatever war Quinn, Kurek, and Wallace are waging – we need to be outside of it.'

'How can we be?' He stared at her in the half-light of the stairwell.

'By focusing on saving as many as we can.'

That seemed to satisfy him somewhat, but he was far from invigorated, and looked like he just wanted to sit there a moment or two longer. Reflecting, maybe, on how that situation had almost gone. On how they'd almost killed Lebedenkov and Kravets. About whether not doing so was the right call.

It was what Jamie was thinking, at least.

And yet, there was still another question lingering between them.

'Why are you here, Wiik?'

He became still, and then looked at her. 'What do you mean?'

'Why did you take this case?'

'I had to,' he said, refusing to look at her.

'What does Falk have on you?'

'Nothing,' he said quickly, trying to get up.

Jamie put her hand on his shoulder now, no trepidation, and forced him back down.

'Bullshit,' she said. 'I could smell this being a bad idea from a hundred miles – as soon as Falk told me what had happened and how Bolstad wanted to handle it – I knew it was going to be a fuck-up and nothing but trouble.'

'So why did *you* come?' He narrowed his eyes at her now, his tone accusing.

'Because ...' She swallowed. 'Because I wanted to help—'

'Now who's lying.' He sighed then and looked up at the grated catwalk above them. The next landing. 'If you don't want to tell me, that's fine. But don't expect a straight answer from me in return for lying to me, Jamie.' He met her eye then, and she was the one to look away.

'It's not that I want to lie, Wiik.' She exhaled. 'I just don't know if telling you will ...'

'Will what?'

'Put you in danger.'

He laughed then. 'You're kidding, right? Look where we are.'

She cracked a smile then. 'I guess you're right.'

'So what is it? Why are you here? Because Falk had you on the hook before she even looked at me.'

Jamie didn't know if she was more nervous about saying

this or when she had a gun to someone's head. 'It's my father.'

'What about him?'

'He …'

Wiik stared at her intensely, waiting.

'He didn't kill himself, Wiik.'

'What are you talking about, Jamie?' he said dismissively. 'I saw the photos – read the crime scene report.'

'You read the report?' She was surprised. 'When did you — why did you read the report?'

'It was back in January – before I contacted you,' he said, widening his mouth into a respectful half-smile. 'During the Angel Maker case – I checked out the original investigation, found out what had happened, read the report. Saw the photos.'

'You never said.' Jamie found her voice small then.

'I didn't know what to say … "Nice to meet you, I'm sorry your father killed himself"?'

Jamie set her jaw. 'You never said "nice to meet you".'

Wiik sighed.

Jamie never was good at jokes. And they always seemed to come out at the worst times.

'Look, Jamie, if Falk has spun you some story to get you to come out here—'

'No, Wiik, that's not it.' She found her voice then. 'It was Claesson – he came to my house. Told me about the case my father was working at the time.'

Wiik had little respect for Claesson, and his word seemed to mean nothing to him either. 'He wasn't working any cases, Jamie.'

'Yes, he was!' She nearly yelled it. 'That's what I mean, Wiik – it's all been covered up, or—'

'Do you hear what you're saying?'

'Yes, I do. I've been looking into this, and you're right – there were no active cases that he was working on. There's nothing. But Claesson said that he *was* working something – but it wasn't official, or it was need-to-know, or, or … Don't look at me like that.'

'Like what?'

'Like I'm crazy.'

'I know you want to believe that—'

'My father was killed, Wiik! Murdered. Do you get that? Do you understand what I'm saying? He didn't put a gun in his mouth and pull that trigger. He was murdered. Someone came into our house, and they did that. To him. And made it look like he'd done it to himself.'

'And I suppose they fed him two bottles of whisky, too? His blood-alcohol level was through the roof on the toxicology report.'

Jamie's jaw was aching she was clenching it so hard. 'I don't know all the details, alright? And I know how it sounds – but Claesson told me that there were other bodies – that my father asked him to look into, quietly – ones that appeared as suicides, but weren't. Just made to look that way. And my father was the last of them. And Falk knows something about it.'

'What does she know?' Wiik looked at her with a certain amount of scepticism.

'She wouldn't say – but I know Bolstad have something on her – and I know she knew this wasn't going to be a cut-and-dry case. Bolstad are twisting her arm to get us here, playing along.'

'Is that what we're doing? Playing along?'

'You know what I mean.'

'No, I don't, Jamie.'

She took a breath, feeling anger rising in her. 'Bolstad wanted this handled in a certain way – by Wallace. And to make that happen, they needed a police force that would play ball – and that's why they came to Falk. Because they know her – because they've got shit on her. They can twist her arm. And they did – to get her to send two detectives out here to make it all look like it was above board.'

Wiik watched, waiting for her to go on.

'But any detective worth their badge could see that this wasn't kosher. That Bolstad was working an angle here, and whoever came out to see to this thing would end up being complicit in whatever cover-up they were attempting. So, she needed someone whose arm *she* could twist.'

'And that's us?' Wiik raised an eyebrow. 'You think Falk walked us into this buzz-saw intentionally?'

'No – I think Falk thought we'd come out here, we'd look around, Bolstad would sweep up the mess and deal with Reyes' killer, and then deliver their proof that the case had "solved itself" for us to choke down after the fact. Then we'd just go home in the knowledge we'd helped Bolstad keep their heads above water.'

'And what was Falk going to give you for doing that? Because I've only known you a few months, but I can already say with confidence that you'd never let something like that go.'

Jamie didn't know if that was a compliment or an insult. 'A name.'

Wiik scoffed again. 'A name. So you're doing all this for a name?'

'Yes.'

'Whose name?'

'If I knew that, I wouldn't be here.'

'So Falk could give you the name of someone who's been dead twenty years and then *boom,* you're at another roadblock.'

Jamie stood up, not wanting to look at him anymore. 'I don't fucking know, alright? But everyone I talk to knows *nothing* about it. And Claesson doesn't know shit either. Falk is the *only* one who does. Or at least the only one willing to talk about it. So, if I do this for her, she'll owe me.'

'If you do *what* for her, Jamie?'

'Solve this case!'

'Solve it? We'll be lucky to get out alive!'

'Then we do both!' They were screaming at each other then. 'We fucking find out who's doing this, we put them on the fucking ground, cuff their hands behind their backs, read them their goddamn rights, and then we go home!' Jamie raised a finger and pointed at the wall.

'You and I both know that there's no way in hell Wallace is letting the killer walk of this thing alive. Not now, especially. And if you get in the middle of that …'

Jamie paused and looked down at him.

He pulled himself to a stance and pushed his pistol back into his jeans. 'All I'm saying, is that if you have the choice between walking away from this with your head still attached to your shoulders, and *not* getting that name from Falk, or putting yourself at risk just to chase a fucking ghost … Then I know you're not stupid enough to choose the second option.'

'And what if I am, Wiik?' Jamie could feel her eyes burning now.

'Then maybe it was pointless me even coming.'

Jamie was stunned for a second. 'Why did you come?'

'For you, Jamie.'

She read the sincerity in his face. 'What are you talking about?'

'You said Falk leveraged you into coming – dangled a name in front of you ...'

'Yeah.'

'Well, she doesn't have anything on me. No way to bribe or blackmail me. No way to get me to do anything I didn't want to. That's what I thought at least. Until ...'

'Until she told you I was coming ...' Jamie finished the sentence for him. 'Jesus, Wiik, I ... I don't know what to say. I didn't want you to ... You didn't have to ...'

'I did.' He forced a smile. Brief as it was. 'Because that's what partners do, Jamie. And I wasn't going to let you go alone.'

Jamie was taken aback. 'I'm sorry, Wiik – I didn't mean to get you into this.'

'You couldn't have known.' Wiik sighed and ran his hand over his head, pressing his hair against his head. 'But I'm glad you told me what we're doing this for, at least.'

'We?'

'We're in this together, Jamie – right now, here. Moving forwards, too, if you need my help, I'm not going anywhere. But if it comes down to it – and we have to make the choice between our lives and what Falk knows about your father, then it's no choice at all. He's gone, Jamie, and whether we know the truth of how it happened or not, it doesn't change that fact. I'm sorry.'

Jamie didn't feel like telling him he didn't understand. 'I already abandoned him once – and it cost me everything. I never saw him again, and I barely spoke to him. My mother told me he didn't want to talk to me, and I believed her. While he was here, in the end, trying to put himself back together. For me. And I'm not going to abandon him again.'

Wiik fell silent now.

'I don't expect you to know what it feels like – but my

whole adult life, everyone told me the sort of man my father was. The sorts of things he did. But that's not how I remember him. And if I can prove that he was the man I remembered, and not the one everyone else did ...' She felt her throat tighten. 'If I can prove that he was working a case, that he didn't kill himself – and if I can find the bastard that did this – and make them pay for it – then you can be damn sure that's what I'm going to do.' She forced herself to breathe. 'And if Falk ends up going down for it – hell, if I have to burn down the whole fucking SPA, I will, Wiik. I'll fucking do it. And no one is going to stop me.'

They stood there in the stairwell in silence.

Eventually, Wiik nodded. 'Okay,' he said.

'Okay?'

'Okay – let's do it. Let's finish this, get the hell off this thing, and find out what happened to your father.' He extended his hand to her, and she stared down at it.

'You're serious?' She met his eye. 'This isn't your fight.'

'That's where you're wrong, Jamie. It's always been my fight. Since the moment you stepped off that plane and started laying waste to Stockholm it's been my fight. And you can be damn sure that I'm going to see it through. If you'll have me.'

She batted his hand out of the way then and put her arms around him, pulling herself against his broad chest.

His arms hovered around her shoulders for a few seconds, and then he let them rest on her back.

After a moment, Jamie released. So did Wiik.

Neither of them looked at the other or spoke.

'Right,' Jamie said after an age of awkward silence. 'We should, uh ...'

'Yeah,' Wiik said, clearing his throat. 'Up or down?'

Jamie looked both ways and thought for a second. 'Up,'

she said then. 'And hopefully, this time we won't need our guns.'

'You willing to bet on that?' Wiik said, falling into step and climbing alongside Jamie.

'No,' she said, pulling her pistol from the back of her jeans and checking the chamber. 'I'm not.'

35

JAMIE PRESSED down on the handle to the door of the lower storeroom and pushed inwards.

It moved an inch and then banged against something. She sighed and then drummed on the metal. 'Vogel – open up, it's us.'

The sound of scraping echoed out to them – for the third door in a row – and then Vogel pulled it open. She took a few steps back until she was level with Ehrling, who was now sporting two fresh black eyes and a swollen nose.

Jamie offered him what she thought was an apologetic smile, and then ushered Rosenberg into the room.

Ehrling came forwards now. 'Sven!' he said, lifting his hands and taking the older man with the white hair by the shoulders. He pulled him into an embrace. 'God, I'm so glad you're alright,' Ehrling finished, releasing him.

Sven Rosenberg, the head engineer, nodded and then seemed to relax now that he was in the company of friends and no longer barricaded in his room.

'Vogel,' Jamie said, watching as the woman pushed a

cooking-oil barrel back in front of the door, 'can you find something for Rosenberg to eat? He must be starved.'

'I'll do it,' Ehrling said from over her shoulder.

'No,' Wiik chimed in. 'We need to speak to you.'

He shrank a little, his hands moving in front of him, washing each other nervously. 'What about?'

Jamie was talking then. 'About Arnold Wallace.'

'What about him?' Ehrling said, stepping back as Wiik came up to stand next to Jamie. He eyed Wiik's hands, ready to dodge another punch if one was coming.

'What's he doing here?' Jamie pressed.

'He's, uh – a corporate risk assessor, and—'

'You can drop the act,' Jamie said tiredly. 'We know Wallace is Bolstad's fixer. Or one of them at least. He's here to mop up the mess, and we're just here to make Bolstad's clean-up operation look legitimate.'

'Though there's not much chance of that now,' Wiik grunted, folding his arms.

Jamie went on. 'So, just tell us what you *really* know, and more importantly, how you're wrapped up in it all. Because we just spoke to Colm Quinn, and they're getting ready to jump ship. Literally.'

Ehrling didn't seem to follow the last bit, but by the way he was looking at Jamie and Wiik's expressions, he seemed to understand they weren't about to swallow another corporate-approved line.

He sighed, then shook his head. 'Okay,' he said, dropping his voice a little, as though Wallace would overhear. 'You're right. Wallace is … who Bolstad sends in when things go wrong.'

'Like they did in the UAE?' Jamie took a punt.

Ehrling picked his head up and looked at her. 'You … you know about the UAE?'

'We know something. But why don't you tell us what really happened.'

Ehrling bit his lip.

'We know you were head of operations at a site there, and then you got booted down a few rungs to this place,' Jamie said. 'And I have a feeling that's why Wallace's got you on such a short leash.'

He swallowed. 'I'm not supposed to talk about it ... I signed an NDA and—'

'Fuck your NDA!' Jamie hissed, unable to stop herself. 'People are *dying,* Ehrling. And you have the power to do something about it. Tell us what's going on and we can put a stop to this.'

He remained still for a second, and then nodded. 'Okay – there was an accident. In the UAE. Some local workers had been contracted to do some work – it was a stipulation of the agreement to drill there – and something happened. While moving barrels, the stack came down and two workers were crushed. Things got out of control – quickly.'

'And they sent Wallace in to fix things?'

'The local workers outnumbered us by around two-to-one. We were ordered not to involve the local authorities until the cause of the accident was ascertained.'

'Until Bolstad could prove liability wouldn't fall on them,' Jamie added.

Wiik snorted. 'Until the police could be paid off.'

Ehrling didn't deny either of those assertions. 'The local workers wanted to report it, but we were ordered to stop them from leaving the drill site. It was over a hundred miles from the nearest town – they needed to use the company vehicles, but we stopped them. We were ordered to.'

'What happened then?' Jamie asked.

'Things got heated. Violent. We had to lock ourselves inside the main building until help arrived.'

'Until Wallace arrived?' Jamie leaned in with anticipation.

Ehrling waited, deliberated, and then nodded quickly. 'He came with a handful of Bolstad security personnel—'

'Like his two guards upstairs?' Jamie confirmed.

Ehrling nodded again. 'He managed to quell things.'

'How?'

'For the ones who would take it, he compensated them handsomely – for the stress and upset caused.'

'And the ones who wouldn't?'

'He told them that they could make the trip back to the town if that's what they wanted. That he wouldn't stand in their way. But that if they left the compound, they wouldn't be employed by Bolstad anymore, so they wouldn't be entitled to use the company trucks. They'd have to walk.'

'Then what happened?' Jamie swallowed, knowing the answer already.

'A group of them loaded up on water and food, and set out just before sunset.'

'And never returned?'

Ehrling was silent.

'Or made it to the town.'

He looked down now.

'How many?'

'Sixteen, seventeen, I think,' Ehrling said quietly.

'Jesus Christ,' Jamie muttered, looking at Wiik.

'After that,' Ehrling said, wanting to get it off his chest, 'Wallace shut down the operation, made us all sign NDAs about the accident, and split us all up, shipped us off to different sites around the world. Bolstad is a small company by the industry's standards – and oil is becoming more difficult to drill for. More red tape. More rules. More regulations.

If something like that got out, we'd go under. Every environmental agency in the world is looking to take out an oil company. And every other oil company is waiting for it to happen.' Ehrling stopped wringing his hands and held them out to illustrate his point. 'It wouldn't stop, you know? The drilling. If Bolstad went out of business, one of the big companies would swoop in, snap up our rights, our sites, our employees, assets, drills, offices – everything. We're surrounded on all sides, barely keeping our heads above water.'

Jamie found her voice had gone cold. 'Oh, poor Bolstad. The multi-national multi-billion pound oil company that's exploited people and countries for years, bribed, blackmailed, and murdered workers to keep their *heads above water*.' Jamie all but spat on the ground.

'It's not just the oil and the money that's in jeopardy. It's the people. Bolstad employs thousands, and they're invested in hundreds of companies – are vital to economies and industries, and—'

Jamie bared her teeth in disgust. 'And that gives you the excuse to be complicit in the murder of seventeen innocent workers? Gunned down, buried in the desert somewhere without grave markers or funerals – dumped in a hole, or just left to rot in the goddamn sun?'

Ehrling's lip began to quiver. 'I didn't know about that – about what he was doing – back then.'

She just shook her head. 'But you knew this time, didn't you? When you reported what happened to Reyes up the chain, and they told you that Wallace was coming.'

He didn't answer.

'And you weren't on a call with him when Reyes died, were you?'

He stayed silent again.

'He was just making you complicit, you know that? Aligning you with his lies, so you couldn't act against him without incriminating yourself.'

Ehrling wouldn't look at her.

Her mind was whirring then. 'But why are we even here?'

Ehrling looked up this time, but didn't say anything.

'Why didn't Bolstad just handle it themselves? Like in the UAE? Why call *us* in? Why the need for this to look legitimate?' She answered her own question then. 'The girls. Noemi Heikkinen. Her father.'

Ehrling looked at his feet again.

'Heikkinen has a stake in Bolstad – used that to get Noemi and her friends out here on their research trip. And they don't work for Bolstad – they're students, political and environmental activists. They couldn't *be* paid off, made to sign NDAs. So Bolstad had to make it look like they were doing the right thing – for them. For Heikkinen's father. Covering their backs in case it did get out.' She shook her head, everything falling into place. 'Well, Bolstad's not getting out of this cleanly – not this time. And if Wallace thinks he can do whatever the fuck he likes to make that happen, he's got another thing coming.' Jamie was seething now. 'We may be here to make Bolstad look like they're doing the right thing. But they can go fuck themselves if they think we're going to stand idly by while they steamroll this coup or revolt or blood feud or whatever is going on here.'

'What are you going to do?' Ehrling asked, his voice quivering.

'Whatever it takes to stop Wallace. And if that puts Bolstad in the ground, then so be it.'

'And … what about me?'

'You just stay right here,' Jamie ordered, pointing at the

ground. 'You leave this room before we say so, then as far as we're concerned, you're going down with Wallace.'

Ehrling wobbled and then steadied himself against a shelving unit filled with tins. He looked like he was about to throw up.

'You hear me, Ehrling? You've got one shot at getting out of this in one piece, and that's us telling a judge that you did everything in your power to expose the corruption at Bolstad and help us save as many people as we could.'

He nodded, keeping his lips locked shut, no doubt to stop the vomit from bursting from between them.

Jamie took a breath and turned to Wiik. 'Come on – we've got work to do.'

Wiik fell into step with her as they headed for the door again. 'Where to this time?'

'The girls are still out there,' Jamie said, shifting the oil barrel with a grunt and pulling the door open. 'And it just occurred to me that they pose the biggest risk of all to Bolstad.'

'Then we'd better find them,' Wiik said, pulling the door closed behind them.

Jamie nodded, filling her lungs, willing the tiredness from her eyes. 'And fast.'

36

THE LIGHT WOULD HAVE FAILED by now, and night would be all but upon them.

As Jamie climbed the stairs towards the upper crew quarters, she checked her watch. It was after seven in the evening. And her stomach was churning. There was nothing left inside it except bile. She'd not eaten or drunk anything in hours, and fatigue was clawing at the back of her eyes.

And yet somehow, this was when she worked best. When she was at her best. When she was tired, and stinking, and more than a little bit pissed off at the world.

Jamie and Wiik climbed in silence until they reached the floor they needed, and paused at the door.

She pulled her pistol from her belt and held it up, glancing back at Wiik to make sure he'd done the same.

He nodded that he was ready, and Jamie shouldered out of the stairwell and into the corridor, distinctly aware that they were just a few vertical metres below Wallace and the command deck.

They moved silently, closing ground on the girls' door.

Jamie knocked quietly.

No response.

She took a breath, trying to steady her heart, and knocked again, a little harder.

Still nothing.

Jamie tweaked her ears, listening for any movement inside. There was nothing. Just the sound of the storm shaking the platform to its core.

'Hooper? Sevier?' she said into the jamb. 'You in there? It's Inspectors Johansson and Wiik – from Stockholm Polis.'

There was no response.

She reached out for the handle and Wiik backed up, ready to cover the room.

Jamie took a breath, pressed down, and pushed the door inwards.

It yawned into the dark room and banged gently on the wall.

No sound or movement rose from within.

Wiik had his pistol trained on the door and Jamie gave him a quick glance, then plunged inside, covering one side of the room while Wiik slid in behind her and covered the other.

She clicked the light switch on and the room came to life.

Empty.

Wiik checked the bathroom.

Empty too.

'Shit,' Jamie said, walking around it. 'There's nothing here. No bags, no belongings, nothing.'

'Bathroom's cleaned out, too.'

'So where the hell are they?'

Wiik offered her a shrug. 'Looks like they've made a run for it.'

'Where? Where the hell *could* they go?'

'It's a big place.'

'Not that big. And we've been all through the platform in

the last day alone.' Jamie stopped now and looked at him. 'You've got what, the command deck, the upper crew deck, three levels of crew quarters, the cafeteria, medical, storage, and—'

'Maintenance.' Wiik finished for her.

Jamie stared at him. 'It's a hundred and twenty degrees in that room – dark, filthy. And a goddamn maze.'

'Sounds like the perfect place to hold up without being disturbed,' Wiik added.

Jamie didn't like that idea. 'No, they must be moving around – keeping their ears open. I'd bet they're in the lower crew quarters. We didn't search them all – didn't think to.'

He couldn't argue, but that clearly wasn't the conclusion he'd come to.

'We just need to look again. Go room by room this time.'

He nodded after a few seconds. 'Okay. Let's go deck by deck. Every room. And we either find them ...'

'Or Kurek.' Jamie tightened the grip on her pistol.

Wiik ran his hand over his head, pushing back his hair again. He opened his mouth to speak, but before he could, he was cut off.

Jamie and Wiik both flinched as the tannoy whined and then settled.

The hair on the back of her neck stood up as Wallace's smug drone cut the air around them.

'*Detectives*,' Wallace said, not a hint of fear or trepidation in his voice, '*I trust you're still alive.*' He paused, then chuckled a little. '*Of course you are. Because now you're armed. You can ... protect yourselves.*'

Jamie and Wiik both looked at each other, unnerved by the emphasis he put on that word.

'*I know this probably hasn't been a typical case for you – and for that I can only apologise. On behalf of Bolstad and myself. This is not the Bolstad experience we feel you really deceive.'*

Wiik had his head turned and Jamie could see his temple vein was back.

'And I'd like to rectify that, if I can,' Wallace went on. *'So why don't you come up to the command deck, and we can sort this all out in a civilised manner? I'll even forgive the deception, the trespassing, and the damage you caused to Bolstad property. For you see, this can – and will – only end one way. Lucky for you, you have the choice of how we get there.'* He paused for a second. *'We can work together, or we can work in opposition. But I assure you we have a common goal, and I'd very much like to reach it amicably. What do you say?'*

Wiik looked at Jamie, and she looked at him.

'I know you have Ehrling's radio with you, so why don't you lift it off your belt, Inspector Johansson, hold it to your lips, and say you're on the way up. I'll even pop the kettle on.'

Wiik looked at Jamie. 'And if we don't?'

'Tick tock,' Wallace said.

Jamie pulled the radio from her belt and held it between her and Wiik.

He shook his head.

Her thumb rested on the call button.

The tannoy crackled as Wallace waited. *'Last chance.'*

Wiik laid his hand on Jamie's wrist.

'Fine,' Wallace said, the pseudo-warmth gone from his voice. *'Have it your way.'* He sighed. *'See you soon, Detectives.'*

The tannoy clicked and then silence reigned.

Jamie lowered the radio and tucked it back on her belt.

Wiik looked around. 'What happens now?'

'I don't know, but it can't be good—'

The words hadn't even left her mouth when the light around them died.

All at once they were plunged into darkness.

Complete, pitch, blinding darkness.

Jamie looked at where she thought Wiik was, and she thought he might be looking back.

Neither of them knew what was going on, but Jamie had a sickening hunch.

And it was telling her one thing.

They'd just been bumped down the food chain, thrown off balance, handicapped.

And now they were being hunted.

37

JAMIE AND WIIK stepped back into the corridor, listening to the wind howl outside, their breath heavy in their ears.

The only illumination they had was coming from their phone torches. Jamie's was half-tucked into her front pocket, Wiik's held at the grip of his gun, his firing hand laid over the wrist of his torch-hand.

They'd been trained for this sort of thing. Not *this* sort of thing. Not exactly. But how to move. How to clear. How not to get killed. And though they'd trained continents apart, they were completely in sync.

Wiik checked the corridor to the left and then swung around, tapping Jamie on the shoulder to let her know to move up.

They had one goal now, and that was to get back downstairs safely. They needed to get back to storage – speak to Ehrling and Vogel, see if there was another way to restore power without storming the command deck.

There was no way they could stumble around blindly in the dark for the next two days.

They closed ground on the stairwell and slowed.

Jamie popped the door an inch and held her ear against the gap.

Silence.

She exhaled, failing to dispel the tension in her shoulders, and then pulled the door wide, swinging her pistol around and checking the stairs leading up, then down.

The bright, pale beam of light from her phone threw shadows off the rails and steps, painting black lines across the bare concrete.

'Clear,' she whispered.

Wiik came in behind her and covered the stairs leading up. 'Go,' he said, motioning her down.

Jamie took the steps quickly but carefully and closed in on the first level of the main crew quarters. She paused briefly at the door and glanced into the darkness, disconcerted more by what she *couldn't* see than by what she could.

Wiik came up on her shoulder. 'You good?' he muttered. It seemed wrong to speak normally. Dangerous, at the very least.

She forced a nod. 'Let's keep going.'

He gave her a reassuring smile. Or at least as reassuring as he could, and then took the lead.

Wiik got two steps before the banging of a door being thrown open echoed up from below.

Wiik and Jamie both froze, both instinctively covering their torches, hurling themselves into darkness.

Neither moved.

The only sound was their muted breath and the near-inaudible clacking of their pistols.

Wiik stepped slowly back.

Jamie could just make him out in the darkness, his face a faint outline in the orange glow bleeding through his fingers. He nodded towards the door behind Jamie, and she agreed.

Neither of them had any intention of crossing someone in the darkness. It could have been the girls – but the likely answer was much worse. Kurek. Møller. Wallace. You could take your pick. They were all out for blood.

Jamie eased the door open, the metal handle slick in her sweaty palm, and stepped into the corridor of the main crew quarters.

They knew this corridor to be empty – everyone had vacated now. Boykov, Reyes, Møller, Kravets, Rosenberg, Lebedenkov, Kurek, Quinn. They all had rooms on this floor, but none of them should have been there. Jamie had to tread carefully. She couldn't afford to put a foot wrong here.

Wiik guided the door to the frame as quietly as possible and then touched Jamie on the shoulder again.

She pressed on into the darkness, muzzle of her pistol facing what could have been an endless chasm. There was no way to tell.

She didn't even know if she was moving in a straight line or not. She was just creeping forwards, sweat beading on her forehead and running into her eyes, making them sting.

Her hands were shaking – one around her pistol, the other laid across her hips, covering the torch. She didn't want to alert whoever was below them to their presence – didn't want the glare filtering through the window and into the stairwell.

But this was just crazy. She couldn't see a damn thing. And there was no noise here. Nothing.

They had to keep moving, and faster. Shuffling like this they were sitting ducks – whether they'd managed to avoid being murdered once already or not.

Jamie could sense Wiik at her flank now, his upper arm resting on her shoulder for guidance.

His toe clipped her heel.

She could hear him breathing fast and shallow.

Jamie's hand twitched, then moved.

They had to go.

She pulled her fingers free of the torch and up to her face to wipe away the sweat.

Light exploded from her phone torch and doused the room.

Everything stood still for a moment, Jamie's brain faltering, identifying what she was looking at.

A shape.

A man.

A mask.

A Bolstad parka.

In front of her.

Arms wound up.

Hands.

Around—

Fuck!

The guy unwound, his face obscured by a black cold-weather balaclava, and the crowbar in his hands whistled through the air, swinging in a dangerous arc towards Jamie's head.

She folded her legs underneath her and dived out of its path, feeling the metal hitting her plait an inch above the nape of her neck

But Wiik wasn't quick enough.

The sound of metal hitting bone was unmistakable.

Wiik howled.

His gun came free and flew into the darkness, the crowbar smashing through his knuckles and breaking them.

He spun to the floor, clutching his wrist.

Jamie's fingers hit the steel grate below her and she was on her knees, staring right at the guy's work boots and her own empty hands. Shit, where was her pistol? Had she dropped it when she'd thrown herself down? She couldn't see it.

The boots parted and stepped back and she looked up, seeing the man wind up another swing, pulling the crowbar overhead, ready to cave in her skull.

It rose above her and she reacted on instinct. She didn't have time to turn and run, to dodge, to do anything except move forwards.

She raked in a hard breath and launched herself at him, leading with her shoulder, putting it right into the guy's gut.

He grunted and took a step backwards, crowbar still raised, and Jamie kept coming, using the space between them to sling her knee right between his legs.

It connected and the crowbar wobbled in the air, his elbows dropping as his body threatened to fold in half with the pain.

Jamie was in front of him now, the crowbar held in his left hand, the other groping at his crotch.

He swung the weapon upwards, wildly, going for a body shot.

She blocked, close enough to take the impact of his forearm against her own.

Pain rippled through her right arm and threatened to throw her off balance as she searched for a weak spot – somewhere to throw a punch. She was too close to kick him now. Close enough to smell his stinking breath, to see the whites of his eyes flashing in the frantic beam of her torch.

And then they grew bigger, closer, and before she even realised what was happening, her world blinked out of focus and she was stumbling backwards.

Pain erupted through her face, spreading from her cheek through her nose and making her eyes loll in her head.

The man drew his head back, the brutal headbutt having caught Jamie off guard, and steadied himself.

Jamie's heels caught on the ground and she fell backwards, feeling the heat of blood on her face.

She landed hard, coughed, spluttered, and then spat blood over her chin, clutching at her face.

Jamie watched him come through her fingers, the slow sidling gait as he let the crowbar fall from his grip. He reached unhurriedly behind his back and withdrew a long, awful knife.

Jamie fought to make out the details, to tell if it was the one that had already tasted her blood once before.

But she couldn't. She could only make out his outline carved in the light coming off her hip. His glowing eyes full of murder and death.

He was over her now, and there was nothing she could do.

She could feel Wiik's foot moving against her ribs, hear him trying to get to his feet, trying to move, groaning and hissing, still cradling his mangled hand.

But all Jamie could do was watch.

Watch as this brute bore down on her, ready to sink the blade into her body.

In that moment, she knew it. This was how she was going to die.

This was how it was going to end. And her body would be dumped into the ocean along with Wiik's, and no one would ever know what had happened to them.

Jamie's breath halted in her chest and she just watched.

Waiting for the end.

The knife rose, twisting in his hand like it had a mind of its own, pointing its tip right at her soft, exposed gut.

His eyes settled there, finding the place he wanted to stab her first, raising his hand.

And then they narrowed, and moved upwards.

A noise sounded overhead and Jamie craned her neck backwards, feeling the blood from her nose run over her cheeks and into her eyes.

A shape surged from the darkness, and voices filled the corridor.

Jamie rolled sideways out of the way, Wiik shunting himself the other, and watched as the newcomer charged down the killer in the mask.

The blade glinted in the air, and then was shoved aloft, the newcomer's hand around the killer's wrist. They wrestled like that, like two bears, sending flecks of spittle in all directions as they warred for ground.

And then, in the confusion of bodies and shattered light, Jamie saw a face.

The newcomer twisted his head back so she could see him clearly now – Sasha Kravets.

She blinked hard then smeared the blood from her eyes to make sure they weren't betraying her.

He had one hand around the killer's throat, the other around the killer's wrist. His head had been forced around, and Jamie could see fingers around his own jaw, digging into his cheek. He had one eye screwed shut in strain, his teeth clenched as he drove the killer back an inch at a time.

He locked eyes with Jamie then and she saw his mouth form a word – 'Run.'

Jamie didn't need telling twice. Wiik was down, hand broken; she was half-blind and could still feel blood running from her cheek. They'd both been disarmed. They needed to get to their feet at least, find their weapons, kelp Kravets.

She couldn't believe it, still.

But there wasn't time to question it.

She twisted onto her hip and scrambled to a shaky stance,

hawking blood from her throat, and searching for Wiik's jacket in the strobing darkness as her arms blotted out the beam of light. 'Wiik!' she croaked, choking on her own blood.

His good hand reached out, waving for her to grab it.

She took hold, staining it red with her blood, and turned, watching as Kravets shoved the killer back, and then landed a sharp right cross.

The killer's hand came free of Kravets's throat and then they were apart.

The knife flashed between them and Kravets jumped back, the blade narrowly missing his stomach.

The killer was moving then.

Footsteps, heavy, fading.

Jamie watched as the killer fled, and Kravets looked back once more.

'Go!' he ordered, pointing them towards the stairs. Then he took off after the killer.

But Jamie wasn't about to let him go alone.

'Stay here,' she called to Wiik, already pulling her hand from his grasp.

She went after him, finding strength with every step.

Jamie spotted her pistol on the ground a few metres ahead and snatched it up, running her sleeve roughly across her face, succeeding only in soaking her jacket in the process. Her entire head was throbbing, her eye already beginning to swell shut.

But it didn't matter. Kravets needed her help. He wouldn't be able to take on the killer—

Jamie got through the door at the end of the corridor and staggered to a halt.

There on the ground in front of her was Kravets, face down, hands folded awkwardly under him.

Jamie stopped and brought her pistol up, scanning the corridor ahead – the one that joined the crew quarters to the cafeteria and medical wing – and saw nothing.

She steadied her breathing and knelt, keeping her eyes up. 'Kravets?' she asked, putting her hand on his shoulder and shaking him a little. Was he knocked out?

Jamie lowered her pistol slightly, putting her hand under the big Serbian's arm, and rolled him onto his back. 'Kravets?' she asked again, pulling her phone free of her pocket now and shining the light on his face.

She fell back, recoiling in shock. His eyes were pointing in different directions, one deeply bloodshot, his mouth agape and at an odd angle, a deep wound under the corner of his jaw below his ear pumping near-black blood over his shoulder.

'Jesus,' Jamie said, all her strength leaving her. She slumped sideways, into an exhausted heap, pistol still in hand, and breathed hard, nausea rising in her. There was no point trying to do anything – the killer had put the knife right up through his neck, severing the optic nerve, and into his brain.

Kravets was dead.

He was dead because he'd tried to protect them.

Because he'd tried to help.

'Jamie?' Wiik was calling now, but Jamie didn't look up. She just kept her eyes on Kravets, feeling the blood drip from her cheek.

'Jamie? Jamie? Jamie!' Wiik appeared through the doorway behind her, his left hand against his stomach, holding his fumbled pistol in his right. 'Are you alright? What happened? Is Kravets—?'

'Dead,' Jamie said, her voice devoid of any life too.

'Jesus fucking Christ,' he said, going to a knee, panting hard.

Jamie glanced over at his hand, his fingers folded into a strange claw shape.

'Your face …' Wiik said then. 'You're bleeding.'

Jamie huffed sardonically, watching as the droplets fell from her chin onto her thigh, the red splotch there widening, shining in the light from her torch.

'We need to go,' Wiik said. 'Come on. We can't do anything for him now.'

He was grabbing her by the elbow then and guiding her to her feet.

They seemed not to belong to her anymore.

But they moved all the same.

Ungainly and heavy.

Like her mind, suddenly. Everything was in disarray. Her brain wasn't working anymore. All it seemed to be able to do was produce Kravets's silent scream, his wall-eyes, the thick substance oozing from his wound. The image was seared there, flashing in front of her eyes as Wiik steered her into the stairwell and down once more.

Her pistol banged against her hip, cold and uncomfortable in her grasp.

She felt like dropping it. Like just letting go.

But she knew she couldn't.

She still had enough sense to know she'd need it.

So while everything else in her body and mind failed her, her grip tightened on her gun.

And if nothing else, that reminded her that there was still work to do.

And that this thing was still far from over.

38

JAMIE SLEPT FACING THE DOOR.

She was huddled into a corner, her knees against her chest, arms folded into a knot against her thighs, gun in her hand.

She jolted into consciousness twice in the night, her pistol flying out to attention, hand shaking violently, only to find that she was in total darkness, the only sounds around her those of the others in the room. Wiik, a few metres to her left, breathing fast and shallow. Ehrling and Vogel, sleeping side by side, and Rosenberg somewhere on the other side of the room, snoring softly.

It took her a while to get back to sleep both times, disoriented by the lack of light, in pain from her face. It was aching, throbbing, and smarting all at once. She'd found a steel tray that showed her reflection well enough to see that the killer had split her cheek directly under her left eye. The centre had risen up, yellowed and gashed, and a deep purple circle had formed around it, swelling and distorting her vision.

Though Wiik had definitely had the worst of it. By

Ehrling's best guess, the strike from the crowbar had broken his outer three metacarpals, and probably turned a few of the bones in his wrist into gravel.

The best Ehrling could do was splint the wrist and hand straight and bind it with cling film. It was either that or aluminium foil. That was all that was available.

There was no way to tell when dawn had arrived, but when Jamie opened her eyes, the constant crashing of the storm seemed to have subsided to a distant howl. She blinked herself clear, winced, and then looked at her watch.

It was a little after seven.

Jamie sighed and rolled onto her side, pushing herself to her feet. She cracked her back painfully, her leg almost completely numb from sitting on a sack of rice all night, and fished her phone from her pocket.

She clicked the unlock button, but the screen didn't light up.

Dead.

Great.

She couldn't see shit.

Jamie pulled the two-way radio from her belt and clicked the talk button, causing the little green screen to light up, throwing a dim glow on her immediate surroundings.

Jamie kicked gently outwards, nudging Wiik's leg with her toe.

His eyes shot open, and he sat up, squinting into the darkness.

He reached down to push himself up, and hissed and swore under his breath as he jabbed himself in the thigh with the wooden mixing spoon Ehrling had splinted his hand with.

Jamie proffered her hand.

Wiik handed her his pistol with his good hand, and then she helped him up.

He took it back, tucking it into his belt. Their holsters were still upstairs in their rooms, along with their clothes. And though Jamie felt like she *really* needed to change her shirt – and shower too – she felt like going there was tempting fate. No, there'd be no more blundering around in the dark.

Wiik looked as dishevelled as Jamie felt in the dim glow of the two-way. His usually pristine hair and clean-shaven jaw had disappeared, and a thick layer of stubble had rooted itself on his face.

He stared at her in silence and Jamie stared back, neither quite knowing which way to turn next.

Or at least pretending. The truth was, they knew exactly what needed to be done. Just the thought of hiding here for a few more days seemed a lot more appealing. And safe.

A few seconds later, Jamie knelt next to Ehrling and shook him awake. 'Hey,' she said, keeping her voice low – everyone else deserved to sleep through as much of this nightmare as possible. 'Ehrling.'

He roused, his eyes opening a little, then widening. 'What – what is it?' he croaked.

'How do we get the power back on?' Jamie asked quickly. That was priority one. The next thing after that was dealing with Kravets's body. They couldn't just leave him there. Not after he'd saved both their lives.

'Uh,' he said, thrown by the question at first. 'You, uh – it's controlled from the, uh …'

Vogel rolled over then, awake now too, and more alert than her boss. 'From the command deck – the whole system can be controlled from there. Lights, heating, everything. One of the terminals will have—'

'No command deck,' Jamie said. 'We can't risk it.

Wallace will have thought of that – he probably cut the power to lure us there.'

It seemed almost ridiculous to suggest that Wallace would lay a trap like that – downright medieval. But here Jamie and Wiik were, bloodied and broken, and they had no way to tell whether it was Wallace's man who'd done it to them. It could quite easily have been his second bodyguard who'd attacked them in the dark. If it wasn't Kurek or Møller.

'Okay ...' Vogel said, sitting up now. 'Uh, what about down in maintenance? Direct generator reboot?' She asked the question to Ehrling more than saying it to Jamie and Wiik.

'That could work,' Ehrling confirmed. 'So long as they switch it to manual mode, first – should be an easy job. Just a few switches.' He looked at Jamie now. 'I can walk you through it over the radio.'

Jamie swallowed, biting her bottom lip to keep her jaw from quivering. 'Uh,' she started, clearing her throat. She'd already been through maintenance once and barely got out alive. 'Any other ways – on a specific floor, maybe? Breakers? Fuse boxes?'

'You could open all the doors and windows?' Ehrling offered, half in jest. 'The crew quarters all have windows – so if you open all the doors it should be light enough to see, at least.'

'And the corridors then – there are some external doors,' Vogel added. 'But it's going to drop twenty degrees the second you do. Last readings I saw said the temperature was down to minus ten with the storm, and the wind chill was minus twenty-four, I think.'

'So we'll freeze the bastards out,' Jamie said, nodding as she confirmed the plan. She had no intention of going back down to maintenance unless she absolutely had to. And sending

Wiik in there felt like condemning him to death. He could barely shoot with two hands – she'd seen him at the range, faced him in a shoot off and won with a *resounding* victory – and with one, he'd not be able to hit water if he leapt off the helideck.

No, they'd just wrap up, brace the cold, and get all those doors open. If it got down to minus twenty-odd, then at least they'd have one thing in their favour.

'Tell us about the lifeboat,' Wiik said out of the blue.

Jamie banished images of Kravets's body lying in the corridors above them, and got back on topic. 'Quinn said he and Krav—' She cut herself off. '... And Lebedenkov, were going to use it to get off the platform.'

'The emergency craft?' Ehrling said, a little surprised. 'That's ... I mean, it's basically suicide.'

'Pretty sure we said the same thing,' Jamie replied.

'It's not designed as a "boat" that could take you some-where – it's just designed to stay afloat until rescue arrives, for use in case of a platform fire, mostly. It's stocked with rations, emergency supplies, a saltwater purifier, life jackets, floatation packs, a GPS beacon. But it doesn't even have a propulsion system, just some oars. And I doubt Quinn is in any fit shape to row anywhere.'

'I don't think that really matters to them,' Jamie said. 'They just want to get off this thing. Quinn's got a target on his back. And apparently, so did Kravets.'

Ehrling didn't comment.

'Any reason that Kurek would be targeting Quinn and his crew?' Wiik asked.

Ehrling looked down, then shook his head. 'No, I thought they were quite friendly. Kurek often joined in their card games from what I knew. Maybe it was a disagreement over that?'

'Quinn said that Reyes owed Kurek some money and apparently it caused some friction,' Wiik added.

'I can't say,' Ehrling said. 'But if they're willing to risk putting themselves out to sea on that emergency craft, then they must truly believe that staying on board is worse.'

Those words seemed to hang in the air for a long time.

'Can the craft be launched at any time?' Wiik asked after a few seconds.

'Usually, yes,' Ehrling said. 'There is a control unit on the craft to operate the winch that lowers it. But if Wallace has shut down the entire system, then power will need to be restored before it can be operated. It can be done by hand – but the skene module is a hundred feet off the water and the handle is on the platform.'

'So someone would have to stay behind?' Jamie was surprised by that.

Ehrling nodded gravely. 'Yes, that duty falls to the head of operations.' He smiled wanly.

Jamie swallowed, looking at the pale outline of Ehrling's face in the darkness – the broken nose and the two black eyes from where Wiik had socked him. She'd thought so little of him, and yet he was utterly serious. He'd give his life up to save those on board. And despite herself, she was beginning to warm to him.

She often held herself in high moral regard – higher than she probably should. Everyone had skeletons in their closet and Jamie was no exception. She was just lucky that'd she'd managed to flee most of hers, leaving them in England.

It seemed not everyone else was so fortunate.

Jamie processed all the information, then turned to Wiik. 'If Quinn is still planning to get off this thing, then he'll have to go for the manual override down in maintenance. He can talk, but I doubt he can convince Lebedenkov to stay behind while he makes a run for it.'

Wiik nodded in agreement. 'We should get up there – tell him about Kravets if he doesn't know already, and then make sure he's not stupid enough to try for the override.'

'After you, then,' Jamie said, gesturing to the door.

But strangely, neither of them seemed keen to take the lead.

39

Once Jamie and Wiik had located a pair of handheld torches in the next storeroom over, they felt slightly better.

Slightly.

Even though the sun was up, things still felt dark and dank.

The storm had done its worst, but the whole platform was cold now, the horizontal rain having seeped through every crack and seam. It seemed to have beaded on the insides of the walls, and had left streaks.

Jamie ran her fingers along the once-dry concrete in the stairwell as they ascended, brushing across wet lines where drops had run. She smeared it along as they wound back up towards Kravets's body.

Wiik was ahead, torch in his good hand, teeth permanently bared against the pain. Quite frankly, Jamie didn't know how he wasn't screaming. Though the sheen of sweat on his forehead and the laboured breathing was enough to tell her that he was just one knock away from it.

He paused at the door and waited for Jamie.

She came up behind him and settled herself, pulling her

pistol free of her waistband and dragging back the slide until a bullet slid into the chamber. She glanced over at Wiik, who was eyeing it nervously. He could only hold one thing now, so she was shooting for the both of them.

Jamie pulled the torch up and held it so that the light was positioned below the heel of her hand. With her right laid across the top of her left wrist, the barrel of her gun and the torch body ran parallel, cutting a swathe of brilliance in the darkness.

'Ready?' Wiik asked, opening the door anyway.

It swung wide, and Jamie stepped into the corridor that contained Kravets's body.

She shuddered, the air in there near freezing. Down below, they'd been in storage, over the top of maintenance practically. All the heat generated seeped up through the floor. But up here, locked off from that, the temperature had plunged. When Wallace had killed the power, he'd killed the heating too, by the way it felt.

Wiik stepped in next to her, hunching over, his breath frosting in front of his face. 'Jesus,' he muttered, 'guess we don't need to open the windows after all.'

Jamie set her teeth. She hadn't really thought that was a practical solution. It was just facing the idea of delving back into the deadly maze of steam pipes and chugging boilers was almost too much to face.

She didn't consider herself a frightened person. The opposite. There wasn't much that shook her, but there was bravery, and then there was stupidity. She'd barely made it out of there once before. Running back in was only going to tempt fate. No, if she could stay out of there, she was damn well going to.

Jamie slowed, facing the flashlight down towards Kravets. Or where Kravets's should have been.

'He's gone,' Wiik said.

Jamie swallowed. 'I can see that.' She let her beam trace the trail of blood, following the glinting liquid that coated the floor. It headed off towards medical. She clamped her jaw shut to stop it from shaking. Though she wasn't sure it was from the cold.

They pressed on, picking up speed, and came up on medical, wondering whether the blood trail leading under the door to the room Quinn and Lebedenkov occupied was a good or bad thing.

Jamie neared, the corridor bathed in a bleak light. There was an outer hatch at the end of the corridor and a porthole window threw just enough light on the interior to get her bearings. But little more.

Even so, she could see that the door was ajar.

The door that had been barricaded previously.

She slowed and glanced back at Wiik, motioning for him to knock his torch off by running her thumb across her throat. He held it against his thigh and fumbled for the switch.

Jamie clicked hers off, tucked it into her jeans, and held her pistol in both hands. Behind her, Wiik fumbled his own pistol out of his waistband and used his thigh to push the slide back.

Once Jamie was satisfied they were both ready, she pressed forwards, closing ground quickly.

She walked heel to toe, keeping noise to a minimum. Though she hoped if anyone was inside waiting to pounce on them, the remnants of the storm would dampen their footsteps sufficiently for them to get the drop on the killer.

Jamie slowed for half a step just before the door, making sure Wiik was right on her shoulder. She lifted her left hand from the grip and signalled for him to cover the right-hand side of the room. He nodded confirmation and Jamie raked in a deep breath.

She fucking hated this part.

A second later, she threw her shoulder into the door, darted in, and took one big step to the left, sweeping her muzzle across the room. She could sense Wiik behind her mirroring her movements.

'Clear,' Jamie announced, lowering her pistol.

'Clear,' Wiik echoed, dropping his to his side and turning to her, seemingly out of breath from just that small exertion.

All that was there was the empty reclining chair smeared with Quinn's blood, and the half-eaten meals they'd been choking down.

Jamie squinted around in the dim light coming in from the small windows set above the counter at the back and checked for any sign of what might have happened.

She saw it then, that the blood trail continued around the chair and under the door that joined into the room that they'd used to store Reyes' and Boykov's bodies.

Wiik followed her eye line and lifted his pistol back to attention.

They both converged on the door, straining their ears for any hint of what lay beyond.

But there was nothing. No sound. No movement.

She tightened her grip on her pistol again, weighing her options.

Wiik was across the frame from her, waiting on her lead.

She lowered her off-hand, and gently rapped on the door.

Nothing.

'Quinn?' she called softly into the wood. 'You in there? It's Inspector Johansson.'

Still no response.

Wiik gave himself a little more room and moved in front of the door, nodding towards the handle, pistol raised.

Jamie's hand closed around it and she exhaled, focusing and tracing the movement back to her grip, the way her feet were going to move, how they were going to divide the room.

Then she pushed down and felt Wiik swoop past her.

She was right on him and they both entered, ready to put bullets into anything that moved.

But nothing did.

It was a room of death.

They both winced at the smell, recoiled at the scene.

There was a thin light bleeding in through a small window on the left-hand wall, painting everything in a dim and ghostly light.

On the floor, there were two body bags. Reyes and Boykov.

Their eyes drifted up, to the other corpses in the room.

The fresh corpses.

On the steel table that they'd first laid Reyes on was Sasha Kravets. He was flat on his back, eyes staring blankly at the ceiling. A deep, near-black pool of blood had formed under him, covering most of the table and dripping onto the floor.

At his side was Colm Quinn, sitting on a stool, legs soaked with his own blood, slumped over his friend and co-worker. One of his arms was folded under him, his face resting in the crook of his elbow, his other across Kravets's chest, fingers weakly stretched in the air.

Jamie and Wiik both stared down at them. Wondering what kind of person would sneak up on a man while he was grieving for his friend, and slice his throat.

Wiik let out a long, loud sigh and hung his head, closing his eyes.

Jamie's reaction was less restrained. 'God-fucking-dammit!' she yelled, turning and launching her boot into a steel roll-top bin in the corner.

Wiik jumped.

Then Quinn jumped.

Then Wiik jumped again and Jamie nearly fell over.

'Christ!' Quinn yelled, sitting upright on the stool and throwing his hands up.

Jamie and Wiik both had their pistols shoved in his face on reflex.

'Don't shoot!' Quinn pleaded.

Jamie lowered hers first, breathing hard. 'We thought you were dead!' she said, unable to catch her breath.

Quinn cleared his throat and rubbed his swollen eyes. 'As good as,' he said, wincing at his wounds as he shifted on his chair. 'The hell happened to your face?'

Jamie touched her swollen cheek instinctively and hissed at the pain. 'Had a run-in with the guy who …' She looked at Kravets, realising how insensitive the comment was.

Quinn's mouth became a thin line. 'Miro found him last night,' Quinn said darkly. 'You didn't see what happened, did you?' He looked hopeful then.

Jamie swallowed. 'No,' she answered. 'But he … he saved our lives.'

Quinn coughed, then looked away. 'Aye, he was good like that. He was, uh, a good friend. It's a damn fucking shame. It really is.' He thumped lightly on Kravets's broad chest.

'Where is Lebedenkov?' Jamie asked then.

'He's, uh … the lights,' Quinn said, glancing up at the darkened strip light above them. 'The electric is off. He went down to maintenance to try and fix it, so we can launch … What time is it?' Quinn asked, twisting round to look at the clock above the locked storeroom. It read just about half-past seven.

'Maintenance?' Jamie choked out.

'I'll need to meet him soon,' Quinn said, trying to get himself to a stance. He looked like he was about to collapse.

'Don't go anywhere,' Jamie ordered him.

He sat back down. 'I have to,' he said. 'He's meeting me at the boat at eight.'

'You stay here,' Jamie said, knowing what was coming next and already hating it. She looked at Wiik. 'We'll ...' She could barely say it. 'We'll find Lebedenkov, then we'll come back for you, okay?'

Quinn looked from one to the other.

'We've got some people downstairs – they're safe. And as soon as the storm breaks, rescue is coming.'

Quinn stared at Jamie. 'I won't make it that long.'

'You will,' she said. 'That's a promise. I'm not going to let anyone else die, okay? Just don't do anything until we get back.'

Quinn thought it over, and then nodded slowly, reaching for his pocket. 'Alright,' he said quietly, pulling a pill bottle to his mouth. He flicked the top up with his thumb and emptied a few pills onto his tongue, swallowing them painfully.

'What are those?' Wiik asked, his seemingly naturally accusative tone still as strong as ever.

'Painkillers,' Quinn said. 'Why, you want some?' He broke into a weak grin.

'Yes,' Wiik said flatly, snatching the bottle from his hand and squinting at the label, brow still slicked with sweat. 'I just hope they're strong.'

40

THE STAIRS DOWN felt like a descent into hell.

The frigid air began to warm and warm until they were at the bottom of the platform.

Jamie had forgotten how loud the sea was down here. How the waves crashing against the legs made the whole floor vibrate. How the constant din made it feel like there was broken glass inside your skull and someone was shaking it.

Jamie stepped out of the stairwell and into the corridor where this had all begun. To her left she could see the hatch to the lower submersible pod where the killer had hanged Reyes' body, the porthole window throwing a gloomy light down the corridor. On her right, the door she'd escaped through. From maintenance.

She swallowed, her feet unwilling to move. The churn and chug from the room was audible from here, the darkness beyond the door already making her feel claustrophobic.

'Ready?' Wiik asked, not looking back. He was moving quickly, still breathing hard.

Jamie shook it off and jogged to catch up, her calf still

throbbing, the pain there a constant reminder of what was yet to come.

She glanced up at Wiik as they closed ground on the door. He was hunched over, cradling his mangled left hand against his stomach, pistol swinging in his right, eyes fixed on their destination. His chin was held up, jaw clenched, his face moist with sweat, eyes wild, pain plaguing his every thought and movement. He reminded her of an old lion. One who'd been gored by a buffalo or tangled with a younger male. Who'd barely got out of there alive, but one whose duties hadn't left them. One who needed to protect the pride. Needed to go on.

She respected him for it. But it frightened her even more.

Jamie could hold a torch, and her gun, but Wiik could barely stay on his feet. And the pill bottle he'd taken from Quinn, along with the load he'd stuffed into his mouth, weren't alleviating her fears much.

The door was there then, and Wiik was trying to move the lever handle with his good elbow, grunting as he did.

Jamie looked down the barrel of his loaded gun as he tried to manoeuvre his arm into the right position.

'Let me,' she said quickly, shouldering him out of the way.

He grunted in frustrated agreement and stepped back, using the hammer of his pistol to scratch the side of his head.

She fastened her grip around the handle and took another look at him. Blotchy cheeks, hair a mess, eyes wide and twitching. Pain and rage riding high in him. Senses dimmed by the pills. The taste of revenge on his tongue. And a loaded weapon in his sweat-soaked grip.

I should do this alone. Those were the words she wanted to say. Should have said. *You wait here. I don't want you in there. You're going to be a liability. I'm afraid your finger's going to slip and you'll put a bullet in me.* Any of them would have been good. All of them would have been better. But just then, she couldn't. The thought of leaving what little support Wiik offered at the threshold …

'Okay,' she said instead, pulling the hatch open, her voice choked and small. She nodded. To herself. To Wiik.

And they went in.

Inside was dark and hot.

Jamie drew a lungful of soupy air. It felt like her eyeballs were being pressed into her head. Like she'd just run ten miles. Like someone was holding a hairdryer on her face.

Wiik leaned awkwardly on the wall and reached out, smacking the butt of his gun into the square light switch.

The button clicked, but nothing happened. As expected.

He grunted again, this time in disapproval. Though the tone was almost indistinguishable from the one outside.

They stood, bathed in the eye-achingly dark red glow of the emergency lights sitting atop the boilers and generators. They were all still running, but Wallace had culled the power to the rest of the platform. Jamie figured they ran on their own closed circuit, battery backups maybe, a diesel generator … It didn't matter. It wasn't why they were here.

It would have seemed easiest to call out for Lebedenkov. To yell his name, and tell him they were there to … to what? Save him? Protect him?

But announcing their position seemed like a stupid thing to do. Especially considering their recent brush with the killer and how easily he'd dispensed with Kravets.

Jamie exhaled and pulled her radio off her belt, pressing the call button with her thumb. 'Ehrling? Ehrling, come in. It's Johansson.' She kept her voice low, the growl of the room around them enough to drown out her voice.

'*Inspector?*' Ehrling's voice came back a few seconds later. '*Are you alright?*'

'Yeah,' she said, feeling the plastic creak under her grip. 'We're in maintenance – where are we going?'

'*The control panel is in the back-left quadrant of the room.*'

She glanced at Wiik. He just scowled.

'You're going to have to do better than that,' Jamie said. 'The whole place is dark, and it's a maze.'

'*Right, of course,*' he said, clearing his throat. '*If you came in through the inner door, take a right, go down to the back wall, and then follow it. If you see two large cone-shaped boiler-stills, you're on the right track. Go around them, and look for a control unit with lights and switches – it's about the size of a desk, slanting upwards – and above it there'll be a panel with breaker switches. That's what you're looking for.*'

Jamie nodded, mostly to herself. 'Okay. I'll call you when we're there.'

'*Good luck.*'

Jamie lowered the radio and stashed it on her belt, wiping the sweat from her hand on the thigh of her jeans.

She looked back at Wiik, and then out at the red room in front of them. She could make out the railings in front of her, the walls of boilers and pipes. Enough to see. To navigate.

She took her pistol in both hands, and then stepped forwards, heading right, following Ehrling's directions.

Jamie passed what she thought was the section of piping she'd vaulted over, burning herself in the process, and pushed on again, right to the back of the room.

Wiik was huffing and panting behind her, his footsteps uneven and dragging.

They reached the back of the room, and Jamie blinked

herself clear, trying to discern shadow from solid in the dark. She reached up and ran the back of her hand across her eyes, trying to get the sweat out of them. They were stinging.

The path turned to the left and Jamie followed it, Wiik behind her.

He was sucking in deep lungfuls of hot air now, trying to catch his breath.

She looked at him – he seemed ready to collapse. They needed to find Lebedenkov. Quickly.

What did Ehrling say? Follow the back wall.

She stuck to it and moved, squinting, willing the sweat to run around her eyes, not into them.

Her ears were ringing now, too, the noise around disorienting as they moved through puddles of pure darkness, pushing towards wherever the fuck that back-left quadrant was supposed to be.

She heard Wiik clip his toe on the grate underfoot and stumble into the railing beside her.

His gun clanged against the metal and his arm slid across the top of it.

He caught himself, the rail against his ribs, legs under him in a twisted mess, and looked up at her.

She could see the pain in his face, the way his body was barely clinging on.

Jamie decided then.

It wasn't worth it. Wiik's life was more important to her that Lebedenkov's. And she didn't care how that sounded.

She went towards him, scooping him into her arms, and pulled him to his feet. His grip tightened around her, arm falling across her back, pistol still in hand.

'Come on,' she said, bearing his weight, 'let's get you out of here. We can figure out what to do when you're—'

But she didn't get to finish.

A deafening clap rang out. Then another. Then another.

Jamie pulled in a sharp breath and for a moment, she thought that Wiik had accidentally pulled the trigger.

A wash of nausea ran up through her guts, and the feeling of the sweat on her spine made her shudder.

Then she realised it wasn't Wiik's pistol. But it was close.

'Lebedenkov,' Wiik muttered, a glimmer of focus in his eyes.

He pushed away from Jamie, wobbled, and then loped forwards, pistol raised and swinging.

'Wiik!' Jamie called after him, taking off in his wake. 'Hey!'

He passed a walkway on his left, stopped, brandished his gun into it for a second, and then ran on, slowing at the next to do the same. Then again.

Jamie slowed, looking on ahead, seeing a column of steam pipes rising into the ceiling. And to the left of them, the cone-shaped boilers.

'Wiik!' Jamie yelled now, knowing he was heading for a dead end.

But he was deaf to her, blinded by whatever mix of pain and anger was powering him.

She picked up speed again, reeling him in.

He stopped, turned around, realising the walkway ended ahead, and met Jamie head-on. He threw his gun out, motioning her to turn around. 'Go!' he commanded.

'Wiik, slow down,' Jamie said, dodging his flailing weapon.

He shoved past her and took off again with even more haste.

Jamie was breathing hard, her heart pounding in her throat.

She pushed the hair off her forehead and took off after him again.

He turned right suddenly and disappeared down a side-path.

She was right on his heels now. Trying to keep up. Keeping her eyes fixed on his coat. His broad shoulders.

Right. Left.

Jamie heard it then, footsteps, and froze, her head snapping up, her pistol going with it.

The walkways splayed ahead, and she caught a snatch of a body moving past the end of the left-hand one. Just a flash. There and gone.

The footsteps receded, swallowed by the noise in the room.

'Shit,' she breathed. 'Wiik!' she hissed, turning back to find him ... gone. Jamie swallowed, looking down the path ahead. It split off in two again, the cone-shaped boilers towering on her right now, separated from her by a row of electrical units and wiring.

This was the last thing she wanted.

But she had to keep moving.

Wiik had heard Ehrling's instructions. He'd know where to go.

She hoped.

Jamie set off, keeping her eyes on the boilers, and moved through the maze, pausing every second or two to listen for any hint of Wiik's panting, grunting, anything.

But she heard nothing but the continual churn of electricity and heat around her.

She took a right again and found the cones dead ahead.

Her eyes drifted to their left, and she saw the unit facing away from her, but unmistakable. The slanted surface, the solid bank of switches.

She ran, moving around it, hoping not to find what she knew she would.

Jamie slowed, sank forwards, hands on knees, chest heaving. 'Fuck!' she screamed, pounding on her thigh with her fist.

There, slumped against the base of the control panel, was Lebedenkov. With three bullet wounds in his back. Right between his shoulder blades. All three shots had a close grouping, right where the heart would be. Close range. Ruthless. An execution by any other name.

She had no doubt he was dead, his vacant eyes staring into the darkness enough to confirm that.

He had one hand crushed under his hulking body, the other bent awkwardly above his head.

'Wiik!' Jamie yelled, not looking up. 'Wiiiiik!'

Footsteps sounded in front of her, and she stood straight, pistol at the ready.

Wiik was standing there, and raised his one good hand. 'It's me.'

Jamie swallowed and lowered her gun, staring down at Lebedenkov. 'We were too late.'

'Kurek?' Wiik asked across the body in front of them.

Jamie looked down at Lebedenkov. 'He was standing at the panel. Kurek must have come up behind him with Reid's gun. Put three in his back.'

Wiik nodded. 'Any sign of Kurek?'

'I saw someone moving in the opposite direction, heading for the door, but I couldn't make out who they were.'

'Did you go after them?'

Jamie shook her head. 'No – I learned that lesson once already.'

Wiik said nothing.

They were one step behind Kurek again. He'd got Reyes,

Kravets, Lebedenkov, and now Quinn was all that was left. And in his weakened state, Jamie didn't think he'd put up much of a fight.

She watched Wiik, as he made an effort to stuff his pistol into the front of his belt with his one good hand. His eyes had grown glazed and heavy, the painkillers he'd popped taking full hold now.

He was swaying in front of her. And was trying to put a loaded gun into his trousers.

'Jesus,' she said, reaching out and taking it off him. 'You're going to blow your balls off.' Jamie put hers down on the control unit in front of her, held Wiik's aloft and ejected the magazine. She pulled back the slide, popping the round out of the chamber, and then thumbed it back into the magazine before snapping it back into the pistol. She handed it back to him, grip first, and he took it, nodding quickly.

Jamie didn't need to remind him why doing that was necessary. You never carry a pistol with a round in the chamber unless you're intent on firing it.

She picked her own weapon up off the control unit and repeated the steps. Eject mag. Eject bullet. Load mag. Insert mag.

It was muscle memory now. And the easiest way not to shoot yourself. They drummed it into you during firearms training.

Jamie sighed and pushed her pistol into the back of her jeans again, freeing her hands for the task ahead.

She knelt and put her arms under Lebedenkov's and did her best to roll him over. Wiik just stood back.

The man slumped onto his back, revealing a spray of black across the front of the control unit.

Jamie felt like she should say something, but she didn't know what. She couldn't even close his eyes. The muscle

tension in someone's eyelids just made them pop back open
until rigor mortis set in. So they just left him lying there, his
shirt soaked with blood where the pressure from the bullets
had blown through the front of his chest, and focused on the
panel instead.

Jamie pulled the radio from her belt, keen on getting this
done and getting out of there, and lifted it to her mouth.
'Ehrling, come in – we're at the control unit.'

'*Inspector,*' came a shaky reply. '*We heard gunshots – are
you … are you alright?*'

Jamie let off the talk button, gathered herself, and then
pressed it again. 'Yeah, we're fine. Can you walk us through
the reboot?'

'*What happened? Is anyone hurt? Do you need me to—*'

'The reboot,' Jamie cut in, her voice barbed. 'Just – just
walk us through it. Please.'

Wiik was looking at her, the pleading tone in her voice
stark.

After a moment, Ehrling came back, his voice calm.
'*Okay, Inspector. Just tell me when you're ready.*'

Jamie clenched her jaw. That was the same damn tone the
counsellor the Met had made her see had taken. She didn't
like it then. And she didn't like it now. She had every fucking
right to be on the bitter edge right now. And it always felt
patronising. She was practically straddling someone's corpse.
'Ready when you are,' she forced out through gritted teeth,
trying not to meet Lebedenkov's endless stare.

'*Okay then,*' Ehrling said. '*Let's get these lights back on,
shall we? Restore some normality.*'

Jamie sucked in a deep breath, felt the sweat run down
her temple and under her collar, and thought how nothing
could have been further from the truth.

41

THE LIGHTS SEEMED BLINDING. After blundering around in the dark for the best part of a day, Jamie felt like she could barely open her eyes.

Wiik was trailing behind now, suffering with his hand, the pills, everything. Neither of them had really slept in the last few days, and they'd subsisted on coffee and snacks. Jamie's stomach had all but shrivelled, but she was intact. Except for her face, but that was superficial. Painful and swollen. But superficial.

Wiik, though … His hand was basically a bag of broken bones until they could get it X-rayed and pinned back together. Hell, it was being held in position by a wooden spoon and cling film, for fuck's sake!

He paused at the top of the stairs and leaned against the wall, breathing hard.

Jamie thought if there was anything in his stomach, he would have thrown up.

'You good?' she asked, knowing the answer would be a lie.

He managed a nod, and Jamie dragged her eyes from him, focusing on the door ahead. They had to keep moving. The killer was already ahead of them. They didn't have time for this.

Jamie pushed the door open and set off, moving quickly. Now that the lights were on, there was nowhere to hide. 'Quinn!' she called out, listening for a response. It was just one turn in the corridor ahead, and then they were there. 'Quinn!'

But he didn't answer.

Jamie picked up her pace, circled wide towards the corner, and laid her hand on the grip of her pistol behind her back. She slowed, breathing steadily, and peeked around. Clear.

She kept moving, towards the wide-open door into medical.

'Quinn?' she tried again, listening for any movement. There'd been no gunshots, no sound of footsteps. There was no sound of fighting, or even of dripping blood. There was just the distant rumble of the fading storm giving its last against the outside of the platform.

Jamie crossed the threshold and went inside. Room one, clear.

The room with the bodies next.

The door was open, too. She could see Kravets's body on the table, Quinn's stool next to it.

But no Quinn.

He was gone.

'Shit,' Jamie sighed, her hands planted on the doorframe. She pushed back and turned towards the corridor again, just in time to see Wiik stumble into it and slump against the open door. He had his eyes closed, his skin pale, dark bags carved into his cheeks.

'Quinn's going for the lifeboat,' Jamie announced, not even looking at Wiik. If she did, she knew she'd leave Quinn to the wolves and stay here with him.

'Okay,' Wiik forced out. 'Let's …' But he didn't get to finish before his knees began to buckle and he collapsed.

Jamie swooped in and caught him, folding under him as his weight dropped onto her.

They both went to the ground and Jamie gasped as Wiik's elbow lodged itself into her stomach.

She had to use her heel against the wall to push herself free, pulling her radio off her belt. 'Ehrling,' she wheezed. 'Come in!'

'*Detective, what's wrong?*' he asked quickly, his voice crackling in the silent room.

'It's Wiik, he's down.'

'*Shot?*'

'No, no,' Jamie squeezed out, wriggling free. 'It's his hand – he took some painkillers – but, I don't know – he's just – he collapsed.' Jamie was on her knees now, rolling Wiik over. 'I need you up here, now,' Jamie said.

His eyes were mostly closed, unfocused.

'*Where are you?*' Ehrling answered.

'Medical.'

'*Okay,*' he said, not a hint of hesitation there. '*We're on the way.*' He clicked off for a moment, and then came back on, his voice shaking like he was running. '*Is he breathing?*'

'Yes,' Jamie answered, watching his chest rise and fall.

'*Fast? Slow? Shallow?*'

'Uh, normal, I think – maybe a little fast.' Her throat had tightened, strangling her voice.

'*Pulse?*'

She pushed her fingers against his neck. 'Elevated.'

'*Is he responsive?*'

'Wiik?' Jamie asked, leaning in. 'Wiik? You hear me?' She pushed her fingers into his left hand. 'Squeeze if you can hear me.'

He did – barely – his chin moving like he was trying to speak.

'Yes,' Jamie said into the radio then. 'Sort of – he can't speak.'

She heard Vogel's voice in the background then. '*Shock?*'

'*No,*' Ehrling said to her. '*Likely exhaustion mixed with prolonged pain response. Heightened cortisol levels. Inspector?*'

'I'm here,' Jamie answered, keeping her eyes fixed on Wiik. His neck was shining with sweat and he'd begun to shiver.

'*Does he have goose pimples?*'

'Goose pimples?' Jamie was thrown by the question for a moment. 'Uh, yeah – yeah, he does.'

'*We're on the way. We'll be there in a moment.*'

'Is he going to be okay?'

'*We'll be right there. Just try to keep him alert.*'

Jamie dropped the radio and took Wiik by the shoulders then. 'Hey, stay with me,' she said, shaking him gently.

He squeezed his eyes together and champed like he was trying to moisten his tongue to speak. And then his face seemed to relax and his eyes fluttered.

'Wiik?'

Nothing.

'Wiik?' She shook him harder.

There was a noise in front of her. She ripped her pistol from her jeans and levelled it at the figure in the doorway.

Ehrling was standing there, hands up. And behind him, Vogel and Rosenberg. Ehrling and Rosenberg were the trained first-aiders. And Vogel came to help too, no doubt. Either that or she didn't want to be left downstairs alone.

If Jamie wasn't so focused on Wiik, she might have thought more about it. But it barely entered her mind.

Jamie lowered the gun and Ehrling came in, the others right on his shoulder.

She moved backwards to give them room and then Rosenberg and Ehrling knelt either side of Wiik and looked him over, speaking quickly. One felt his pulse, the other checked his breathing, opened his eyelids to look at his pupils.

Then they lifted him up and laid him on the consultation chair in the middle of the room.

Jamie stepped towards the door, next to Vogel, pistol still in her hand.

Ehrling and Rosenberg worked quickly, fishing in cupboards and cabinets to get exactly what they needed. In under a minute, they had a blood-pressure cuff on Wiik's arm, an IV stand and fluids bag set up, and Ehrling was prepping a syringe, filling it with a mixture of liquids.

'What is that?' Jamie asked as he drew from the third bottle.

'A vitamin cocktail and a low-dose sedative to help reduce the excess cortisol in his blood.' He met Jamie's eye and smiled reassuringly at her. 'He'll be fine – it's just the stress his body has gone through, the pain, the constant movement, combined with a lack of sleep. Once his hand is reset and he's had some rest, he'll be okay.'

Jamie was frozen for a moment as her brain weighed it up.

'Thank you,' Jamie she said, taking one last look at Wiik.

'Inspector?' Ehrling called after her as she disappeared through the door. 'Where are you going?'

But she didn't answer.

She was already running.

Too many people had already died.

And she wasn't about to let one more go.

If Kurek was after Quinn, then she'd do everything she damn well could to stop him.

42

JAMIE THREW the door open and braced herself against the wind.

She took a step forwards, two to the side, and then straightened out, fighting it with every stride.

The rain had cleared now, but the storm was still fierce and cold enough to make her eyes ache.

Jamie looked around, alone on the platform, and saw the skene tower rising up in front of her, connected to the main drilling platform by a narrow catwalk.

A thin spurt of smoke was shooting out of the top of the tower chimney, swirling away in the last of the storm.

The sky was a mottled grey and moving fast above it.

Jamie ploughed on, shielding her eyes from the wind with her arm, still clutching her pistol.

There was no sign of Quinn.

There was no sign of anyone.

She quickened her pace, forcing herself into an awkward, windswept run.

The concrete platform came to an end, and she was at the mouth of the catwalk suddenly.

It was black steel, two metres wide, hemmed in by bright yellow rails.

And there, about three-quarters of the way along, was Quinn. He was hunched over, clinging to the right-hand rail. One of his arms was hooked over it, another clutching his stomach. He was shuffling forwards. Slowly. Painfully.

He must have seen the lights come back on and made a break for it, assuming Lebedenkov had succeeded.

Jamie checked her watch. It was eight now.

The sky had lightened enough to see the horizon, but there was no sign of the sun. Just endless, thick clouds and a flat, cold light spread out across the desolate ocean.

It looked like crushed slate beneath her feet.

'Quinn!' she yelled, her voice carried away on the wind.

Jamie took a step forwards, onto the catwalk, and felt like she'd just stepped onto a canoe. The whole thing was moving and twisting.

No wonder Quinn was clinging to the rail.

Jamie swore and fought for balance, her other foot joining the first.

She steadied herself, feeling the whole catwalk rippling, and reached back, pushing her pistol into her waistband, throwing her arms wide for balance.

Jamie shuffled as quickly as she could towards Quinn.

She yelled his name again, making up ground.

The catwalk must have been twenty metres long. Totally unsupported.

The metal groaned under her.

'Quinn!' She was halfway now, still moving, and closing the distance.

Quinn lifted his head and turned to look at her.

Jamie took two big steps, lost her balance, and reached out for the rail, steadying herself.

She bounced, from one side to the other, drawing level with him, clinging to the bar opposite.

Quinn stared at her with pain in his eyes. He'd put on a Bolstad parka and the fur-lined hood flapped around his head.

Underneath, he was wearing a knitted sweater and jeans, both of which were red with blood.

'Are you okay?!' she screamed, barely able to hear it herself over the wind. It was at her back now, whipping her hair around her face.

'Where's Miro?' he screamed back.

Miroslav Lebedenkov. Jamie's mouth opened, moved uselessly for a second, and then she closed it, taking a breath. 'I'm sorry, Quinn!'

'He's dead, isn't he?' He hung his head and shook it, forcing himself a little more upright. He got his legs under him and laid his back across the rail so he was facing her fully. 'How?'

'Shot!' Jamie answered. 'But the power is on – you need to come back inside, okay?'

'No!' He gritted his teeth and tried to turn back towards the skene tower.

From here, Jamie could see the nose of a white craft jutting out from behind the chimney. It was swinging around in the wind, and by what she could see, would be no more than a matchbox among the waves below.

'We can keep you safe!' Jamie pleaded, turning back to him.

But he wasn't listening. He started moving again, hauling himself along.

Jamie stepped forwards, lurching across the metal grating, and slamming into the opposite rail, right behind Quinn.

She reached out for him, her eyes streaming in the wind, making a grab for his shoulder.

Her fingers grazed the material, and she took another step, finding it this time.

He stopped and turned back, face stricken with fear. 'Let go!' he bellowed.

'I can't do that, Quinn!'

'If I stay here, he'll kill me!'

'I won't let that happen!'

'He'll kill you too!'

'We'll handle Kurek! You have to trust me!'

His eyes widened as she said the name, then searched her face for a second.

Before either of them could say anything else, the whole catwalk shook and they both slumped against the metal, fighting for balance.

Though it wasn't the wind that had done it. Jamie knew the feeling – she'd felt it herself not minutes before.

New weight on the catwalk.

Jamie spun in place, feeling the bar hard against her back as she rolled across it, ready to face Kurek.

Except it wasn't him.

Jamie stared at the two figures gingerly making their way towards them.

Wallace and his bodyguard.

And they hadn't come for Quinn.

They'd come for her.

Her gun was in her hand a second later and out in front of her.

Then Wallace's guard was holding his.

He was six-foot-plus with close-cropped hair. His black suit and woollen coat looked out of place out here, but his intentions were clear enough.

Wallace took a step towards them, one hand on the rail,

the other reaching out to quell his guard. He laid a hand on his wrists and pushed the gun down.

Wallace did his best to stand straight, his black Bolstad coat buffeting behind him like a cape. 'Inspector!' he called.

Jamie had to strain to hear him.

'Make this easy on yourself!'

What? He just expected Jamie to lower her gun? Let Wallace's man shoot her? No way. Even if she was ninety-nine per cent sure she'd miss any shot she did take. Hell, she could hardly hold her arm straight.

'Do you really want to die for him?'

For … him? Jamie's brain twigged a second too late. She tried to twist around, but Quinn was already on her.

She felt his body hit hers, his breath hot on her neck as he reached over her shoulder, going for her gun.

Jamie tried to get free, but his other hand was already on her wrist, dragging it from the railing, pinning it across her chest.

She could feel his fingers digging into her skin on her other wrist as he tried to pull the pistol free, but she wasn't giving in so easily. Jamie bucked backwards, throwing her hip into Quinn, and he doubled over a little, his grip coming loose.

There was a moment of relief as she felt space between them, but then it was ripped away just as quickly as Quinn's fist flew out of nowhere and connected with the side of her head.

She saw blackness, and when she regained herself, her right hand was waving in front of her, fingers empty, the nose of her pistol already pressed against her temple.

Jamie's whole face was vibrating as she fought to fill her lungs, her eyes struggling to focus.

The numbness receded then and the pain came in big,

swollen waves, exploding from the corner of her jaw and up into her skull.

She heard Quinn's voice in her ear, distant over the sharp ringing from the blow. 'You take one step and I'll blow her fucking head off!'

Jamie moved her jaw stiffly, trying to wrangle her tongue, and looked up, squinting at Wallace and his guard.

Wallace didn't look alarmed, though. He didn't even look phased. 'Come now, Quinn!' He took a careful step, his guard moving with him, half in front of him, ready to take a bullet if one came. 'Don't be stupid.'

The big man had his legs splayed against the wind for support, but Wallace held on to the rail, his white hair flying around his head in wispy strands.

'Not another step!' Quinn roared, making Jamie wince. She could feel warm flecks of saliva hitting her ear and neck. 'I'll do it! I'll kill her!'

'Then kill her,' Wallace said, no more than ten metres away.

Jamie's brain was firing on all cylinders again now, but she didn't dare move. Not with a loaded gun to her head.

'You think,' Wallace said, 'that it matters to me? You and I had a deal, Quinn, and you chose to go back on that. Which means you're not getting off this platform, and neither is Inspector Johansson. So whether you put a bullet in her head, or I do, it makes no difference.'

'I held up my end!' Quinn roared back, making Jamie's ear ring. 'How was I supposed to know Reyes would cross us? I did what I had to!'

She could see Wallace's eyes narrow. 'You're a fool, Quinn, and I was just as much a fool to trust you. Going after Reyes like that – you put *everything* at risk. Everything! You should have let me deal with it. And then it would have been done *right*!'

'You would have fucked us over the first second you could!'

'And you've only succeeded now in doing it to yourself. Reyes, Kravets, Lebedenkov – your friends – they died for what, Quinn? To keep up your ruse?' He scoffed. 'You really thought that Inspector Johansson here could have done anything for you? Could have *protected* you? From *us*?' He shook his head. 'No one can protect you, Quinn. You're going to die here.'

Jamie's mind was working overtime, trying to process, trying to understand, looking for some way out of this. Quinn had killed Reyes – because his deal with Wallace had gone sideways. Because ... because they'd switched out the seal for the worn one. To kill Reyes? No, that didn't make any sense. To ... to cause a spill? And Reyes had been in on it, but he'd fallen for Noemi, told her everything, double-crossed Quinn and the others. Prevented the spill from happening.

And Quinn had killed him for it.

It all made sense finally.

But why was Wallace in league with Quinn to sabotage their own drill? It would put Bolstad under. For good.

Fuck! It was impossible to think with a gun to your head. A loaded gun. A gun with a bullet in the chamber, ready to ... wait ... Jamie swallowed, tried to stop herself from shuddering. A bullet in the chamber ...

She had to think. Faster than Quinn was.

Was there a bullet in the chamber? No, of course there was. Why wouldn't there be? She thought back. Back to medical. She'd taken her gun out there, pointed it at Ehrling. Had she chambered a round? No, she didn't think she had.

What about before that? There'd definitely been a bullet in the chamber in maintenance. She knew that.

Wiik. Yes, she'd taken the bullet out of *Wiik's* gun because he was going to shoot himself in the testicles. She'd taken it off him, popped the bullet out, put it in the magazine and given it back to him …

Then she did the same with hers.

She did the same with hers.

But did she chamber a round after that? Fuck, she couldn't remember.

Jamie looked up at Wallace, watched as he touched his guard on the arm. He moved in front of Wallace fully, his hands flexing on the grip of his pistol. He was taking aim.

Quinn's grip tightened on her, the muzzle biting into the skin of her temple. This was it. She had to gamble. Her life depended on it.

Her right hand was free, hanging at her side.

She had to do it. It was either try and get shot, or do nothing and get shot.

Fuck.

Jamie tensed.

Fuck!

Now or never.

She slung her elbow backwards as hard as she could. It impacted just above Quinn's hip bone, right where he'd been stabbed.

She felt him convulse behind her. Felt the muzzle ram against the side of her head. Heard the hammer fall on an empty chamber.

A sharp, metallic click.

But no bang.

No bullet.

Jamie dove forwards, spinning from Quinn's embrace.

He still had his hand on her wrist and twirled her as she fell.

She watched as he rose up behind her, and then as the bullets struck him. One. Two. Three. In the chest. Close grouping.

Lebedenkov's body flashed in her mind.

Quinn released her and fumbled her pistol, staggering backwards.

Jamie landed hard on her back, watched as Quinn's heels hooked on the metal grating and he went sprawling.

'Shoot her!' Wallace's voice echoed from over Jamie's head.

She didn't need to look to know.

Her legs scissored, and she flipped over, listening as more shots echoed. As bullets pinged off the steel around her.

She scrambled, rolled, then threw herself towards her only hope of getting out of this.

Her body clattered into Quinn's and she dragged herself over him, hand stretching out for her pistol.

Sparks exploded off the grate inches from her face, and she winced, screwing her eyes closed, reaching blindly.

Then she felt it. The familiar ripple of the grip, the sleek body, and snatched it up.

Jamie held it skyward, saw it cut out against the sky for an instant, and reached up, snapping the slide back and listening as a bullet slotted itself into the chamber.

She sucked in a breath and dragged herself upright, an instant of focus seizing her as she put Wallace's guard right between the sights.

There was a plume of light from his gun.

Then one from Jamie's.

Pop. Pop. Pop. Pop.

Her finger bounced off the grip as she fired. Two, three, four – she lost count.

She could see stars, ghosts of the flash, and a black shape through it.

Jamie blinked furiously, regaining her vision just in time to see that pristine black suit and dress coat hitting the walkway.

She choked out a breath, looked down, searching for holes, and forced herself to breathe, trying to get to her feet, fighting the wind.

When she looked up again, Wallace was on her.

She pulled the gun to attention for a second time, still reeling, on her hands and knees, and felt it knocked free of her gasp in a flurry of tailored wool.

Wallace's polished shoe connected with the barrel and sent it spinning into the air.

It careened over the side and disappeared.

She watched it go, unable to react before his hands were on her neck and was driven backwards again.

Jamie rolled up onto her heels, trying to stand before he took her down, and tripped over Quinn's body.

She landed hard, flat on her back, with Arnold Wallace on top of her.

The impact would have kicked the air clean out of her lungs had his thumbs not been on her windpipe.

Jamie spluttered, beating at his shoulders, but he was straddling her stomach, crushing her throat.

All she could see were black spots dancing across the tiger-striped sky. And Wallace's face. The pointed features, the wispy white hair, the unassuming countenance reshaped into an evil snarl.

She wasn't leaving that platform alive.

He was going to make sure of it.

She twisted and writhed, her mind betraying her.

But it was no good. He had a vice hold, and though she scratched at his wrists, pulled at his hands, grabbed for his face, he didn't relent.

Jamie's eyes went to the right, back towards the platform. Wiik. Wiik! Where was Wiik? Why wasn't he there? Why wasn't anyone there?

She saw Quinn then, staring right back at her, his eyes wide and vacant and dead.

And she saw her future.

She'd be joining him in a minute.

She'd have to lie here for another minute, maybe more, as Wallace choked the life out of her. Feeling the world fade away as her body used up the trapped oxygen. Until her brain shut down.

Until her heart gave out.

Pain rippled through her arms and legs, her head feeling like it was about to explode with pressure.

Her cheeks burnt, eyes bulging.

Tears streamed from them.

And Wallace pressed on.

She could feel the rough grating under her heels as she raked them around, trying to think. To fight. To do anything.

One of her knees flew upwards, hit Wallace in the back.

She felt the pressure increase on her neck, felt something click inside it. More pain. More black spots.

Wallace shifted his weight, moving higher on her body, putting all his weight on her neck.

She threw her knee up again and felt it hit Wallace in the ribs.

He squirmed, his mouth opening in some sort of pain – maybe he called out – Jamie didn't know. All she could hear was crashing waves. Or maybe it was the blood in her ears. She couldn't tell.

But she kept kneeing.

Again. Again. One leg, then the other. Right. Left. With everything she had.

Pain shot through her back then as her spine curved upwards, free of the floor, and landed again.

She lifted her leg this time, looking past Wallace's head, and saw her toe there.

He was practically on her chest now, his knees under her arms. High enough ... high enough to ...

Jamie summoned everything she had left and kicked her leg upwards, outside Wallace's shoulder, and bent it down in front of him. Her hip screamed at the angle, her laces hooking under his chin.

And then they were moving. Tumbling.

She put everything she had into it, forcing her body upright, and Wallace back.

His eyes widened as he fell backwards, and Jamie felt her shoulder begin to lift, her hands fastening around his wrists as she pushed him down onto his back, his legs still around her ribs.

The hold on her neck loosened, and she kicked out, pulling away at the same time, forcing him free of her throat.

Air surged into her lungs like liquid fire and her arms flailed, grabbing for the rail behind her.

She gasped madly, pulling herself around, away from Wallace, and onto her side.

Jamie felt his fingers on her leg as he clawed his way back up towards her. To finish the job.

She kicked again, not even looking, and felt her heel hit something

Wallace grunted, slumped backwards, thudded against the opposite railing.

The whole catwalk was swinging underneath them, turning Jamie sick.

She coughed violently, spraying blood over the back of her hands, and listened to the scrabbling of Wallace behind her, getting to his feet.

She felt pain. Terror. She was going to die here. Alone.

No.

No. No. No! She wasn't. That's not why she came here, and she wasn't going to let it end like this.

Jamie turned back to face him, watched as he got up against the rail, like a boxer on the ropes, and launched himself across the gap.

She felt the cold metal of the bar in her grip, measured the distance, and threw her boot out as hard as she could, striking Wallace square in the stomach. He impaled himself on it, doubled over the top, and bared his teeth.

But that wasn't enough.

Not for him.

She pulled it free, turned and launched her other leg straight up into his face, feeling the grim crunch of bone against her heel.

Wallace went back, arms windmilling, and struck the rail.

Blood spurted from his mouth and nose, his feet leaving the ground.

In a flutter of black and crimson, he was gone, and Jamie Johansson was alone on the catwalk.

She held her breath, choking on her own blood, and sobbed, watching it splatter over the bright yellow rail.

She watched it form thick, dark droplets, and peel itself free of the paint, dripping into the jagged ocean below.

Following Arnold Wallace into the frozen depths.

43

Jamie didn't know how long it took her to gather herself up and find her feet.

She crawled most of the way back to the platform, not trusting herself not to go over, too.

When she reached solid ground, she made it to her feet, and stumbled waywardly towards the main building.

She had no radio, no gun. And nothing left to give.

She needed to get inside, back to medical. To Wiik, and Ehrling, and Rosenberg, and Vogel. To safety.

It's all she could think about.

Her throat was raw, and every few steps she spat more blood onto the concrete. She didn't know if it was from where Wallace had choked her or the blow Quinn had dealt, but she could feel it pooling around her tongue all the same.

The hatch swam out of the blur towards her, and she saw her hands reach for it, barely within her own control.

Jamie twisted the handle, her fingers numb and stiff, and pulled.

It swung heavily and almost pulled her off balance.

She took a step back, swayed, and then moved into the gap, freezing as she did.

Her heart beat hard against the inside of her ribs, blood dripping from her lips.

There, in front of her, was Orn Møller.

He filled the corridor, his eyebrows fastened into a deep 'V', fists clenched, ready to swing.

Jamie breathed hard, felt tears in the corner of her eyes. 'Please,' she croaked, meeting his glare. 'I can't …'

But he didn't come forwards. Didn't attack. He just stood there. Silently. As though deciding what to do.

And then, slowly, from behind him, they appeared. First, the curly red hair of Ashleigh Hooper on his left, her face distrustful. And then the fine features of Paméla Sevier on his right. Both hovering at his massive shoulders.

No one said anything.

And then, from behind Sevier, Jamie saw her.

Stepping slowly out. The pale skin. The white-blonde hair. The electric-blue eyes. Dirty-faced, tired, frightened, but alive.

'Noemi Heikkinen,' Jamie said – she wasn't even sure if it was out loud. She could only taste metal.

She felt the frame begin to slip from her grasp, darkness invading her field of vision.

And then she crumbled.

44

EHRLING PRESSED A COLD, wet cloth to Jamie's face, and she recoiled painfully.

'Ow,' she said, screwing up her eye and wincing. Her cheek was throbbing, her jaw was aching, her throat felt like it was full of hot embers, and her ear was ringing so loudly she didn't know if she'd ever hear right again.

Ehrling pulled the compress back, inhaling with a soft hiss. 'I'm sorry,' he said, 'but I've got to clean you up.' It was that same semi-condescending tone, like she was a child refusing to eat her vegetables. Except she wasn't, and this wasn't over some piece of soggy fucking broccoli. She'd just had the shit kicked out of her. Again. And almost had her head blown off. Again. And once more, got into more trouble than her job was worth.

'I'm fine,' Jamie muttered, her voice like gravel.

'If you don't let me, then I can't see whether you're injured or not.'

'I'm fine,' Jamie insisted, dragging her eyes away from Noemi Heikkinen for a moment.

He saw the look on her face and backed away.

In fact, Jamie was pretty far from okay. One of her back molars had been loosened by Quinn's punch. Another one, that is. To join the one on the other side that was already loose from another fight that came as a result of a string of bad calls. She pulled her tongue off it, grimaced, and then looked back at Noemi Heikkinen.

Everyone was waiting patiently for her to start.

They were gathered on the command deck. Jamie, and a now-conscious Wiik, who'd been given another good dose of painkillers. He was sitting on a chair with a bag of fluids clipped to the collar of his coat. His eyes were glazed and his hand bandaged, but at least he was awake. Which was something.

Otherwise, Vogel, Ehrling, and Rosenberg were there. As was Møller, Hooper, Sevier, and finally, Noemi Heikkinen.

Jamie and Wiik were sitting in front of the desk, looking inwards, the storm breaking behind them through the window, and Heikkinen was on a chair in front of what had been Wallace's room. Orn Møller was standing at her shoulder, arms folded ominously, face still bruised, while Hooper and Sevier were leaning against the wall behind him.

'Noemi,' Jamie forced out, holding her fingers against her crushed throat. Damn, it hurt so much to speak. 'Can you tell … us … what' – she swallowed painfully – 'happened?'

The girl was kneading her hands in her lap. She seemed in fine health, but her face was grubby with dust and grime, and her hair thick and greasy. She glanced up at Møller, who was staring at Jamie. After a few seconds of silence, he gave a slight nod.

Noemi Heikkinen let out a long breath, her bright blue eyes swelling with tears, and then she began. 'Alejandro was

... He was good, okay?' she said quickly, her voice high pitched and sweet, her accent lilting the words.

She didn't appear to want to go on until everyone acknowledged that fact with a nod.

'He didn't want to do it – to go along with it. But he couldn't stop. He wasn't allowed. So ... so I did it for him. I stopped it.' She paused again, looking at everyone in the room. 'And that's why they killed him.'

Møller put his hand on her shoulder now.

Jamie knew who was responsible for Reyes' death by now, but she needed Heikkinen to say it. And for everyone to hear it. 'Who?' Jamie croaked. 'Who killed him?'

'It was Lebedenkov,' she said. 'But Quinn was the one who told him to. He was the one who was in charge of it all.'

Vogel spoke up now, her voice hard. She was angry that anyone had taken the liberty of hatching a scheme of any kind on her platform. 'In charge of what?'

'They ... they were planning to cause a spill – by swapping out a new seal for an old one.'

Jamie nodded along, hoping she'd keep going.

'They made Alejandro do it. He didn't want to. He knew the damage it was going to cause.'

Jamie bit her lip. So, it was Quinn's plan to change the seal, not the engineers. But why?

Ehrling spoke then. 'To the company?'

'The ocean.' Hooper answered that one, the harsh tone of incredulousness in her voice unmistakable and more than enough to keep Ehrling from interjecting again.

Jamie tried to clear her throat, winced at the pain, then managed a few words. 'Why did they do it, Noemi?'

'They wanted to cause a spill so that Bolstad would go under,' she said then. 'There was another company trying to buy them, Alejandro said. Some guy from the company –

someone high up approached Quinn, offered to pay him to sabotage it. To force Bolstad to sell.'

Jamie's eyebrows raised a little. Corporate espionage? That was an angle she hadn't considered. 'Was his name Arnold Wallace?'

'I don't know,' Heikkinen said.

But Jamie would have bet anything it was. She'd heard the words. *We had a deal, Quinn.* So they scheme to have the seal blow, cause an international incident. Bolstad's stock tanks, they get bought out, and Wallace gets a slick new promotion with the new company. And Quinn and his crew would all get nice pay cheques and bonuses for their trouble.

Except Alejandro Reyes fell in love with an environmentalist. He tells her about the plan, gets cold feet. She tries to convince him to back out. He refuses, fearing for his life. She does it anyway, goes behind his back. And then ultimately puts a target on it.

'Why were you on the lower submersible platform?' Jamie asked then.

'We were getting off the rig,' Heikkinen said quickly. 'Quinn knew what we'd done, and we wanted to get away. We were going to go the following morning, before the sun came up.'

Jamie slotted all the missing puzzle pieces into place. Knowing something was up, Quinn dispatched Lebedenkov to kill them both off. Either to keep the plan quiet, or maybe to try and cause enough of a scandal that Bolstad would go under anyway.

Wallace, seeing things going sideways, gets himself dispatched to clean the mess up … With the intention of taking care of Quinn and his crew. Plugging the leaks before they got out. Which included Heikkinen. Møller's face … Jamie remembered. He'd tangled with Shane Reid, Wallace's man, who was looking for Heikkinen. But he wouldn't give her up.

She'd got him all wrong, she thought, looking at the big guy with his hand on Heikkinen's shoulder.

The files taken from her room, the missing seal, that had to be Wallace, too, tying up loose ends. And no doubt he'd ordered Quinn to be killed in his room, but Quinn fought him off. Then, he arranged to meet Quinn on the drill deck, probably under the guise of calling a truce, ready to brandish the seal in his face, use it as leverage. But then Reid had been ambushed by Kravets after he disabled the camera …

Then Wallace killed the power, and sent his man after them in the dark. All of them. Quinn, Kravets, Lebedenkov, Jamie, Wiik … Hell, he probably would have killed every single person onboard to keep things quiet. The thought sent a shiver down her spine.

And all along, Quinn was playing Jamie against Wallace, using her as a buffer, diverting her attention towards the engineers, throwing up a smoke screen while he and Kravets and Lebedenkov made a run for it.

It made her feel sick. The whole fucking thing. And for what? Money. At the cost of dumping billions of gallons of oil into the ocean. Causing untold, irreparable damage. All for money. And power.

She hated corporations. A law unto themselves. Who killed and exploited and extorted to get what they wanted. Business claimed to be civilised, but it was more like the wild west than anything else.

Money did ugly things to people. She'd witnessed that time and time again.

Jamie turned her attention back to Heikkinen. 'How did you get off the submersible deck?' Jamie asked, eyeing the timid girl in front of her.

'There's an, uh, shelf – kind of thing – that runs along the wall, around to maintenance, it's—'

'I know it,' Jamie said. 'Intimately.' Damn, she had a will to survive. She wouldn't have guessed, but she had to give it to her. 'So where have you been until now?'

'Hiding,' she answered. 'In maintenance, in storage. The lower crew quarters. Wherever people weren't. I was afraid that Quinn would find me, and …' She trailed off then.

Storage? 'I was down in storage a few days ago – was it you who snuck up on me and then ran?'

Heikkinen met her eye, then nodded quickly. 'I was going to say something, but … I didn't know who you were, and … I thought maybe you'd come to …'

Kill her. That was what she didn't have it in her to say. 'And Møller? How does he figure into this?'

'Orn saved me,' Heikkinen said. 'I hoped he would help me. And he did. I found him, and he kept me safe. Didn't tell anyone I was alive. Not even …' She looked over at the two girls behind Møller, who were displaying a mixture of relief and sourness.

'And you cut him free in the lower crew quarters?'

Heikkinen nodded again.

'And the marks on your face?' Jamie asked Møller then. 'Wallace's man?'

He lifted his chin. 'Caught me coming up from storage. Asked where I'd been. Didn't like my answer.'

'And that's why you had the knife? To protect yourself?' Her eyes drifted to Heikkinen. 'And Noemi.' She looked up at Hooper and Sevier, who'd gone missing days before. 'And the girls.' She drew a painful breath. 'You've been looking after them all this time?'

He huffed. 'Someone had to.'

Jamie met his eye. She didn't have the fight in her to take

issue with that remark. And she definitely couldn't talk anymore. She could taste blood in the back of her throat again. 'Thank you,' she forced out. 'It's over now. You're safe.' She looked around the room, her eyes coming to rest on her broken partner. 'We're all safe.'

THE SKY WAS clear and blue, and the air was cold.

Jamie was standing on the helideck, staring into the open cabin of the Eurocopter that would be taking her and Wiik back to Sweden in a few minutes.

Below, on the main drilling platform, two more helicopters sat, marked with the SPA logo. Little figures moved around in white forensic overalls like bugs.

'Johansson.'

She turned to see Ingrid Falk walking towards her. Her short black hair was turning in the breeze, her long woollen coat pinned to her slim legs.

'A word,' Falk said, coming to a halt under the slowly bouncing rotors of the chopper.

Jamie nodded. Her throat was still aching horribly, though she could force out a few words if she needed to.

'Preliminary forensics reports have come back,' she said, squinting into the afternoon sun. 'What do you want first?'

Jamie didn't answer. She just stared at her.

'Let's go from the top. The knife wounds on Alejandro

Reyes' body were matched to a knife found in maintenance, near Miroslav Lebedenkov's body.'

And my leg, I bet, Jamie felt like saying. She stayed quiet instead, shifted her weight from side to side, feeling the bandage bristle against her jeans.

'The wounds on both Colm Quinn and Sasha Kravets's bodies were matched to a blade found in the executive quarters, inside a suitcase where you said the bodyguards' belongings were. Combat knife, military issue. We don't know if it's the murder weapon, but the shape and size are a strong match.'

Jamie figured it was a standard part of what Bolstad issued to their security personnel. It could have belonged to either of Wallace's guards. Maybe it'd be the murder weapon, or maybe the real murder weapon was on the bottom of the ocean, along with Wallace's second heavy. Not like it really mattered now.

'We're fairly confident that ballistics from the bullet wounds on both Colm Quinn and Miroslav Lebedenkov's body can be matched to the same make and model of pistol we recovered from the drill deck, near to where you said you found Shane Reid's body. The same pistol that all Bolstad security personnel are issued with. It will be enough to make a strong case. Strong enough to be able to subpoena Arnold Wallace's bank records to follow-up on the corporate espionage theory. Bolstad will likely go down for this.'

Falk let that hang in the air as if it was some sort of solace to Jamie.

It wasn't.

'Doesn't much matter now, though, does it,' Jamie muttered, still scowling.

'You did a good thing, Jamie,' Falk said. 'If not for you …. a lot more people could have died.'

Somehow, she didn't feel like talking anymore. And it wasn't because her throat felt like it was full of blood and broken glass, either.

She had almost helped Quinn escape. Had almost helped a murderer escape. Until the last moment she thought he was innocent ...

There was a bitter taste on her tongue that she couldn't shift. Jamie sighed. At least they were all dead now.

She grimaced at that thought. At how glad of it she was.

'What about Kurek?' she asked, staring out at the unnervingly still ocean. He was the last piece of the puzzle. The missing piece.

'No sign of him,' Falk answered, standing next to her. 'We've searched the entire platform. Found blood in several places, but we're yet to match it to anyone. If he's alive, he's not here. But I don't know how he could have got off. The more likely answer is that he's—'

'Dead.' Jamie sighed. 'Quinn probably killed him so he could use him as a scapegoat. Dead men can't defend themselves.'

Falk didn't add anything further. She just stood there, looking sheepish.

'How's Wiik?' Jamie asked after a moment.

'In pain,' Falk said. 'He's being attended to, but he'll need surgery. We'll be taking off soon. Are you coming back now or do you want to catch a ride with the forensics team when they're done?'

'I'm coming,' Jamie answered. She didn't want to spend one second longer than she absolutely had to on this place.

'When we get back ...' Falk started, looking at Jamie's bruised and swollen face. 'I think you should take some time off. You've earned it.'

Jamie snorted. 'You know we almost died.' She met

Falk's eye. 'You almost got us killed. You sent us here to be pawns in Bolstad's game – but really you were just putting our heads in a noose. I hope you know that.'

Falk broke eye contact. It was all the answer Jamie needed.

'You're both alive,' she said then. 'That's what matters.'

'What matters,' Jamie started, unable to keep the bile from her voice, 'is that you deliver on what you owe me. You promised me a name for doing this.'

Falk stiffened a little.

Jamie knew what she was thinking – that Bolstad had told Falk to dispatch two detectives that would fall in line. They needed a pair of yes-men that'd take a back seat to Wallace's supposed 'fixing', not an international scandal and a pile of dead bodies. But Jamie couldn't help that. It was Wallace who'd arranged Bolstad's demise long before Jamie and Wiik had even got involved. They were just in the way from the start, and if it hadn't been Wallace going over that rail, it would have been Jamie and Wiik. Dead or alive. And Falk would have had a phone call saying the mysterious killer had taken their lives too.

'You know,' Falk said, almost wistful, 'I never intended to end up like this – in anyone's debt. But … in this job, there are hard choices to make.'

Jamie ground her teeth, then shuddered at the pain of her loose molar. She knew more about hard choices than Falk ever would with her desk-hunched posture, groomed appearance, and scar-free skin.

'Long ago, I was given a choice like that, and it meant letting someone corrupt, and corruptible, assume power – assume control of my post – or step into it myself,' Falk went on.

'And that gives you the right,' Jamie muttered, 'to be

corrupt yourself? Because you were *less* corrupt than the alternative?'

'I don't expect you to understand.'

'Good. Because I don't.'

'Your father wouldn't have, either. He lived in a black-and-white world, too.'

Jamie was about three seconds from knocking her fucking head off. 'The name, Falk.'

'It's not that simple, Johansson.' She put her hands in her pockets, her voice quivering a little. 'Bolstad is just one piece of a much larger whole. The only one you can see right now. But this runs so much deeper. What your father was doing before he …' She either had to say *killed himself* and lie, or *was murdered* and admit the truth. ' … That investigation – it was going to hurt a lot of people. And if you take up that fight again, you will be too.'

Jamie watched her spew bullshit, hands locked in fists in her pockets.

'And if you do – I won't be able to protect you. Just like then, there will be people who will try to stop you. Who will do anything to make sure that happens. Once you open this door, Jamie, you'll have to walk through it. And there'll be no coming back. You'll end careers, lives. Mine included.' She looked at Jamie again then.

'I could end yours now,' Jamie growled. 'In a fucking heartbeat. And I will if you don't give me that name.'

'Imperium Holdings.' She exhaled, like just saying the words was sealing her fate. 'They have a big stake in Bolstad, as well as a lot of other companies around the world. Energy. Commerce. Banking. Agriculture. Manufacturing. There's not an industry they don't have their fingers in. In Sweden, at the very least.'

'That's not good enough, Falk. I need more. You know more.'

'There's a man,' she said, looking at the ground. 'I met him, once.'

'Who?'

'He deals with things on Imperium's behalf. People. People who are in their way.'

'What's his name?'

'Sandbech.'

'Sandbech.' Jamie let it ring.

'I don't think it's his real name – but it's all I have.'

'Did he kill my father?'

'I know your father was looking into him – when he … died.'

Jamie swallowed, her heart beating slow and hard in her temples.

'Can I give you some advice, Jamie? Some advice I wish your father would have taken when I gave it to him twenty years ago?'

'No,' Jamie said.

'Drop it. Leave this alone. Take some time off, get rested, and then, if you want to come back, you can. Or if you want to move on, I'll write you a glowing recommendation. But please, please, Jamie, don't go after this. If you do – if you take up the same fight that your father did – then I'm afraid you'll end up like him.'

She processed that. End up like him? What did that even mean? Probably something different to Falk than it did to Jamie. 'Thank you,' she said, turning to face Falk, reading the sincerity in her eyes. The fear. 'But you know, letting things go really isn't in my blood.'

EPILOGUE

INGRID FALK LET herself into her apartment a little after dark a week later.

It had been raining, and her coat was soaked through.

She stepped through the door, slipped her jacket off, and hung it on the hook next to the door, and then laid her umbrella next to it.

A puddle began to spread from its point across the dark wooden floor.

Falk stepped in and then stopped, her hand half in her bag, fingers still entwined with her keys. 'You,' she breathed, staring at the man sitting in the armchair next to the window.

He was in his sixties, tall, and strongly built. His tailored grey suit hung well on him, a thick curl of silver chest hair peeking out of the top of his unbuttoned white shirt. He had his legs crossed, a book in his lap, taken from Falk's bookcase to his right. His face was shadowed, but she would have known him anywhere.

Her eyes fell on the gleaming silver pistol drowned in the light of the reading lamp on the table next to him, silencer already attached.

She swallowed. 'I tried,' she said, her voice thin and quaking. 'Tell them I tried.'

'Come now, Ingrid. You know I'm no messenger,' he said, voice languid. 'And we're long past grovelling.'

'It wasn't me. It was your man, Wallace. He was the one who—'

'Wallace is not *our* man. We have no men. And if we did, they certainly wouldn't be of his sort.' He laid the book next to the gun and laced his fingers around his knee, bouncing his foot casually. 'Put simply, you have failed. We asked a simple favour of you, and you failed.'

'I didn't,' she pleaded. 'I couldn't have known what would happen.'

'You were asked to supply a pair of detectives who could take direction,' the man say softly. 'You failed to do that.'

'Wallace was double-crossing Bolstad, anyway! It wouldn't have mattered!' Her voice was growing shrill.

The man lifted a hand and held it flat, motioning downwards to quieten her.

Falk fell silent.

'If Wallace thought he was smart enough to betray us and get away with it, then he was more of a fool than we ever thought. We would have dealt with Wallace correctly, after the fact. Now, the whole thing is a complete mess.'

'He would have killed them if they hadn't—'

'So they would have died. Should have. And we would have dealt with it, afterwards. You had one job, Ingrid. And you couldn't manage it. We need someone in your position who *can* manage these sorts of things.'

Falk realised then that there was another sound in the apartment. A sound of gushing water.

The room was dim, but she could see steam rising from a

crack in the bathroom door, glowing faintly in the light from the lamp next to the armchair.

Her lip began to quiver. She knew what was coming.

'Ingrid,' the man said, voice quiet and warm. 'You know what happens next.'

She couldn't find her voice.

'And like with all the others, you have a choice. Your way, or mine.'

She could feel her hands shaking.

The pistol was in his hand then, laid on his knee. His other hand extended, turned over, and opened, palm to the ceiling.

In it, was a razor blade.

AUTHOR'S NOTE

There seems to be a rhythm to this for me now. That I become excited by the idea of writing a novel, plot lines surge and evolve in my head, and then I begin with gusto. By around a third of the way through I begin to slow my pace, take a step back from the story, reflect, do some editing and reimagining, and then as I reach the final third, things begin to accelerate again until the finale.

Then, once it's done, I feel exhausted and think I'll take a few weeks off, to give myself some time. But that night, usually I'm thinking about the next book again.

But I like that, in a way. It reminds me that I enjoy this. Because I do – this isn't my 'job' yet. I don't make enough doing this to stop working a nine-to-five. So right now it is purely for enjoyment. And I want it to feel that way for you, too. Not that I'm simply pushing novels out the door to keep the lights on. Because that's not the case.

So let's talk about *Rising Tide* then. Hopefully you've never read a novel like it – or at least one with the same setting!

I feel myself gravitating more towards the raw thriller and

suspense aspects of the genre rather than grounding things within the procedural side of crime. I recognise that there are many authors who do the latter far better than me. Who have the kind of experience that lends itself to that truly factual style of crime writing. Whereas I feel my writing is magnetised towards a different true north, and I'm enjoying exploring that. I hope you are too.

This novel places detectives in a non-police setting, and I hope that it felt refreshing in some ways. Many of the events that occurred in this story were beyond the control of our heroes, too. This was a novel that saw them placed in a reactive state, rather than an active one. And that in a way, was fun to explore, too. If you've read *Angel Maker*, then you saw Jamie and Wiik as cool, collected people in charge of an unfolding investigation. Sure, there were some bits that got away from them! But for the most part, they were deciding what to do next and where to go. Trains laying their own tracks. In *Rising Tide*, however, it was the opposite. They were thrust into a situation that forced them to switch to a survival-mode of sorts. Where people were dying around them, plots were advancing out of sight, and for the most part, they were scrabbling for answers, fighting for their lives, and trying to tread water as the tide rose around them… Yeah, that's probably not as artful as I hoped, but hopefully it felt new enough that it kept you reading to the end!

Because that's always what I want to deliver. Each case that Jamie is involved in needs to feel different in my mind, otherwise I don't think I'd enjoy writing it.

Each new book forces an evolution of character for me. *Angel Maker* was a big breakout moment for Jamie as she returned to face some demons she'd buried, and finally stepped into her father's shoes. Solving a case he didn't was a way for her to get closure, too, and really allowed her to come to terms with the way her life turned out. Knowing how her father felt in the end, discovering the truth about who happened, in both the Angel Maker case, and after – that changed Jamie, in a big way. She could finally begin to rebuild her life, knowing the man her father was.

But then, to learn of the revelation that Claesson laid at her feet, well, that opened a whole new chapter. One that was continued here.

And while there wasn't a lot of progression on *that* story-line in these pages, there is more than you might think. Not only did Jamie learn the name of the man who may have killed her father, but she also placed herself on Bolstad's radar. And while she did her part to expose the plot going on – and ultimately foiled it – had Wallace killed Quinn and Jamie, he would have returned to his life, and the plot to sink Bolstad would have gone through. But as Jamie made sure that didn't happen, Bolstad will come under fire, and will no doubt go under. And that'll be a blow to Imperium. And as far as they're concerned, those meddling detectives from Stockholm are to probably blame.

So, in a way, this novel has done something for Jamie that got her closer to her father's killer – and that's sticking her nose into Imperium's business. Whether she knew that was what she was doing or not.

We move then, into book three in the series, *Old Blood*, with Imperium looking to remove a rather dynastic thorn from their side! Oh, how will Jamie deal with that? And the bigger question, is will Stockholm Polis stand by her or will Imperium do their part to prevent that?

I like the idea of standalone novels – of new readers coming to the series at every turn – and I hope that's the case, that some of you reading this are here for the first time. That would be wonderful! And I hope that there was enough for you to enjoy without having read the other books. Though the real pleasure for me comes with stringing together the novels in a way that really gives an insight into Jamie's changing life.

Even now she carries with her the things from the prequels. And those characters that developed there will come back around at some point.

I have so many ideas for where to take Jamie, and for other characters, too. There are other kinds of stories I want to tell – ones I want to set in this 'universe' as well – ones which overlap with Jamie's world. I don't know that Wiik or Roper or Brock or Hassan or Elliot will get their own series, but perhaps someone will push to the forefront.

For now, Jamie has a good amount of road ahead of her, and by the time you read *Old Blood*, I'll have some more concrete ideas in place. I think, though, I'm going to give Jamie a break, whatever happens. I've enacted a lot of horrible things on her in the last year or two of her life, and she deserves some rest, a good friend, maybe. A little bit of a quieter life. But, alas, you know how things can get in those 'quiet' places, where much goes unseen by the law and the rest of the world. Wouldn't it just be Jamie's luck, huh, to land in a small, tranquil little town, just to find out that it holds some dark, chilling, awful, terrible, torrid, and just plain terrifying secrets?

Oh well, we'll just have to see how that goes, won't we?

My very best,

Morgan

OLD BLOOD

Book 3 in the DI Jamie Johansson Series

When a series of accidents unfolds in front of Jamie, claiming the lives of those around her, she knows that it's anything except coincidence.

With the bruises from the last case still bright on her skin, and her partner still recovering, Jamie is on the back foot. But that doesn't mean she's backing down.

Imperium Holdings are responsible for the death of her father, and who knows how many others. They have their hooks into every inch of the city, and while no one else seems to want to face the truth, Jamie knows that they have Stockholm in a choke hold. From the politicians to the police and everything in between, there's no one beyond Imperium's reach.

When an ultimatum is forced upon Jamie, she has to make the biggest decision of her life: abandon everything she's ever believed in and let it go, or stand up to Imperium, and face things head on.

All she has is a name, and the taste of blood in her mouth, but that's enough.

Imperium have put down detectives before — Jamie knows that better than anyone. But they've never met anyone like her. Someone who truly has nothing to lose.

She's learned from her father's mistakes, and she knows what lies ahead. There's no denying that it's going to be the fight of her life.

She just hopes she's ready for it.

———

Old Blood is the hotly anticipated third instalment of the DI Jamie Johansson series, and sees her tackle her toughest challenge yet. With no one single crime to pursue, and a twenty-year-old axe to grind, Jamie will be pushed to her limits as she tries to find closure for her father's death. They say living well is the best revenge, but Jamie never learned how to do that. All she knows is justice, and without the confines of the law to guide her, she'll have to seek her own kind. No matter how bloody.

Old Blood, book 3 in the DI Jamie Johansson Series, is out now!

WANT MORE JAMIE?

Keep reading to discover *Your Word* the first DI Jamie Johansson short story, just a little something extra to get you excited for *Old Blood!*

Your Word

Jamie Johansson smelt like grease. Not all the time. Just then. But by damn did she stink.

She let herself into her apartment building after dark and closed the door behind her, leaning back against it, feeling the glass cool against her scalp. Her hair was thick and unclean, her skin covered with a film that she felt like she'd need wire wool to get off.

Jamie blinked herself clear and hauled her half-numb right leg behind her as she made for the stairs. As she dragged it up towards the first floor she made a mental note that if a suspect made a break for it through a drainage tunnel again, she'd follow her partner's lead and try to head him off.

Not dive in after him.

Jesus – why did she have to live on the fourth floor?

Get a top-floor apartment, Jamie. Stairs are good for you, Jamie. You have to keep fit, Jamie.

She grimaced as she got to two, staring up at the next flight and pausing for breath.

As the tired throbbing behind her eyes receded, another noise filled her head. One that she couldn't ignore.

Down the corridor to her left, she could hear shouting. Muted by a door. But unmistakable.

She hobbled towards it.

Two speakers. One man. One woman.

His voice booming, angry. Hers shrill, upset. Frantic.

Jamie paused and swallowed.

Scared.

She quickened her pace, zeroing on the door in question, 2C, and paused at it, listening at the wood.

'—and all you do is sit around all day, spending my money, buying shit online, *wasting* your life!'

She could hear heavy footsteps as he tramped around the apartment.

Jamie held fast, kept listening.

The woman was yelling then. 'You told me not to work! You said you loved it when I was here, at home, waiting for you—'

'Because I thought you'd have enough sense to have dinner waiting on the table for me every night. That you'd be *grateful* for what I gave you. Except this place looks like shit! You look like shit! If I wanted to marry a pig, I would have done, and it would have given me a lot less fucking grief!'

'Oliver, I—'

And then Jamie heard it. The curtailed words, the sharp slap of the back of a hand hitting an unsuspecting cheek.

It reached her ears and an instant later her fist was pounding on the door.

The room beyond fell quiet.

Jamie hammered again. 'Stockholm Polis, open the door,' she called.

There was hushed murmuring, and then footsteps approached hurriedly.

They paused just the other side of the door, and then there was silence. A second later, a door inside the apartment closed, and the one in front of Jamie opened, revealing the man she knew had to be Oliver.

He was about six foot, middle-aged, with a narrow head, thin glasses, a pointed chin, and the kind of shit-eating false grin you'd like to wipe off with a cricket bat.

'Yes?' he asked, reaching up and pushing his glasses up his nose.

'Detective Inspector Jamie Johansson,' Jamie said curtly, not returning the smile. 'Everything alright in there?'

Terrible question, but, going on the offensive this soon was a good way to get the door slammed in your face.

'Fine. Thank you,' he said, noticing the grime on Jamie's face, and probably the smell too, judging by how his nose was twitching. 'What can I do for you… Inspector?'

'Can you describe for me the situation that just occurred in there?'

'Why?'

'Because I'd like to hear your version of events.'

He stared at her, assessing his options.

'Or I could come back in a few minutes, I live just upstairs,' Jamie said then, almost as a throwaway remark. 'I can come back anytime, actually.'

She wondered if that would be enough.

Jamie glanced past him and into the apartment. It was bigger than hers – open plan. Lots of white and exposed wood. Expensive decor and furniture.

Oliver was in a suit, too. Navy blue with a white open-collared shirt. It was tailored. Not a cheap two-piece from the local outlet, that was for sure. The guy had money, and he made sure his wife knew that. A solicitor, maybe?

'That won't be necessary,' Oliver said then. 'My wife and I were just having a discussion. She is a passionate woman.' He flashed Jamie a brief smile and her skin squirmed under her collar. 'She, uh,' he said, closing his eyes and shaking his head before lacing the act with a little, innocent laugh, 'dropped her mug of tea... If you heard something, you know?'

Jamie leaned around him. 'I don't see any spilt tea.'

'It was empty.' He held on to the smile.

'I don't see any shards.'

'The mug was enamel.'

Jamie stared up at Oliver, not buying a word of it. 'And your wife? Where is she now?'

'In the bedroom, I suspect. She wasn't feeling well.'

'That's why she dropped the mug, then.'

He nodded, smiled again. More skin-squirm. 'Of course – that makes sense.'

'It usually does,' Jamie said, nodding. 'Okay, Oliver, well, I just thought I'd check in to make sure everything was okay. My hearing is pretty good, but sometimes I mistake one noise for another, you know? But better to be safe than sorry.'

'Indeed. Now, if you don't mind, I'm just about to cook dinner.'

'For you and your wife.'

'Of course. She's had a long day,' he said, feigning compassion. 'And she deserves to be... taken care of.'

'Everyone does,' Jamie said, resisting the urge to do something her badge prohibited. 'Lucky for you there's a detective who lives in the building. You *take care* of your wife, then I *take care* of you.'

'My tax money hard at work.' He moved backwards from the threshold and nodded a quick goodbye, then closed the door in her face.

Jamie sighed and hung her head. 'You have no idea.'

Three days passed and all was quiet in apartment 2C. Jamie wasn't naive enough to think that Oliver Hedlund had seen the light and chosen a better path. He'd just learned to *take care* of his wife more quietly.

Jamie had taken the liberty of looking him up.

She lingered on the second landing each time she passed, keeping her ears pricked for anything that would let her kick the door down. But she'd heard nothing.

It was before eight in the morning when she approached the main door.

A woman was approaching from the other side, walking hurriedly, carrying a plastic bag from the local shop.

Jamie stood back and let her enter. She was in her forties, slight, with long dark hair tied into a low ponytail. Her skin was pale, her eyes held low, submissive. But it wasn't that which caught Jamie's eye. It was that she was wearing a patterned scarf, dual wound to cover her neck and knotted at the side. And that it didn't go with the drab sweater and jeans she was wearing.

'Mrs Hedlund,' Jamie said as she passed.

The woman paused, looked back at Jamie with fright in her eyes. 'Yes?' she said, voice quiet and cautious.

Jamie hadn't really thought this far ahead. 'I'm Detective Inspector Jamie Johansson,' Jamie said then. 'With Stockholm Polis. I don't know if you know who I am, but I came to your door a few days ago…'

Jamie watched as her grip tightened on her shopping bag, her bottom lip folding into her mouth with apprehension.

Jamie knew what was coming next, and headed her off. 'Look,' she said. 'I know you probably don't want to talk to me – but if there's anything you ever need…' She fished a card from her pocket and held it out. 'I'm right upstairs, and my personal number is on there. Just call. Anytime. Day or night, okay? And I'll come running.'

The woman stared down at it like it was coated in arsenic. 'Really,' she said, 'there's no need.'

Jamie kept holding it out.

The woman wanted to take it. She would have walked away otherwise.

Jamie leaned forwards then and dropped it into her bag of shopping. 'Just put it somewhere… safe.' She smiled at Linnea Hedlund. 'Just in case.'

And then the woman was gone, and Jamie was left standing in the brightening light of the coming day.

Jamie stepped onto the fourth floor at nineteen minutes past eight, her stomach rumbling. But she knew that she had nothing appetising in her fridge, and didn't know if she could be bothered to go to the shop.

She let herself in on autopilot, dropping her keys onto the table next to the door, and swung it shut behind her.

A dull slap rang out, and then she felt it crack her square in the back, right between the shoulders.

Jamie stumbled forwards, snatching at her breath, pain rippling through her chest, and reached out for the wall to steady herself. She turned quickly, still bent over, winded, and watched as Oliver Hedlund stepped into her hallway.

Before she could say a word, he flicked a little white card at her, sneering as he did. 'You can take this back,' he grunted as it pinged off Jamie's thigh and spun to the floor. 'And don't ever speak to my wife again.'

Jamie drew a breath and dragged herself upright, resisting the urge to pull her pistol from the holster on her ribs and shove it in his face. 'You know I'm a police officer, right?' she choked out, her lungs still stunned.

'So then take me in,' he said, cockiness oozing from his every pore. 'I'll just say you arrested me for no good reason – that you've got a vendetta. And frankly, it's your word against mine.'

Jamie caught her breath, watching the man, holding herself back. He knew what he was doing, had this all mapped out. Whatever she did now, he'd have a way of weaselling out of it. Of that much she was sure.

'I'm glad we understand each other,' he said then, stepping back through the doorway. 'And if I see you anywhere near me or my wife, I'll make your life very difficult. Got it?'

Jamie kept his gaze but didn't say a word.

After a few seconds, he broke eye contact and strode away, expensive leather loafers squeaking on the tiles.

The Wine Cellar was a cocktail bar situated just three hundred metres from the law firm that Oliver Hedlund worked at. Jamie had been spot on with her guess that he was a solicitor. He gave off that stench of needing to be in control. And his profession gave him just that.

Hedlund and his co-workers exited the bar at a little after ten. It was a weekday, after all.

They exchanged some jokes, laughed on the kerb for a minute or two, and then dispersed. The two guys he was with lived in the opposite direction and walked off together, leaving Oliver to make his way home. Just a kilometre and a half away. It would take him around fifteen minutes to walk.

Maybe a little more if he'd had a few to drink. And tonight, he had.

The street was quiet, and Oliver walked languidly, pulling his phone from his pocket and squinting down at it with one eye closed.

A figure swept up behind him then, overtaking on his right before he even realised they were there, black hood pulled up tightly around their face, and threw their shoulder into him.

He swore in shock and staggered, the stranger grabbing the phone from his hand and bolting right down an alleyway.

Oliver Hedlund regained himself, looked around for anyone that might help, and then took up the chase.

No one was around to follow.

He huffed and panted, the alleyway darkening around him as the reach of the streetlights dimmed behind.

His heavy breathing morphed into a laugh then and he slowed, sagging a little as he caught his breath. A moment later he stood straight and smoothed his grey silk paisley tie against his stomach. 'Dead end!' he called to the figure who was standing in front of him, staring at the steel gate and locked chains in front of them.

A drainpipe dripped somewhere in the darkness, the stench of rotting food thick in the air.

'Hand it over,' Hedlund demanded. 'And maybe I'll have the police go easy on you.'

The figure turned slowly then, and peeled the hood back from their head.

'You,' Hedlund said, laughing. 'Jesus, I knew you were stupid, but I didn't think you'd be *this* stupid.' He shook his head. 'You're done. You're fucking *done.*'

Jamie Johansson stared back at him, still holding his phone in her hand, an image of a practically nude 'fitness model' displaying proudly on his Instagram feed. She must have been half his age. Probably less.

He held his hand out. 'Phone. Now,' he said, pulling his shoulders back, raising his chin.

Jamie came forwards slowly, holding it out.

He reached forwards, ready to take it.

And in the darkness, didn't see her move.

She stepped into her left foot, swung her right around in a shallow arc, and felt the laces of her boot connect with the side of his left knee.

The whites of his eyes flashed, and he crumpled, calling out.

Jamie stepped forwards then, taking his still-outstretched hand from the air, bending it backwards at the elbow until she had it twisted up next to his ear.

His back arched away from her, the filthy water on the alley floor soaking into the fine wool of his suit trousers.

Oliver Hedlund tried to squeal but a quick jerk of his hand killed it in his throat.

'Shut it,' she said, feeling the tendons in his wrist and forearm strain.

He obliged. 'You – you can't do this, you're a police officer,' he squeezed out through gritted teeth.

'So then report me. They'll bring me in and I'll just say you've got a vendetta against me because I interrupted you while you were hitting your wife.' She gave his wrist a little tweak and he whimpered a little. 'And believe me, I've asked around about you, and I've got a dozen people who'll happily testify to what a petty, arrogant piece of shit you are. So do it, see what happens.'

He was silent.

Jamie exhaled. 'That's what I thought.'

And then she flattened his knuckles against the top of his

forearm and listened with a certain grim satisfaction as the bones in his wrist snapped.

She released him then and watched as he flopped forwards onto his belly, mewling, and tried to crawl away.

'Oh, and Oliver?' Jamie said, standing over him. He didn't turn around to look at her, but she knew his was listening. 'You think about filing a report about this, and, well, it'll be your word against mine.' Jamie watched for a moment as he clawed his way through a filthy puddle in a miserable attempt to escape, and then turned away. 'And if you ever think about laying a *finger* on your wife or threatening me again, I'll make sure the next alley you go down really is a *dead end.*'

———

Get Old Blood, book 3 in the DI Jamie Johansson series now!

To stay up to date with everything Jamie, follow me on Facebook @morgangreeneauthor or head to my website and join my mailing list at morgangreene.co.uk

ALSO BY MORGAN GREENE

The DS Johansson Prequel Trilogy:
Bare Skin (Book 1)
Fresh Meat (Book 2)
Idle Hands (Book 3)

The DS Johansson Prequel Trilogy Boxset

————

The DI Jamie Johansson Series
Angel Maker (Book 1)
Rising Tide (Book 2)
Old Blood (Book 3)

Death Chorus (Book 4)
Quiet Wolf (Book 5)
Ice Queen (Book 6)